"McLean's first novel takes the reader on a terrific journey through the machinations of Boston law. *Under Fire* is a compelling legal thriller with vivid characters and a case that ignites our interest practically on the first page. McLean, a law professor and former criminal prosecutor, knows her stuff and, even better, knows how to translate it to fiction."   —*Booklist*

"*Under Fire* is a riveting read. I know the word 'riveting' is hackneyed. Maybe I should say sticky, because I couldn't put it down. I was up till two A.M. this morning finishing it."   —Lucia St. Clair Robson,
New York Times bestselling author of
Last Train from Cuernavaca

"This fast-paced debut legal thriller by a former criminal prosecutor offers an interesting immigrant twist. It should appeal to Richard North Patterson fans."
—*Library Journal* on *Under Fire*

"On your shelf of legal thrillers, move the Grishams aside and make room for Margaret McLean. She's got all the knowledge of an insider and—more important—all the skills of a great storyteller. She'll take you into the offices and the holding cells and the courtrooms, and you'll believe every detail and nuance. Then she'll start to heighten and tighten and twist and turn, and you won't be able to put the book down."
—William Martin,
New York Times bestselling author of
City of Dreams, on *Under Fire*

Forge Books by Margaret McLean

Under Fire
Under Oath

MARGARET McLEAN

UNDER FIRE

A TOM DOHERTY ASSOCIATES BOOK | NEW YORK

UNDER FIRE

A Forge Book
Published by Tom Doherty Associates, LLC
175 Fifth Avenue
New York, NY 10010

www.tor-forge.com

Forge® is a registered trademark of Tom Doherty Associates, LLC.

ISBN 978-0-7653-6641-2

First Edition: June 2011
First Mass Market Edition: December 2012

Printed in the United States of America

0 9 8 7 6 5 4 3 2 1

For my daughter, Sarah Barcomb, with love—
you are my muse and inspiration

The one thing that doesn't abide by majority rule is a person's conscience.

—Harper Lee
To Kill a Mockingbird

ACKNOWLEDGMENTS

First and foremost, I wish to thank my three children—Sarah, Dave, and Kate Barcomb—for their patience and encouragement. I can finally answer your persistent question: When's the book going to be done, Mom? Here it is. I must also extend a heartfelt thank-you to my parents, Robert and Carol McLean, and my brother, Robby.

I had the time of my life researching fires for the opening scene and investigation. Thank you to the Massachusetts Department of Fire Services, the Boston Fire Department, and the Norwell Fire Department. A special thank-you to State Police Sergeant Paul Zipper, who educated me on the details of investigating fires. Thank you to State Police Lieutenant Martin Foly for such a warm welcome at his unit and for helping me with the homicide detective character. I appreciated learning so much about ballistics from Captain John Busa of the Massachusetts State Police and Sergeant James O'Shea of the Boston Police Department. Thank you to Mike Mazza, Sergeant Paul Horgan, and Milo for teaching me the details of canine investigations. I enjoyed learning about what goes on at the firehouse from Frank Latosek "Firefighter Frank" up in New Hampshire. A very special thanks to my friends on Rescue One in Boston: Lieutenant Rick Connelly, Steve Cloonan, Marty Fernandes, and John Centrino. I had a great time spending the day with all of you!

Thank you to the Honorable Santo J. Ruma for sharing stories about the old West End of Boston. Many thanks to Aida Faye for teaching me about Senegal and the Muslim faith. I also enjoyed learning the real estate/development angle from Mark Dickenson, Walter "Budge" Upton, and James Lydon. Thank you to Anthony Amaru for helping me think through the subplot.

Thank you to all my friends and supporters at Mystery Writers of America—a wonderful organization for writers. My Monday night writers group deserves a huge round of applause: Paula Munier, Stephen D. Rogers, Andy McAleer, Vaughn Hardacker, and Jeff Walters. Thank you for bearing with me, chapter by chapter, and providing me with such fabulous insight into the craft of writing. Another thank-you to my daughter Sarah for all her meticulous editing and telling me exactly what she thinks about the work in progress: both the good and the bad.

At last, thank you to my agent, Susan Gleason, and my editor, Bob Gleason, and all of you at Tor/Forge who believe in this book.

UNDER FIRE

1

There's something sinister about black smoke—the way it creeps up, closes in, and chokes the life right out of you. Jack Fogerty had to conquer it head on. He jammed the steel Halligan between the knob and frame and yanked sideways. The wooden door splintered and popped open. Smoke billowed from the Senegalese Market and enveloped him. Jack twisted his regulator and went on air. Fire alarms blared.

Please God help me save them. Tell me where they are. The woman and boy lived upstairs above the store. Jack and his partner, Andy, plowed through the dense smoke, hugging the wall and staying low. Where was the stairwell up? Should be in front. *Save them.* It was his calling in life, a driving force passed down by generations of firemen—his father, grandfather, great-grandfather.

Orange flames engulfed a shelf in the back and spread upward. Glass jars shattered. Not much time before the fire burned a hole through the ceiling, reached the second floor, and banked back down.

Jack studied his thermal imaging camera to navigate through the smoke. He pointed the screen from side to side and scanned the wall crammed to the ceiling with shelving and products. No way up. Could the stairs be to the left? Where was the engine company with the lines? White indicated heat, and the image of white flame off to his left had doubled. *God help me save them.*

Jack tripped and fell sideways into a wall of glass jars. Pain tore through his elbow. Andy pulled him to his feet, and they moved along the right-hand wall. He scoured up and down with his camera. Nothing. *An explosion.* A battery of cans pounded the floor. Find the stairs or they will die. Jack stumbled again. Sweat trickled down his back.

A gap appeared between the shelving, and the image of a doorknob came up on screen. *Locked.* Andy squeezed beside him and wedged the Halligan into the wood frame. The door flew open. Smoke poured into a steep stairwell leading up. Jack slammed the door and bounded up the stairs with Andy at his side.

They entered the hallway of an apartment. Did he hear footsteps? A white image appeared on the thermal screen. It looked like someone moving away.

"Hey!" Jack yelled as loudly as he could through his air mask, but the figure kept running until it disappeared off screen.

Jack swung the camera to the right, revealing dark images of a couch, desk, chairs . . . a living room? A figure appeared near the corner diagonally across from them. He saw scurrying, lots of movement. Another white blur. Were there three altogether?

Andy leaned into him. "You grab that one. I'll take the camera and do a left-hand search down the hall. Meet you back here."

Jack nodded and handed off the camera. The yellow flashlight clipped to his waist provided little illumination. He entered the living room with his right hand on the wall. *A flash.* Something exploded in his stomach, knocking him to the floor. Glass shattered.

Jack's head felt dizzy, and his insides contracted in excruciating pain as he sat up. Had he been shot? A hot, sticky liquid plastered his stomach. Get them out of here and ignore the pain. He bit down and discerned movement a few feet away. Jack sprang from a squatting position and grabbed hold of an arm.

"My son! He ran that way." The woman doubled over, coughing.

"Get down on your hands and knees. Now!" he shouted. An explosion thundered close by and shook the building. Dishes smashed onto the floor. The fire had made its way up. The hot, sticky liquid oozed over his hip and down both legs. *Blood*. Where was Andy?

"Malick!" the woman screamed.

A body crashed into Jack's side. He felt searing pain. *The son*. He clenched his teeth and grabbed the boy. "Where's the other one?"

"Nobody else." The woman wheezed and coughed.

"Sure?"

She nodded and hacked again.

"Is there another way out up here?" They couldn't go back down; that exit would be blocked by fire and smoke.

The woman gagged and exploded into another coughing fit. He couldn't tell if she nodded or shook her head. She pointed toward the hallway, and Jack saw the orange glow. Fire. *Where the hell was Andy?*

"Down!" Jack made them crawl along the living room wall. Get them to a window. He prayed they'd be there with a ladder or the rescue box. Where the hell was the engine with the lines? Flames crackled in another room. Windows shattered. They had less than a minute to get out. *Hot as hell*. Jack vomited a thick, bloody-tasting sludge into his air mask, nearly blocking the regulator. Had to get them out and find Andy. *God help me save them.*

The boy collapsed. Jack dropped his Halligan and scooped him up in both arms. He was heavy. *Give me strength.* The woman smacked her forehead against the floor as she gasped for air. Couldn't carry them both. Jack heaved the boy over his shoulder, tore off his glove, and held the woman's hand in his. He willed himself forward as his eyesight faded in shades of red and army green. *Somebody help us.*

"Jack!" Andy appeared like a blurred apparition crawling toward them along the wall.

"I found the son. Passed out." Jack rolled the limp boy into Andy's arms and released the woman's hand. He motioned toward the window. Andy hesitated. Jack pushed him away.

He vomited more sludge and blood, blocking his regulator. Jack fought the urge to tear the useless air mask from his face. His eyelids curled shut. *Please God lead them out.*

The pulsating beep of an alarm hammered into his head. A fireman's PASS device had activated. Someone wasn't moving. Not Andy. *Please not Andy.* The beeping reached a crescendo and then faded.

Jack was lost and swimming through the black smoke as hard as he could. Heat radiated through his gear, roasting his flesh. In his mind he willed the woman, boy, and Andy out the window and onto a ladder. *Please God help them. Please . . . please . . . please.*

An invisible force pulled him up like a swirling funnel cloud. *Maureen, John, Brian, Steve, . . . the baby on the way.* He knew right then she would be a girl. The last words of the Fireman's Prayer flowed through his mind:

> And if according to my fate
> I am to lose my life,
> bless with your protective hand
> my children and my wife.

2

The heat bore down on Sarah Lynch as she roller-bladed toward the pier. The sun scorched her shoulders and calves. Perspiration drenched her long red ponytail. She had to stop and catch her breath.

Sarah tipped her head back and drained the water bottle. *Another funeral.* This time, she wasn't required to attend. She felt the urge to turn around and slip back into the routine she had carefully carved out for herself: playing in three coed hockey leagues and teaching ice skating. The routine carried her from an early morning shower to her pillow at night. It filled her brain with fluff.

Sarah skated through the swarm of pedestrians on the Northern Avenue footbridge past James Hook Lobster. This mid-July day felt different from the rest. The roasting heat didn't come from the sun that afternoon. It radiated up from the heart of the people. Someone had poured an accelerant across the city and ignited a firestorm. Anger. Hatred. Shock. The fireman was one of their own.

The crowds thickened and pressed against her. It was so hot. She finally reached the federal courthouse where two Boston fire trucks extended their long ladders above the curved glass entrance. An enormous American flag stretched between the rescue boxes on top, and a lone fire truck idled below the flag with lights flashing.

"Sarah?"

She turned to see State Police Sergeant Frank Brady, the lead fire investigator for the state fire marshal's office. Frank was fit and stood about six feet, two inches tall. He had dark hair and luminous green eyes, but his best feature, the wide, magnetic grin, was absent that day.

"Long time no see." He placed his hands on her shoulders and kissed her cheek. "I miss you."

"Yeah, me too." Sarah heard her own voice waver. She should've returned his phone calls and e-mails. She'd been that way with all her old friends until they eventually gave up trying. "I've been meaning to call . . ."

"I know, I know. No worries, right?" Frank patted her back. "It's good to see you now." He gave her a tiny smile before turning serious again. "What're you doing here? Did you know him?" He pointed toward the fire truck.

"I'm here to watch, pay my respects." She wasn't quite sure why she had rollerbladed across town to be here. *Another funeral.*

"Gonna be huge, over twenty thousand firemen. They're lining up right over there and marching to St. Vincent's." Frank motioned toward Boston's World Trade Center on Seaport Boulevard. "Then it's over to Florian Hall afterward."

"Such a tragedy." Sarah eyed the fire truck idling under the flag. Why did it have to happen? Was it really God's will as the priests claimed? She didn't know, would never figure it out, and no longer wanted to try. But Sarah did know that someone was out there, probably next to that truck, drowning in the first stage of grief. Sarah remembered the shortness of breath, the nausea, the ringing in her ears.

"Boston hasn't seen anything like this before. Shot down in the line of duty." Frank wiped sweat from his brow. "We could use your help on this one. Nobody's been 'Lynched' in Suffolk County since you left the DA's office."

Lynched. Sarah hadn't heard that for a long time. It

had suited her well back in those days as a prosecutor, created headlines. Would she have been assigned to this one?

"Can you believe I'm heading up the fire investigation? First time Boston asked for our help in years."

"Really?" Sarah knew about the friction between the Boston Fire Department and the state police. They must've determined it was a conflict of interest for the Boston arson investigators. And the case was so emotional. How could anyone shoot a fireman? It had weighed on her mind from the time the story broke. "Do you have a good case?" She had to yell over the drumming of the helicopter blades.

"The facts are pretty straightforward, but—" He paused and pinched his lower lip. "It's different. You know, we arrested a black lady from Senegal. She's Muslim, too."

Sarah considered his words: *a black lady from Senegal*. In her experience as a prosecutor, most arsons and murders were committed by men.

Frank nodded. "She set the place on fire for the insurance because they were about to foreclose on her store. The fire department got there too quick, so she started shooting." Frank shook his head. "The lady shot Jack Fogerty, the first fireman on scene. After that, he continued rescuing her and her son. Got 'em to safety first and then he died. Unbelievable. How could somebody just shoot a fireman like that?"

Sarah recalled the fireman's family pictures in the *Boston Globe*. The children were so young. "I'm sorry for his wife and kids. Now she's a widow, and they've lost a dad."

"And she's pregnant too. Fourth child." Frank's gaze lingered on the truck. He appeared lost in thought for a moment. "You working?"

"Sort of." Sarah didn't feel like getting into her daily routine. It sounded so meaningless. "I may apply for an assistant coaching job at Boston College." She shrugged. "Up in the air."

"Not practicing law?"

The question jolted her. Sarah should've known it was coming. People always asked when she'd resume her law career, especially old colleagues.

"Sarah?"

"I prefer the ice." She couldn't think of anything better to say.

"You're a star, I'll give you that. We all rooted for you in the Olympics. Silver medalist and all. I'm proud of you."

"Yeah . . . thanks." And she should be proud. Sarah had achieved something most others could only dream about. Making the Olympic team, winning the silver. But, when it was all said and done, she knew the truth: hockey was her great escape. She looked up. Frank was rambling, and she could barely hear him through the noise.

". . . a real winner in the courtroom, so fiery, so talented." Frank studied her. "How long's it been?"

"Four years." *A lifetime ago.* The thought of practicing law again made her shudder. "I can't go back. My heart's not in it." Sarah still had nightmares about a gun, shots firing, and the most important person in her life . . . *falling.*

Frank looked into her eyes. "I'm sorry about what went down. Life's not fair sometimes. It shouldn't have happened to John . . . or you. I don't know how—"

Sarah raised her palms. She couldn't talk about it anymore.

"Understand." Frank nodded several times. "Still single?"

"Haven't found the right one." *The right one was dead.*

A siren blared and four Boston Police cruisers with pulsating blue lights proceeded toward them. The Boston fire commissioner, department chiefs, and officers marched in perfect parallel columns of two in their dress blues, white caps and gloves, and black bands running across gold badges. The color guard came next with its array of national, state, and fire department flags, followed by the piper band's steady drumbeat and solemn chords. The lone fire truck pulled out.

One woman caused all this?

Frank pointed toward the courthouse. "Fogerty's men will ride with him on Rescue One for the last time to the church and then to the cemetery. They're the honor guard with the red shoulder cords. See the men marching right beside the truck?"

Sarah shielded her eyes. "With the gold cords?"

Frank nodded. "Pallbearers. They were real close to him, part of his working group, some of his best friends."

The gold letters spelling *Boston Fire* glowed against the red fire truck. The reds and golds swirled together. The casket assumed center stage atop the truck, draped in an American flag and surrounded on all four sides by large fanned bouquets of red roses mixed with baby's breath. The casket loomed past Sarah in slow motion. It gave her chills. She watched until it was nothing more than a small red, white, and blue rectangle in the distance.

"I'm heading over to the church. Nice to see you again, Sarah."

"Tell everyone I said hello." She hugged him. "Good luck on the case."

"Thanks." Frank walked several paces and turned back. "Sarah? Aren't you related to Buddy Clancy?"

"My uncle. Why?"

"He's got the case."

Nick Marinelli needed this case. It was meant to be.

He stood in a single-file rank between Massachusetts Governor Ryan Noterman and Suffolk County District Attorney Martin Wright. The funeral procession would soon be passing before them and through the grand entrance of St. Vincent's Church. Sweat soaked his black hair, and the white dress shirt clung to his chest and back like a wet rag. The sun scorched his eyelids, yet he barely noticed. It was the heat from within that blistered.

Governor Noterman cocked his head. "Everything all set for the arraignment tomorrow?" He had a powerful voice.

"We're ready." Nick hated politicians and wished he wasn't wedged next to this suave African American with his magnanimous personality. Noterman was a second-term Democrat, known for his tax increases, steep budget cuts, and hiring freezes. As a result, Nick's unit at the DA's office had been cut in half. They were all overworked and underpaid. Noterman's solution: casino gambling, which would rescue the state from a financial doomsday. Nick knew he lived for the limelight, and here he was, front and center.

The governor rocked back on his heels. "How's the case coming along?"

"Fine." Nick refused to elaborate. The evidence appeared solid, but something frightened him. It wasn't quite right, and he couldn't figure out why.

Governor Noterman filled his cheeks with air and slowly released it.

The DA leaned across Nick and addressed the governor in his thick Boston accent: "Got a solid one."

Solid. Nick despised that word. It made him think of granite, something hard and impenetrable. One time he dropped a dumbbell on his mother's granite countertop and it cracked. They had to replace the whole thing.

"Your office better win this one, Marty, or you'll never get that IAFF endorsement when you throw your hat in for AG."

"Not worried in the least over the union. They wanted Marinelli and that's who they got." The DA snickered. "You're the one who needs the unions for that casino of yours."

"Back pocket." The governor eyed Nick. "And how old are you?"

"Thirty."

He whistled.

"Our best arson guy." The DA clasped Nick's shoulder. "Gets the convictions, and that's hard to do because the evidence burns up. Arson investigators love him and so does my union."

"*Your union.*" The governor rolled his eyes. "I hear you come from a family of firefighters, Nick."

"Can't even count 'em all." His Italian relatives had been calling around the clock. They pressured him for details he couldn't provide.

"I know about your father. A shame."

"That's why I specialize in arson." *And you know nothing about my father.*

"What about the homicide?"

"He's in good hands with Detective Callahan." The DA raised his voice over the news helicopters.

Governor Noterman shouted back, "I hear the accused retained Buddy Clancy."

Disgust clouded the DA's face. "And it won't take Clancy long to play up the race card. No offense, but we got a black Muslim woman here."

"You're in for quite a battle." The governor wiped his face with a handkerchief. "You can't let Clancy get away with it. This has nothing to do with race, religion, or the fact that it's a woman. Absolutely nothing." He glanced quickly at Nick and lowered his voice. "Trust me. It'll get real ugly if you lose." He gestured toward the crowds. "These people are out for blood. There's too much at . . ."

Nick couldn't hear the rest, and he didn't want to. He couldn't wait to get away from the politicians and back to work.

"Preeesent . . . arms!" a commander shouted.

All saluted as the tribute fire truck pulled up to the church. The twelve members of the honor guard lifted the casket and passed it to the pallbearers, who carried it between the ranks of dignitaries into the church.

Nick followed suit. His gaze rested on the family in the front pew—the pregnant widow with her three little boys. *God help them through this.* He had to survive the trial pressure for about a year. They would struggle a lifetime.

Nick would land a conviction for them—not the governor, DA, or the union. He would do it for Jack Fogerty's wife and boys and the little baby he'd never hold in his arms.

3

Sarah cut left and plowed through the hole. Two bodies closing in. Time was running out. Hard right. Her thighs burned. She held her breath. Only seconds remained. *Do it now.*

Sarah dug her skates into the ice and fired a backhand wrist shot at the net. Score!

She circled around and high-fived her teammates. The win felt exhilarating, and, as usual, Sarah was the only female on the team.

"Way to go, Hottie!" The right wing slapped her on the back.

"Hey, who's that?" The goalie pointed up the ice with his stick.

Sarah turned to see a white-haired character dressed in a plaid suit and red bow tie skating toward her with L.L. Bean black and tan leather skates dating back to the 1950s.

"Oh my God." It was her uncle, Buddy Clancy. She blinked several times, but he kept coming. "Uncle Buddy, what are you doing?"

"Looking for my favorite niece."

"Can't you wait 'til I get off the ice?"

"Nope."

Both teams and the refs stood motionless, staring at him. Why was he here? *The fireman's case.* She had planned to call earlier and ask how he could possibly defend this one. Instead, she had rushed home after the funeral to get ready for her hockey game.

"Great game, Sarah." Uncle Buddy grinned. "Played tough, plowed your way right through the line."

"Is this about—"

"Come on." He cut her off with a wave of the hand. "Let's skate for a bit, like we used to. I remember taking you to this rink not long after you learned to walk. You're thirty-two now, so thirty years ago? I held your hand and you wouldn't let . . ."

Sarah skated beside him as he reminisced. She knew all about his style. Uncle Buddy had such a sugary, grandfatherly way about him. She'd seen him entice just the right words from a witness's mouth. *Case-winning words.* He could charm a jury like no other, and here he was laying it on with her. Did he need her help now? After all, he had inspired her to go to law school and pursue litigation. *No way, she couldn't do it.* Sarah loved her uncle, but she wanted nothing to do with his case.

"And I remember your first peewee hockey game. You looked like a little ruffian in all that equipment. Your mother blamed me for encouraging you to play a boy's sport, but I knew you had it—"

"Uncle Buddy?" Sarah glided ahead and skated backwards, facing him. "Why did you take the case?"

"What case?"

"Come on. I know you too well."

"I guess you do." His lips formed a tiny, resigned-looking pout. He skated for a moment with his hands clasped behind his back. "It's a sad one."

"I'd say so. A fireman was shot and killed. He was my age, Uncle Buddy, with a family." She studied him. What could he possibly say to that?

"Yes, yes. I know." Uncle Buddy looked into her eyes. "I've been practicing law for a long time, Sarah. There's something unique about this one and the woman who stands accused. It's like this: she's the perfect puzzle piece, the right colors and shape, but wedged into the wrong spot."

4

"**I'm not making** any promises, Uncle Buddy." Sarah sidestepped around her jeep. She planned to politely decline the case after their jailhouse interview with his client and make it back in time to teach her after-school skating lessons. She wasn't ready to dive back into law, and there was no way in hell she could defend this woman. Her speech had been rehearsed earlier in the locker-room mirror.

"Just give her a chance." Uncle Buddy stepped out of the car and adjusted his gray fedora.

Sarah grunted. She was trained to despise the accused from day one. And now, after losing John, how could she have sympathy for anyone accused of murder? Frank and Mike Callahan knew exactly what they were doing when they made this arrest.

"Listen to her story."

"The fireman was doing his job, rescuing people in the middle of a fire."

"Nice opening line for the other side."

"What do you expect? I'm a trained prosecutor, Uncle Buddy." Sarah felt herself slipping into argument mode. "I'm not cut out for criminal defense work. In fact, I don't even like it."

"How do you know?"

"Because they're all guilty." It seemed like it, according to her experience in the gang unit. The police usually got it right in the first place. Thanks to lawyers like her uncle, bad guys would get off on technicalities.

"They brainwashed you at the DA's office," Uncle Buddy said.

"No, I think you've been brainwashed over the years by your crazy clients."

"Aww, come on. All good folks, some lost their way, that's all." He smiled. "Go on in and get a spot in line. I'll gather a few things here."

"Sure." Sarah headed toward the jail and sighed when she joined the long line of people waiting to pass through security. What was she doing here? No way in hell could she defend a case like this. She had to be firm with Uncle Buddy.

"Clancy!" a guard yelled. "I told you from now on you're to leave your dog in the car."

Sarah turned around, along with everyone else in line, to see Uncle Buddy clutching the leash of his golden retriever. *Here we go again.*

"*My dog* has a name."

The guard raised his hands and bellowed, "Well, I *forgot* it."

"How could you?" Uncle Buddy clucked his tongue. "Give you a hint." He addressed all the people in line. "Who served on the big bench from 1972 until his death in 2005?"

"No clue." The guard rolled his eyes.

"Come on. A conservative Supreme Court justice?"

"Rehnquist!" a young man shouted.

"Bingo!" Uncle Buddy gave him a high five.

The guard huffed. "I should've figured you'd name your dog after a judge. But, why a conservative? Aren't you a liberal Dem?"

Uncle Buddy laughed. "Rehnquist is the ideal conservative. He never says a word."

Sarah felt Rehnquist's tail rapping against her leg. He liked the story about his name. She reached down and stroked his head.

The guard folded his arms. "Seriously, he can't go up

with you, and I'm not going to babysit him all morning like last time."

"Just a few minutes?" Uncle Buddy pouted. "Rehnquist hates being all alone in the car."

The guard sighed. "Clancy."

"Come on, he can sniff out all the drug dealers." Uncle Buddy raised his eyebrows. "And I'll share some of my candy with you. Got the good stuff from Phillips."

"Rocky Road bars?"

Uncle Buddy nodded.

"Make it quick then." The guard snatched the leash and instructed Rehnquist to sit off to the side.

Uncle Buddy always gets his way, Sarah thought. She fished her keys and cell phone from her pockets, placed them in the plastic box, and tossed her purse on the security belt.

Uncle Buddy dropped his large tattered briefcase on the belt. A buzzer went off. Rehnquist barked.

"Dammit!" The guard raised the old briefcase. "It's always a three-ring circus with you, Clancy."

"My lucky briefcase is not for sale. It's forty-six years old, and I've won more cases with it than I can count."

"Gimme a break. You lost plenty over the years." The guard reached in and extracted a crinkled brown paper bag. "I'm more concerned about the knife you got in here."

Sarah felt the urge to defend her uncle. "It's a mistake, probably evidence from another case. Right, Uncle Buddy?" She could see him forgetting something like that. At least it wasn't a gun.

"Oh no." Uncle Buddy waved a finger. "I planned on bringing it up."

"What?" Sarah couldn't believe he said that. *A knife.* Was he planning the great escape? Another Alcatraz?

"Your client's in custody. They can't have knives."

The guard raised his voice, causing several people to crane their necks and watch the charade again.

"Fuss, fuss, fuss. In the old days we could walk right through with the tip of a hat. Why, I could bring three dogs, ten knives, and carry a gun if I wanted."

Leave it to Uncle Buddy, Sarah thought, *always something.* And he did everything for a reason, like his choice of bow ties for himself and Rehnquist. This one had black and white pinstripes. The inmate tie. What was he up to with the knife?

Uncle Buddy reached in the bag and lifted a shallow metal bowl decorated with brilliant red trumpet-shaped flowers. Next, he pulled out a spoon, a fork, and a butter knife.

Sarah stifled a laugh. "Are you planning on having lunch up there, Uncle Buddy?"

"I'd say it's a little early to be thinking about the last meal," the guard said. "Unless you plan on tanking, Clancy."

"I had a question or two about my client's dinnerware, that's all." Uncle Buddy raised the bowl.

"Clancy. Clancy. Clancy. You can never make it easy on us. You can take that bowl in, but the rest of it stays with me."

"Much obliged." Uncle Buddy grabbed his briefcase, and stuffed the bowl back inside. "I didn't care about the silverware; it's mine," he whispered to Sarah. "You see, if I had brought this big metal bowl by itself, he would've confiscated it as a potential weapon."

"You're good." Sarah couldn't help but admire her uncle. She secured her purse strap across her shoulder. "Why is the bowl important?"

Uncle Buddy raised his eyebrows like he had the answer to a puzzle, but she had to figure it out. That's why her uncle had fascinated her for as long as she could remember.

Sarah followed him into the visitors' area toward a figure in handcuffs sitting behind a small conference table wearing an orange jail-issue jumpsuit. The woman raised her head, and Sarah uttered a tiny gasp. She was stunning. Her thick hair flowed down to her waist in an abundance of African braids. Tiny colorful beads adorned each braid at the bottom. She had an exquisite, narrow face with beautiful skin and large chestnut eyes.

As they gazed at each other, Sarah recognized the look of immense sadness. It was an image she saw in herself over the past four years. How did this beautiful woman end up here?

"Good morning, Amina." Mr. Clancy removed his hat. "Please meet my niece, Sarah Lynch. Sarah, this is Amina Diallo."

Amina stood, leaned forward, and kissed Sarah twice, once on each cheek. She felt clumsy with the handcuffs. Sarah stiffened. Perhaps Amina shouldn't have kissed her. People didn't do that over here. She knew that, but she wasn't thinking straight. The nausea crept into her throat. Amina was so exhausted she had trouble catching her breath. Her ears rang and the tiny black spots appeared again.

"You okay?" Mr. Clancy placed a gentle hand on Amina's arm and guided her back into her chair.

Amina rested her head between her knees and gagged. "My son?" The words gushed out.

"Malick will be alright." Mr. Clancy's voice was calming. He reminded Amina of her father. "Good news. He'll be released from the hospital this afternoon, and they'll place him with a local family. I'll make sure he's safe." His eyes crinkled with many lines. "Promise."

"Is he a suspect?" Amina clasped her hands on her knees and pressed them hard against her lips. She had prayed all night for Malick. She heard Mr. Clancy sit down; the metal chair creaked.

"The police ruled him out."

"Thank you, God," Amina whispered. "Thank you, God." She closed her eyes for a moment before lifting her head. "I am worried for Malick. Only fifteen. He's all alone over here." The image of her limp son in the fireman's arms flashed before her. It burned a hole in her heart. Malick had appeared dead with his head flopped back, mouth wide open. *Dead.* Her only child. *Dead.* Amina's breathing became shallow.

Mr. Clancy squeezed her hands as if he could read her thoughts. "It's okay. We'll get through this together."

Sarah opened a legal pad and clicked the button on her pen. "We might as well get started."

Amina inhaled and regarded Mr. Clancy's niece. Sarah wore a stiff black suit and sat up straight with her pen poised, ready to go. She looked like a doctor preparing for surgery. Mr. Clancy had spoken highly of Sarah's legal skills, yet she seemed uncomfortable and out of place.

"Can you tell me about the events leading up to the fire?" Sarah asked.

No. Please no. Amina began to shake. The bile rose from the pit of her stomach up to her throat. Amina wanted to tell Sarah she couldn't remember a thing, but the words wouldn't come out. Her jaw had locked.

Sarah clicked her pen against the tabletop as she waited for an answer. When none came, she sighed. "Okay, let's back up then. The lender was about to foreclose on your building?"

Amina managed a nod. *The foreclosure again.* The police had questioned her until her head spun. She should've just let it go. *Started over.*

Sarah read something from her notes. "So, the store was on the first floor, and you and Malick lived on the second floor, up above?"

"Mmmm." *Upstairs sleeping.* Amina had to get Malick out . . . and then she couldn't find him. He wasn't in his bedroom, not in the hall . . .

Amina saw Sarah's mouth moving. She must've asked another question. *Concentrate.* Amina rubbed her temples. The handcuffs scraped against her chin.

"When did you purchase the property?" Sarah's voice sounded distant.

Amina remembered signing the papers. She had taken her time, used her most beautiful penmanship—a big curly *A* and *D*. She finally owned her home and store. The first woman in her family to do it. So many years of hard work, saving money, sacrificing. Amina recalled having such high hopes that her husband would join them. That day she felt on top of the world. Amina couldn't remember the last time she felt like that.

"You don't recall when?" Sarah glanced at her uncle.

"When . . . what?" Amina felt dazed.

"Not to worry, we can look that stuff up." Mr. Clancy smiled at her, *a knowing smile*.

"What happened with the mortgage?" Sarah shifted in her seat.

"I don't know." Amina looked away. *She didn't know, that was the truth*.

"When did you stop paying?"

Judgmental. Yes. Sarah was judgmental. Why didn't she *pay*? A simple question. Amina remembered the day her landlord put the building up for sale and presented her with an eviction notice. She recalled panicking. How could she find another location for her market and afford the rent? All Amina's customers were local.

A week later, a well-dressed man stopped in and asked for a bowl of yassa au roulet. "This is the best chicken I've ever had." He requested a refill and came back the following day. His name was Mark LaSpada. He knew the building was for sale and asked many questions. When Amina expressed concern over moving, Mr. LaSpada came up with a solution: she could buy the building herself. *Me?* Amina recalled laughing out loud. Who could believe it? But Mr. LaSpada worked the numbers. He made everything so easy. Amina came up with money for the down payment, and that's when she signed the papers. The monthly mortgage would be the same as her previous rent. And it was, until the payments doubled after a year, and a few months later, they went up again. Mr. LaSpada said not to worry, we'll fix it. *He lied.*

Sarah leaned across the table. "What's his name?"

"Whose?" Amina didn't know she'd spoken a word out loud. Perhaps she had without realizing it? Was she delirious?

"Your mortgage broker."

"Right." Amina's gaze dropped to her lap. "Mark LaSpada." Her words were barely audible.

"What did he do?" Sarah cocked her head.

"Nothing. He never returned my phone calls." Amina chewed on her lower lip. *They say I started the fire for insurance money because the lender was about to foreclose. That's all.* Amina looked at Mr. Clancy for help. Tears ran down her cheeks.

Mr. Clancy curled his lips into a slight smile as if he understood her despair. "I hear you're a terrific cook?"

Amina nodded. She could talk about food, that was

safe. She swallowed back the lump in her throat. *Calm down and concentrate.* "You'd like my bouidienne."

"What's that?" Sarah twirled the pen between her fingers.

"Fish stew over rice." Amina imagined sautéing the onions, tomatoes, parsley, stirring . . .

"Sounds delicious." Sarah smiled for the first time.

"Yes, you see, in addition to the store, I had a little deli. Up front. I'd make sandwiches . . . wraps, but on each day of the week I would feature a hot dish." Amina pictured people stopping in for their favorites. On Tuesdays she always made her yassa au roulet de la casamance, her mother's barbecued chicken smothered in onion and lemon sauce over rice. On Fridays she served avocat aux crevettes, avocado stuffed with shrimp. Amina could almost smell the sweet and spicy aromas from the recipes passed down through her family.

"What else did you sell at the market?" Sarah scratched something down on her pad.

"Uh . . . I've added things over the years." Amina drew a blank. She was so tired. Up all night. *Don't think about the fire.* "I'm sorry, what did you ask me?"

"What types of products did you sell?"

"Oh." Amina inhaled. "We have West African . . . uhh . . . different types of couscous, spices, oils, sweets." Amina pictured the narrow aisles, which she'd taken such care stacking and organizing. "Nine years." Panic gripped her. She wrung her hands so hard her fingers hurt. "They wanted it all."

Sarah leaned over the table. "Who's they?"

Amina froze. She couldn't talk about this anymore. What if she said the wrong thing? *Don't ask me. Please don't ask me.* She closed her eyes and saw the dense smoke, jars smashing on the floor, Malick's head flopped back.

Sarah asked another question, yet Amina blocked it from her mind. *Stop.* She wished she could cover her ears with both hands, but the steel cuffs prevented that. "My son. I have ruined his life." Amina doubled over and cried.

Mr. Clancy placed a hand on her shoulder. "You're a good mother, Amina. Nobody can take that away." Sarah slid a plastic packet of tissues next to her. She cried for several minutes before wiping her eyes.

"Hey, let's not forget the bowl, Sarah." Mr. Clancy reached into his briefcase, and pulled out a dinner bowl.

Amina's favorite dinner bowl.

"Somebody dropped it off at my office yesterday. Anonymously." Mr. Clancy rested it on the table. His knuckles were knobby like her father's.

Amina gazed at her bowl. "Danny."

"Who's that?" Sarah asked.

"A homeless man who comes around collecting cans on Wednesday nights." Amina pictured his slow gait; one leg was shorter than the other. Sometimes she could hear the rattling grocery cart from a block away. "Danny." She sighed. "Loves the thiou a la wande, my meat stew. I serve it the Senegalese way. Malick and I have enjoyed sharing that meal with him for years." *Never again.*

"What is the Senegalese way?" Sarah asked.

"Well . . . I lay out a rug and place the bowl in the center. We sit around and dip into the stew. Like this." Amina demonstrated using three fingers. "We have coffee and dessert after. Danny likes my banana glace."

Mr. Clancy's stomach growled. "Now I'm hungry."

"What kind are these?" Sarah rotated the bowl and traced a red flower with her index finger.

"The flowers of the African tulip tree."

"Well, my dear. We must be on our way. Rehnquist's waiting downstairs, and we have lots of work ahead. I'll check up on Malick and come back tomorrow. You have my word."

"Thank you." Amina was relieved to see them go. Thank God they didn't ask her more details about the fire. She was too drained to think straight. *The fire.* She shivered. What would she tell them?

Sarah wondered why Uncle Buddy ended the meeting so abruptly. She was also surprised he hadn't come armed with pen and legal pad. At the DA's office, Sarah had gathered all the information she could in the initial interview. Perhaps he'd already done that, but she doubted it.

"What do you think?" Uncle Buddy asked when they were walking back to the car with Rehnquist.

"Amina has a unique background, coming over here from Senegal, working her tail off. I'll give you that. But you'll have a jury full of people with interesting stories. Amina's isn't going to be enough to override the fact that a fireman was shot and killed in the line of duty."

"Did you pay attention to her body language?"

Sarah pictured the interview. "Came across nervous, couldn't talk about the fire."

"What does that tell you?"

"That she's guilty."

"Mercy." Uncle Buddy cupped his forehead. "She really has been brainwashed, Rehnquist." He paused. "Step out of the prosecutor's shoes for a minute. I think Amina's afraid. There's more to her story."

"If you think so, then why didn't you ask?" Sarah would've spent twice as long, peppering this woman with questions.

"She's not ready to tell us."

Sarah sighed, frustrated with him. "How could you possibly know that if you didn't ask?"

"If you ask the right question at the wrong time, you'll get the wrong answer."

Perhaps Uncle Buddy was afraid of the truth. How could he defend Amina if he learned for certain that she committed arson and killed a fireman? Then what?

"Why did you make such a big deal about that bowl?" Sarah questioned whether the charade with the guard was worth it.

"Ahhh, Rehnquist, what am I going to do with her?" Uncle Buddy gave his dog a hardy pat. "The heart of this case is right here in the bowl. Let me show you." He handed Sarah Rehnquist's leash, set his briefcase down, and raised the bowl up high with both hands. Sunlight bounced around the engraved flowers. "Do you know anyone who would invite a homeless man in to share a special family meal once a week?"

Sarah considered his remark. Would she do that? Probably not. "Actually, I can't think of anybody. You got me there."

"That's right." Uncle Buddy handed the bowl to Sarah. "Here we have a very compassionate woman. So, my question to you and a jury would be: does Amina have it in her? Could she commit arson and murder a fireman? My instincts say no."

5

Nick slipped into the large First Session Courtroom and headed toward the prosecutor's table. The arraignment would be filmed live, and he was the face of justice. Nick had to exude confidence in the prosecution's case, so that the raw, bleeding city could begin to heal. A flawless court hearing was essential to the process.

A court officer opened the door. "I'm letting the press in at eight thirty. Judge wants to move it, prisoner's here."

"Got extra security?"

The court officer walked out without answering.

Nick hoped so. He knew the governor had placed a hiring freeze on court officers too. The firemen would be attending in droves. *Angry droves.* He tossed his file down. The doors flew open and banged closed. Footsteps sprinted down the aisle.

Nick turned around and saw his former boss from the gang unit, Sarah Lynch. "What on earth are you doing here?"

"My uncle's finishing a trial in Cambridge, so I agreed to handle the arraignment." Sarah placed a big tattered brown briefcase on the defense table. It didn't appear to belong to her.

Nick couldn't believe it. Sarah? Pinch-hitting for the defense? And this, of all cases?

"Hallway's packed with firemen already." She adjusted her blue fitted skirt.

Nick stared at her without knowing what to say. Sarah was smart and beautiful, and her voice was soothing, like a late-night radio disc jockey. He used to close his eyes and listen to her charm the jury. God, she was good.

"Nick? You look like you've seen a ghost."

"Well, I haven't heard from you since—"

"John's funeral. Four years ago."

"Right." Nick felt guilty. He should've called her more over the years, checked up on her. John Burke's senseless murder had thrown Sarah over the edge. She was standing right next to him when he got shot. Sarah was unreachable after the funeral. Nick meant to call again after he'd seen her play in the Olympics. Perhaps he should give her a hug now. He opened his file instead.

"What do you have?" she asked.

"Initial police and fire reports. I can't believe you're handling this. Are you working with your uncle now?" Nick was well aware of Clancy's reputation, a master at his craft. He could find a pinprick in a case and tear it into a canyon.

Sarah fiddled with the worn handle on the briefcase. "I'm weighing my options."

"Really? Come back to the DA's office. Enough time has passed. What happened to John wasn't your fault."

She appeared lost in thought. "Not everyone believes that, Nick."

"So what? Come back and prove them wrong. Show those shortsighted bastards what you're all about. You're a fighter, Sarah. You were tough as nails in the Olympics." Nick remembered her getting the most penalties.

"What're you asking for today?" Sarah pulled out a legal pad.

Nick noticed the swift change of subject. He decided not to press her further. "Sarah. You think I'd let a murderer off on personal?"

"My uncle wasn't expecting personal recognizance, but something reasonable. Let's say . . . five hundred?

We'll set a pretrial date with enough time for you to present your case to the grand jury."

"Out of your mind?" Nick deliberately picked a phrase *she* would've used when they worked together. "I'm requesting this one held without bail."

"We're talking no prior record."

Nick figured her uncle had rehearsed this with her. "What about the trespassing and wanton destruction of property charges?"

"Those were dismissed. Amina is a single mother raising a teenaged son."

Not the single mother bullshit again. "A foreigner, risk of flight."

Sarah raised her eyebrows. "Amina has a green card. She's an immigrant small business owner who works hard and has strong ties in the community."

"So what?" Nick was tired of her charade. Sarah used to hear the same old excuses back in the gang unit. In fact, they used to joke about it together. "Look, I got a dead fireman on my hands. I'm requesting Amina Diallo be held without bail, and that's my final say."

"But—"

Nick watched her lips moving. A good acting job, but not spoken from the heart. He knew the real Sarah, a fierce advocate for being tough on crime. She didn't know what she was doing.

"Sarah." Nick touched her arm with his fingertips. "As a friend and former colleague, let me tell you, this is not the case to get involved in. Take a hard look at these reports." He handed her the thick stack. "We have Frank Brady on the arson and Mike Callahan heading up the homicide. The best of the best."

Sarah fanned her thumb up through the corners of the reports. "I ran into Frank at the funeral. He said you have an open-and-shut case." She unclasped her briefcase again and pulled out a manila folder and . . . a shiny metal bowl decorated with tropical flowers.

"What's that for?" Nick wondered if she planned on eating lunch at the courthouse—*with her own bowl*?

"Nothing." She tucked it back in. "You know, Nick, there may be more to this case. Remember all the bad blood between the state police fire investigators and the Boston guys? Think about all the political pressure on Frank to make the arrest and land a conviction. The governor's been making one press conference after another. Did anyone look beyond this one woman?"

That's her uncle talking. "I'd say Frank was especially meticulous with his investigation, given the political heat. And Callahan's been working around the clock on the homicide. You know them both, Sarah. Very conscientious."

"But what about you?"

"Me?"

"Yeah, don't you think it's too personal?" Sarah paused. "A fireman died." She paused again. "Given what happened to your father?"

Nick felt the anger burning in his gut as if Sarah had doused it with gasoline. Since when had she asked about his father? *How's he doing? Who takes care of him? How hard was it to grow up with a disfigured dad condemned to a wheelchair? Little kids were afraid to look at him—the bogey man without a face.*

"Nick?"

"I'm thoroughly convinced they arrested the right one, and I wish we had the death penalty."

Cole Sollier had prepared for this arraignment like no other. He squeezed onto the courtroom bench jammed with bleary-eyed firemen. Someone would pay for the man in the casket. His fingers worked the ziplock plastic bag in his coat pocket and plunged into the oily kalamata black olives.

What happened? The plan had been well thought-out. They came too soon. He placed an olive on his tongue and pressed it against the roof of his mouth, extracting salt and oil. Now the mistake was his to fix.

Cole rolled the olive from the tip to the back of his tongue. The simple motion diverted his mind from the searing pain in his stomach. His back molars penetrated the flesh and stopped at the pit. She would be taken care of. *They promised.*

"All rise!" a court officer said. "The Brighton Division of the Boston Municipal Court is now in session. The Honorable Richard A. Rouley presiding."

Amina felt the scorching hatred of the crowd. She kept her eyes down, and was relieved Sarah had brought her a headscarf to wear in public. She couldn't look at those people. The sheriff squeezed her arm hard, cutting off the circulation. He would make her face them, force her eyelids all the way open. The woman deputy would've stripped her naked for this. Amina shuddered at the thought of rough fingers pulling her apart. Yanking, prodding, spitting. *Please don't be here, Malick. You can't see this.*

"Burn in hell you fucking Muslim whore!"

The courtroom erupted with jeers. All the firemen stood, and several pushed into the aisles.

"Bring back the death penalty!" a woman shouted.

Amina jerked. They want to *kill me.* Right here. She had a sudden premonition, a vision of blood everywhere. Her body turned frigid. Was she prepared to die?

"Order!" The judge pounded his gavel. "Remove those

two." From the corner of her eye, Amina watched as court officers struggled with a big woman and a fireman shouting profanities.

"Now the rest of you sit down!" the judge yelled.

Could he stop them? Amina heard rustling from the gallery, but the shouting had ceased.

"Your Honor, may I have permission to join Ms. Diallo on the other side of the wall, in the criminal dock?" Sarah's voice rang out.

"You may, counselor."

She wants to stand beside *me*? Amina watched in disbelief as Sarah made her way into the dock through the swinging wooden door on the side.

"It's okay," Sarah whispered. She placed a hand on Amina's shoulder and left it there. *A brave move.* Amina was speechless.

The clerk rose. "First on the list of arraignments for Wednesday, July twenty-fourth is criminal complaint number 11-CR-1633, Commonwealth versus Amina Diallo. Addressing count one, burning of a dwelling place in violation of Massachusetts General Laws, Chapter 266, Section 1. How do you plead?"

The clerk stared; the crowd stared. They were all waiting for an answer. Amina's words caught in her throat. They accused her of burning. Burning the store, burning her home upstairs . . . while Malick lay sleeping.

The judge huffed. "What's the matter? Do we need an interpreter here?"

"No, Your Honor," Sarah said. She then whispered into Amina's ear: "Just say 'not guilty.' "

Just say not guilty. What if she said guilty? What would happen then? Would it be best for Malick? Amina scanned the crowd. Would they still want to kill her?

Sarah nudged her.

"Not guilty." Amina had to force the words out.

"Liar!"

The gallery burst into chaos again.

"Order!" The judge banged the gavel until the shouting subsided.

"Addressing count two, alleging the crime of murder in violation of Massachusetts General Laws, Chapter 265, Section 1. How do you plead?"

Amina closed her eyes and pictured the fireman carrying Malick over his shoulders. His name was Jack Fogerty. He had willed himself to stay alive in order to rescue them. Amina knew it from the moment he whipped off his glove and held her by the hand. He guided them right through the black smoke. They would've died. *Breathe.* Amina's chest constricted. *Breathe.*

"Amina, you have to answer again." Sarah's voice sounded far away.

"Not guilty." *And that was all she had to say.*

"Murderer!"

"Terrorist!"

"Question of bail, Commonwealth?" The judge yelled over multiple shouts from the gallery.

"Yes, Your Honor." *A confident male voice. The prosecutor.*

"I'll hear you."

"The commonwealth is requesting that the defendant, Amina Diallo—"

A woman screamed.

"He's got a gun!"

A resounding blast. Amina fell.

A man sitting near the front dove into the criminal dock.

Judge Rouley ducked under the bench.

People screamed.

Nick turned to see a man with a handgun sprinting

down the center aisle. He slammed through the court-room doors and disappeared. Another gunshot came from the hallway, followed by more screaming.

A moment of silence shrouded the courtroom until a court officer barged in. "Anybody hurt?"

"The Muslim got shot!" a voice called out.

"Call an ambulance!"

Nick scanned the area where Sarah and Amina had been standing moments before. A sheriff's deputy stood still, looking down. Blood spatters dotted his face and uniform. Deep red rivulets dripped down the wall. An array of sirens screamed outside.

Nick headed toward the dock.

"No, stay back!" the deputy yelled.

Nick felt helpless and numb. He couldn't see what they were doing behind the high wall. "Is she going to make it?"

"If they stop the bleeding."

Nick's jaw muscles clenched. This wasn't the ending anyone wanted. It was his job to win a conviction for the family through the criminal justice system.

"Everyone stay seated!" A Boston cop jogged down the aisle, followed by paramedics wheeling a stretcher.

Frank Brady emerged from behind the dock with his hands, pants, and shirt covered in blood. Nick had re-membered him slipping into the front row just before the judge came on the bench.

Nick stood on tiptoe, straining to see.

"Ready for transport. Coming through!" The cop ran back down the aisle with his arms up.

The door to the side of the dock flew open as the para-medics wheeled a body.

"Clear the courtroom!" The cop smacked his billy club. "Turn off the goddamn cameras."

"Is it safe to come out?" an old man's voice cackled.

"Clear."

Nick watched the judge crawl out from under the bench.

"Deputy Graves!" Judge Rouley marched toward the dock.

The deputy with blood spatters on his face and shirt jumped. "Yes, Your Honor?"

"How'd this happen in *my* courtroom?"

"Don't know. Me and Deputy Simons were standing with the prisoner over here and—"

"Where's Simons?"

"Down in lockup."

"What's he doing there?"

"Taking the prisoner back down."

A sick feeling came over Nick. He sprinted toward the dock and peered over the wall. Blood all over the rug. Blood on the deputy's boots. Blood soaked the police and fire reports he had given Sarah.

"Mr. Marinelli?" The sheriff's deputy grabbed his arm.

"You said Simons was down in lockup with the prisoner."

"Yeah."

"But Amina Diallo went out on the stretcher, remember?"

The sheriff's deputy stared at him.

"Did you hear me?" Nick felt himself perspiring. "You said *the prisoner*, but you meant to say—"

"Prisoner's in lockup."

Nick's mouth went dry, his body chilled. "Who was on that stretcher?"

"Sarah Lynch."

6

Two male faces crowded Sarah's vision. Lights, wires, and beeping monitors filled the spaces beyond. Her body bounced and rocked from side to side. A siren wailed and raging pain ran the length of her left arm. "Where . . . ?"

"On the way to the hospital."

"My arm's killing."

"Hang in there."

An IV tube pierced her skin. "What happened?"

"You got shot."

The word *shot* pinged from wall to wall like an echo. *Shot.* She felt her eyes closing again. *Shot.* Same sound, like four years ago. *Shot.*

Three hours later, Sarah woke up in a pale green hospital room, looking up at a bow tie dotted with yellow smiley faces. "Uncle Buddy?"

"Thank God you're okay." He stroked his white hair.

"She's awake!" Her mother dashed toward the bed, followed by her father and five brothers. "How're you feeling, sweetheart?"

Sarah didn't feel anything except thirsty.

"You got shot right in the courtroom!" her youngest brother yelled. "It's all over TV. You're famous again, like when you were in the Olympics."

Shot. She could've been killed. Nausea crept into her throat. Shot. *In court.* Sarah recalled standing in the dock next to Amina. An explosion as she fell . . . screams . . . blood. Wait, they both went down. Amina? What happened to Amina?

Her mother brushed her cheek. "Sarah?"

"What about Amina?"

"She's alright," Uncle Buddy said.

"She get shot?" Sarah remembered all the blood.

"No."

Thank God. Sarah was relieved but felt numb again. She took the bullet this time. Last time it had been John, but he died. *Instantly*. Both times, too close. Sarah bit her lower lip until it hurt. She was still alive. If she hadn't been standing next to Amina in the criminal dock, would it have gone down differently? Amina might be dead.

Sarah's arm throbbed like hell. She was afraid to look.

"You'll be okay." Her father motioned to the white gauze covering her left arm. He must have sensed her fear. "Nicked artery and tissue damage. Take a little time, but it'll heal."

"Who did it?" Sarah imagined a distraught fireman being tackled to the ground.

"Don't know." Her mother's face tightened. "He's still on the loose."

"What?" Sarah jolted forward. Pain shot through her arm. "You mean some guy snuck a gun through security and then got away?"

Uncle Buddy grimaced. "He wrestled the gun from a court officer, fired, and took off. Cut right through everybody in the hallway. There were no court officers or security guards stationed out there, so he got away." He paused. "They'll catch him."

"I hope so. Got a bad feeling about this one." Her mother glared at Uncle Buddy.

"They're in a *huge* fight because you got shot," her brother whispered. "Mom's been on his case wicked bad."

Sarah could picture the two of them going at it, brother

and sister. Uncle Buddy didn't stand a chance today. "I'd like to speak with Uncle Buddy a moment. Alone."

"Don't let him use that fancy lawyer talk." Her mother shuffled them out and pointed at Uncle Buddy. "God forbid you ask *my daughter* to handle something small for you. Oh no. Gotta be a huge murder case where everybody despises—*hates*—your client. She killed a fireman, for Christ's sake. You should be ashamed of yourself. After all Sarah went through before?" She slammed the door.

Uncle Buddy sat in a chair next to the bed and rubbed his eyes. He looked exhausted. "I'm sorry, Sarah."

"Not your fault." She could tell her uncle felt guilty. If he hadn't been tied up on the other trial in Cambridge, he would've been standing in her place, next to Amina. Perhaps he would've been over to the left a little more and that would be it for him. Sarah couldn't figure it out. That's why she had immersed herself in hockey, so she could stop analyzing. She replayed the arraignment in her mind. "Why do you think . . ."

"I don't have an answer."

"Is it the right question?"

"I think so."

"Wrong time?"

Uncle Buddy smiled and his eyes crinkled in that warm, comforting way of his.

Sarah's head felt groggy. She focused on the rain falling outside her window. "First time I set foot in a courtroom after four years, and I almost got taken out." She sighed. "I think I'll apply for that job coaching women's hockey at BC."

"That what you want?"

Uncle Buddy could make her think by simply raising a question. And she didn't feel like thinking. *Not today, not tomorrow.* What did she want? *Just got shot.* To stay alive? Or perhaps not. She imagined John, his deep belly laugh, the way he used to tickle her.

"You're a talented lawyer," Uncle Buddy said.

Lawyer. Sarah focused on that word. It sounded cold, intellectual. Why had she applied to law school? Influenced by Uncle Buddy and all his courtroom glory? Yes, of course. But had she considered other options? Not really. She thought back to her first day as a prosecutor in the Boston Municipal Court. *Frantic.* Sarah had started the day with a slew of bail arguments in the first session, throwing out random dollar amounts to the judge, not knowing what she was doing. She moved on to an overload of pretrial conferences in the grungy hallway surrounded by gangs of ham-and-egger criminal lawyers in mismatched suits. She plea-bargained domestics, OUIs, and assault and batteries until they became a blur. The supervisor kept tossing her manila folders and criminal records: *get rid of these.* It was all about cleaning house.

Sarah eventually graduated from the district court chaos to handling more serious cases in superior court. She thrived in the courtroom, where there were so many creative ways to win points with the jury and land a conviction.

"I could go back to the DA's office?"

"The DA's office? Sure, with your big machete." Uncle Buddy grabbed a wet umbrella and made a swinging motion. "Clean up the streets of Boston."

Wasn't that a good thing? "I'd be practicing law again."

"And what does it mean to practice law?"

Why was he asking her that? Sarah shrugged. "Arguing cases before the jury. Getting convictions. You know." Her head ached. She didn't feel like elaborating.

"You didn't answer my question."

And who's on trial? "Come on, Uncle Buddy. I'm tired. I just got shot. It's the defense side I'm uncomfortable with. That's for you, not me." Sarah recalled the angry masses at the funeral procession and the hatred spewing from the people in court. *A force raging out of control.* They had called Amina a whore, a terrorist. It had taken courage to enter the dock and stand by her. *And that's when she got shot.*

Uncle Buddy twirled the umbrella, tossed it to the ceiling, and caught it like a baton. "Which hockey game did you enjoy more, the one against Sweden or Switzerland?"

Sarah knew the answers were in his questions. "Sweden."

"But you lost."

"We played tough, weren't supposed to win."

"Ahhh." He spun the umbrella up behind his back and caught it again.

"Watch the IV lines Unc—"

"Now think of Amina's case. Who's supposed to win?"

"Handpicked from my garden just for you." Frank arranged the bouquet of pink coneflowers and yellow black-eyed Susans on Sarah's bedside stand.

"Thank you." Sarah sipped her ginger ale. She had slept several hours and felt somewhat better. At least the headache was gone. "Rumor has it you vaulted over the dock and stopped me from bleeding to death."

"You owe me. Ruined a brand new shirt and pants."

"I'm sure the state police'll foot the bill."

Frank smiled and sat down.

"Any leads on who shot me?" Sarah couldn't believe the shooter escaped.

"Not yet. Boston PD's working on it. I still can't

believe it happened, but they were short on security. It boils down to all the governor's budget cuts."

Sarah fingered her bandage, contemplating the scenario for the hundredth time. She couldn't stop asking herself the "why" questions. Perhaps Frank had answers. "Do you think someone was targeting Amina?"

"Looks that way. Emotions were running so high after the funeral. They think it was a fireman."

"It's the second time."

"What?"

Sarah watched Frank's eyes register. He knew exactly what she meant. "I was walking right next to John when that asshole shot and killed him four years ago. Alive one second, dead the next. God, he meant the world to me."

"I know."

"It was my fault."

"Sarah." Frank reached across the bed and squeezed her hand. "John knew the risks. He was an Assistant D.A. longer than you."

She pulled away. "I arranged the meeting, and it turned out to be a setup."

"Don't blame yourself."

How could she not? "We were supposed to meet a key witness near Upham's Corner. The guy said he was too scared to come in. I should've known better." Sarah wished she could erase her mistake. The witness had lied, and they walked right into it. The shots echoed through her ears.

"You were doing your job. Remember, John went voluntarily."

"He had second thoughts. I'm the one who convinced him. I needed that witness to win my case." Sarah bit her lip as tears rolled down her cheek. "I killed him."

"No you didn't. Come on."

"And then I ran away from it all. Played hockey and worked out until I couldn't think anymore." Sarah had driven her mind and body to the point of sheer exhaustion. That's how she'd made the Olympic team.

"Your way of coping."

"Quitting." Sarah had known the truth for a long time, but immersed herself in her routine whenever it surfaced. She was a coward when she left the DA's office. "I should've stayed and fought it out. John's killer was never brought to justice."

"You need rest."

Sarah had heard those words before. Rest? No way. Resting gave her mind free rein and that meant dwelling on how things should've been. She'd rather dive back into hockey. No more thinking. Everyone would understand. They always did. Except Uncle Buddy, he liked making her think. And why was that? Sarah gazed at the black umbrella leaning against the wall. Her uncle was providing her with a way to get back on her feet, something to fight for, something meaningful. He couldn't have predicted she'd get shot in the process, but that's why he grabbed her off the rink. *Rescued her.*

"Sarah?"

"Is this case really that strong against Amina?"

Frank got up, walked to the window, and peered at the Boston skyline. "I wouldn't take it on if I were you. It's too emotional. The Boston cops and firemen will never forgive you. They'll take it personally."

Frank was right about them; she'd played on their team. "But not you, Frank. You wouldn't hold it against me."

"No."

Frank was different; Sarah knew that. Despite his flaws, he believed in justice, which went far beyond locking people up. She looked over his shoulder and could see the glass buildings reflecting orange as the setting sun broke through the remaining rain clouds. "Do you really think Amina did it?"

Frank turned from the window and looked her square in the eyes. "I do."

Sarah felt the conviction in his words. She pressed a button, adjusting the bed to an upright position. "Perhaps this was a classic rush to judgment, Frank. Have you thought about that? The Boston Fire Department lost one of their own, and they hated having to call you in on the arson. I'm sure it was the governor's decision." Sarah hit her left arm on the bed rail and grimaced in pain.

"You okay?"

Sarah nodded, but her arm still throbbed. "And the firefighter's union is leaning on the governor, mayor, and the DA. I know all about the political pressure—I lived with it."

"No question I'm up to my eyeballs in pressure, but that doesn't mean I compromised my investigation."

She knew he'd say that. "My uncle and I reviewed the reports. Looks like two points of origin for the fire, and the ballistics evidence isn't solid."

"Sarah, I can't discuss the case with you." Frank sounded curt. "I'd better leave and let you rest."

She studied the umbrella again. *The underdog.*

"Did you speak with Amina?" Sarah knew Frank's strength came from his superior interviewing skills. He had a way with people, just like Uncle Buddy.

"Course."

"Did you know that once a week Amina shares a meal with a homeless man? A special Senegalese meal. With her son there and everything. Did you know that, Frank?"

He tapped his fingers on his cheek.

"Your reputation's built on knowing someone's story inside and out?"

"That small fact won't make a difference here."

"Because you've already set your mind against Amina."

"Based on my investigation, she's guilty."

"But this is one less question asked, one less fact you know about." Sarah fixed her gaze on Frank, locking eye contact, and, at the same time, locking her will.

Cole tore the lid from a plastic tub of black olives and wedged it between his legs. The cement seawall felt hard and cold through his jeans, and the thick mist penetrated his worn leather jacket and sweatshirt. A bitter wind skimmed off the surf, slinging salt beads that clung to his chapped lips and stung his eyes. It smelled like sulfur and muck, reminding him of digging for clams with his mother years ago.

The sun had set and the water appeared black in spots. Black like the olives. *And smoke.* Sometimes the blackness caused him to see imaginary red blotches. Is that what happened? *Another olive. Another mistake.*

Cole bit through the salty flesh, down to the pit. That woman didn't know what she was up against. Why did she do it? He propelled the pit between puckered lips and watched it arc up, out, and down into the gray foam. His fingers plunged into the oily tub, grasping more olives. In rapid succession, he chewed and spit, chewed and spit.

A breaker slammed against the wall, showering Cole's head with frigid water. His nostrils bubbled and dripped. He licked the salt water from his lips and chin.

Another pit sailed off the tip of his tongue. He rubbed away the itch in his eyes.

Cole stared for a long time into the gray-black sea, spitting pits and ignoring the pain. He nibbled another olive with his front teeth and flicked the pit into the surf with his thumb and middle finger. They promised to take care of her. What if he hadn't made it out? He sucked another olive before clenching down, cracking the pit in two.

7

Amina was surprised to see Sarah waiting for her in the visitors' area. A large bandage bulged from beneath her blouse around her left arm. Five days had passed since the shooting.

"Hello, Amina." This time Sarah kissed her once on each cheek. It was a small gesture, an ordinary greeting in Senegal, yet it caught Amina by surprise. She sensed a change.

"I'm sorry about your arm." Amina sat across from Sarah at the small table. Sarah wore jeans and sneakers, and came empty-handed: no briefcase or legal pad. Was she planning on quitting? Amina wouldn't blame her.

"I'll be alright." Sarah raised her injured arm. "Could've been worse."

Much worse. Sarah had been knocked off her feet and ended up on top of her. At first, Amina thought she'd been hit, when the blood stain expanded like bright red tentacles across her dress. *Right in the chest area.* Amina had been convinced she was going to die until someone yanked her arm, nearly tearing it from its socket, and dragged her until her head hit a wooden post. She rolled onto her stomach and watched them working on Sarah, the source of all the blood. Sarah had been shot, Amina realized. *Because she was standing in the wrong place. Sarah had shunned the raging mob and joined the Muslim, the terrorist . . . the one who murdered a fireman.* It was supposed to be Amina lying across the courtroom rug bleeding, not Sarah.

Amina reached across the table with her cuffed hands and touched Sarah's fingers. "It meant the world to me when you came inside the criminal area. Facing that crowd . . ." Amina cringed. "Thank you for standing by me."

Sarah squeezed her hands in return. "I did it because I believe in you, Amina."

Amina appreciated Sarah's passion, but she knew it would be a losing battle. The hatred spewing from the people spoke volumes.

Sarah leaned back and crossed her ankles. "Where are you from in Senegal?"

Amina noted the change of subject and the casual tone in her voice. "Khombole is where I grew up. It's outside the city of Dakar, in the region of Thies." Amina pictured her hometown with its open-air market where she often walked with her mother and sisters to buy vegetables, rice, and millet.

"What's it like?"

"Rural. Around twelve thousand people live in Khombole. Most of us speak Wolof, which is a native language, and French." No one had expressed much interest in Amina's country other than a few customers inquiring about her Senegalese cuisine. Except Danny, her homeless friend. He couldn't get enough. "Why do you ask?"

"Because I'd like to learn more about you. It will help me with your case."

"I see." It would be painful for Amina to talk about Khombole, but Sarah had stood up for her, had gotten shot. Besides, she thought, it may be best for Malick. Going forward, she had to be strong for her son. "Back home it's very hot and dry most of the time, but we have a rainy season from May to September." Amina recalled all the childhood chores she had to get through in the heat of the day. *Forever sweeping, carrying water.* "I didn't grow up with the luxuries you have here, not even close."

"Tell me."

"For one thing, we didn't have running water. Every morning I'd walk to the town faucet with my sisters and girl cousins; sometimes my mother and aunts would come too. But it was fun, because we'd see all our friends. You see, no one had water." Amina pictured all the women and girls wearing colorful dresses and wraps with showy patterns of flowers, palm fronds, or animals. They had to wait their turn at the common faucet. Her mom and aunts gossiped, while the children took advantage of the free time to play games. She liked the smooth cement near the faucet where the balls bounced the best.

"I can't imagine life without running water." Sarah ran her fingers through her hair. "Did everyone fill up buckets, and go back and forth all day?"

"We'd carry the water back in a siwo. It's a giant bowl-shaped pan with handles on the side. You roll a cloth, coil it into a circle, and place it directly on your head. The siwo balances on top."

"You carried water on your heads?" Sarah stifled a laugh. "Without spilling? There's no way I could do that."

"Of course you would. All the girls learn very young. You start practicing at age three or four. Siwos come in all sizes." Amina remembered fooling around and having races, and with that came the accidents. The water would spill. And then came the chorus of moms and aunts all yelling at once.

"Tell me about your family."

Amina smiled. *That would take forever.* "We live together as a big extended family: uncles, aunts, cousins, grandparents, and so on."

"All in one house?" Sarah raised her index finger.

"Sort of. We have a giant sandy courtyard in the center with apartments all around." Amina hesitated. "It's ahh . . ."

"What?"

"Different."

"How so?"

"In Senegal many families are polygamous. Our faith allows a man to have up to four wives as long as he treats them equally. So my father had two wives, and his three brothers each have two."

"You're telling me all those people live together?"

"Yes, it's a big compound. The men all have their own rooms, but the women have to share one room with their children. It's tight, but you just sleep there. You take turns with the other wife staying alone with your husband. Of course, when it's your turn with him, you must prepare all the meals and take care of him, like wash his feet at the end of the day. The other wife gets the day off. It's only fair."

Sarah cocked her head. "I can't imagine sharing like that. Were there fights over the men?"

"No, not really. The women would argue more over the children. If there was a fight, they'd get involved and bicker over who started it, or who was teasing who, stuff like that." Amina recalled the chaos. She pictured children running everywhere, playing, laughing, doing chores. Amina had wanted more children. The heavy sadness enveloped her again.

"It must've been noisy all the time."

"Oh yes. We also had chickens, goats, and sheep roaming free in the courtyard."

Sarah wrinkled her nose. "No way."

Amina nodded. "The children must clean up after the animals. I constantly sifted sand as a child. In fact, I still dream about sifting sand."

Sarah smiled. "What brought you to Boston?"

"A cultural exchange program." *The opportunity of a lifetime.* Amina recalled jumping up and down and twirling around the courtyard when the letter came. If she hadn't come to the United States, where would she be now? Working in Dakar? Perhaps she'd be home cooking dinner with her mother and Aunt Fatou, who'd be calling out orders. *Come on girls. Fan the fire. Shuck more beans.*

"Through your school?"

"What?"

"Was the exchange program through your college?"

"Oh, yes, sorry." Amina's mind had drifted. "I graduated from Cheikh Anta Diop University in Dakar and applied for the program after that." She sighed. "I never dreamed of getting in. They don't take many applicants, and so many apply. After three years I gave up, got married, and then my visa came through."

"Oh." Sarah paused. "What happened with your husband?"

"Lamine wanted me to go." Amina recalled staying up nearly the whole night with Lamine, making plans. They had been so foolishly hopeful. "Coming over here to work is an opportunity you can't pass up." She felt the lump growing in her throat. "The opportunity . . . You have no idea." She tried to hold the tears in, but they spilled out and trickled down her cheek. "I can't talk about Lamine, especially now."

"I understand." Sarah spoke just above a whisper. "I also had . . ." She paused and looked at her watch. "Our time's about up. My uncle and I will be here tomorrow with Malick."

"Thank you." Amina wiped her face on her arm. She hoped Malick remembered what to say and wouldn't try to help her. *He couldn't.* Malick had a future; he had hope. Amina's life was over.

She followed the guard back through the hallway to the cell block and wondered what Sarah had been about to tell her. It sounded personal. This time Amina felt more comfortable around her. Sarah wasn't as rigid and concerned about getting all her facts straight. It appeared as if she wanted to be there, to simply talk and listen. But Amina knew Sarah would get around to asking more about the events leading up to the fire. It was inevitable, and Amina hadn't yet figured out what to say.

The guard gave her a hard shove. The cell door slammed shut.

8

"**All rrrise! The** Suffolk Superior Court is in session, the Honorable Conrad J. Killam presiding."

Sarah stood with Amina. It was a chilly Tuesday morning in late March, and the first day of trial. She had endured nine months of trial prep since she'd made her decision to defend the case with her uncle Buddy. Nick had attained his indictments before the grand jury, transferring the case to the superior court.

Judge Killam barged out of his lobby, double chin bobbing. His black robe appeared neatly pressed as did his gelled gray hair with the asymmetrical comb-over.

"Be seated!"

Sarah glanced back, willing the courtroom doors to open. Uncle Buddy was late. Firemen and members of the press packed the spectators' gallery. The governor sat in the front row with the grieving widow on his right and the president of the firemen's union on his left. Sarah could see right through the governor's charade. It was all about press coverage and union endorsements. New England Cable News was filming parts of the trial live.

"Commonwealth ready for trial?" Judge Killam poured himself a glass of water.

Nick rose. "Yes, Your Honor."

Sarah felt the sudden rush of adrenaline. She had gotten her feet wet arguing pretrial motions with Uncle Buddy. But trying this case before a jury meant diving underwater. And that would feel like taking a plunge in Boston Harbor with the L Street Brownies on New Year's Day. Was she really ready?

The judge zeroed in on Uncle Buddy's empty seat. He spread his hands, stood up, and leaned over his bench. "Attorney Lynch?"

Sarah rose and forced a respectful smile. "Good morning, Your Honor." All eyes and the damn TV camera focused on her. "My cocounsel of record has been slightly detained. I'm requesting a brief—"

"Court Officer!" Judge Killam banged his gavel. "Bring that jury in right now. We'll start without him."

Sarah attempted to appear calm. Uncle Buddy knew

Judge Killam ascended the throne exactly at nine. They had endured a full day of jury selection on Monday, and the judge was raring to go. Clerk Kelly gave her a sympathetic glance as he straightened the papers in his file.

"What if something bad happened?" Amina said. She wore a pale-blue suit and matching headscarf. Sarah had tried talking her out of the scarf to dilute feelings of prejudice toward Muslims, but her client had insisted.

"Don't worry. He'll be here," Sarah whispered.

The jurors filed in and focused on Amina and her headscarf. Sarah returned each searching stare with a nod and a smile.

The courtroom doors banged open, followed by the squish-squash of wet rubber galoshes. An out-of-breath Uncle Buddy flopped his tattered briefcase on the defense table and it slid off the other end.

"Your Honor, ladies and gentlemen of the jury, Mr. Marinelli, my apologies, please." He whipped off his winter parka and unraveled the red, white, and blue New England Patriots scarf from around his neck, revealing a star-spangled bow tie.

Judge Killam sprang from his chair. "Once again, Clancy, you've demonstrated a blatant disrespect for my courtroom. What's your excuse?"

"I got lost."

"Did I hear you correctly? Your office is right over the bridge in Charlestown. You've been to my courtroom countless times. How on earth could you get lost and miss Center Plaza?"

"Your Honor, it's that Big Dig." Uncle Buddy turned around and looked right at the governor. "And they still can't get it right. I hit a detour after the bridge and ended up way over by the Common. That's all one-ways going the other way. Had to circle around and head back up this way, but I hit more one-ways that sent me back the other way again."

Sarah watched the jurors nodding along with her uncle.

"The Big Dig is over, Clancy."

"That's what I thought!" He stretched his arms out wide.

"This is inexcusable. You were late for the last trial when your bus got hit by a duck boat. Remember?"

"But that was the duck boat's fault."

"I don't care whose fault it was, Clancy. It seems we have a pattern here."

"Pattern? I've never been hit by a duck boat before. And that was the last time—"

"A pattern of being late!"

"Oh. Most respectfully, Your Honor, I wouldn't—"

"From now on, you will take the *early* bus. Is . . . that . . . clear?"

"Yes, of course. I'll save money on parking." Several jurors nodded again.

"And, perhaps some lives too." Judge Killam wagged his finger. "I've seen you drive, Clancy, and it isn't pretty."

Uncle Buddy snapped off his galoshes, while Amina poured him a glass of water. Sarah recalled his advice to their client on the previous day, "Pour us a glass of water, it'll make you appear courteous. Remember, the jurors notice all the details." Sarah marveled at the way her uncle could endear himself to a jury. His tardiness and Big Dig excuse had eased the tension that choked the courtroom that morning.

Uncle Buddy turned and whispered in Sarah's ear. "When it's your turn, just talk to them, nothing fancy. Let Nick do all the huffing and puffing. Our job is to keep it simple. We're not going to win this with a flashy opening statement. We have to earn their trust over time. Don't overstate the facts and make promises we can't deliver."

"Got it." Sarah knew Nick's emotional opening would be an impossible act to follow.

"Show them how important their role is. Amina's fate is in their hands. This may be the biggest decision of their lives, let them know that."

"I will." Sarah gazed at the stone-faced jurors. How could she get through to them? They demanded hard proof that Amina didn't do it. She read it in their eyes.

"Remember." Uncle Buddy winked. "We're the underdog."

Clerk Kelly read the criminal indictment. "And now, will the juror in seat number five please exchange places with the juror in seat number one?"

Sarah's expectations rose when a well-dressed African American man assumed the foreperson's chair in seat number one. He owned a computer store in Roxbury. He and Amina were small business owners and minorities.

"Commonwealth?" Judge Killam folded his hands.

Sarah watched Nick rise and pivot toward the spectators' gallery. He looked like a warrior, ready for battle. This case was personal for him. He came from a family loaded with firefighters. She pictured his maimed father and shivered. Perhaps it was too personal.

9

Nick held eye contact with the widow and exchanged a silent promise for justice. He ignored the governor, who was seated next to her. Nick's opening statement was crucial. He had to hook them from the start, prove that the defendant murdered a fireman in the most horrific way.

He glanced at the defense table and had to contain his fury over Clancy's joke about getting lost because of the Big Dig. No question it was a ploy to shift the focus away from the emotional impact of Nick's opening statement. Who on that jury hadn't been lost due to Boston's ongoing construction and one-way streets modeled after cow paths? Clancy had made himself look like an ordinary guy, one of them, and they fell for it. The second he set foot in the courtroom, Clancy played the game and played it well. Now he had Sarah on his side.

Nick took a deep breath. *Keep your eye on the ball.* It's what Nick's dad used to say when he had coached him in baseball years ago. Nick pictured the wheelchair. *Focus.*

"Good morning, ladies and gentlemen. Nicholas Marinelli for the commonwealth." He gazed into the eyes of each juror. "This case is about Jack Fogerty, a Boston firefighter murdered in the line of duty." Nick spoke slowly, with a deep, grave voice.

"Here we have three little boys, anxious to go camping." Nick raised a poster-sized photograph. "John, age eight, Brian, who's six, and Stevie, three. They'd just finished packing the minivan with tents, fishing poles, and all sorts of gear."

"And this is their daddy." Nick pointed to a muscular man kneeling on one knee with his arms around the two older boys and the youngest leaning against his chest. "Yes, this is Jack. God rest his soul." The sun reflected off his cropped, rusty hair.

"After Jack's pregnant wife, Maureen, snapped this picture, Jack joined his buddies at the firehouse for one last tour of duty before the family vacation. He chatted nonstop that night about teaching the boys to fish, pitch a tent, light a campfire . . ." A woman's soft hiccupping sobs drifted through the courtroom.

Nick looked back at Maureen and recalled the lone bagpipe with its sad melody floating on the summer breeze over Jack's casket. Maureen and each little boy had placed a red rose on top. She held the last stem with the fullest bloom to her abdomen, kissed it, and laid it with the others. A gift from the unborn child. Five beautiful roses fanned across the gleaming mahogany.

"Jack did not make that camping trip. He missed the birth of his first baby girl. In fact, Jack will never see his wife and boys again in this life. Why?" Nick raised his hands, which were balled into fists. "Because the evidence will prove beyond a reasonable doubt that Amina Diallo maliciously and intentionally started a fire in her store on July twentieth of last year. Without a second thought, Jack charged into that smoke-filled building to save the defendant and her son. And what did she do in return?" Nick snapped his index finger at the defendant like a pointed gun. "Amina Diallo took his life. She killed him. The evidence will show that she deliberately shot Jack in cold blood as he reached out to help her, and that this shooting was a premeditated act of malice amounting to murder in the first degree."

Perspiration dripped from Nick's forehead and traveled back behind his ears as he outlined the damning evidence. Passion burned through his limbs, cramping muscles. Nick prayed he could hook the jurors. He exchanged eye contact with the foreperson. *God, he had to win.*

Derrick Martin had watched Marinelli's hair uncoil and pop out like little springs all over his head. Marinelli was a passionate lawyer who believed in his case above everything else.

He wondered whether it was fate that he was chosen to be foreperson. Derrick almost told the judge he wasn't qualified to serve. Twenty-three years ago he let the justice system down when he witnessed a shooting, never came forward, and the victim ended up paralyzed. Derrick was nineteen years old then, yet the guilt still lingered. Maybe this was his chance to redeem himself. It was Derrick's duty to lead the jury to the right verdict. According to all those people facing him in the packed gallery, including the governor, that meant convicting the Muslim who murdered a fireman, husband, and father of four.

Why had he been picked over the others? Because he ran his own computer business, and it looked good for Judge Killam to pick a well-dressed black man in this high-profile case. After all, the defendant was black too. The judge's decision to make him switch seats had angered the big man from Dorchester who was forced to move. That guy was your typical loudmouth blowhard with a thick Boston accent, and, to make matters worse, he called himself *Quahog*. Why would anyone want to be named after a big, ugly clam? Where'd he come up with that? Did he make a lot of clam chowder

with quahogs? Thank God they hadn't been sequestered.

He glanced around the jury box. Derrick had never
worked with such a diverse group of people all at once.
They also had a Dominican barber, a FedEx driver, an
Italian woman who had sixteen grandkids, a young
blond waitress, a liberal lady with crazy outfits who
just moved to Boston from Cambridge, a quiet Asian
librarian, and several yuppies. They would have to
somehow pull together and make a decision. *God.*

Derrick focused on Sarah Lynch as she gripped the
edge of the defense table and pulled herself up. His
mother's name was Sarah too. He wondered how she
would manage to address them after such an emotional
opening by Marinelli. What could Sarah possibly say?
He watched Clancy rise and pat her on the back. He
whispered something and she nodded. Words of encouragement?

"This is the most difficult moment I've faced in my
years practicing law. Attorney Clancy and I feel for
Jack Fogerty, his wife, and children. We too are seeking
justice for him in our vigorous pursuit of the truth."
Sarah looked right at Derrick as if she relied on him to
help her. But how could he? She'd have to give him
something to run with. Marinelli had all his facts lined
up in perfect order. If they followed the prosecution's
recipe, they could bake the perfect chocolate cake, a
crowd-pleaser.

"Please pay careful attention to all the evidence and
keep an open mind. Each element of a criminal offense
must be proven beyond a reasonable doubt. As Judge
Killam explained, the Commonwealth bears that heavy
burden of proof."

Derrick studied the dark-featured defendant with her
face partially shadowed by the headscarf as if she had

something to hide. Had Sarah and Clancy asked their client if she'd burned her store and shot a fireman? Was she claiming someone else did it? Was she going to testify?

"As you listen to the Commonwealth's case, ask yourselves, are the witnesses credible? Are there other avenues that weren't investigated? Was this a classic rush to judgment?"

Sarah centered herself before the jury and outlined evidence she and Clancy planned to present. Derrick noticed she was less detailed than Marinelli; she presented the case like she was preparing an Italian meal, a little of this, a little of that.

"The Commonwealth will not be able to prove beyond a reasonable doubt that Amina committed these crimes. After you deliberate and weigh all the evidence, I trust you will uphold justice and—" Sarah paused and rubbed her temples. "You know . . ."

Derrick listened to her voice trail off. She sounded like she'd lost her train of thought. An awkward moment of silence followed. Derrick looked at Clancy sitting at the defense table with his hands folded. Would he come to his niece's rescue? Perhaps she had doubts about taking the case. What was going on?

"What I'm about to say is . . . well, I'm not even sure I can articulate what I'd like to say here." Derrick noticed her voice had dropped an octave, as if she'd forgotten about the courtroom and was in the midst of a regular conversation.

"You've heard an outline of both sides and you're probably wondering why I . . . we . . . took this case. Nine months ago, my uncle whisked me off the hockey rink asking for help, but I wanted nothing to do with it." She shook her head. "I'm a former prosecutor, you know? Lock 'em all up, throw away the key. That was my mentality. So I told my uncle I couldn't defend a case like this. *No way.* That is, until I met Amina, got to know her, heard her story." Sarah walked behind Amina and gripped the back of her chair.

"Throughout this trial, you'll hear bits and pieces of Amina's story too. She was a simple, hardworking immigrant mother. Raising her son has always been her top priority. It's all she talks about. Amina . . . here, let me show you." Sarah walked around her client's chair, reached into a paper shopping bag, and pulled out a large metal bowl painted with red flowers.

"This belongs to Amina." Sarah displayed the bowl before the jury. "Amina always treasured her African dinner bowl. Once a week she prepared a special Senegalese meal in this bowl and invited a homeless man in to share it with her son and her." Sarah peered into the pattern as if searching for answers. "Most people wouldn't take the time to do that. Others would be afraid to let a strange homeless man into the house." Her words were almost whispered and barely audible.

"Would this kind woman set a fire with her son sleeping upstairs? Would she shoot the fireman who was coming to rescue them?"

Derrick felt Sarah's passion surge throughout the courtroom as strong as Marinelli's. She believed in her client.

"The facts of this case do not fit Amina Diallo. That's why my uncle and I believe in her. Thank you."

Derrick watched Sarah take her seat and place the bowl on her table. He scanned his row of jurors—some were still squinting at the brilliant bowl. Had they already made up their minds? Would they give her a chance? The blowhard from Dorchester met his gaze. *Quahog.* What was he thinking?

10

"**Commonwealth, call your** first witness," Judge Killam said.

Quahog Robowski sat in chair number five. His real name was Robert, but he had scribbled "Quahog" on his jury questionnaire. He thought about using his formal name for court, but decided against it. Quahog's what people had called him ever since he was a newborn when his brother said, "That baby's butt-ugly like a quahog!" Forty-four years of being named after a clam. He did love clam chowder, and you couldn't make it without the big quahogs.

Quahog had been forced to exchange seats with the black guy. Like he wasn't good enough to be foreman? Street smarts are what made you a good judge of people. Quahog grew up in Southie's Old Colony Housing Project and had seen it all. Could tell right off the bat if somebody did it or not.

And this one did it. Quahog studied the defendant with her wacky braids beneath the weird blue veil. It was all bullshit. Her lawyers were trying to make her out to be some poor immigrant Arab from Africa. During jury selection, Judge Killam had asked all potential jurors if they had feelings of prejudice against Muslims. Quahog hadn't responded, but no one else did either.

He watched Marinelli carrying a legal pad to a podium just past the jury box. He seemed a bit intense, but who wouldn't be? Poor guy was tag-teamed by two lawyers for the black Arab terrorist. Didn't seem fair, two against one. There was Clancy with the bow tie and Big Dig, and the tall, hot-looking redhead. She'd made a

big deal about some stupid bowl. Quahog didn't care
how many homeless people the Arab fed.

"Commonwealth calls Timothy Murray," Marinelli
said.

A man in his early twenties walked down the aisle
and was sworn in by Clerk Kelly. His hair resembled a
seventies-style mop similar to Shaggy on *Scooby Doo*.
That kid wouldn't last long in Quahog's neighborhood.

Marinelli smiled. "Please introduce yourself to the
ladies and gentlemen of the jury."

"Uh, Tim Murray."

"Where do you live?"

"Orient Avenue in East Boston."

"Are you in school?"

"Yeah. I go to . . . a senior . . . BU." He wiped sweat
from his brow. "Communications major."

Quahog chortled. What kinda faggot major was that?
Communications? This kid was so nervous he could
barely talk. No wonder real Americans weren't getting
jobs. *Communications.*

"At approximately 12:20 a.m. on Thursday, July
twentieth, what were you doing?"

Communications glanced at his watch. "I'd been out
in Faneuil Hall and was walking home from the T
when I noticed this orange glow in the Senegalese Market. I ran to the window. The place was on fire. Then a
woman saw me and—"

"Objection, nonresponsive." The Arab's redhead lawyer jumped up.

Judge Killam nodded. "Sustained."

Quahog groaned as Marinelli questioned the witness about the exact location of the store. No wonder
trials took forever. Just let Communications tell his
story.

Marinelli glanced in Quahog's direction. "Can you describe the Senegalese Market?"

"It was like a corner store that sold mostly African stuff. I'd go in there sometimes, especially when she had the spicy lamb kebabs with rice."

Quahog wouldn't be caught dead eating that crap. He preferred the pub grub they made at O'Brien's. Nothin' better than the homemade pot roast with french fries and gravy.

"Your Honor, may I approach the witness?" Marinelli grabbed a photograph.

"You may."

He showed the picture to the defense and handed it to Communications. "Recognize this?"

"That's the Senegalese Market before it burned down."

"Your Honor, I'm offering this photograph into evidence as Commonwealth's exhibit number one."

"So admitted."

Quahog's stomach growled. The fat lady wedged in next to him with the armful of silver bangles gave him a long look. What was that for? He wished he could make his stomach growl again. Just his luck being stuck next to her. Quahog glanced at the clock. When would they break for lunch? The morning recess wasn't long enough, and they had the same stale Munchkins, only coconut leftover.

Marinelli strolled back to his podium. "Can you describe the fire in more detail?"

"High flames in the back left-hand corner, like six feet or so. Sorta looked like the big potato chip rack was burning."

This time Clancy rose. "Why, it seems as though the witness is guessing."

"Are you objecting, Clancy?"

"Absolutely."

"Then say so." Judge Killam turned to the jury. "Sustained. Please disregard the last sentence."

Quahog didn't get it. So what if the kid saw chips burning? Why didn't the defense want us to hear that? He'd remember it on purpose: chips, chips, chips. Salt and vinegar, barbeque, sour cream and onion. Oh, to lean back in his swivel chair and crunch away. And a beer to go with them would be a great thing.

Marinelli looked at Quahog again as if he'd read his mind about the beer and chips. "Mr. Murray, were you familiar with the interior of the store?"

"Yeah."

"To the best of your recollection and without guessing, what was located in the area of the store where you saw the flames?"

"The chips. They were on this high wire rack that stood off by itself in the corner.

Marinelli nodded. "What did you observe next?"

"I saw a woman running away from the fire, uhh, and toward me. Like she was heading to the front door. When she got close, she glanced at me and ran away."

"Can you describe her?"

"Long black braids like the lady who owned the store. Her." He pointed at the Arab.

"Your Honor, may the record reflect the witness has identified the defendant, Amina Diallo."

"It may so reflect."

"Can you describe what the defendant did when she looked at you?"

"Her eyes got real wide as if she was shocked to see me standing there. Like I'd caught her in the act."

The redhead and Clancy shot up together. "Objection!"

"Sustained. Please disregard everything after 'her eyes got real wide.'"

Quahog couldn't believe the judge sided with them again. They jumped up every time it got a little hairy for their client. Made the Arab look even more guilty.

"Did the defendant do anything else?"

"She just stared at me for a second or so with this shocked look on her face and ran off to the right."

"What did you do next?"

"I pounded on the window and yelled, 'Wait!' I tried getting in the front door, but it was locked. The lady never came back, so I ran into the street to find help but there was nobody around except this homeless guy across the street. My cell was out of juice so I ran back down Waldemar Ave. toward the T."

"What happened next?"

"About halfway down the next block, I saw this big fire truck coming toward me. It didn't have its siren on, so I figured it was coming back from the accident I'd seen earlier near the T stop. I flagged it down. They stopped, and I told them about the fire and that a lady and her son lived upstairs."

"What happened after that?"

"They headed toward the store. I saw two firemen break through the front door with a crowbar or something, and I think two others ran around back."

"Did they spray water on the fire?"

"No, those guys just ran in. Another truck had the hoses, but it took them a while to get there."

Could Quahog do that? Risk his life for some whacked Arab?

Marinelli flipped a page in his pad. "What else did you observe?"

"I saw them rescue the lady and her son down one of the ladders from the second story." He paused and looked at the Arab. "They were definitely lucky. I mean, pretty much right after they got them out the whole place went up. The firemen risked their lives just going in there."

And one was murdered. Quahog scanned the rows of firemen in the gallery with the black bands on their badges. He hoped the union was taking good care of the widow and Jack Fogerty's family. Pipe fitters would've.

"Nothing further, Your Honor."

Quahog studied the Arab. Of course she was guilty: she was the only one arrested. She didn't care that her son was upstairs sleeping. The towelheads were all whackos. They trained the women to strap bombs under their dresses and blow up schools. Capable of anything. No doubt it was her running away after she lit the chips. Didn't expect to see Communications standing there. If the Arab didn't do it, she would've opened that door and asked him for help. The redhead and Clancy were paid big bucks to defend her. Oil money.

Amina felt the frigid gazes from all directions. She focused on a loose paperclip near Sarah's pile of documents. She couldn't bear to look at anyone, especially the jurors. *Caught in the act.* The words stung. She couldn't remember anything from the testimony except for that. *Caught in the act.* Amina felt her chest tighten. *Breathe.* Her lungs felt like cement.

Mr. Clancy patted her lightly on the arm, and eased out from behind the defense table. He rubbed his lower back with both hands. Amina noticed the jurors watching him now.

"Ahh, Mr. Murray. My niece and I thank you for taking the time to join us this morning."

"Uh . . . sure." The student sat straight-backed, holding on to the podium with both hands. Amina heard the uncertainty in his voice.

"I must apologize in advance." Mr. Clancy pointed to his right ear. "I'm a little hard of hearing, so bear with me. Oh, to be back in your shoes again. How old are you?"

"Just turned twenty-one two weeks ago."

"You like BU?"

"Love it."

"Good for you. Go to the Beanpot?"

"Every game."

"So, you're a hockey fan. Great tournament, but a disappointing final, huh?"

"Yeah, thought for sure we'd beat Boston College."

"Did you know my niece played hockey on the Olympic team?"

The student shot Sarah a big smile. "Wow. The Olympics?"

Marinelli rose halfway. "Objection, Your Honor. This line of questioning has nothing to do with the trial."

"I agree. Enough with the hockey, Clancy."

"I'm sorry, Your Honor. You know, it's the last case before my retirement kicks in. Guess I got carried away."

The judge wagged his index finger. "That's what you said the last time."

A muffled laugh came from the direction of the jury box. Without much effort, Mr. Clancy had diffused the tense atmosphere created by the prosecutor. Amina felt her lungs loosen up. She could breathe again.

"They've got the heat cranked up in here. Dries out the eyes." Mr. Clancy rubbed his eyelids. "Wear contacts?"

"I do. Heat dries them right out."

"Makes the contacts a little blurry too. Like they get after you've been wearing 'em all day?"

"Definitely."

"Back to the person you saw in the store. The eyes were wide open?"

"Yeah."

"Wide like when you're afraid of something?"

"I'd say so."

"Any communication between the two of you?"

"No."

"Offer to help?"

"Didn't have a chance. I would've if she opened the door."

"So the answer's no?"

The student paused. "That's correct."

"Is it possible this person was afraid of you?"

"No reason to be."

"There's a fire in the building and a man with his face plastered against the window. Isn't that a little scary?" Mr. Clancy circled in toward the stand, keeping his eyes on both the witness and the jury box.

"Under those circumstances, it's possible she could've been afraid of me." He shrugged. "Suppose so."

"Maybe this person thought *you* started the fire?"

Marinelli jumped up. "Objection, calls for speculation."

"Oh, come on judge, the witness was speculating up a storm on direct."

"And you could've objected. Sustained."

Amina admired how Mr. Clancy created a different picture with the same words. It reminded her of drawing game squares in the sand in her Khombole courtyard. The girls would throw a pebble and hop from square to square. When they had a winner, they could smooth the sand with their hands and start fresh. That's what Mr. Clancy did in the courtroom. He smoothed the sand.

"You were out with friends earlier in Faneuil Hall?" Mr. Clancy asked.

"Yeah."

"What happened to them?"

The student cracked a smile. "They got lucky."

"Ahhh . . . girls. Which bar?"

"Bell in Hand."

"Great spot. The Bell was around in my day. Fact, Paul Revere kicked back a few there."

"I believe he did."

"Everybody drinking, having a good time?"

"Oh, yeah."

"Well, except for you at the end?"

"Right. No luck with the girls."

"How'd you get in?"

"To the bar?"

"Yeah, weren't you underage?"

The student blushed. "Uhh . . . I don't think they were checking IDs."

"Wearing your contacts?" Mr. Clancy blinked several times.

"Don't remember."

"You wouldn't wear glasses picking up chicks?"

He smiled. "Would've been wearing contacts."

"When you were at the scene of the fire, were you able to see anyone in the upstairs apartment?"

"No."

"There were no lights on in the building, correct?"

"Don't think so."

"Was it smoky inside the store when you first arrived?"

"There was smoke, but not as much as when the firemen knocked the door open."

"I'm a little confused about something." Mr. Clancy glanced at Amina and Sarah. "Maybe I was daydreaming during Mr. Marinelli's questioning or it's the dementia kicking in. How were you able to obtain a clear view of the *person in the store* through the smoke with no interior lighting?"

The student looked down before answering. "Must've been from the streetlights shining in."

Mr. Clancy sighed. "There's no streetlight in front of the store."

"I think there was one."

"Hmmm. I bet Mr. Marinelli's picture will help us here. Thank God for Mr. Marinelli and his pictures. Your Honor, may I see Commonwealth's exhibit number one?"

"You may."

Mr. Clancy took the photograph from the clerk and handed it to the witness. "Thank you kindly, Mr. Kelly. Now, take a good look at that picture. Are there any streetlights in front of the store?"

The student studied the photograph. "No."

"Did you see the person in the store for very long?"

"As soon as she saw me she ran away."

"So, a second or two?"

The student looked up at the ceiling and over at Marinelli. "Umm . . . that's about right, I guess."

"Did this person carry a flashlight?"

"No."

"Interesting." Mr. Clancy nodded several times, appearing perplexed, just like the witness had. "Were you able to see behind the building from your vantage point?"

"No."

"Did you look at the roof?"

"No."

"Did you see anybody start that fire?"

"No."

"Course not," Mr. Clancy said.

"Objection." Marinelli rose. "Your Honor, I'm requesting that you instruct Attorney Clancy to refrain from commentary."

"Sustained. Put a question before the witness, Clancy."

"Apologies, apologies. It slips out at times." Mr. Clancy nodded at the judge and faced the witness again. "When you first spotted the fire, do you know how long it had been burning—without guessing?"

"I'd have no way of knowing."

"Of course you wouldn't. Thank you for your help today." Mr. Clancy grinned, and walked back toward Sarah and Amina. He stopped halfway and tapped his forehead. "Oh! I forgot a question. Thank God I thought of it before sitting down." He turned to the jurors. "Always happens to me. I remember stuff soon as I sit down, you see. By then it's too late." He spun around and faced the witness again. "Mr. Murray, you mentioned seeing a homeless man across the street?"

"Yeah, when I went back to look for help."

"Did you approach him?"

"No."

"Talk to him?"

"No."

"Ever see him again?"

"I don't recall. With all the commotion and fire trucks, I forgot all about him."

"Thank you again. No further questions." Mr. Clancy made eye contact with the jurors and sat down.

"Any redirect, Commonwealth?" Judge Killam said.

"Yes, Your Honor." Marinelli slid out from behind his table with arms swinging. There he goes, Amina thought, stomping all over the smooth sand. She pictured him in heavy work boots.

"Mr. Murray, did you try to get inside the Senegalese Market?"

"Yes."

"What happened when you tried?"

"The door was locked."

"Did you see any evidence of forced entry at the store?"

Sarah popped up. "Objection, leading."

"Sustained."

"Score!" Mr. Clancy whispered.

"What did the windows look like?"

"Weren't broken far as I could see."

"How did the firemen get in?"

"They had to force the door open with a tool."

Amina knew what the prosecutor was getting at: Malick and she were the only ones home, so who else could've started the fire? There was no evidence of a break-in. Marinelli leered at her. *I've got you cornered.* That's what his eyes said. Amina gazed into the jury box. They were watching.

Judge Killam checked the courtroom clock. "Mr. Clancy?"

"Your Honor, ladies and gentlemen of the jury, and Mr. Murray, I have no further questions. Please have a very pleasant lunch."

Judge Killam smiled broadly. "Very well, Mr. Clancy. The courtroom will stand adjourned until ten past two." He turned to the jury. "Please do not discuss or read anything pertaining to this case."

Amina noticed several jurors smiling at Mr. Clancy. They were hungry and appeared relieved for the break. Marinelli would've kept going, and they knew that. Mr. Clancy had smoothed the sand again.

Buddy joined Sarah and Amina as the judge and jurors filed out of the courtroom. Marinelli's questions had spilled over into the sacred lunchtime recess. *A big no-no.* Stomachs growled in full force in that jury box. Their concentration was down to zero. The judge also yearned for his three-course hot meal at the Federalist.

Buddy watched Sarah place a reassuring hand on Amina's shoulder. His niece had a soft side, which was often overshadowed by her tough exterior as a prosecutor and a hockey player. Amina's case was good for her.

"I liked your opening statement with the bowl," he said, after Amina had been escorted out by a guard.

"Think it worked? It felt like I was lecturing to a bunch of marble statues."

"It's a start. You have some of them thinking and the bowl will serve as a focal point, physical evidence of Amina's kindness. We should leave it right here throughout the trial." Buddy pushed the bowl to the corner of the defense table closest to the jury.

"Speaking of the bowl, we should reinterview Amina's homeless friend. I wonder if he's the same guy who was hanging around at the time of the fire?" Sarah made a notation on her pad.

"You're right." Buddy's investigator had located and spoken with Amina's friend, but he denied knowing anything about the fire. "See? New things always come out at trial. I say we talk to him ourselves, forget the investigator."

"Us?"

"Sure, let's ask Amina which night he collects the cans in her neighborhood, and we'll go over together." Buddy noticed Sarah appeared hesitant. The last time she'd gone out to meet a witness, a gang member shot her colleague. Buddy wanted nothing more than to help Sarah come to terms with her past and move on. "Lunch?"

"I should stay and review my notes."

"Hogwash. You need energy."

"Okay, you're treating then." Sarah grabbed her coat. "By the way, great job with the cross, even though you embarrassed me with all that nonsense about the Olympics."

Buddy snapped on his galoshes. "Oh, I planned that. I'm hoping they'll put two and two together, connect the Olympics with the courthouse shooting, have more sympathy for you and, BINGO, root for Amina. I also made you blush, which is always good, and that big man in seat number five grew up with a hockey stick in his hand. I guarantee it. He's the one who calls himself Quahog. Remember his jury questionnaire? Probably plays in the beer and puck leagues several nights a week."

Sarah nodded. "The pipe fitter from Dorchester. Quahog. Wonder where he came up with that name?"

"Quahog's all bent out of shape because Judge Killam made him switch seats with the black guy." Buddy chuckled. "Doesn't like the liberal Cambridge type sitting next to him, and she can't stand him either."

"The art teacher?"

"You got it."

"How'd you notice all that?"

Buddy pressed his hands together. "Most important piece of advice I'll give you: know your jury. Learn to read their body language. By the time we present our case, we should know what color toilet paper each prefers."

Sarah laughed. "I wouldn't go that far."

"It's true." Buddy tossed his fedora in the air and caught it on his fingertip. "Let's grab some clam chowder in honor of our friend Quahog."

Buddy and Sarah entered the hallway, which bustled with people waiting for elevators. A television reporter interviewed Marinelli using light poles and two cameras. Buddy wasn't surprised when Sergeant Brady saw them and made a beeline toward Sarah.

"Hello Frank," Sarah said. "Made it through my first opening statement on defense."

"And I heard you made a big to-do about that bowl again. It's too bad I'm sequestered out here. I'd love to see you on the other side." Frank shook hands with Buddy. "You stole her from us."

"No, my niece finally saw the light." Buddy pointed at the bright television lights. "What about you?"

"Me?"

"Yeah, are you and Nick ready to dismiss this dog and pony show?"

"Not a chance."

Buddy cupped his hand on Frank's shoulder. "Think about it. You'll be better off in the long run if you save face now. Your first witness turned out to be a flop."

"We're going to win, and you know it, Clancy."

"Don't count on it."

"Attorney Clancy!" A reporter stuck a microphone under his chin. "Are you planning to get your client off?"

"Of course we are, because she's innocent. Amina Diallo should never have been arrested in the first place. This whole trial is a charade. You saw the governor sitting out there. It's all about publicity."

Shouting came from the direction of the courtroom. Buddy turned around to see a court officer running down the hall. "Everybody clear out now! Take the stairwells." He stopped when he saw them. "Got a bomb in there."

11

At **3:00 p.m.**, Nick whisked through the Boston Fire Department headquarters. He passed the empty first bay; Rescue One had been called to the courthouse for the bomb. What next?

He bounded up the stairs three at a time and entered the firehouse kitchen. Andy Larson sat at the cafeteria-style Formica table with his chin resting between calloused knuckles. He was in his early fifties, had a large rugged face and huge biceps.

"Heard they got a live one." Andy spoke with a hoarse Boston accent.

Nick sat across from him. "Yeah, bomb squad found a homemade bomb made out of a tennis ball with a note attached to it. Somebody rolled it under the defendant's chair during the lunch break."

"Wow. Who'd attach a note to a bomb? What'd it say?"

"Don't know yet. They think it was a publicity stunt."

"Court canceled?"

"We're on standby." Nick hoped it would be, but with Judge Killam anything could happen. He pictured the old judge holding midnight court.

Andy released a long breath. "Quiet 'round here."

The firehouse cat leaped on the table, squeezing between Andy's elbows. He scratched under her chin. "Jack loved Maxine, you know. He was the one who rescued her from that building we imploded several years back. Been with us ever since."

Nick rubbed the cat's arched back. It was good to hear Andy talking again. Nick had difficulty extracting his story. Andy often forgot details and mixed up the sequence of events that occurred on the night of the fire. He had to get it together or Clancy would have a field day.

Nick pointed to a whiteboard that contained instructions in red magic marker about feeding the cat. "How come Maxine's not allowed table scraps?"

"Poor thing has cancer, so we all chipped in for the treatments. Now we have to feed her through an IV tube." Andy sighed. "Maybe we should've put her to sleep. Everybody thought of Maxine as Jack's cat, so we had to do what we could."

"I'm sure Jack would appreciate it."

Andy stroked the cat. "I think she's dying of a broken heart. Maybe we should just let her go." Andy gazed out the window at the new Rose Kennedy Greenway along Atlantic Avenue. "Everybody misses Jack. He was the life of the firehouse. Can't believe he's gone."

Nick felt Andy's grief. "I'd like to know more about him."

"Jack. Mouth was always running. When he told a joke it took him forever to get to the punch line. Typical Irish guy from Southie. God, what I'd give now." Andy rubbed his eyes. "I can't get up there in front of all those people and remember what I'm supposed to say."

"You'll get through this. Clancy and Sarah have to be extra careful and treat you with kid gloves. If they don't, the jury will take it out on their client." Nick secretly hoped they'd go after Andy. He wanted the jury to despise Amina Diallo. Nick recalled seeing a ray of hope in her eyes when Clancy had cross-examined his first witness. He imagined himself with a giant red fire extinguisher, spraying directly into her face, spraying until that hope went out.

"I don't know." Andy's face sunk between his hands

until his handlebar mustache stretched sideways, and his chin rested on the cat's back. "It's all a black hole. What the hell was I thinking splitting up?"

Nick leaned over the table. "You and Jack were doing your job, trying to rescue people. You *both* split up, remember? It was a mutual decision."

"Was it? I don't remember a goddamned thing."

"You just told—"

"It all happened so fast, you know?"

Nick bit his upper lip. That was all he needed, more uncertainty. Sarah had managed to get through to the jurors in her opening statement. She appeared so sincere talking about the damn flower bowl in that seductive voice of hers. Nick caught several flickers of doubt in their eyes. That's all it would take. *One flicker.* And Clancy had muddied the BU student's identification of the defendant, planting the seed that someone else committed the arson. Maybe it was that homeless man lurking out there? Nick hated Clancy. The old codger lived for distorting the truth and tricking witnesses into doubting themselves.

"Andy, we'll go over your testimony again in the morning. Whatever you do, testify with conviction. Okay?"

Andy looked away without answering. "Here they come." He pointed out the window at the long fire truck pulling into the bay. "You sure I won't have to get up there this afternoon? I'm not ready."

Nick wondered if Andy had heard anything he said. "If Judge Killam resumes the trial, his court officer will go on strike. You'll be on first thing tomorrow morning."

Rescue One's four-man crew stormed into the kitchen carrying subs from J. Pace. "Hey, Nick, we watched you all morning on TV 'til the bomb."

Nick shook hands with the men. "All clear?"

"Yup, and here we are again." One of the old-timers tossed a *Boston Herald* down on the table. "Back in the seventies, all we did was fight fires and grab bombs. Those were the days, my friend."

"Pop goes the Arab."

"What?" Nick said.

"Pop goes the Arab. The note."

"Is that what it said?" Nick glanced around the room at the snickering firemen. Nick figured whoever wrote the note must've seen Amina's headscarf and thought she was an Arab.

"Yeah—the reporters'll have a field day."

"Unbelievable." Andy laughed as the others sat beside him and talked over each other.

"They were aiming for her chair."

"Can blow her ass through the roof far as I'm concerned."

"Yeah, put a stick of dynamite—"

"That's enough." Lieutenant Draak unwrapped a steaming meatball sub for Andy. "Here, eat her while she's hot."

Somebody snickered. "Always gotta protect the foreigner."

"Hey Nick, how come you didn't object more when Clancy was beatin' on that BU kid?" a fireman said. "It was so obvious the Arab was runnin' away after she poured the gas and tossed the match. I'm surprised she didn't pop right then and there. Those braids would've gone right up."

The group burst into laughter.

Nick raised his hands. "Don't talk about what you watched on TV. Andy's a witness. He's not supposed to hear any trial testimony." Would they refrain from rehashing it all as soon as he left? *Not a chance.* "It'll help if you talk about Jack, recall the funny stories."

"We got plenty of them."

"What about that hot-lookin' redhead lawyer? What's up with the bowl and the bum?"

"Pop."

Nick waited for the laughter to die down again. "Does anybody remember seeing a homeless man at the fire scene?"

"Oh yeah."

The quick response surprised him. "You do?"

"Came up on TV today."

"But do you remember seeing the homeless man at the time of the fire?"

"Nobody does. We all just heard about it on TV."

Of course. The damn TV again.

"What about Tight-ass? It's his job to find witnesses, right?" A fireman walked across the room demonstrating a bowlegged walk. Nick knew they were mocking the state police. They never referred to Frank Brady by name, only "Tight-ass."

Nick chose to ignore the question. "Get some rest, Andy. I'm going back to the office." He grabbed his coat, and headed toward the stairs.

"Oh, Nick? Chief wants to see you. I think it has to do with the governor. He's all bent out of shape over some comment Clancy made on TV."

And he almost got away.

Jeanette Giganti needed to go back.

As soon as court was canceled, she avoided reporters and walked from Center Plaza toward Beacon Hill and the Charles River. When she reached her destination, she balled her hands in her pockets, and stared up at the giant billboard that read, "If you lived here, you'd be home now." *If you lived here.*

Jeanette had lived there forty-six years ago. They were an immigrant Italian family with six kids squeezed into the first floor of a five-story brick tenement on Chambers Street. Her father was a pushcart peddler, who sold fruits and vegetables near the north building of Faneuil Hall.

They moved out of the old neighborhood and into East Boston on the eve of her sweet-sixteenth birthday. A memory as vivid as the births of her children and the deaths of her parents. It was the only time she saw her father cry.

If you lived here, you'd be home now. Jeanette stared up at the sign until she no longer saw it. Narrow streets, rusty bicycles, kids playing kick the can and agates. She savored the aroma of Italian gravy intermingled with the Jewish bakeries and Polish delis. An old world and a loud one. Jeanette smiled as she remembered the babies crying all hours of the night, men singing as they walked home from the social clubs, and the big mommas yelling out the windows in Italian or that thick Irish brogue. *So long ago.*

Was it fate she'd been picked for this jury? The case had seemed so straightforward in the beginning, and now, it made her reflect on her past. Who was this young immigrant mother standing trial? *Amina Diallo.* Her name had a beautiful ring. *Amina Diallo.* Beautiful, like the woman herself. Jeanette visualized Sarah raising the African dinner bowl with the delicate red flowers painted all around. Jeanette wouldn't dream of serving a homeless man in her own home with her family. And that made her sad.

Jeanette's gaze shifted from the big sign to the water-stained concrete towers of Charles River Place, which were supposed to be upscale condominiums. *If you lived here, you'd be home now.* How could anyone call *that* a home? She couldn't picture clotheslines hanging from those sterile black balconies. Jeanette was willing to bet that very few would even recognize their neighbors to the left and right.

It all happened so fast. The old West End. *Gone forever*. The neighborhood was only a third of a square mile nestled between Beacon Hill and the North End. Jeanette counted eight elementary schools with bustling playgrounds where children shared traditions, secrets, and every so often came to blows.

She recalled it was a rainy day in 1968 when the city came barging in with their bulldozers and wrecking balls. They obliterated the West End: demolished homes and businesses, tore up lives. The city declared the area blighted and took it under eminent domain.

Seven thousand poor immigrant families. Immigrants who had become citizens and taxpayers. Immigrants who owned tiny corner stores like Mini White's with the long counter of penny candy where you could always find a row of dirty-faced children standing on tiptoes. A penny for the handful of *semenza* from the whisky jar. What happened to the old Jewish couple who owned it? How could they fight city hall, the governor, or anybody else? The lucky ones scraped up enough money and started over in the South End, Eastie, or Somerville. But there were those who couldn't make it. *If you lived here.*

Jeanette started walking toward the nearest T station. Everyone viewed her as the soft-spoken Italian lady in her late sixties, a secretary nearing retirement, a good Catholic mother and grandmother. *The perfect juror.* Would they ever dream she poured cement mix into the gas tank of a wrecking crane?

12

"**What are we** up against, Uncle Buddy?" Sarah lifted her coffee cup, which left a ring on one of the fire reports scattered across her desk. "Pop goes the Arab. Who would do something like this?" She recalled the hurt in Amina's eyes when they told her about the bomb with its attached note.

"Prejudice. I've seen it take multiple forms over the years." Uncle Buddy buttoned his overcoat to head home for the evening. "Some folks just thrive on it."

"I thought we'd progressed." Sarah recalled growing up in Charlestown during school desegregation and forced busing. She had attended private Catholic school, but had witnessed her share of bullying based on race or color.

"Two steps forward, one step back." Uncle Buddy demonstrated with a giant step backward, knocking into a side table.

"Watch the—" Sarah jumped up, but he spun around just in time to catch the falling lamp. "Good save, Uncle Buddy. Do you think Judge Killam will declare a mistrial tomorrow?" The story about the bomb had leaked to the media.

"I think this was a publicity stunt." He centered the lamp back on the table. "It would be a waste of the court's time if they started the process all over every time someone pulled a prank. Killam will probably threaten to close the trial off to the public if anything happens again, and I'm sure he'll speak with the jury first thing."

"What's our position?" Sarah knew most jurors would catch something about the bomb and note on TV.

"We don't want a mistrial. Besides, it may work in our favor by creating sympathy for Amina, which we desperately need tomorrow with Nick's fireman on the stand. I imagine some of the women will have the same appalled reaction you had." He straightened the lampshade. "Let's see . . . the pediatric nurse, the nice little Italian lady from the North End, the liberal gal with all the silver bracelets who sits next to Quahog . . . possibly the young waitress."

"The foreperson too, I bet." Sarah had received good vibes from him.

"Definitely. He's seen his share of that crap." Uncle Buddy put his plaid driving cap on. "I think he's rooting for you, Sarah. I can read it in his body language. He liked your opening with the story about Amina sharing meals with the homeless man."

"He's taking his job very seriously. I see him concentrating and taking notes."

"That's good for us. Concentration often leads to reasonable doubt." Uncle Buddy tapped his lip with his index finger. "Hmmm . . . I'll wear my Red Sox bow tie tomorrow. Can you guess why?"

"Because opening day's around the corner?"

"Nope."

"One of Nick's witnesses is a Yankee fan?" It usually had something to do with a witness.

"Boy, do I wish. Guess again."

"Uncle Buddy, I have no idea."

He flashed the one-up-on-you grin. It meant he knew something no one else did.

"What?"

"Antiliano Estrella."

"What a name. I'm surprised you pronounced it right.

He's the good-looking Dominican juror in seat number three?"

Uncle Buddy winked. "Antiliano owns a barbershop in Jamaica Plain, and cuts hair for all the Dominican ballplayers on the Red Sox."

"Wow. I remember the part about the barbershop on his questionnaire, but how'd you know the rest?"

"The *Globe* ran an article on him a few months back. I remembered and looked it up on the computer." Her uncle appeared proud of himself; someone must've Googled it for him. "I guarantee Antiliano's keeping everyone entertained with his stories. We want him on our side." He checked his watch. "Gosh, I'm two hours late for dinner. Where's Rehnquist?"

"Sleeping under my desk."

"Come on, boy." He whistled and the dog circled around the desk, wagging his tail.

"You're both going to get it from Aunt Margaret."

"Yeah and she's tougher than Judge Killam. He makes me take the bus; she'll throw us both under the bus."

Sarah laughed as Uncle Buddy and Rehnquist rushed out the door. She made herself a bag of microwave popcorn, and was about to pull the sides open when the office doorbell rang. Sarah peered out the window at Amina's son, Malick, a tall, skinny teenager. He reminded Sarah of her youngest brother, who was probably doing his homework a few blocks over. Malick must have been watching the news about the bomb in court. She felt sorry for him.

"Come on in." Sarah showed him to the client chair on the opposite side of her paper-strewn desk.

"Somebody's trying to kill my mother." His gaze shifted from Sarah's face to his lap. "They already tried shooting her. Now they got a bomb. Can they get her in jail?"

Sarah opened her mouth but couldn't find the words. How could she respond? "This was just a publicity stunt. Your mother's protected. They have guards." It was a weak answer. She hadn't dreamed that counseling Amina's son would be part of the job.

His large brown eyes searched her face. "Gimme a break. There were guards in court, but the guy almost killed her and got away with it. He's still out there."

"The police haven't stopped looking for the shooter." Sarah felt a tingle in her arm where she was shot. She often wondered how hard they were looking. Did a hysterical fireman do it? Someone who had been close to Jack? Were the police covering for him?

Malick stood and circled around the chair. "Everyone hates my mother. Cops all want her dead for killing that fireman."

Sarah studied him. Did he think his mother did it? Or did he actually *see* his mother do it?

"If you win this, how do we know they won't kill my mom when she gets out?" He grabbed a crystal paperweight from Sarah's desk, and tossed it from one hand to the other.

"You can't think like that. Please put that thing down."

Malick tossed it back on the desk. "Why couldn't we just move out? Let the foreclosure happen. She could've saved money and set up another store someday. I would've helped." He gestured with his hands as he spoke.

"She knows that. Your mother talks about you all the time, how you helped her." Sarah knew Amina loved her son more than anything in the world.

"It's not fair to me." He kicked the metal wastepaper basket next to the desk. Sarah watched it fly across the room and topple over.

She leaped to her feet. "Calm down, Malick."

"My mother's in jail for murder."

"Pick it up, have a seat, and we'll talk."

Malick gathered the spilled trash and replaced the basket. "Sorry, but how do you think *I* feel?"

Sarah pointed to the empty chair and he slumped down again, resting his head in his hands. She waited, listening to his sobs.

"I'm sorry, Malick." She handed him a box of tissues. It was the least she could do.

"It's not fair." He wiped his eyes. "Why can't my mom be normal like everyone else? Work, work, work. She's always in that store. And, she's into these stupid online groups. Like, she spends so much time trying to change things she just can't change."

"Like what?"

"I don't know. All sorts of stuff. Like the beggar kids in Dakar who get sent out on the streets by the masters. It's not her problem to fix. She should be figuring out how to get my dad back. If he were here, this wouldn't have happened. You know, this didn't have to happen. It's just not fair. Everyone hates me now too."

"I understand. It's not fair to you." The other kids were probably giving Malick a hard time at school, insulting his mother with all kinds of names. Sarah wondered what Amina did about the beggar kids. She'd have to remember to ask her.

"Did you speak with your mother today?" Sarah opened the bag of popcorn and offered him some. He waved it away.

"She told me not to worry, that you'd take care of everything."

Sarah couldn't hold his gaze. Winning this one would be a long shot—the odds were stacked against Amina. "We need to discuss what happened the night of the fire."

"She doesn't want me involved."

"Why not?"

Malick chewed on the tie of his hooded sweatshirt. "My mom doesn't trust anybody. Thinks the DA will trick me and I'll say the wrong thing. Then the cops'll charge me with helping her burn the place."

Sarah wondered what *saying the wrong thing* really meant.

"I don't care what my mom says. I'm gonna testify. Because it's *my* decision, not *hers*. Somebody set that fire. My mom didn't shoot the fireman." Conviction and passion permeated his voice.

"What happened the night of the fire?"

"Already told the cops."

"I need to hear it from you."

Malick stared at the wall behind her. "Someone else was there."

The olives were running low. Cole had been parked on the street watching the law office all evening. At times he had to curl on his side to ease the pain. What about the boy? Only fifteen years old. *A liability.* He dipped his finger in the plastic tub and circled the inner rim. Olives up to the knuckle. Why was he here? To fix it. Fix it. Fix it.

Only one to blame this time. He stirred the slippery black olives and thought about his mother.

13

Derrick sat in the foreperson's chair on the second day of the trial. Security and reporters swarmed the courthouse.

"Did you hear about the note?" Christine Dindy leaned toward him. She worked for Children's Hospital as a pediatric nurse.

"Yeah, it's disturbing." Derrick felt uncomfortable discussing it, but who hadn't gone home and watched TV? The networks highlighted the homemade bomb with its attached note as their breaking news story. *Pop goes the Arab.* It made him sick. Amina wasn't even an Arab. She was from Africa, a Muslim. Derrick removed his glasses and rubbed his eyes. How could anybody concentrate?

"I almost feel sorry for her." Christine nodded toward Amina Diallo in her flowing beige dress with gold trim and a matching headscarf. "Hope nobody tries to go after us."

"If it gets any worse, we may be sequestered."

She grimaced. "I heard they don't do that anymore."

"Costs the state too much."

"Yeah." Christine looked at Sarah. "I wonder how she really feels about this one, with everybody against her client. Look at all the firemen sitting out there. Clancy's broken in by now, but this has got to be tough on her."

"I agree." Derrick watched Sarah whispering to her uncle. She appeared poised and ready to go in her tailored maroon suit, which complemented her red hair. How did she feel deep down? Sarah was a fighter, and Derrick couldn't help but admire her.

"Clancy's a Red Sox fan," Christine whispered. "Check out the bow tie."

Derrick smiled. He'd already noticed the Red Sox bow tie and matching Red Sox socks. They'd been discussing the Sox in the conference room during breaks. It was fun listening to stories about the players from Antiliano.

"At least Clancy was on time this morning. He must've taken that bus," Christine said.

Clerk Kelly approached the first witness, who was obviously a fireman, with his pressed blue uniform and handlebar mustache. Derrick thought the man looked exhausted, with sagging dark circles beneath his eyes.

"Do you swear to tell the truth, the whole truth, and nothing but the truth, so help you God?"

The man cleared his throat. "I do."

Marinelli assumed his usual position at the podium. He also appeared calm and unfazed by the previous day's events. "Please introduce yourself to the ladies and gentlemen of the jury."

"Andy Larson."

"Are you employed?"

"Boston Fire Department, thirty-four years."

Derrick wondered if the fireman's slow, husky voice was natural or the result of months of anxiety and grieving.

"Is this your first time testifying in court?"

"Ahh, yeah."

"Are you nervous?"

"Been worried about it months on end. Can't sleep at night." Andy looked at the jurors for the first time. Derrick nodded back.

"Andy, what do you do for the Boston Fire Department?"

"Serve on rescue."

"What does that mean?"

Andy cleared his throat. "Okay . . . well in the fire department we have the engine, ladder, tower, rescue, and the marine units. I'm with Rescue One, the second oldest fire rescue company in the country."

Derrick noticed how his words came out flat and in rapid succession as if the testimony had been rehearsed many times.

"What are your duties with Rescue One?"

"Search and rescue."

"Can you describe the truck?"

"Sure. Uh, like a giant toolbox. Got the jaws of life, jacks, rakes, hooks to pull down ceilings . . . all kinds of tools for forcible entry."

"Do you recall Wednesday, July nineteenth of last year?"

Andy's eyes widened. "Ahh—okay."

Derrick thought he appeared off guard for a moment.

"Were you on duty that day?"

Andy pulled one side of his mustache down and chewed on the end. "Working a twenty-four, which would take us into Thursday morning when the fire occurred."

"Who were you working with?"

"Umm . . ." He wiped the perspiration from his brow with the back of his hand. "Me, Lieutenant Draak, Art Gramer, and, you know." He closed his eyes and paused.

"Who else?"

"Jack—Jack Fogerty."

"Andy, can you tell us about Jack?"

He gripped his water glass with both hands and drained half of it. Both ends of his mustache dripped. "Repeat the question?"

"Please tell us about Jack."

"Oh. Yeah. Jack." Andy twirled the wet mustache around his index finger and looked like he was trying to remember what to say. "Uhh, long jokes, always running off at the mouth, so on."

"Can you tell us more?"

"Couldn't cook. Yeah, couldn't cook. One time he strained our homemade chicken stock right down the drain because he forgot to place a pan underneath. He's the only fireman I've ever seen start a grease fire in the house kitchen. So we'd send him out for takeout when it was his turn to make dinner."

Several jurors chuckled. Derrick laughed to help Andy along. He felt sorry for him.

"Are you familiar with Jack's family life?"

"I . . ." Andy's eyes lingered on Jack's widow and son in the gallery. "Jack loved his boys, always taking them places, playing sports, coaching. Dad of the year, you know? And . . . and the best husband too. Jack and Maureen grew up together in Southie. They were high school sweethearts who were meant to be togeth—" His voice cracked. "That night, before we got the call, he just couldn't stop . . . couldn't stop . . ."

"Couldn't stop what?"

"Talking. God. About the boys." Andy pursed his lips. "They were his life. And Maureen." Andy looked out at Jack's wife who was crying and holding her son. "He loved you."

Andy rested his forehead on his fist. "Gimme a minute."

Marinelli nodded. "Take your time. I know this is difficult for you."

Derrick noticed Christine wiping a tear from the corner of her eye. Sarah appeared to be sympathizing with Andy as she sat perfectly still with her head tilted a bit to the side. How could she defend such an emotional case? Derrick knew she had a soft side. It came out when she mentioned the African bowl in her opening statement. He looked at Amina and wondered what she was thinking about.

Marinelli flipped a page in his legal pad. "Andy, what were you doing at approximately 12:20 a.m. on July twentieth?"

Andy nodded several times and took a deep breath. "We responded to a call near the Suffolk Downs T stop in East Boston. Car accident, small fire. As we were heading back, a man waved us down. He told us there was—"

"Objection." Sarah rose to her feet. "Hearsay."

"Sustained."

Marinelli nodded. "As a result of a conversation with the man who waved you down, what did you do?"

"Drove down Waldemar Ave. The Senegalese Market was on fire. We jumped into our gear, grabbed tools and the thermal camera. Me and Jack forced entry through the front door with a Halligan, while Lieutenant Draak ran around back. Art put his gear on outside the truck because he was driving."

"Where was the fire located?"

"Back left corner, first floor."

"What were your observations when you broke through the front door?"

"Visibility was pretty much zero with the smoke, but we could still make out the orange glow of the fire. I remember smelling gas."

"What did you do next?"

"We stayed down low and started with a right-hand search."

"What's that?"

"In a fire you have to move with your hand against the wall or you'll get disoriented. Here, we were trying to find a way up fast as we could. Jack was looking for a door or stairs with the camera."

"Can you describe how the thermal imaging camera operates?"

"Detects heat. The images are black, white, and shades of gray. It's like . . . when you point it at a person, his image will come up white on the screen. A warm door knob will appear grayish-white. The camera helps us navigate in the dark to find victims or hot spots behind doors and walls."

"What happened next?"

"Jack found a locked door. I opened it with the Halligan and we headed upstairs. I remember closing the door behind us to block the rising smoke. Uh, second floor was pitch-black. The door at the top of the stairs opened into a hallway with a living room on the right. The camera screen showed somebody going in the opposite direction, straight down the hallway. When Jack pointed the screen into the living room we saw another person, maybe twenty feet away off to the right."

Derrick noticed Andy's increased momentum. His words came out faster, as if he was back in the fire, racing to find the occupants.

"What did you do?"

"We made the split-second decision to separate. That was it. I'll regret it the rest of my life." Andy looked into the gallery at Jack's widow and pinched the bridge of his nose. "This is real hard. He was my partner and I let him down. I let Maureen and the family down too. I'm so sorry," he said, in a soft voice.

Clerk Kelly refilled Andy's water glass. Derrick observed the anguish in the man's eyes. Could he have saved Jack if they hadn't split up? If they had stayed together, maybe they'd both be dead. Why would anyone shoot a fireman? His gaze lingered on the stoic, yet striking, Amina Diallo. Did she really have it in her?

Marinelli waited for Andy to make eye contact with him. "Your Honor, may the witness approach the diagram?"

"He may."

Andy walked over to a poster-sized floor plan of an apartment layout and picked up a long black pointer.

"Where did you go when you separated from Jack?"

"Up this way to the left. Toward the one we saw running down the hall. Jack went to the right, into the living room over here." He tapped the living room on the lower right part of the diagram.

"Who had the camera?"

"Oh, me. I grabbed it because the one who ran down the hall was out of sight at that point. We agreed to meet back in the same spot."

"Was Jack carrying anything other than his Halligan tool?"

"He had a flashlight clipped to his waist."

"Was it turned on?"

"Course."

"What did you do next?"

"Headed to the front bedroom on the left. Checked out good. Empty. Then, as I was heading out, taking a left back into the hallway, I heard a loud bang coming from the living room that sounded like a gun firing. I pointed the camera in the direction of the noise and saw—" Andy paused and looked at Amina sitting next to Sarah and Clancy. She returned Andy's gaze. Derrick thought he saw her flinch.

Marinelli raised his voice. "What did you see on your camera screen?"

"I saw her." Andy extended the black stick toward Amina. "Pointing a gun."

"Objection!" Sarah and Clancy jumped up and spoke simultaneously. "Objection, move to strike!"

"Sidebar?" Sarah said.

Judge Killam nodded. "You may approach."

Derrick and Christine exchanged glances. He wished they could discuss the trial. All three attorneys scurried to the other side of the bench and huddled close to the judge. Sarah's face burned bright red as she leaned in to make her argument. Derrick wondered why she seemed so surprised. Didn't they know this was coming?

Andy continued staring at Amina, squeezing the pointer until his knuckles turned white. He appeared ready to leap across the courtroom with stick in hand, leading the charge against her. Derrick wondered if all the firemen would follow suit. Their outrage was evident through clenched jaws and folded arms. He imagined the TV camera had zoomed in on the black stick pointing at Amina.

After the sidebar all attorneys resumed their positions. Sarah was unable to mask her anger, and Amina kept mouthing, "He's lying." Derrick watched Clancy place a hand on Amina's shoulder and whisper something. The old lawyer was the only one who appeared unfazed.

Judge Killam turned to the jury. "The objection is overruled."

Marinelli looked overly pleased with himself. "Andy, describe in more detail what you saw on the camera screen."

"I saw that woman pointing a gun in Jack's direction. It was a black-and-white image, but I know it was her. She's the one I saw."

Derrick saw Marinelli make eye contact with each juror as if to say *I told you so*. He wondered what Clancy would do on cross. Derrick watched him lean back and adjust the Red Sox bow tie with his chin slightly raised as if that little tidbit of damning testimony meant nothing at all.

"Where was the defendant located when you saw her pointing the gun?"

"At the far end of the living room in the right corner. She was diagonally across the room from where I was standing."

"Where was Jack?"

"He was crawling toward her along the living room wall from the opposite corner."

"Andy, what did you do next?"

"By instinct I headed toward Jack and tripped over something and may've blacked out. Hard to remember. I got up, grabbed the camera and my Halligan, and headed toward Jack."

Marinelli paused. "Did you check any other rooms?"

"No. Oh wait, I did check the kitchen, which was down the hall on the left. It was on fire and burning pretty good. I didn't see anyone and closed the door. I checked the back bedroom opposite the kitchen on the right. It was also on fire, but not as bad. The curtains were burning, along with a chair next to the window. I scanned the room with the camera, checked under the bed, didn't find anybody. Then I opened a door leading into a bathroom."

"Did you check in there?"

"Yeah. It was very smoky, but empty. The bathroom had another door which opened back into the hallway."

Derrick scratched his head. It didn't make sense. How come Andy hadn't rushed over to his partner after hearing a shot and seeing the gun?

"What did you do next?"

"I went back down the hall and took a left into the living room. There were two entrances to the living room from the hallway. One up here near the bath-room." He pointed to the upper left-hand corner of the living room. "And one down here next to the stairwell where we first came in."

"Okay." Marinelli rubbed his chin. "Could you see anything on your camera screen?"

"Yes. I saw Jack moving slowly along the far living room wall carrying that . . . that African lady's teen-aged son over his shoulders. The kid was unconscious. The lady was bent over, coughing, but Jack held her by the hand. I remember that. He held her by the hand."

"Where were they heading?"

"To a window off the front of the building. You see, there were no windows on the interior walls. They were located off the front and back of the building."

"What happened next?"

"I ran over to Jack, and he placed the son in my arms and said, 'I found the boy passed out.' He motioned us on. We were about fifteen, twenty feet away from the window at that point. I dropped the camera, hauled the kid up over my shoulder, and led the lady by her arm. Jack stayed where he was. I tried to get him to come with us, but he wouldn't."

"What were the conditions like inside the apartment at that point?"

"Pretty bad. I was afraid they'd die of smoke inhala-tion. Luckily a ladder got raised to the window. I ended up handing the kid off to the guys from the East Boston ladder company. They helped the lady down too."

"What did you do next?"

"I ran back for Jack. I remember his PASS device beeping. It goes off when a fireman stops moving." He covered his ears. "I can still hear it beeping today . . . every day, every night."

"Did you find Jack?"

"Yeah. Two firemen joined me and we carried Jack to the window, got him into the rescue box. They took him down. I saw somebody performing CPR on Jack right there in the box. I guess he wasn't breathing. The paramedics put him on a stretcher and into an ambulance, but it made no difference." Andy yanked his hair with both hands. "Jack was dead by then."

"Objection." Sarah rose. "Move to strike the last sentence. The witness lacks personal knowledge of Jack's condition at that point."

"Sustained." Judge Killam turned to the jury. "The last sentence spoken by the witness is stricken from the record. I'm instructing you to ignore it."

Derrick noticed that Sarah rose halfway when Andy said he guessed Jack wasn't breathing. She changed her mind for some reason and sat back down. How could Andy know Jack wasn't breathing? Why had she objected in one instance and not the other?

"What did you do next?"

"I went down the ladder and asked about Jack. They told me—"

Clancy stood this time. "Objection, that's hearsay."

"Sustained."

"Did anything else happen?"

"A paramedic bandaged the cut on my forehead, which I must've gotten from coming down on the corner of that table when I tripped. After that I filled out an incident report and helped at the scene."

"When did you find out about Jack's condition?"

"About two hours later. Lieutenant Draak sat us down at the firehouse and told us."

"No further questions."

Derrick watched Marinelli return to his seat; the courtroom remained silent. Amina Diallo appeared to be staring into space, lost in thought. Derrick thought

he saw her lips moving, and wondered if she was praying. He looked at Clancy and waited for the old man to
rise.

Judge Killam cleared his throat extra loud and long.
"Do you plan to cross-examine this witness, Clancy?"

Sarah rose. "I'm handling the cross, Your Honor."

Derrick was surprised. He figured Clancy would perform all the cross-examinations. He'd handled the first
witness with such expertise. What could Sarah possibly
get out of Andy to help their case?

The judge studied the courtroom clock. "How long
do you intend to be?"

"About forty-five minutes."

"We'll take a brief morning—"

"All rise!" the court officer said.

Derrick looked at Sarah and then at Jack's widow as
he filed out behind Christine and the rest of the jurors
in his row. This case had everything from homemade
bombs to witnesses breaking down on the stand. Andy
had struggled up there. Derrick wondered how it would
feel to testify in a packed courtroom and look out at
the victim's family, praying you get all the facts right.

He thought back to the shooting he had witnessed
years ago. If only he'd been half as brave as Andy. But
that was different, he assured himself. If Derrick had
gone to the cops, he may not have lived to take the stand.
Now he had a family, a thriving computer business, and
people respected him. Derrick breathed in deeply and
sighed. The trial had dredged up the past, and he couldn't
help but think about the man in the wheelchair still waiting for the witness to come forward.

Derrick and Christine walked in silence to the stale
coffee line in the conference room. The other jurors appeared contemplative as well. How many others had
skeletons in the closet? What were they thinking?

14

Get up and *do it*. That's what Sarah repeated to herself as she approached Andy. Why had Uncle Buddy insisted she handle this cross-examination? Because she'd evoke more sympathy with her soft feminine touch? Hardly. Everybody loved firemen.

Andy knotted his fingers as she closed in. Their eyes met. His were large and blue and sad. Sarah wished she didn't have to do this. Andy lost his partner and friend like she had lost John. *One gunshot*. She knew what he was going through, the guilt, the self-doubt. If only he could've done things differently. If only he had stayed with Jack. If only she hadn't insisted on meeting that witness with John. *If only . . .*

Sarah assumed her position and drew a breath. *Concentrate*. Andy had struggled on the stand to get all the facts right. The jurors knew it. She had to be careful, they liked Andy. Several women had dabbed their eyes when Andy talked about Jack's widow and children. Sarah had to achieve the perfect balance: remain sympathetic while poking holes in his testimony. She glanced at the foreperson. He looked back at her with laser intensity.

"Mr. Larson? May I call you Andy?" Sarah softened her words.

"Sure."

"I'm sorry for your loss."

Andy nodded.

"When you respond to a fire, you must perform your job as fast as possible?"

"Uh huh, but you got to take certain safety precautions, like staying low, moving along a wall, and making sure you don't trip over something."

"People can die within minutes of smoke inhalation?"

"Right. It's the smoke that kills most people, not the actual flames."

"I see." Sarah inched closer to the witness, keeping her shoulders angled toward the jury. She wanted to start with the basics and create a rhythm. "On July twentieth, did you have your sirens on when you approached the Senegalese Market?"

"Uhh . . . no, because we were flagged down and the store was right down the street."

"Were there any lights on inside the building when you arrived?"

"No."

"Did the roof have any lighting?"

"Not that I recall."

"The moon out?"

"Was a dark night."

"Do your helmets have lights?"

"No."

"The only lights you and Jack carried were the flashlights clipped to your waists?"

"That's correct."

"Once you were inside the building, it was too dark and smoky to see with the naked eye?" Sarah had to establish the setting. Most people didn't realize that visibility went down to zero during a fire.

Andy nodded. "Couldn't see anything without the camera."

"When you and Jack first arrived in the upstairs apartment, you saw someone moving down the hallway on the camera screen?"

"We did."

"What color hair did this person have?"

"It's a black-and-white image. No way you could tell that."

"A human body glows white, like a ghost?"

"Right."

"Was the figure male or female?"

"Couldn't tell."

"Where did this person go?"

"Whoever it was must've ended up going in the living room through the second entrance. Had to be the African lady because Jack said he found the son passed out, unconscious. So it had to be her."

"But, you're not certain without guessing?"

"Makes sense to me."

Sarah had to raise the possibility that someone else may have been upstairs during the fire. But who? And why? The jurors would demand answers.

"You lost track of the person who ran down the hall?" Sarah inched forward again.

"Just temporarily. We rescued the only two occupants in the house."

"Is it possible the person you lost track of ran into the back bedroom?"

"Doubt it, because I didn't see anybody in there."

Sarah detected sarcasm in Andy's tone. She had to pursue another line of questioning, go on the offensive. Uncle Buddy always pursued his cross-examinations out of chronological order, touching on various high points and leaving them hanging in the air. Let the jurors connect the dots later, he had advised.

"After you made it out of the building, a paramedic attended to your head wound?"

"Yeah."

"Did you speak with any police officers at the scene?"

"No."

"You mentioned filling out an incident report?"

"Yes."

"You filled out that report before leaving the fire scene?"

"Yeah, my lieutenant's a stickler on reports. He wants us to have them done ASAP for the 920 guys, the arson investigators."

Sarah inched closer to the witness. "So, you completed your report before you knew what happened to Jack?"

Andy cracked his knuckles. "Yeah."

"At that point all you knew was that Jack had trouble breathing and had to be rushed to the hospital?"

"Right."

Sarah pursed her lips. "In your report you left out the part about seeing Amina pointing a gun?"

Andy hesitated and looked at Nick, who remained neutral. Nick must've known this line of questioning was coming. Sarah wondered if he knew Andy would take the stand this morning and claim he saw Amina pointing a gun.

Andy cleared his throat and stared into his lap. "I guess I left it out."

Sarah walked to her table and picked up the one-page report. "I don't want you to guess. Would you like to see your report to refresh your recollection?"

"I can explain."

Sarah couldn't let him explain anything for the same reason she never asked a *why* question during cross. Uncle Buddy never relinquished control to the witness. "Andy, you prepared the incident report within an hour after you exited the burning building?"

"About an hour."

"Okay. Were the events you described in your report clearer to you back then than they are today?"

"My memory's about the same."

"Your memory is as clear today as it was nine months ago?"

"Yup."

"You never wrote down a word in your report about seeing Amina pointing a gun?" Sarah waved the paper in the air. She watched the jurors' eyes shifting from her to Andy as they waited for an answer.

"Not at the time."

"Did you write any supplemental reports including the information?"

Andy twisted his mustache. "No."

Sarah grabbed two scrap papers from her desk and pretended to read from one. "You didn't mention the gun to the paramedic who treated you?"

Andy's line of vision moved from his lap to the paper in Sarah's hand. "I guess not. No."

Sarah glanced at the other paper and eyed Andy. "Did you mention the gun to any police officers?"

Andy glanced at the second paper and shrugged. "I don't recall."

"Did you speak with Detective Callahan from homicide?"

"Yeah."

"Did you tell Detective Callahan that you saw Amina pointing a gun?"

"I don't recall. By the time I met with him I was all messed up."

Sarah watched the jury. They appeared pensive, not one jotted down a note. "When you wrote the incident report, you didn't know that Jack had been shot?"

"No."

"You never mentioned that you saw a gun to *anyone* at the fire scene?"

Andy rested his face in his hands. He appeared

frustrated, defeated. "I don't remember. I might've." He sighed and looked to the jury for help.

Sarah knew she had to be careful. Maybe it was best to move on, she'd made her point. A forty-something woman with short brassy hair presented Sarah with a frigid stare. The icy eyes spoke volumes. Why did it always seem to be another woman? Sarah walked a few paces and forced herself to concentrate on the next group of questions.

"When you checked the back bedroom, the curtains were on fire?"

"Yes."

"A chair was burning too?"

"Right."

"That chair was next to the window?"

"Yes."

"Was the window open?"

"It may've been. Not sure."

"There's access to the roof from that window, correct?"

"Don't know."

Sarah made eye contact with the foreperson, who squinted through his glasses as he listened. She hoped he could navigate through the emotional cloud and latch on to the blatant inconsistencies in Andy's testimony. How could he omit mentioning the part about the gun to everyone at the scene?

Sarah looked at Andy again and raised her voice, "That person you first saw moving down the hall could've entered the back bedroom, escaped out the window, and climbed up to the roof?"

"Objection." Nick rose. "Calls for speculation. The witness was uncertain about access to the roof."

Judge Killam cocked his head. "Sustained."

Sarah waited a moment before moving on. Even

though her question hadn't been allowed, it hovered in the air and raised a possibility.

"The fire in the back bedroom burned near the window, right?"

"Uhh, yes."

"Did it appear that the fire had just started in that bedroom?"

"Hard to say."

"Is it possible somebody had just set that fire?"

"I'd have no way of knowing."

"Could someone have set that fire from the window and escaped onto the roof?"

Nick popped up with mouth wide open and arms spread. "Your Honor, Ms. Lynch is overstepping her bounds. This line of questioning is outrageously speculative."

Judge Killam leaned over his bench and locked eyes with Sarah. "Sustained! Move along."

Sarah paced for a moment to let the possibilities sink in. "You moved from the bedroom directly into a bathroom?"

"Yes."

"Was that bathroom on fire?"

"It was smoky." Andy fiddled with his mustache again.

"Andy, you tripped and fell right after you ran out of that front bedroom across from the living room?"

He leaned back, folded his arms, and scowled. "You obviously weren't listening. I tripped after I saw your client with a gun and I ran to help Jack."

Sarah hadn't wanted him to mention Amina and the gun again. The more times it was brought up, the stronger the image would become for the jurors. However, she wanted him to read his scanty report out loud and this presented her with an opportunity. "According to your incident report you tripped after you ran out of the front bedroom."

"No."

Bingo. That's just what she wanted. Sarah marched over to Nick and showed him the copy of Andy's report. "Your Honor, may I approach the witness?"

"You may."

"Andy, I'm handing you a copy of your incident report dated July twentieth. Please read the second paragraph out loud."

He grabbed the paper, rolled his eyes, and read from the report. "Structure fire. Two stories. Forced entry through front door. Fire first floor, A/B corner. Found stairwell to second-floor apartment. Saw occupant head down hall, another in living room. Checked front bedroom on left, empty. Heard a loud bang. Sustained injury exiting front bedroom. Checked kitchen, back bedroom, and bathroom for occupants. Fire in kitchen and back bedroom near window along B wall. Found FF J. Fogerty in living room along C wall with two occupants."

"Did you black out when you tripped?" Sarah asked.

"I'm not sure, that part's a little blurry."

"Blurry? Are other parts of that night *blurry*?"

Andy closed his eyes and cupped his hands over his ears. "I don't know. I just don't know. Okay? I'm sorry. I'm so sorry for everything. I can't do this no more."

Sarah's heart sank. She shouldn't have asked that last question. Uncle Buddy would've sat down after Andy blurted out the word "blurry." What a beautiful word for the defense. Why had she felt compelled to ask it? The jurors sympathized with Andy, she read it in their tight lips and lined foreheads. This was not how she wanted to wrap up her cross-examination. She was only doing her job. Why couldn't they understand? Sarah had to ask pointed questions surrounding the sketchy identification of Amina pointing a gun. Andy was the only eyewitness.

Andy rested his forehead in cupped fingers. What more could Sarah ask of him? Let him go, her instincts told her. "Thank you. No further questions." Sarah watched Nick leap to his feet before she retreated one step to her table.

"Andy, please explain why you neglected to write the part about seeing Amina Diallo pointing a gun in your incident report?" Nick pointed his entire arm at Amina.

Andy wiggled forward in his chair and addressed the jury. "Okay. I tried to explain before, but *that lady lawyer* wouldn't let me. The fire report was only supposed to be a brief summary, and I wrote it up quickly at the scene. I'm trained in rescue and fire suppression, not in writing reports for trial. My mind was focused on Jack that night. They carried him off in a goddamned ambulance, and the next thing I know, he's dead. Sometimes things become clearer later on."

"What do you mean by that?" Nick asked.

"Well, I had to sit down and go over the events in my head and make sense of it all. I saw that woman." Andy gestured toward Amina several times with his index finger. "*That woman*, pointing a gun on the screen. The image sticks out in my mind and it will always be with me until the day I die."

"No further questions."

Sarah stood. "Recross, Your Honor?"

"As long as you limit your questions to what Mr. Marinelli asked on redirect. And make it brief because it's almost time for lunch."

"I will, Your Honor." Sarah maneuvered around her

table. "Mr. Larson, you just testified that the image you saw on the black-and-white camera screen became clear later on?"

"Yes."

"You were running at the time?"

"I was moving."

"The image flashed across the screen for a split second as you were moving?"

Andy paused for a moment. "I saw it for a couple seconds."

"Did the person you saw on the screen have short hair or long hair?"

Andy looked at Amina. "Long."

"Was this person wearing glasses?"

Sarah watched Andy study her client again. "I don't think so."

"Are you sure?"

"I can't be positive."

"When you glanced at the image on the screen as you were moving, either before or after you tripped, you weren't exactly clear about what you saw *at that point* in time, correct?"

Andy regarded Nick and waited as if he hoped for an objection. His face reddened. "It was later on that I realized she was pointing a gun."

"After you saw this image on the screen, you didn't continue in Jack's direction."

"I headed toward Jack and tripped. After that I must've seen him moving. I thought he was okay."

"So you headed in the opposite direction to check the kitchen, back bedroom, and bathroom?"

"Just doing my job, lady."

"Mr. Larson, I know this is hard for you, but I'm also trying to do my job. I have one last question, and I want you to think about it before you provide an answer. Did your mind suddenly become clear after you reviewed your testimony over and over with Mr. Marinelli?"

Nick shot to his feet. "Objection!"

"Sustained."

"Nothing further. Thank you, Mr. Larson."

15

Uncle Buddy stretched his galoshes over his shoes. "Come to the Federalist and have a bite."

Sarah watched the guard escort Amina back to her holding cell for lunch. "We should be discussing strategy after Andy's surprise revelation that Amina was pointing a gun."

"My dear, we must rest our brains or we'll be burned out by three o'clock. Beautiful job on cross."

"Thanks, but you would've sat down earlier. I can't seem to stop myself from asking that extra question."

"Sarah, Sarah, Sarah. You're too hard on yourself. Cross-examination is an art and it takes years to master. I would've lacked the willpower to sit down at your age too."

"Yeah, I guess." Sarah tried to picture a young Uncle Buddy, but couldn't. He had looked and dressed the same for as long as she could remember.

"The Federalist is calling."

"Not for me." Sarah sighed. "We also have Amina's son, Malick, saying someone else was in the apartment during the fire. How come he's just coming out with it now? Why not tell the police first thing?"

"Ahhh." Uncle Buddy rubbed his hands together.

"Could be all sorts of reasons. I'm sure Amina knows, but she's not ready to tell us." He turned toward the gallery and nudged her. "Here comes your *friend* again."

Sarah knew who was coming without looking up. "Maybe Frank's worried he missed something in his arson investigation, or he's wondering what we have up our sleeve."

"That's not all he's interested in." Uncle Buddy winked.

Sarah felt herself blushing as her uncle squeaked down the aisle in his galoshes. "No scotch, Uncle Buddy, you'll be snoring all afternoon."

"Why hello, Sergeant Braaady," Uncle Buddy said. "Are you coming to work a deal with us? Amina may agree to straight probation, but I doubt it. She maintains her innocence like a beacon shining in the night."

"Life without parole."

"You're still on that kick? No kidding. Even after your fireman's *foggy* visions? Wait a minute. Blurry. That's the word he used. *Blurrrry.* Lucky for you he got off the stand or we would've been hearing about the Sugar Plum Fairy." Uncle Buddy fluttered his fingers, performed a pirouette, and curtseyed. "Dear, dear, you must be in denial," he said, as he pointed a toe and danced through the door.

Frank shook his head. "Your uncle missed his calling. With the ballet moves and the quick jabs, he should've been a boxer." He leaned over Sarah's shoulder. "I snuck you lunch. The DA's office had extras." He placed a long, white bag from Pi Alley on top of her papers. "An Italian sub and chocolate chip cookie for dessert."

Sarah was starving and appreciated his lunch, but fell for the grin. "Very risky, consorting with the enemy."

The grin widened. "Especially with Nick ready to explode out there."

"He stormed out without even looking at me." Sarah unwrapped the oversized sub. "So, who coached Andy Larson?"

"Nobody. The guy experienced major trauma when he lost his partner. I'm sure he saw your client pointing a gun and blocked it out. Repressed memory."

"Oh, come on, Frank. Who buys that crap?"

He regarded her for a moment. "You know, Sarah, life isn't always so black-and-white."

"Exactly. Now, explain that to Nick." Sarah spread the white sub wrapping over her papers and smoothed it with her palm. "Amina's case is far from being black-and-white. That's why I had to go after Andy. Nick takes it too personally."

"He's under all sorts of scrutiny from the union. You should see it out there. As soon as Nick steps from the courtroom, they surround him like a pack of coyotes. They're worse than the media, because you can't ignore the union."

"Part of the job." Sarah took a bite of her sub and washed it down with water.

"I suppose, but Nick has his personal issues. His father's maimed from an arson fire. The roof caved in on him."

Sarah imagined the fire, a man trapped beneath rubble, unable to move. She thought back to her days supervising Nick. He stayed late, listened to her critiques, won cases. And that was all that mattered.

"Did you ever give him any time?" Frank asked.

"Time? What are you talking about?"

"Your personal time. Did you sit down over lunch or a beer and ask him about his life outside the office? That type of thing?"

The desire to make an excuse washed over her. "I was always swamped assigning cases, and then I had

my own trials to deal with. Nick could hold his own."
Sarah considered Frank's words. *Take the time. Listen
to their stories*, as Uncle Buddy emphasized. Maybe
that's where she'd gone astray. Why hadn't she sympathized with Nick a little more?

Frank placed a hand on her shoulder and smiled. "I
was impressed how you learned about Amina and her
dinners with the homeless man. I missed that in my investigation, remember?"

Sarah watched him lift Amina's African bowl from
the table and turn it in his hands. She thought about
Amina and her life in Senegal, going to and from the
town faucet collecting water. She had wanted a better
life over here for Malick. Sarah wondered who else
could have been in that upstairs apartment during the
fire. Had Malick made it up? They had to dig deeper
and find the truth for Amina's sake, but also for Andy
and all the firemen.

"A penny for your thoughts?" Frank set the bowl
back down.

"My mind's drifting. I'm exhausted."

Frank's cell phone rang. It sounded like he was
speaking with someone from the governor's office.

Sarah detected a long sigh when the call ended.
"Somebody sounds nervous at the state house," she
said.

"The governor wants to make sure I've done my
job." Frank pursed his lips.

"Is Noterman typically this hands on?"

"Never." Frank tapped his cell phone against his lips
several times. "He's all over Nick too. I think Noterman
needs the positive publicity right now. Lately, we've heard
nothing but negative press, with his plans to raise the
gas tax, the sales tax again, increase tolls."

"He's making the state appear desperate for the revenue, so he can push his casino bill through this time." Sarah recalled all the uproar over legalized gambling when the governor tried to get it passed through the legislature the first time. It was defeated.

Frank nodded. "He's got an agenda. No doubt about it."

"If he wants his casino so badly, he'll have to mobilize the unions." Sarah tilted her head, causing a gob of pickles and tomatoes to spill from the sub down the front of her suit. "Can't believe I did that."

"Me either, you're always so polished." Frank smiled. "Must be a side of you I've yet to discover."

"The clumsy part, you mean?"

"Yeah, very cute."

"Cute? I won't be so *cute* when I'm cross-examining you."

"You really think you're ready to play hardball?"

"I'm up for the challenge." She rewrapped the other half of the sub, stuffed it in her briefcase, and grabbed a blank legal pad. "Thanks for lunch. I have to run and see Amina now."

Sarah darted into the hallway and nearly collided with Nick.

"Can I have a word with you, please?" Nick's breath smelled like sour cream and onion chips, and his voice sounded muffled through gritted teeth.

"I'm in a rush." Sarah wasn't ready for this. She panicked and angled away from him. She noticed the group of firemen and union officials gathered by the elevators, watching them.

"You're not squirming out of this one." Nick sidestepped in front of her. "How dare you attack my reputation by saying I coached Andy."

By instinct, Sarah counterattacked. "I find it interesting how he changed his story to bolster *your* case."

"I didn't *tell* him what to say, Sarah."

"Power of suggestion."

"You're a coldhearted bitch." Nick raised his voice, causing more people to stop and stare. "The way you attacked Andy after he lost his partner? You'll do whatever it takes to win. You obviously haven't learned from your mistake."

Sarah felt her stomach muscles tense. He was referring to her old case, *her mistake* that cost John his life. She wanted to throw her arms around Nick's waist, and tackle him down hard on the floor. "You're the one making the mistake now, Nick, and you don't even know it. All you care about is how you look in front of the press and the union." She turned her back on him and walked away. This time, though, she had to fight back tears.

Amina heard Sarah coming. Her high heels clicked along the tile floor. Amina shoved her lunch tray aside. She couldn't touch the soggy grilled cheese and cold french fries today. Andy's testimony took her back to that terrifying night. She couldn't stop thinking about the fireman. *Jack Fogerty.* He had carried Malick and somehow managed to hold her hand. What was he feeling at that moment? Did he know he was about to die? Her heart ached for his children. Amina was the last person to hold their father's hand.

The cell door clanged open for Sarah and clanged shut again. Amina winced; she hated that sound. Was Sarah here to rehash Andy's testimony about the fire? Amina eyed her legal pad. That was the last thing she felt like talking about.

"How are you doing?" Sarah's hair appeared disheveled. Long red strands had dislodged from her French braid.

Amina released a long sigh. She recalled Andy's black stick pointing at her. *She's the one I saw.* "It's useless. The jurors have judged me already."

"It's not useless. We haven't even presented our case yet." Sarah sat beside her on the steel bench. "Malick believes someone else was there during the fire."

"No." Amina crossed her arms. She could not let Malick get involved. "My son did not see anybody that night. He passed out from the smoke and can't remember a thing."

"You're sure?"

"Positive, and I don't want him repeating any of this nonsense to the police."

"But if Malick can help your case, we may want him to take the stand."

"That is out of the question. I'm his mother. Don't I have any say?" Amina raised her voice—she had to remain firm. "Malick must go back."

"Back where?" Sarah brushed hair from her eyes. "To Senegal?"

"Yes. He must live with his father now, with Lamine."

Sarah closed her legal pad and set it down on the other side of the bench. "Tell me about Lamine." Her voice had changed pitch. It was much softer now.

Amina regarded Sarah for a moment. Should she tell her? It was a story Amina hadn't shared with anyone besides family. After what happened to Lamine, she had closed herself off to others, gotten bitter. *Why?* Because it was all so unfair. Completely unfair. Amina had coped by doing whatever it took to survive over here. What more could she have done? When she tried to do something good, a little charity work, it had backfired too.

Amina observed Sarah waiting patiently. *Tell her*. It was time to let go.

"Here, let me fix your braid. Turn that way." Amina squared Sarah's head in her palms and removed the elastic band at the bottom.

"Thank you." Sarah fluffed the loose pieces. "I didn't realize how much it had fallen apart."

"I don't think your hair would've made it through the afternoon."

"You're probably right."

Amina started in the center of Sarah's back and began pulling the old braid apart. "Do you have a brush?"

"No."

"That's okay." Amina combed her fingers through Sarah's thick, wavy hair and gently worked out the knots. "Lamine." Amina felt the familiar ache. "What would you like to know?"

"Anything." Sarah tipped her head back while Amina worked her fingers from underneath. "Anything you want."

Amina closed her eyes. "Lamine has the gift of music. He was born a griot." She pictured her husband with his tender eyes that saw into the soul. "In our tradition, a griot plays the tama, he's also a singer, a dancer, . . . a storyteller. He communicates with the people. Through music."

Sarah dipped her chin forward as Amina combed the silky hair at the nape of her neck. "What's a tama?"

"The tama is a talking drum. Centuries old. Through the rhythm of the tama the griot speaks to us. In the old days of the kings, the griot would be there always, next to the king. He'd counsel the king through bad times, give advice . . . lift the king's spirit. If there was a battle, the griot would lead with his tama to give the warriors courage." Amina imagined the griots of old, beating out a wartime rhythm and singing in Wolof.

"What does the drum look like?"

"It has a shape like this." Amina released Sarah's hair, and outlined an hourglass shape with her hands. "Comes in different sizes. The tama is made of wood with iguana or sometimes goat skin stretched over the two ends to make the playing surfaces. Let's see . . . those ends are laced together by strings which run up and down the drum. The tama is held here, under the armpit, so, when it's played, the strings are squeezed." She moved her arm in and out like Lamine did. "The squeezing changes the sound and meaning of the music. It's hard to explain, but the music from the tama is a language in itself. Sometimes you don't really hear it, you just feel it."

"Do you play the tama with your hands?"

"Drumstick and fingers. Like, if I'm holding the tama in my right arm, I'd use my right fingers and the drumstick in the other hand." Amina demonstrated fluttering her fingers and snapping her left wrist. "Of course, only men are allowed to play the tama, and you must be a griot. It is bad luck for me to touch it."

"How did you and Lamine meet?"

"We met in Dakar. He was playing his tama in a group with four other men, including my cousin. My girlfriends and I started dancing." Amina recalled how they had been dancing in a giant circle around the group. Lamine had reached out to her with the alluring beat of his tama. She felt the heat in his music and the passion in his eyes. And Amina was drawn in, closer and closer to Lamine. He played for her and only her. *A feeling of ecstasy.*

Amina gathered Sarah's hair again. "We dated for about eight months. I loved every minute with Lamine.

He's very intelligent, and makes me laugh. But when he'd play his tama for me, I'd be consumed. It was so . . . beautiful. Every day, I couldn't wait to get out of work to be with him." Amina smiled at the faded memories. "He eventually asked me to get married, and I set my price." Amina paused as Sarah jerked her head around. She looked confused. "In Senegal it is symbolic that a man must send money to his bride-to-be. The women set the price. It's called *le dot*."

"You're kidding." Sarah clapped a hand on her thigh. "I wish we had that over here. How do you set a price?"

"Well, I knew the prices set by my cousins when they got married, and I asked around. When I finally came up with a number, I raised it even higher." Amina laughed. "Poor Lamine."

"No, good for you." Sarah laughed with her. "Did Lamine meet your price?"

"Yes. Lamine was lucky to have a good job working in customs, but he also had to ask his family for more." Amina separated a handful of Sarah's hair at the top of her head, and raised it up high.

"What did you do with the money?"

"I kept some, but I gave most of it to my family: my mother, grandmother, aunts, and some cousins. When I have babies, they'll give me gifts worth double what I gave them. It's like an investment. I must also give back to Lamine's family by bringing them gifts. Of course, when somebody gets the opportunity to come over here and work, we send money back home. It's the right thing to do." Amina used three fingers to divide the hair into three equal pieces. "Families take care of each other."

"How long were you married when you came over here?"

"Only six months." Amina pulled and began weaving the top pieces together. "Lean forward a little."

Sarah shifted. "I can't imagine leaving him like that. Have you seen Lamine since?"

"Yes, he came over on a visitor's visa. After my internship, we rented an apartment in Mattapan. I worked as a night receptionist at the Meridien hotel, because of my French, and braided hair in a beauty salon during the day. Lamine worked in construction or landscaping where he was paid under the table. He also joined a reggae band, so he played in a few clubs here and there. After a year of working, saving money, we had Malick."

"When did you get the idea to start your own business?"

"I'd say, when Malick was a baby." Amina gathered hair from both sides of Sarah's face, and added it to the braid. "We felt there was a need for an African store, so we planned to run it together and live upstairs. We originally found a spot in Mattapan, which was very affordable, but the area . . . I didn't realize."

"Crime?"

"Gangs, shootings, stabbings. In Senegal we have crime, but I've never seen anything this bad. I mean, nobody had guns back home. And, it was an African neighborhood . . . you'd think they would've left us alone." Amina remembered feeling vulnerable every time she had to walk home at night. "We were so naïve to think we could run a business there." She continued working the excess hair into the braid down to Sarah's shoulders.

"I'm sensing something happened," Sarah said. "Amina, if it's too painful, we don't have to talk about it."

Amina tugged downward on the braid, making it lie flat. "Mmmm. You should know this. It is why Lamine is no longer here. It is why I'm alone. If this . . . things would've been different." Amina felt tears trickling from the corners of her eyes. She wiped her face across the top of her shoulder. "We've had bad fortune."

Sarah mumbled something inaudible.

"What?" Amina leaned over Sarah's head.

"Nothing. Really, go ahead."

"It happened when Malick turned six. We wanted to surprise him with a bike, a two-wheeler. I suggested a used one, but Lamine insisted it had to be brand-new. So, we went to the Target and picked out the best bike. It was bright blue with silver streaks. The night before Malick's birthday, Lamine got a rag and some wax and buffed that bike for over an hour." Amina remembered him humming.

"Malick must've loved it."

"Oh yes. He loved that bike . . . he loved that bike." Amina felt the tears welling in her eyes again. "So we found a long parking lot up the street where Lamime taught him how to ride." She pictured her husband running alongside Malick and his bike. *Don't look down. Keep your eyes straight ahead! Crash. You almost had it! Come on, let's try again.*

"Malick finally got it, so he always wanted to ride. One time he rode down the sidewalk, a bit faster than usual. I jogged behind him, trying to keep up, you know?" She pictured his blue bike wobbling along up ahead. "A gang of kids came out of nowhere. Knocked him right off that bike and stole it. Broad daylight. Just like that." She snapped her fingers. "There he was, a little kid, my son, lying on the sidewalk, crying. His knee was skinned and everything. I ran as fast as I could, yelling the whole time. But they didn't care. Those kids just ran away with the bike." She remembered them laughing.

Amina ran her fingers underneath the braid. "When Lamine got home from work, he insisted on getting that bike back. I told him not to. We could get another one."

"You should've gone to the police."

"I guess." Amina wrapped the elastic several times around the small end of the braid. "So when Lamine went up there, to where they hung out, . . . they jumped him. One kid pulled a machete and went after him. Lamine . . . Lamine was just trying to defend himself. He ended up in some sort of struggle. You know, to get the knife away? Trust me, Lamine isn't a violent man. I don't know exactly what happened, but the kid with the machete ended up getting cut pretty bad. The police came and they took the kid's side against Lamine. They all said Lamine went crazy with the machete because he wanted the bike back. They lied and said they just found the bike in the street."

Amina drew a deep breath. "Lamine was arrested for a machete attack, ended up in jail, and then got deported." Amina smoothed the sides of the braid, but her fingers were shaking. "There, it's all done."

"I'm sorry, Amina," Sarah whispered, and then turned around and looked into her eyes. "I'm so sorry."

The cell door clanged. "Time for court," the guard said.

16

Stay awake, Buddy ordered himself. Perhaps he shouldn't have had that scotch at lunchtime. It had been a long, drawn-out afternoon in court. Nick had questioned Art Gramer, Rescue One's driver, on the stand for what felt like an eternity. The fireman hadn't witnessed anything significant, but he scored the sympathy vote with the jury.

Now, it was past ten at night. Buddy had been driving around East Boston for nearly two hours with Sarah and Rehnquist, searching for Amina's homeless friend. They had to keep trying. The chances were good they'd locate him. The recycling bins were placed outside on Wednesday nights for Thursday morning pick-up.

"Let's go back to the office. We're never going to find him, Uncle Buddy. It's getting late, past your bedtime."

"Look who's talking?" He nudged Sarah, who appeared sleepy, with her feet on the dashboard. Rehnquist whimpered in the backseat, his head resting on her shoulder. "Sarah, see the new bridge, the Lenny Zakim?" Buddy pointed out the car window to the lighted, symmetrical blue cables in the distance.

She finished a long yawn. "Yeah?"

"It's an illusion. One spire is twenty-seven feet taller than the other, but they appear exactly the same."

Sarah gazed at the Boston skyline. "Cool. What made you think of that?"

"Amina's case, you see? The prosecution built what appears to be the perfect bridge, and we have to show it's an illusion."

"Ohhh—I knew you had a reason." She reached back and stroked under Rehnquist's chin. "You make it sound so easy. How are we going to do it? The jurors crave motive. If Amina didn't set that fire, then who did?"

"That's why we're here." Buddy pulled up to a Dunkin' Donuts drive-thru and ordered more coffee and a blueberry muffin for Rehnquist. "We have to be scrappers. Come out to the streets with our picks and shovels."

They parked next to the burned shell of the Senegalese Market. Sarah blew on her coffee, and stared up at the store for a long time.

"What are you thinking about?" Buddy often wondered where Sarah's thoughts drifted during her prolonged periods of silence.

She rested her temple against the window. "Can you ever get rid of guilt? Or does it linger in your gut for the rest of your life?"

"It can stay with you for years, maybe a lifetime." As he suspected, she was dwelling on that case four years ago when her friend was shot and killed. Nick had reopened the wound earlier in the hallway. When Buddy heard about the confrontation, his first thought was to protect Sarah by calling Nick and speaking his mind. But he refrained. Sarah was well-equipped to fight her own battles, and Buddy could only imagine the pressure Nick had to deal with now.

"You know it then?" Sarah faced him.

"What?" Buddy's mind had drifted with thoughts of Nick and the trial.

"That lingering guilt."

"Too well." Buddy would never be able to purge those guilty feelings for Sarah, but he could draw from his many years of doing criminal defense work. "Got a guy off a murder charge some time ago. Dalton O'Reilly. He was charged with killing his girlfriend. First day home, Dalton O'Reilly killed his entire family and himself. Two little kids."

"Oh my God. That's awful." Sarah sat up. "But you had no way of knowing . . ." Her voice trailed off.

"That's what my friends and family told me, but it didn't do any good. I can still feel the guilt nestled somewhere in the back of my throat. When it rises up, I have to swallow it down again. You learn to deal with it."

"I guess." Sarah fingered her braid and stared up at the singed red sign of the Senegalese Market. "I can't stop thinking about Amina and her husband . . . the talking drum . . . the bike. How did she manage to raise her son all alone? Without giving up and going back home?"

"Amina's a survivor." Buddy had defended characters like Amina in the past. Survival often took precedence over the law.

"There's more to her story too."

"Always is." Buddy smiled at his niece.

"Look." Sarah pointed out the back window. "Wonder if it's him."

Buddy twisted and saw a bearded man with frizzy gray hair pushing a shopping cart filled with bottles and cans. Bulging black trash bags hung over the sides and end of the cart. "Let's give it a go." They stepped out and headed toward him. Buddy clipped Rehnquist's leash to his collar, and wondered why Sarah brought her large shoulder bag.

"Good evening, sir." Buddy tipped his hat.

The homeless man eyed them and grunted.

"Where'd you serve?" Buddy asked.

"Khe Sanh. First Battalion, Twenty-sixth Marines." His voice sounded hoarse.

Buddy whistled. "You like it black, then." He gave him a hot coffee and extended his hand. "Buddy Clancy."

"Danny Sullivan." He took the coffee in his worn tan knit gloves which were cut off below the knuckles, exposing chafed fingers and dirt-packed nails.

Buddy recognized the desperation in Danny's eyes as they shook hands. His breath smelled like sour milk, a sure sign of infected teeth. The matted hair reminded Buddy of a stray dog he'd taken in as a kid. "Danny, this is my niece, Sarah Lynch."

"Thank you for your service." Sarah shook Danny's hand and held onto it like she would a long time acquaintance's.

"Two tours of duty. Did what I was told to do. God wanted me to experience hell to appreciate heaven. My guardian angel brought me back from that hellhole they call Vietnam. A miracle. Now I'm home where they'll kill you on the streets over a can."

"I hear you." Buddy extended the pack of cigarettes he had purchased earlier to break the ice. "Smoke?"

Danny helped himself and Buddy lit it up for him. He inhaled long and hard. "Nice-lookin' dog. I like the bow tie."

Buddy smiled. "Thank you. This is Rehnquist. He's friendly."

Danny squatted down and spoke softly to Rehnquist as he stroked him with both hands. Buddy made small talk about the brutal winter and spring training. He planned on easing Danny into the topic of the fire.

"Do you know anything about that fire?" Sarah pointed to the boarded-up market. Buddy wished she hadn't been so direct, but he knew she couldn't help herself: it was the old prosecutor in her.

Danny flicked the cigarette butt on the sidewalk and waved his hand in dismissal. "I figured you two were out here because you wanted something. Always the same thing; nobody cares about the homeless. I don't know nothing." Danny pushed his cart.

Sarah followed him. "What about the lady who lived there with her son?"

"Most people just walk by us like we're invisible." Danny slogged toward the next recycling bin. "A homeless guy gets killed, and it doesn't even make the newspapers."

Buddy recognized the truth in Danny's statement.

Sometimes the homeless got in the way and paid for it with their lives.

"Did you know the lady?" Sarah asked.

"Nope."

Sarah reached the bin first, gathered an armful of cans, and emptied them into a bag hanging from his cart.

"Thank you."

"I'd like to show you something." She unbuckled her shoulder bag and pulled out Amina's African dinner bowl. "This belongs to a friend of mine."

Danny gazed at the bowl without speaking. Buddy caught a glimpse of recognition in his eyes. It looked like they had the guy who dropped the bowl off, but did he witness anything?

"My friend, Amina, needs all the help she can get right now." Sarah gripped the bowl and extended it again. "You said nobody cares about the homeless, but Amina did. I don't know of anyone else who—"

"Summertime. The market went up."

Buddy was proud of his niece. It was her sincerity that had broken the barrier with Danny. If anyone could get through to those jurors, Sarah could do it.

"What'd you see?" she asked.

"It was like any other night, and then all of a sudden, I looked, and saw flames shootin' up."

"Did you notice anyone or anything out of the ordinary before the fire?" Sarah spoke slowly and with emphasis.

"Nope, nothing at all."

"What about after the fire started. Did you see anyone outside the store?"

"Nobody. Fire trucks came."

Buddy exchanged eye contact with Sarah. He must have missed the BU student. "How many trucks?"

"Only one at first. Fell right out of the sky like a medevac. I think God up and dropped it there to put out the fire."

Sarah placed the bowl back in her bag and helped Danny pick bottles and cans from a garbage barrel. "Did you see anyone escape from the building?"

"Oh, I saw the escape." He raised his hands toward the market. "And the miracle."

"You did?" Sarah raised her eyebrows. "Tell us about it."

"They escaped right out the upstairs window."

Buddy cocked his head. "Who's *they*?"

"Amina and her son. Got rescued through the window. Miracle they made it out alive. A fireman died in there."

Buddy watched Sarah's shoulders sag. She wanted to hear about an arsonist escaping with matches in one hand and a can of lighter fluid in the other. It was never that easy. "Where were you when you saw the fire, Danny?"

"'Cross the street, in one of my homes."

"Homes?" Sarah looked perplexed.

Danny laughed, which sounded more like a series of wheezes. "Got plenty to choose from these days with all the places getting boarded up around here. I prefer the open air. Safer, where they can't corner you inside. He knows what I mean." Danny rubbed Rehnquist's head and pointed with an elbow. "Right over there's where I was."

Buddy, Sarah, and Rehnquist followed Danny across the street, and peered into a narrow alley, which was blocked by a Dumpster at the other end. The dim illumination of a streetlight revealed a television with rabbit-eared antennas perched on top of an inverted plant stand. The frayed cord wasn't plugged into anything. A sunken couch faced the TV. A birdcage without a bird hung from a long nail wedged in the cracked brick wall. It smelled of mold and urine.

Danny nodded. "And she always had these cloth napkins." He squared his hands in the air as if smoothing out an invisible napkin. "I'd get an ice-cold can of Coke too."

"I understand you enjoyed Amina's desserts?" Sarah smiled at him.

Danny looked like he was watching something in his empty birdcage. "Sometimes I'd leave tulips on her front stoop. My way of sayin' thanks."

"Did Amina have you over for dinner on the night of the fire?" Buddy asked.

"It was the last time." Danny took a long drag and stared across the street at the market.

Sarah followed his gaze. "What time did you have dinner that night?"

"Pawned my watch." Danny scratched his scalp with all ten fingers. "Let me think. Market closed at seven, so sometime after that."

Buddy tossed several cans in the cart and handed Danny the pack of cigarettes along with several folded McDonald's gift certificates. "Take care of yourself."

"God bless. God bless."

"Thank you." Sarah shook Danny's hand again. "Now *we* need a miracle."

"You'll get your miracle, too, young lady. Be patient. God's got his plan for everybody. Thought he'd take me in Khe Sanh during the siege. He wanted me here. It was a miracle."

As they headed toward the car, Buddy heard the rattle of the cart moving toward the next cluster of garbage bags and bins. He replayed the conversation in his head.

Sarah nudged him. "Why would Amina take the time to make Danny a Senegalese meal if she planned to light her place on fire a short time later? If she knew Danny camped out there in the alley, why do it on a Wednesday night? Why take the risk with him as a potential witness? Uncle Buddy?"

Buddy heard her, but something bothered him. It felt like they were missing a piece of the puzzle. He turned and watched Danny squat and dig through a trash bag. "Here, hold on to Rehnquist." Something compelled him to head back and ask one last question. "Tell me again, what was the miracle during the fire?"

Danny's face lit up. "The angel."

Bingo. Buddy exchanged a knowing look with Sarah, who had joined them again. "What angel?" he asked.

"The angel came for that fireman, took his soul straight up to heaven. The Angel of Death. We knew it well in Khe Sanh."

"Where did you see this angel?" Sarah asked.

Danny rose and spread his arms. "Flew right across the roof. It was a miracle."

"When?" Her eyes widened. "During the fire?"

"Yeah. Rose right out of the smoke like a ghost. I figure it was right after the fireman died."

Buddy tried to visualize the scene. Was Danny crazy, or did he really see a figure running across the roof and think it was an angel? "Was it a male or female angel?"

"I really couldn't tell from down below, but I saw the wings."

Sarah wrinkled her brow. "Which way did it fly?"

"Flew down the row of buildings and disappeared."

Buddy hadn't heard anything quite like this before. He wondered what the jurors would think of an angel with wings. "Do you remember what the angel was wearing?"

"Maybe silver or gray. Flew pretty fast. It wanted me to see, I know that. Stopped in midflight and looked right at me. It kind of hovered for a second like a hummingbird and flew on its way again." Danny placed a hand on Sarah's shoulder. "Angels are messengers of God, my dear."

"What do you think the message was?" she asked.

"The truth. Angels will show us the truth if we're willing to see it. They help us find our way." Danny pointed to the apartment above the market. "The fireman was lost up there, and the angel guided him out."

"I see," Buddy said. "Did you tell anyone else about the fire or the angel?"

"I didn't tell that tall guy who came around asking questions."

"I bet that was Murphy. Large ears that kind of stick out?" Buddy described their part-time investigator.

"Yeah."

"Did anyone else question you?" Sarah asked.

"Dark-haired man came around end of the summer. Didn't tell him about the angel either."

"A cop?" Buddy wondered who else was interested.

"Didn't say, but I don't think so. Wasn't the type."

Sarah squinted. "What do you mean by that?"

"The eyes." Danny pointed to his own eyes. "You can judge a man by his eyes. And those eyes held demons."

17

Jeanette Giganti smoothed her floral dress before taking her seat in the jury box.

"Pretty." The blond waitress smiled as she sat beside Jeanette. She appeared to be close to twenty, so young and inexperienced for such a serious case.

"Thank you. I made it myself."

"Cool."

Jeanette regarded the girl's faded jeans with the frayed holes. Inappropriate for court, but she probably didn't know any better. Too bad the girls weren't into sewing anymore. This generation seemed so busy with their electronic gadgets and cell phones. Jeanette didn't even own a computer. Life had become too fast-paced.

Marinelli announced his next witness with zeal. Jeanette admired the young prosecutor's Italian passion, just like her father. She had thumbed through her old West End photographs the previous day. What a courageous man her father had been, emigrating from Sicily at age seventeen without a penny in his pocket. He met her mother on the day he set foot in the West End, and they were married in less than a year. Perhaps that's why he was attached to the old neighborhood and so saddened when the politicians used eminent domain to take it all away. It was a great place to live. Life was simple. People trusted one another.

Jeanette gazed at Amina's brown headscarf with its tiny blue flowers that matched her dress. She must have made it herself. Jeanette imagined Amina was simple too. Simple and hardworking and sad.

"Good morning." Marinelli smiled at a muscular

fireman who appeared to be in his early fifties. "Please introduce yourself to the jury."

"Paul Draak." He spoke with a deep, authoritative voice.

"Where do you work?"

"I'm a lieutenant for the Boston Fire Department on Rescue One."

Jeanette listened to him describe the chain of events leading up to the fire. She caught glimpses of the lingering guilt in his voice and eyes, especially when he looked at the young widow. Jack was one of his men, his responsibility. That fire would change his life forever, just like it had changed Andy's life. Jeanette looked over at Amina again.

"Lieutenant, what did you do when you arrived at the fire?"

"I called in a second alarm, grabbed my tools, and ran around the building to attempt entry through the back."

"What did you do next?"

"I popped the lock with my Halligan and pushed in, but there was something blocking the door on the other side. Art, our driver, came around back and started pushing with me."

"What happened?"

"We finally got it open. It was a storage room, stacked to the ceiling with crates of stuff. Looked like she just had a delivery. So we had to create a path in order to get through. Took time. Time we didn't have."

"Did you make it into the store?"

"Eventually, but the fire was raging by then in the back. The engines hadn't arrived with the lines, so we had to run around the building and go through the front."

"What happened next?"

"The engine and ladder companies came. We grabbed a line and fought the fire, while they raised ladders to the second floor. I prayed that my men, Jack Fogerty and Andy Larson, had found the occupants and were on their way out. I knew it wouldn't take long for that fire to vent up to the second story and through the roof."

Jeanette watched the poor widow bury her face in her hands. Her husband had been struggling to rescue Amina and her son when those fire trucks finally came. He must've been thinking about his wife and children when the moment arrived, when he knew he wouldn't make it. Jeanette said the rosary for the young woman. Every night she prayed for her.

"Lieutenant Draak, did you have the occasion to observe the roof of the building?"

He regarded Marinelli for a moment. "Yes. The roof. I took a good look at it before we attempted entry to see if any fire had made its way up and if there were any people."

"Were you able to see the roof?"

"Absolutely. Plenty of illumination from the street-lights up there. It was only two stories high."

"What were your observations?"

"Everything was quiet." Lieutenant Draak leaned forward and raised his voice. "There was nobody on that roof." He poked at the witness stand with his index finger. "Nobody running across it. I would've definitely seen them. We're trained to spot people running from fire scenes."

"Did you see anyone escape from a second-story window?"

Sarah and Clancy sprang to their feet. "Objection, leading question."

"Sustained."

Jeanette could tell the last several questions had been planned and rehearsed to counter the defense theory that a mystery arsonist had escaped out some window and up to the roof. Sarah had raised the possibility that Andy had detected a third person on his camera screen when he and Jack arrived upstairs during the fire. Marinelli wanted them to believe it was Amina all along, that she had circled back around to the living room.

"What were your observations about the windows?"

"There was no activity at any of the windows. Again, as firefighters, we're trained to look at all windows for people who may be trapped inside."

"After you finished fire suppression activities, did you have a conversation with anyone regarding Jack?"

"Fire Commissioner Hurley came up to me with Boston Fire Chaplin, Father Mahoney. I could tell by the looks on their faces it wasn't good." Lieutenant Draak drew a deep breath. "They told me—"

Sarah rose halfway. "Objection, hearsay."

"Sustained."

Marinelli looked like he was getting tired of the objections. Jeanette didn't blame him. It interrupted the flow of the trial. "As a result of the conversation with Commissioner Hurley and Father Mahoney, what did you do?"

"I just stood there." Lieutenant Draak's words came out slow and deliberate. "What they had to say shocked me beyond my imagination. The news was devastating." He stared at Amina.

Jeanette witnessed the anger that Lieutenant Draak directed toward Amina. She peered out at all the firemen in the gallery with the black ribbons on their badges. Solidarity. What an uproar if their verdict came back *not guilty*.

"What did you do next?"

"The hardest thing I've ever done in my life."

Jeanette knew what it was. There was no easy way. She had relayed similar news to a friend, news that broke the heart.

"What was that?" Marinelli lowered his voice.

Lieutenant Draak faced the jurors. "Telling Maureen Fogerty that her husband was gone. I wanted to be the one because we're close family friends and Jack was *my responsibility*. It was around two in the morning when we pulled up in the red chief's car. I could tell she knew by the way she looked at me."

"How did you do it?"

"We sat her down. Father Mahoney and Fire Commissioner Hurley came too. I told her Jack had been killed in the line of duty. Maureen . . . she folded up. Lost it. I've never felt so helpless in my life. And then—" His voice cracked. He paused and composed himself. "And then, their little boy came down in his pajamas. The kind with the feet built in. He wanted to know what happened, why mommy was crying. The three of us just stared at him. Nobody had the strength." He paused. "What do you say to a kid?"

Jeanette's eyes welled as she watched Jack's widow crying again. She must've been the one to tell her children. A mother's job. Four months pregnant too. Jeanette recalled having little ones of her own and babies on the way. Those should be joyous times.

"What did you do next?" Marinelli spoke softly.

"We all went over to headquarters and gathered the men together." He licked his lips. "I told them."

"What did you say?"

"That Jack . . . that Jack . . . died of a gunshot wound. *Somebody* shot him in the line of duty." He stared at Amina. "My men, they took it real hard."

"No further questions." Marinelli nodded at the

lieutenant. Jeanette noticed the kindness in the young prosecutor's eyes. Marinelli cared about the widow and his witnesses. He believed in his case.

Sarah rose for cross-examination. She believed in her case too. Clancy patted his niece on the back. Jeanette and Clancy were from the same generation. No doubt he held doors open for the ladies and gave up his seat on the T bus. No one did that anymore.

"I'm going to go over a few things that I'm not so clear on, okay?" Sarah had a sweet voice.

Lieutenant Draak nodded, but appeared defensive and untrusting.

"There's an overhang above the back door?"

"Yes."

"When you were trying to get in, you were standing beneath that overhang?"

"Yeah."

"Hard to get in?"

"Because she had it crammed with junk." The lieutenant pointed at Amina.

"After getting in, you had to move heavy crates?"

"Yes."

"To create a path?" Sarah moved her hands in the shape of an S.

"Right."

"That took several minutes?"

"It did."

"Lieutenant, as you were trying to get in the back entrance, you weren't concentrating on the roof, were you?"

"I kept an eye on the roof."

Jeanette knew Sarah was right. Those firemen weren't paying attention to the roof. They were trying to get in.

"Could you even see the roof from beneath that overhang?"

"I remember seeing it just fine."

"Is it possible someone could've climbed onto the roof from the second-story window and run across while you were busy moving crates?"

The Lieutenant rolled his eyes. "No way. We would've eventually found them stuck up there."

Sarah showed Marinelli two pictures and approached the witness. "Are you familiar with what's depicted in this photograph?"

"Looks like the row of buildings that run up the block next to the Senegalese Market."

She handed him the second picture. "Do you recognize what's depicted in this photograph, marked D2?"

"A fire escape."

"That's the fire escape located at the last building in the row adjacent to the Senegalese Market?"

Lieutenant Draak studied both photos. He looked at Amina again. "If you say so."

"I'm asking *you*, Lieutenant." Sarah spoke slowly.

Lieutenant Draak shuffled the pictures over and over. His jaw tightened. "I know what you're trying to do. Anything to get *her* off."

"Please answer the question, sir. I'm asking whether that fire escape leads from the roof to street level?"

"Guess so."

"I don't want you to guess."

The lieutenant tossed the photos on the podium, one fluttered down on the rug. "I'm sure it leads to street level as most fire escapes do, lady."

"Thank you Lieutenant, nothing further."

Judge Killam leaned forward. "Redirect, counselor?"

Marinelli rose. "No, Your Honor."

Jeanette studied her fellow jurors. Did they care about the fire escape? Had they already decided on guilty verdicts? Jeanette knew there were two sides to every story. She had learned that early in life. However, Sarah and her uncle would have to come up with hard proof of Amina's innocence if they planned to convince this jury.

Cole rolled the olive pit up and down his tongue when the cable channel aired a commercial. His thoughts drifted back to the night before. They were circling like buzzards. He spit the pit in his hand and added it to the pile beneath the bed. What would he do?

Cole tore a strip of dead skin from the middle knuckle on his right hand and popped another olive into his mouth. What did the bum say? What exactly did he see?

The bad air came up again. He twisted to the side and vomited in the lobster pot next to the bed. The bum would never make it to court.

18

Amina knelt in her cell for noontime prayers with her arms extended along the cold cement floor toward Mecca. She praised Allah, the merciful and compassionate, with all her soul, mind, and heart. She repeated part of the Koran's opening *surah* many times: "Guide us in the straight path . . . not the path of those who have incurred Thy wrath and gone astray."

When she finished, Amina rose slowly. Her kneecaps throbbed. Somehow, she and Lamine had gone astray. Otherwise, she wouldn't be facing trial, and he wouldn't have been unfairly deported. She hoped Malick would follow that straight path.

"Chocolate cake here!" Mr. Clancy's voice echoed down the hallway. When he drew near, he looked like a grinning waiter with an orange cafeteria tray balanced above his head.

Sarah followed with a Diet Coke. "We thought you might need some company."

"A special treat for you, my dear." Mr. Clancy lowered the tray, while the guard unlocked the cell door.

"Oh, thank you." Amina appreciated the thoughtfulness. "But I must refrain. Ramadan began today and I have to fast."

"I'm sorry." Mr. Clancy smacked his forehead. "We should've known that."

"No, no it's okay." Amina cared for Mr. Clancy and felt bad she couldn't eat his cake. "I must fast, and make many sacrifices these days."

Mr. Clancy set the tray aside and joined her on the bench. "Tell me about Ramadan."

"Our most holy month. When the prophet Muhammad received his first revelation from God, and then, ten years later, made his migration from Mecca to Medina. It's a time to pray, of course, but also for reflection."

"When do you have to fast?" Sarah squeezed inside as the guard clanged the door shut again.

"From dawn until sundown we can't have any food or drink." Amina felt the hunger pangs, but cherished them now like never before.

"Not even a drop of water?" Mr. Clancy looked shocked.

Amina laughed. "Not a drop."

"And I thought we had it tough." Mr. Clancy addressed Sarah. "Back when I was a kid, we couldn't eat before communion, so we sat there and starved for half a day while the priest said the Sunday Mass in Latin. Your Uncle David passed out once."

Sarah cocked her head. "I can just picture the two of you sitting there, starving, like it was the end of the world."

"That's right. And, we couldn't eat between meals on Ash Wednesday or Good Friday." He raised a finger. "But, I found out later that the Jesuits cheated with milkshakes. Glad my mother never knew."

"Oh, that reminds me." Sarah smoothed her skirt and sat next to Amina on the bench. "Malick mentioned something about your online involvement with certain religious issues?"

"Your blip," Mr. Clancy said.

"*Blog*, Uncle Buddy."

"Ahhh, what's the difference." Mr. Clancy waved his hand.

Amina wondered why they were asking. Did they think her blog had something to do with the fire? She doubted it, but it wouldn't hurt to tell them. "I started a blog about a year ago." She paused; the issue was complex. "When I attended college and worked in Dakar, I felt so sorry for the talibes."

"The what?" Sarah squinted.

"Talibes. They are young boys . . . how do I put this . . . who are supposed to be learning the Koran at a daara, which is an Islamic school. You see, the city has many daaras, and each one is run by a marabout, an Islamic teacher. Unfortunately, there are many corrupt teachers who send the boys out to beg on the streets in order to support the school. It is very sad. They are dressed in rags and so young." Amina recalled seeing some as young as four running in packs toward pedestrians and cars with their large tin cans. They'd beg for coins, rice, trinkets, almost anything.

"Did you raise money for them or something?" Sarah asked.

"No, because the money would fall into the wrong hands. The marabouts are very powerful, and the practice has gone on for a long time. People do not like to change. They are closed-minded, consumed with the old way." Amina recalled the government's poor response to the problem and felt her anger rising again. "I used my blog to raise awareness over here. There are as many as a hundred thousand of these boys begging in the streets of Dakar."

"Gracious, that's terrible." Mr. Clancy brushed stray crumbs from his suit trousers. "Did anything happen as a result?"

"I had quite a positive response, most people had no idea about the practice over here. If this hadn't happened—" Amina gestured toward the steel bars. "I would've taken it further. Perhaps something good would've come out of it."

"I meant, did anything bad happen?" Mr. Clancy asked.

Amina thought back. Anything bad? *Yes.* She'd almost forgotten about the phone call. "A man called the market and accused me of being a traitor to Islam. He sounded like a crazy religious fanatic, making all kinds of threats, demanding I shut down the blog. I hung up on him, and that was that." Amina recalled how shocked she'd felt after listening to him.

"When did this occur?" Sarah asked.

Amina remembered Malick had been at school. "Sometime around mid-June, right before summer vacation."

"So, about a month before the fire?" Mr. Clancy rubbed his chin. "Perhaps it's possible . . . that this fanatic set the fire and shot the fireman?"

"I don't know." Amina's voice trailed off. She bit her lower lip. "I suppose anything's possible."

Sarah exchanged a puzzled look with her uncle.

"We'll take a peek at your phone records." Mr. Clancy checked his watch. "Oh dear. Three minutes until his highness ascends the throne. We've got to skedaddle to the courtroom."

19

Quahog noticed the extra swing in Marinelli's arms that afternoon. The young prosecutor had something significant, like he'd been dealt a strong hand and he knew it. He watched Clancy strategizing with the redhead, *Miss Hockey*, at the defense table. Let the games begin.

"Please introduce yourself to the jury."

"Sergeant Carol O'Brien. I'm the canine handler assigned to the state fire marshal's office."

Quahog liked dogs and women. *He was in for a treat*. This one had cute dimples and a bouncy chest. Marinelli must've had fun prepping her.

"What do you use canines for?"

"To aid us in our search for accelerants, which are liquids capable of fueling a fire. Examples are gasoline, kerosene, acetone, and benzene."

Quahog listened as Marinelli guided her through her specialized training. He sounded like he wanted to cut right to the chase. He had something that would sink the Arab.

Miss Hockey wrote rapid notes in her legal pad.

Quahog had almost fallen off his chair when her uncle mentioned she was an Olympic player. He didn't follow women's hockey, but some of the guys at the pub did and they remembered her as a real hottie who ended up in the penalty box a lot. They all wanted to trade places and stare at her legs all day.

"Sergeant O'Brien, do you work with one dog in particular?"

"I've worked with my black lab, Milo, for eleven years." The dog lady beamed.

Quahog wondered whether he should get another dog to keep his yellow lab, Mr. Bud, company. A black lab just like Milo would be perfect. Better yet, maybe they'd throw in a nice-lookin' dog lady to go with it.

"What kind of training program did Milo go through?"

"He's certified through the Massachusetts State Crime Laboratory, the office of the state fire marshal, and is one of only forty canines nationally certified through the ATF."

The dog had more papers than Quahog. He pictured Milo using the toilet and fetching cans of beer out of the fridge for Monday night football. *A man's best friend.*

"Does Milo have a daily training routine?"

"He lives with me, and we work according to a system of repetition and reward. I place a few drops of an accelerant in the yard or within my house for Milo to find. Sometimes I'll place drops on pennies and toss them around. After he finds them, I feed him Iams chunks. I use the same food every day, and he's never fed without detecting the accelerant."

Quahog pictured Milo eating Iams chunks for breakfast, lunch, and dinner. How boring. Why not sneak the poor thing a hotdog every once in a while? *Man.* To go through life without ever tasting a Fenway Frank? Only twelve more days until the season opener against the Yankees. He hoped to get tickets through Antiliano, the Dominican barber. Popcorn, peanuts, dogs, and beer. His stomach growled.

"How does Milo perform his job?"

"I give him the command, 'See-ek,' and he moves forward, sniffing. He sits down and points with his nose at the greatest source of accelerant. Milo will point and look up at me several times. It's called a passive-alert method. After Milo points, I feed him Iams chunks out of my hand at ground level so he smells the accelerant as he's being fed."

"Do you train with any burned substances?"

"Absolutely." The dog lady shifted sideways to face the jury. From her smooth voice and eye contact, Quahog could tell she had testified many times before. "I use a daisy wheel, which is made from a pair of crossed two-by-four boards. Tin cans with burned substances inside are placed on all four ends. For example, one can may hold fragments of burned carpeting, another may have pieces of charred wood, and so forth. Only one can contains something burned with an accelerant. I spin the wheel, and Milo's job is to find the one *hot* can versus the three *negative* cans. The term *hot* refers to the can containing the accelerant."

"How does Milo perform in his training?"

"Excellent."

Quahog watched her breasts bounce as she faced Marinelli again. He'd like to take her for a ride on that daisy wheel.

"Directing your attention to Thursday, July twentieth of last year, did anything happen?" Marinelli raised his voice as if to inform the jury he was finished with the preliminary bullshit.

"Around 1:45 a.m., Milo and I—"

"Ahhh-chooah."

Quahog jumped. The annoying juror with the New York accent sneezed louder than anyone he'd ever known.

"Ahhh-choooah."

And again. The second one was even louder. Quahog would love to place a drop of gasoline on the New Yorker's tight little ass and watch the dog alert.

". . . spoke at length with Sergeant Frank Brady and with Detective Callahan, who was in charge of the homicide."

Miss Hockey rose. "Objection to the use of the word *homicide*. There is no evidence of a homicide."

"Sustained." Judge Killam faced the jury. "You are to disregard the last word."

Quahog didn't get that one. Wasn't this a murder case? What was wrong with saying homicide? Miss Hockey was at it again with her jabs. Marinelli appeared to have lost his place for a moment. Did she do that on purpose to throw him off? Of course she did. Come on, kid, get back in it. You're way ahead here.

Marinelli straightened. "What did you do after speaking with the investigators?"

"I walked Milo through the small crowd that had gathered near the fire scene to see if he could detect accelerants on anyone's shoes or clothing."

"Did he find anything?"

"Nothing significant."

"What happened next?"

"About an hour later, I met Detective Callahan at the command center, which was a trailer they had set up on scene. Detective Callahan and Sergeant Brady were questioning the defendant, Amina Diallo, inside the trailer."

"What did you do?"

"I took Milo into the trailer and he—"

"Objection!" Both Miss Hockey and Clancy jumped up. "Sidebar, Your Honor?"

Judge Killam nodded and all three lawyers gathered at the other side of the bench. *Another delay tactic by the defense.* That's because they knew Marinelli was about to produce his ace.

Quahog watched the lawyers trot back to their spots and wondered who won that round. Miss Hockey looked like she was ready to check the judge into the boards. He had his answer.

Marinelli grinned. "Once again, please inform the jury what Milo did when you brought him into the trailer?"

The dog lady made eye contact with each juror as if she wanted everybody's undivided attention. "Milo walked right up to Amina Diallo, sat down, and pointed with his nose at the woman's slippers."

Ahhh. Quahog studied the Arab in her long brown veil. *Nabbed by the dog.*

"What did that indicate to you?"

"Objection," Miss Hockey yelled.

"Overruled. The witness may answer."

"It indicated to me that Milo alerted to the presence of an accelerant on the defendant's slippers."

"Objection, move to strike the answer."

Judge Killam raised his voice. "Overruled."

Jab, jab, jab, and it ain't workin', Red. Marinelli's got your number.

"What did you do after Milo alerted to Amina Diallo's slippers?"

"I rewarded Milo with his Iams chunks. Then Detective Callahan and I told the defendant to remove her slippers and she did. I took possession of the slippers, placed them in an evidence can, and ultimately took them to the crime lab for analysis."

"Did you bring them to court today?"

"Yes." Quahog watched the dog lady reach down and produce a large metal can. She opened it and held up a pair of pink ladies' slippers. Marinelli paraded right up to the clerk's table with the can and slippers and slam-dunked them into evidence. *Score.*

"What happened after that?"

"I took Milo to Ms. Diallo's car and he alerted to a floor mat in the back and a pair of ladies' leather gloves in the glove box."

Whoosh. Scored again.

"What happened next?"

"At 10:30 a.m. I left Milo in the car, and proceeded into the Senegalese Market with Sergeant Brady and Detective Callahan to assess the situation." She turned toward the jury again. "It's my responsibility to make sure the building is clear of hazardous debris before deploying Milo."

Quahog studied the stoic Arab. Would they find more evidence against her inside?

"What did you do after that?"

"I placed several calibration drops of fifty percent evaporated gasoline outside the fire scene as a test for Milo. He successfully hit on the drops, so I knew he was ready to go into the building. Oh, I almost forgot, he always relieves himself before he goes in."

Quahog suddenly felt the urge for a bathroom break. He had too much of that stale coffee during lunch. The burnt aftertaste lingered on his tongue.

"What happened next?"

"Milo and I entered the market through the front door. I gave him the command, 'See-ek!' "

"What did Milo do?"

"He went to the back left-hand corner of the market, sat down, and pointed to the floor with his nose."

"I see." Marinelli raised his eyebrows and looked right at Quahog. "What did you do next?"

"I fed him and marked the area with an orange cone."

"What happened next?"

"Milo alerted at two other spots in the same general vicinity."

This time, Quahog stared at the Arab sitting next to Clancy and Miss Hockey. He got Marinelli's point, loud and clear. Left-hand corner: that's where she poured the gas, and she was wearing those ugly pink slippers. The stupid Arab should've ditched the slippers. Communications saw her running from that exact spot too. *Gotcha.*

"What happened next?"

"We conducted a limited search of the upstairs apartment, and Milo alerted to an area in the back bedroom, near the window, in the right-hand corner of the building."

"What did you do after that?"

"I cut samples with a battery-powered saw from each area marked by the orange cones."

"Did Sergeant Brady point anything out to you?"

Clancy and Miss Hockey jumped to their feet. "Objection! Hearsay."

"Sustained."

Quahog wanted to ask the judge what hearsay meant. He had heard the expression on the law shows and various TV trials. Why couldn't they just talk in plain English? It was like a secret society.

"After speaking with Sergeant Brady, what did you do?"

"I recovered what appeared to be a red latex balloon

fragment. It was located in a crack between the floorboards in the original area where Milo alerted. That back left-hand corner, first floor. I placed the red latex in a separate evidence can."

"A piece of red latex balloon." Marinelli rubbed his chin. "What did you do next?"

A popped balloon? How was that significant? Quahog had picked up on the emphasis in Marinelli's words. The dog found it, and now it was a piece of evidence. Had to be important. Otherwise, why bother with it?

Sarah saw the accusation in the jurors' eyes when Nick finished his direct examination. They had appeared especially interested in the red balloon fragment. Some probably had images of Amina tiptoeing downstairs in the middle of the night with a gas can, spilling a few drops on those pink slippers, before tossing the match. Sarah felt like they were sinking, chest deep, in muck. Perhaps they were clinging to loose ends in a desperate attempt to ignore the truth that Amina was guilty.

No, Sarah reminded herself. *Amina's the underdog. Keep fighting.* She forced herself to think about Danny, the homeless man, and his miracle angel. She prayed he could save the case. Was he delusional, or had he really seen someone running across the roof during the fire? Who was the dark-haired man asking questions? Could it be that religious fanatic who made the phone call about Amina's blog? Danny's words still echoed in her ears: *those eyes held demons.*

"Cross-examination?" Judge Killam stared down at the defense table.

"Have fun, Uncle Buddy," Sarah whispered. He winked and headed toward the jury box.

"Thank you for coming this afternoon, Sergeant

O'Brien. You've been very enlightening." Uncle Buddy adjusted his yellow bow tie adorned with black English Terriers.

"Just doing my job."

"Yes. Oh, speaking of that, where's Milo?"

"At home."

"Oh, I see. Did he have a pleasant lunch like the rest of us?"

"No, he has to wait until I get home."

"Oh, what a pity. You're the only one who can feed him?"

"Yes."

"And he can't be fed without sniffing an accelerant?"

"Correct."

Uncle Buddy appeared sad. Over lunch, Sarah had listened to him philosophizing about man's love for dogs. "That's the key to my cross," he repeated several times. "Nothing else matters. You watch."

"Poor Milo must be starving without a morning snack and no lunch?"

"He'll be okay."

"What if you don't make it home until after five?"

Sergeant O'Brien looked down at her hands. "By then he'll be hungry."

"Ever slip him a filet mignon?"

"No."

"How 'bout a Reuben on rye?"

"No."

"A pancake?"

She sighed. "I'd love to, but I can't."

"Only the Iams chunks."

"That's right."

Uncle Buddy began his two-step toward the witness. Sarah admired his natural rhythm, always first on the dance floor for the jitterbug.

"Did you have Milo sniff the shoes of a homeless man at the fire scene?"

"Perhaps. I walked him through the crowd."

"This particular homeless man had grizzly hair and a beard. He would've been guarding a shopping cart full of cans. Do you remember him?"

"No."

Uncle Buddy rubbed his chin between his thumb and index finger. "Lots of firemen when you arrived?"

"Yes."

"How many?"

"Oh . . . I'd say thirty, possibly forty."

"And they were trampling in and out of the Senegalese Market?"

"Yes."

Sarah watched her uncle trample around the courtroom like a fireman in big, clumsy boots. He was good at creating mental images for the jury. Big boots tainting crime scenes.

"Did you instruct Milo to sniff their boots?"

"No."

"It's possible Milo would've detected the presence of accelerants on their boots?"

"Yes."

"That's because they'd been traipsing through the debris inside the building?"

"Some had been inside fighting the fire."

"It's possible to track through fire debris and pick up evidence of an accelerant on your shoes, boots, or *slippers*?"

"Yes."

"You could've picked up debris on the soles of your boots as you walked through the scene?"

"Yes."

"Milo could've alerted to *your* boots that night?"

"If I had walked through debris containing traces of an accelerant, yes."

"So if Milo alerts to someone's shoes or slippers, it doesn't mean they were involved in setting the fire."

"No."

Uncle Buddy grabbed the pink slippers from the clerk's table and removed one from the bag. "Now, perhaps I didn't hear you correctly. I'm getting hard of hearing these days. Did you tell the jurors which part of the slippers Milo alerted to?"

"What do you mean?"

"Top or bottom?" Uncle Buddy dangled the slipper before the jury box and rotated it in his fingertips.

Sarah watched Sergeant O'Brien's cheeks flush red for an instant. "Milo alerted to the bottom."

"Ohhhwww. The bottom." Uncle Buddy turned the rubber tread toward the jury and walked the length of the box. "The soles of both slippers?"

"Yes."

"Don't you think that's rather significant?"

The witness hesitated. "Not necessarily."

Uncle Buddy spread his arms. "Why, if I were to run through fire debris or track through an area where *someone else* dispersed gasoline, the gas would end up on the *bottom* or the soles of my slippers. Correct?"

"It depends."

"Oh, come on. It's common sense that gas would cling to the sole of a slipper."

She sighed. "Yes."

Sarah noticed concentration on several faces in the jury box. Uncle Buddy excelled at taking a piece of what appeared to be damning evidence and flipping it in his favor. If Amina had spread gasoline to commit arson, drops would most likely be detected on the tops of her slippers too. Sarah hoped the jurors got it.

"Milo sniffed Amina's clothing at the command center, right?" Uncle Buddy placed the slipper back in the bag and tossed it on the clerk's table.

"Yes."

"She was dressed in a blue nightgown?"

"I believe so."

"Did you inform the jury whether Milo alerted to anything on that nightgown?"

"Milo did not alert."

"Wow! You mean to say he didn't find a trace of gas or any accelerant on Amina's nightgown following the fire?"

"That's correct."

"Where's that nightgown now, Sergeant?"

"I don't know."

"I'm sure if you found gas on it, you'd have it right here." He rapped the clerk's table.

"We would."

Uncle Buddy clicked his tongue. "You arrived at the fire scene around one forty-five?"

"Yes."

"That was approximately an hour after the fire started?"

"Right."

"So for the first hour, Milo was unable to walk through that crowd and sniff for accelerants?"

"That's correct."

"An arsonist could've come and gone by then."

"Objection!" Marinelli shot up.

"Overruled."

"It's possible," Sergeant O'Brien said.

"By the time you arrived with Milo, the crowd was dispersing?"

"Some people were still there."

Uncle Buddy advanced again. "But you can't say how many had gone home by then?"

"No."

"You weren't present when that fire started, were you?"

"No."

"Did you take Milo door to door to see if any of the neighbors had accelerants on their clothing or slippers?"

"No."

"Did you take Milo up to the roof of the building?"

"No, it was deemed unsafe."

"The buildings are connected?"

"I believe so."

"Did you request access to the rooftops of the other buildings to search with Milo for accelerants?"

"No."

"Hmmm." Uncle Buddy rubbed his chin and shook his head slowly, appearing disappointed. "Sergeant O'Brien, you mentioned on direct examination that *nothing significant* happened when you walked Milo through the crowd?"

"What I meant was Milo alerted but the two people were ruled out for a legitimate reason."

"Milo alerted? Really?" Uncle Buddy twirled toward the jury with his eyes and mouth wide open. Sarah smiled at his theatrics.

"Yes."

"Amazing." He glanced back at Sarah with a shocked, wrinkled brow. She picked up on cue and returned a wide-eyed look of surprise. Now it appeared like Marinelli was hiding relevant information. "Did Milo alert more than once?"

"Two times."

Uncle Buddy extended his right arm forward, raised two fingers, and drew them back and forth like a windshield wiper. "Milo alerted two times. Two times. And you call that *insignificant*?"

Sergeant O'Brien crossed her arms. "The first boy had a Zippo lighter in his pocket, and Milo alerted to that. Sergeant Brady spoke with him, but he must've had a legitimate reason for possessing the lighter. Carrying a lighter is not illegal."

"Plenty of fires have been started with Zippo lighters, right?"

"I'm sure they have."

"Sergeant Brady didn't spend much time with him, did he?" Uncle Buddy asked.

"No."

"Milo alerted a second time?"

"Yes, a man had filled his car with gas that evening. Milo alerted to his hands, shorts, and sneakers."

Uncle Buddy practically fell backward as if blown by a strong gust. "So, you're telling us that a man with gasoline on his hands, shorts, and sneakers was present at the fire scene?"

"Yes."

"You must be aware that most arsonists return to the scene of the fire?"

"Some do."

"Do you recall the man's name?"

"No."

"Humph." Uncle Buddy paraded in a small circle with hands clasped behind his neck. "A man covered in gasoline."

"People fill their own tanks and splash gas all the time."

"Oh, yes they do. They do it all the time." Uncle Buddy nodded toward the jury. "I'm sure the man must've been cuffed and hauled into the station for questioning?"

"No."

"I see, I see." Uncle Buddy pursed his lips. "They already had their suspect. No need to look further."

"Objection!" Nick yelled. "Move to strike."

"Sustained." Judge Killam faced the jury. "Please disregard Attorney Clancy's last statements."

Uncle Buddy smiled. "Oh, pardon me. I got a bit carried away. Sergeant O'Brien, I'll stop here so you can go home and feed Milo a nice big supper. Please give him a pat for me and tell him he did an excellent job."

Cole reached into the oily tub and extracted another olive to take the sulfur taste away. What could they learn from a balloon? The dog found a red balloon fragment that hadn't melted in the fire. *Hard to believe.* He penetrated the salty flesh with his front teeth.

The wind nearly knocked him over backward off the seawall. He extended his arms and rocked from side to side, saving himself from a deadly fall on the jagged rocks below. His mother always said he had good balance. She needed to take her pills. He had to leave and stop dwelling on all the possibilities.

Cole cracked the pit between his molars and picked out the tiny seed from the center. The sweet seeds were tender, exquisite. The best part.

20

Sarah gripped her large Sorelle's coffee with both hands as if holding on for dear life. Thank God for caffeine. She peered out her window and watched several people hovering under umbrellas as they headed home late from work that evening. It felt damp and cold in the office. Uncle Buddy was conserving energy again. What she'd give to be curled up in bed, sipping hot homemade chicken soup and eating apple pie. Not in the cards.

Sarah slumped into her overstuffed leather chair, and stared at the typed fire reports covering her desk. She felt exhausted from a sleepless night dwelling on details. Something felt out of place. They had to find it.

"Here we are!" Uncle Buddy clamored through the front door and into the reception area. He folded his umbrella, while Rehnquist bounded toward Sarah.

"Hey there, Rehnquist." Sarah got up and coddled the prancing dog, kissing him on the head. "If the jury could only meet him." She straightened the bow tie on his collar.

"And here comes Malick." Uncle Buddy pointed out the window with his umbrella tip.

"Wow, a teenager who's on time for something. Imagine that. Okay, Rehnquist. Do your job." Sarah rubbed the dog's ears and headed toward the door. She greeted their client's son, and noticed how haggard he appeared with dark circles under his eyes.

Malick grinned when he saw Rehnquist. It was the first time Sarah had seen him smile.

"A matching tie and everything? What's your name?" Malick stroked under the dog's chin.

"This is our legal assistant, Rehnquist." Uncle Buddy hung his raincoat in the closet. "Rehnquist, meet Malick." He sat in the receptionist's chair and removed his galoshes. "We'll use Sarah's office today. She has the fancy artwork."

"Is that all you like about my office, Uncle Buddy?" Sarah folded her arms and tapped her foot.

"She just refilled the gumdrops in her candy dish," Uncle Buddy whispered to Malick and pointed at the glass bowl in the corner of the desk.

"I heard that." Sarah wagged her finger. Uncle Buddy had a sweet tooth for as long as she could remember. He'd often carry around a bag of jelly beans in his suit pocket. One time they spilled, bouncing all over the courtroom rug during a trial.

"Can I get you anything, Malick? I have blueberry muffins here." Sarah grabbed the white Sorelle's bag from her bookshelf and held it in front of him.

"Thanks." Malick took a muffin and sat down. Rehnquist sat beside him, staring at the muffin with perked ears. He also had a sweet tooth.

Uncle Buddy eased into the other chair and cherry-picked a handful of green gumdrops. "Play chess, Malick?"

"Yeah." Malick broke off a piece of the muffin and fed it to Rehnquist.

"Any good?"

Malick nodded, letting the dog lick each finger. Sarah watched him, wondering what thoughts were running through his mind.

Uncle Buddy slowly chewed his gumdrops. "Trying cases is a lot like chess. All boils down to strategy: you have to really see the board and visualize what your next three moves will be."

Malick fidgeted with the drawstring on his hooded sweatshirt, and reached for Rehnquist again.

"Malick," Sarah spoke softly. "We have a homeless man who claims he saw someone moving across the rooftops during the fire."

"Yeah, and I told you, somebody else was there. But who's gonna believe me? Like it's okay when that fireman lied about seeing my mom pointing a gun. He didn't see that. I swear to God it was somebody else."

"I believe you," Sarah said. "And that other person could've escaped out the upstairs bedroom window. That's why we're making such a big deal out of it."

"But it'll boil down to me and a drunken bum versus the cops and a bunch of firemen. Who's gonna win?"

Sarah glanced at her uncle. Malick was right about that.

"I like betting on the long shots." Uncle Buddy popped three green gumdrops into his mouth and tossed one to Rehnquist, who leaped up and caught it. "But for now, don't think about who's going to win or lose. We're making our way through the middle game. They've captured a few pawns, maybe a knight, that's all."

"So, what's your next move?" Malick asked.

"We have to figure out why someone else was in the apartment that night." This time, Uncle Buddy picked out the red gumdrops. "Let's keep an open mind and think about all the possibilities."

Sarah listened to her uncle philosophizing about chess, and, at the same time, refreshing Malick's memory about whether anyone unusual had come to the store in the past year. She had the feeling Malick was holding back about something, just like his mother was. Uncle Buddy would avoid the direct question but eventually chisel his way to the truth, or at least the path leading up to it.

"Hey, that's not fair, you and Rehnquist ate all the reds." Malick squinted at Uncle Buddy and rotated the glass bowl. "Ask my mom about the lady with the big red briefcase. Well, it wasn't a hard case, but—"

"A large shoulder bag like mine?" Sarah pointed to her bulging black bag leaning against the wall.

"Yeah, and red like the gumdrops." Malick fed an orange gumdrop to Rehnquist.

"What made you think of that particular lady?" Sarah felt like they were grasping at straws.

"Well, I sort of forgot about that lady with all this crap going on, but my mom used to meet with her at the store. A couple times she asked me to work the deli while they sat and had tea."

"Do you remember her name?"

"Uhhh . . . Debbie? Or, wait, I think it was Donna. I never heard her last name."

"Was she hot-lookin'?" Uncle Buddy mimicked an hourglass figure with his hands.

Malick smiled. "Not bad, had blondish hair and wore it back in a ponytail a lot. She was old though."

"*Old.* Like around Sarah's age?" Uncle Buddy winked.

Malick studied Sarah. "Little younger."

Sarah knew her uncle would kid around about that later. *Old.* Thirties were the new twenties, she reminded herself. "What made you think of her just now?"

"She had this real serious look about her. Whenever she talked to my mom, it always put her in a wicked bad mood. The lady took notes too."

"Ahh." Uncle Buddy pointed with both index fingers. "We're talking investigator or reporter. Well, could've been an inexperienced lawyer. Old-timers like me keep it all up here." He tapped his temple. "To hell with notes, they only get lost."

"Did your mom ever mention what they talked about?" Sarah wondered if it had anything to do with Amina's blog about the Koran teachers and the street boys.

"I asked my mom once, but she changed the subject, now that I think of it."

"Is there anything else you can recall about this lady?"

"Well . . ." He lowered his gaze.

Sarah waited. She could tell he was hesitant. Uncle Buddy fished the candy bowl for purples.

"Don't take *all* the purples." Malick reached into the bowl.

"You have to be aggressive in here. You're competing with an old shark," Uncle Buddy said.

Malick grinned as they both went for the purples.

"Anything else about the lady?" Sarah wanted to stay on track.

"My mom stole something out of her bag."

"Stole something?" Sarah nearly knocked her coffee cup over. "You sure?"

"Uh huh. When she went to the bathroom. Nobody else was in the deli. I was stocking shelves toward the back of the store, but I saw her do it."

"What did she take?" Sarah looked at Uncle Buddy chewing his gumdrops in slow motion again as if it helped him concentrate.

"Looked like a couple folders jammed with papers," Malick said. "Freaked me out because my mom would never steal anything. She's like, you know, straight and narrow. She'd kill me if I ever did something like that."

"Did you ask your mom about it?" Sarah watched him crack his knuckles.

"Yeah, later on, I did. She was, like, creeped out that I saw it. I could tell by the look on her face. Like I caught her in the act."

Caught in the act. Sarah had heard those words before. "What did she say?"

"That it was nothing. The papers belonged to her, and then, in typical fashion, she got pissed off at me about something else. The whole thing was weird. If the stuff was really hers, why didn't she just ask for it back? Why'd she have to steal it like that? I don't get it."

"Did anything else happen?" Sarah asked.

"I think the lady found out because she stormed into the store the next day. She was wicked mad and said something to my mom. I didn't hear it all, but my mom followed her out. It looked like she was trying to explain herself. But the lady booked out of there."

"When did that occur in relation to the fire?" Uncle Buddy said.

"About a week or two before."

21

Nick arranged the papers and canisters in a neat row on his table that Friday morning. These lab results were damning evidence of Amina Diallo's guilt. He watched her enter the courtroom wearing a long maroon headscarf. *You're finished now. Clancy can't charm his way around this.* Nick had watched the jurors during Clancy's cross of the canine handler. He had them feeling sorry for the dog. And that's what they were thinking about all night. *The poor starving dog.*

The courtroom doors opened and closed. Nick knew what was coming, but he had to turn around and see for himself. His witness resembled a tall version of Albert Einstein, complete with the bushy white eyebrows and thick, disheveled hair. A bit eccentric, but he's one of the best, Nick reminded himself.

The jurors eyed the peculiar man in the tailored black suit. "Please introduce yourself to the ladies and gentlemen of the jury."

"Professor Marvin Moore." He addressed the jury with a deep, authoritative voice and interlaced his long fingers on the podium.

"What is your occupation?"

"I have three, actually. I'm a forensic chemist, a professor at Northeastern University, and . . ." He smiled and raised his eyebrows. "A magician."

Right out of Harry Potter. Several jurors looked at Nick in bewilderment. He wondered if they could see the exclamation points and question marks on Professor Moore's bow tie. Hopefully not. "What is your training and experience?"

"My first chemistry set was a birthday present when I turned ten, but we must go back even further. You see, with the name Marvin Moore, I aspired to be a famous magician. Note the magical flow: Marvin Moore . . . Harry Houdini?" He sighed. "Ah, but my parents didn't consider magic a noble profession. So, I ended up with a BS degree in chemistry from MIT." He wiggled in his chair.

Here it comes, Nick thought. He raised a hand to stop Marvin, but the effort was in vain.

"I'm most proud of my senior week prank. The city woke up to the MIT dome floating in a mysterious red cloud with a police car perched on top. It made the front page of the *Boston Globe*."

Nick watched an older juror nod as if she recalled Professor Moore's infamous mark on MIT. "What other training did you have in forensic chemistry?"

"I rubbed noses with the staties and feds at their esteemed academies, but fieldwork provides the most experience. I'm a thirty-nine-year veteran chemist at the Boston Police Department's crime lab."

Nick had to rein him in. Judge Killam already cleared his throat once. "Professor Moore, on July twentieth of last year, did you receive anything at the lab?"

"I certainly did. Sergeant Frank Brady arrived with nine sealed evidence cans, which were dated and labeled A through I and marked 'fire 107 Waldemar Ave.'"

Nick guided Professor Moore through the meticulous procedure of preserving the debris and other evidence contained in the cans.

"What did you do next?"

"I performed a bit of magic." He raised his eyebrows several times. "You see, that fire debris has to be transformed into a liquid. So, I took out my magic wand . . ." He stood, reached into his pocket, produced a thin paper strip, and waved it like a symphony conductor. "Voila."

All Professor Moore needed was a top hat and cape to go with the act, and Nick wouldn't put it past him someday. "What is that?"

"Why, it's my magic DeFlex strip. I placed one strip in each can and heated them overnight at a whopping temperature of ninety degrees centigrade. I also set DeFlex strips inside positive and negative control cans. The positive can contained a drop of gasoline and the negative can didn't have any ignitable liquids in it."

"After placing a DeFlex strip in each can, what did you do?"

"I joined my wife in bed for a different kind of magic."

Laughter erupted from the jury box, gallery, and the defense table. Nick felt like strangling the guy. There was no room for humor in this trial.

Judge Killam rapped his gavel. "This is a courtroom, *Professor*."

Nick waved both hands to intervene. "We don't need to know about that."

Professor Moore sat back down, his lips curled with a mischievous grin. Nick felt himself perspiring. You never knew what would emerge from that man's mouth. He had spotted the union president sitting out in the gallery and knew the governor was glued to the television set.

Nick took a deep breath. *Keep going.* "What did you do the next day?"

"I removed the strips from the cans and placed each in a vial containing carbon disulfide, which is a lovely solvent. I mixed the vials on a rocker, and the residue which had collected on the strips was transformed into a liquid form. There you have it: magic. Pure magic."

Nick watched the jurors as Professor Moore described how he performed tests on the liquid in each vial. The foreperson took notes, while Quahog leaned back and closed his eyes from time to time. Some fiddled with their pens, while others appeared amused by the eccentric witness.

"What were the test results?"

Professor Moore waved his lab report. "Here we have it, folks: my final act. The fire debris collected from the back left corner of the store contained gasoline residue. The red fragment found in the same area was latex commonly found in balloons, and it tested positive for gasoline residue. The debris collected from the upstairs bedroom contained acetone residue, which is the main ingredient found in nail polish remover. The pink slippers, leather driving gloves, and automobile floor mat all tested positive for gasoline residue. The comparison samples did not contain any ignitable liquids."

"What did you do after you ran those tests?"

"I prepared my lab report and discussed the results with Sergeant Brady and Detective Callahan."

"No further questions." Nick made eye contact with the foreperson, who would surely share his notes during deliberations. In his previous experience trying arson cases, evidence of poured gasoline sealed the defendant's fate.

"I wonder where he got that bow tie?" Mr. Clancy adjusted his own tie. He and Sarah had joined Amina in her cell again for the lunchtime recess.

"Uncle Buddy, enough with the tie already."

Amina sensed Sarah didn't feel like listening to her uncle's obsession with Professor Moore's bow tie. Sometimes she lacked patience with him. Amina recalled feeling the same way about her father years ago.

"All those exclamation points and question marks." Mr. Clancy shook his head. "Never saw anything like it."

Sarah addressed Amina and changed the subject. "We met with Malick yesterday."

"Malick?" Amina stiffened. She hadn't realized they were meeting. "Why?"

"We had to introduce him to Rehnquist." Mr. Clancy smiled.

"Who's that?" Amina hoped it wasn't another private investigator who would pepper her son with questions.

"My dog."

"Oh, that's right." Amina's relief transformed into guilt. "Malick always begged for a puppy, but with the store and living in the city, I said no. Maybe I should've gone ahead . . . it would've made him so happy." Amina wished she could turn the clock back. What she would give for one more day, just the two of them. *Mother and son.* What she would've done differently if she had known.

"Did you ever play chess with him?" Mr. Clancy asked.

"He used to play with his father a long time ago." Amina remembered Lamine teaching Malick how to play when he was five. She pictured them sitting opposite each other at the kitchen table studying the board. "We played a little here and there." Amina also recalled the many times he asked her to play, and she had replied: "I can't right now, the shelves need to be restocked . . . the books must be balanced . . . the deli prepped and cleaned."

"Could you beat him?" Mr. Clancy asked.

She raised her eyebrows. "In chess? Probably not."

"Then I don't feel so bad. He cleaned my clock on Saturday, but I'm a little rusty." Mr. Clancy recounted some of Malick's moves.

"I can tell you." Sarah raised a finger. "They both had stomachaches from eating all my gumdrops and two bags of popcorn."

"Oh, it was worth it. We had great fun." Mr. Clancy flipped his pen in the air, catching it like a baton. "You know, I explained to Malick that trying cases is similar to chess. You have to concentrate on the board and strategize. Marinelli positioned his rook today with the chemist. He thinks he's lined up to take our knight. We have to block him and grab his knight instead. I'm looking at the board, but I'm not seeing how we can accomplish that right now. I know there's a way. Always is."

"What do you mean?" Amina shifted on the bench. She could tell he was about to ask her something related to the case. It made her nervous.

"Malick mentioned a lady who came into the store?" Mr. Clancy lifted Sarah's briefcase and placed it in his lap. "With a big red one like this."

Amina stared at the briefcase and sat very still without saying a word. Sarah and Mr. Clancy remained silent, waiting for a reaction. *She had to say something.* "I don't know who Malick was talking about. I have many customers. It is—*was* very busy. What did he say?"

"That you met with this woman several times, and when she left, you were always in a bad mood," Sarah said.

"Perhaps she didn't pay her bill. I don't know. I can't remember. Is that all he said?" Amina shifted her gaze from Sarah to Mr. Clancy and back. She knew there was more.

Sarah looked into her eyes. "Malick said you took papers from her briefcase."

Amina flinched, and she knew Sarah caught it. "I can't believe he told you that. Malick doesn't have a clue about what he saw or *thinks he saw.*" Amina cracked her knuckles. "I want him to concentrate on school, not this."

Mr. Clancy raised a finger. "He'd like a dog."

Sarah glanced sideways at her uncle; the comment came from left field. "Why are you back on the dog topic again, Uncle Buddy?"

"Nice cocker spaniel, perhaps?" Mr. Clancy continued in a soft voice. "Or a pug?"

Amina pressed her fingernails into her cheeks. *A dog.* She couldn't get Malick a dog unless she got out of jail. But Amina had to keep her son safe. This was dangerous territory. Should she open the door a crack? Tell them just a little? Some . . . but not everything? Amina could never tell them everything. She regarded Sarah and Mr. Clancy.

"Amina, you can trust us." Sarah draped an arm around her shoulders.

"I got in over my head, I think." Amina exhaled. "A mistake."

"We all make mistakes." Sarah whispered.

"Not like this. I'm in jail and left my son without a mother. I've lost everything." Amina regretted mentioning anything about a mistake. It was a foolish comment. There was nothing anyone could do now. Her situation was hopeless.

"Amina." Sarah leaned forward until her face was inches away. "Remember when you told me about Lamine's music and the healing rhythm?"

"The djpo. It is the healing rhythm of the tama, the talking drum."

"Right, and I know you mentioned that for a reason." Sarah paused. "Did you see something in me? Something that made you think I needed healing?"

Amina had seen the dark chasm in Sarah's eyes. "You lost someone close."

"You're right. John, my colleague. He was the love of my life. He ended up dead because I made a mistake, a misjudgment."

Amina stared at Sarah without speaking. What could she say to that? Someone died because Sarah made a mistake?

"John was shot and killed right next to me." Sarah recoiled as if the words had slapped her. "The guilt swallowed me whole. It engulfed me."

Amina felt for Sarah as she listened to her story. It sounded as if Sarah was relaying details for the first time. Mr. Clancy sat still with his head bowed. Amina could tell the tragedy had affected him as well. He cared for his niece like a father.

"I'll never be able to undo John's death," Sarah continued. "I've come to realize that. I have to move forward and do something meaningful." She reached over and squeezed Amina's hands. "That's why I took your case."

Amina felt Sarah's passion surging through her fingertips.

"Don't give up, Amina," Sarah whispered. "Let us help you."

"Tell us about your mistake," Mr. Clancy said. "Give us a shot."

Amina wanted to believe they could help her. "Do you really think there is hope for me?"

"Yes." Sarah and Mr. Clancy spoke in unison.

Amina decided to press forward. "The lady . . . Donna . . . asked about my mortgage broker and the loan."

Mr. Clancy made eye contact with Sarah. "What'd she want to know?"

"All kinds of things." Amina wished Donna had never come into the market. "She was writing a news article about my neighborhood. The research showed it had the highest number of foreclosures, so she wanted to know more about my mortgage."

"Like what?" Sarah asked.

"Various details, names. I can't remember them all." Amina remembered Donna going on and on about all the people who had lost homes and businesses. "Donna believed something illegal was going on with Mark LaSpada, my mortgage broker, but she wouldn't give me any details."

"Typical." Uncle Buddy rolled his eyes. "Reporters are like doctors. They ask you all kinds of questions and give up very little in return. It's like a secret society they don't want you to be part of."

"That's why I took the papers from her file. I would never do that, but I begged her to share that information. It had to do with me and my store. I was about to lose everything and she knew it. I didn't have the time to sit around and wait for her investigation."

"Do you still have those documents?" Sarah asked.

"Destroyed in the fire."

"Can you remember what they looked like?" Mr. Clancy said.

"Let me think. Some were typed and appeared official with government stamps scattered around. There were notes in Donna's handwriting, some old newspaper articles."

"What'd you do with all that stuff?"

"The wrong thing." *Her biggest mistake.*

"Which was?" Sarah leaned to the side and nearly slipped off the bench.

"I stormed into Mr. LaSpada's office and told him I had proof he was stealing people's homes . . . accused him of lying, cheating. I read out loud from Donna's notes, told him she was writing an article that would expose his entire family, put them in jail. I mentioned various names, and information about another fire. The fire scared him the most."

"Which fire?" Sarah jumped to her feet.

"Somewhere in Quincy. It involved a golf course."

"We can research that one." Mr. Clancy rapped his

knuckles against the steel. "I'd like to know more about the names. Think hard. Can you remember any?"

"Another LaSpada name . . . begins with an *S*." Amina rubbed her temples, trying to remember. She pictured the documents, but couldn't come up with the name.

Sarah paced back and forth in the tiny cell. "Salvatore?"

"Yes. Yes, that's it." Amina was certain. "Who's he?"

"Mark's father." Mr. Clancy spoke with disdain. "The founder of LaSpada Development. The patriarch. He's been around for years, made a fortune on the Big Dig, tight with all the politicians. I wouldn't be surprised if he was up to something."

"And the governor's name, Noterman. I remember it was underlined several times." Amina made an imaginary line with her finger.

"I bet they're up to their ears in shenanigans, and it involves boatloads of money." Mr. Clancy rubbed his thumb and index finger together. "Hmmm. The governor, the governor. Now that intrigues me. I could have some fun with that."

Sarah leaned her forehead against the iron bars. "An open arson investigation from Quincy would have to be right out of Frank's unit. He could've been the lead investigator or at least worked on part of it. I'll ask him. We have to get in touch with her today."

"Who? Donna?" Amina asked.

"Yeah." Sarah turned around and faced her.

"I think she's dead."

22

"**W**hat a character," Christine whispered, as she resumed her seat next to Derrick in the jury box after lunch.

"Whew." Derrick regarded Professor Moore in his black suit and wacky bow tie with the question marks and exclamation points. "Can you imagine working with that guy?"

Christine giggled. "Well, he likes making magic with his wife."

Derrick rolled his eyes. As foreperson, he hoped he could sort it all out by the end of the trial. He watched Sarah whispering to her client, and shuffling through papers at the defense table. How could she and her uncle challenge this MIT wizard with his infallible lab results that seemed to spell Amina Diallo's doom?

Derrick glanced around at his fellow jurors. They appeared anxious to whip through the afternoon. It was almost the weekend. He looked forward to spending time with his kids and catching up on work. Christine was going to take a night shift at Children's Hospital and get paid overtime. Antiliano had a Red Sox haircut lined up for Saturday. Quahog would make it to happy hour at Aces High by five fifteen.

Judge Killam refilled his water glass. "Cross-examination?"

Clancy whispered something to Sarah and pointed to Professor Moore's bow tie. Sarah shook her head and said something in return. He clasped his hands together like a kid about to chomp into a king-sized candy bar.

Sarah smiled; she had a beautiful smile. Derrick noticed how her lip gloss caught the light.

"Good afternoon, Professor Moore." Clancy leaped from his seat, skirted around the defense table, and trotted right up to the witness.

Judge Killam mumbled, "This oughta be good." Derrick looked up at the bench and caught the judge's eye. Perhaps the old codger had a sense of humor after all.

Clancy bent forward and squinted. "Great tie, just terrific. Are those question marks and exclamation points?"

"They certainly are."

Clancy looked at the jury in disbelief. "Where'd you get it?"

"I'm not telling."

"Why not?"

"Because you'll go out and buy one."

Derrick laughed along with the rest of the jurors. It was a battle of the bow ties.

"Oh, come on. I wouldn't do such a thing."

"You would."

"I wouldn't."

"Enough with the tie!" Judge Killam banged the gavel. "Move on."

"My apologies, Your Honor." Clancy walked back toward the jury box and faced the witness again.

"Can you tell me how many firemen traipsed into the building with their big boots?"

Professor Moore leaned back in his chair. "Of course not."

"Can you say how many fire investigators went in and out?"

He adjusted his bow tie. "Why . . . no."

Derrick imagined the Senegalese Market with the firemen trampling in and out, hose lines everywhere.

How could they preserve a fire scene for evidence collection? The task seemed impossible.

"Did you monitor the evidence collection?" Clancy sidestepped and moved forward.

"I didn't have to. Sergeant Brady is a *very* competent investigator."

"Get to the fire scene at all?"

"No."

"Making magic with your wife that night?"

"Objection!"

"Sustained."

"With my bow tie on."

Derrick laughed. That was a good one.

Judge Killam turned to the witness. "Sir, when the objection is sustained, *don't answer*."

"My apologies this time, Your Honor." He winked at the jury. "I couldn't help myself."

Clancy marched ahead several steps. "Professor, did you *ever* go to the Senegalese Market?"

"No."

Derrick noticed how Clancy never missed a beat even when the witness upstaged him. He possessed the rhythm of a natural performer while getting his point across.

"Hmmm. Professor, you can only perform tests on the evidence they bring to you, correct?"

"That's right."

"Did they give you any samples from the roof of the building?"

"I don't believe so."

"Test any firemen's boots?"

"Oh, no. They need their boots to fight fires."

"Those boots could've contained gasoline residue."

Professor Moore wrinkled his nose. "Among other things. It's possible."

"Any shoes from the folks at the scene?"

"No." Professor Moore adjusted his bow tie to the left.

"The neighbor's nightshirt?"

"No." He readjusted his tie to the right. Derrick figured he was attempting to tease Clancy with the tie.

Clancy pointed into the gallery in the direction of the mayor, who happened to be in attendance that day. "Collect any clothes from *the Democrats*?"

Professor Moore laughed. "Good one. No."

"And the Republicans?"

"Nothing."

"Hmmm. And, what about the governor? He seems awfully interested in this case. Did you collect—"

"Objection!" Marinelli jumped to his feet. "Relevance?"

"This is cross-examination," Judge Killam rubbed his chin. "But, I'll sustain your objection. "Move along, Clancy."

"I'm simply trying to make my point." Clancy appeared taken aback. "How 'bout O.J.'s missing glove? Did you test that?"

"No." Professor Moore laughed again.

"It's possible any of those items could've tested positive for gasoline residue?"

"Yes. Well, I'm uncertain about O.J.'s glove."

Clancy raised his voice. "Are you aware there's a self-service gas station right up the street from the Senegalese Market?"

"I wasn't aware of that, but it's good to know in case I need a fill-up when I'm over that way."

"Customers could've tracked gasoline residue into the store after filling their tanks?"

"I suppose it's possible."

Derrick inched forward. Clancy had a point. Anyone

could've tracked gasoline into that store with a station up the street. Gas could seep into the floor mats and remain on a pair of driving gloves. People filled their tanks and gas always dripped from the nozzle afterward. He'd spilled gas on his own shoes plenty of times. But customers tracking gasoline into the store would only leave very small amounts behind.

Clancy anchored his thumbs beneath his red suspenders and raised his voice. "Your tests inform us of the presence of ignitable liquid residues in a given sample, right?"

"Yes."

Clancy raised his index finger. "Okay, but they don't provide *amounts* of the ignitable liquid residue."

"That's right."

Clancy zigzagged toward the witness. "So, you can't tell us whether the samples from the store contained a gallon of gasoline or a drop smaller than a dime."

"That's correct."

"Or a bead the size of a pinhead?" He moved forward again.

"Right."

"A particle on a pebble tracked in by a pup?"

Professor Moore drummed his long fingers. "Very imaginative. I suppose *that* pebble could contain all sorts of stuff."

"How 'bout a customer who pumps gas up the street, gets the munchies, and fingers the potato chip bags?"

"What about him?"

Clancy raised his hands and wiggled all ten fingers. "Gas on the fingers may leave *residue* behind?"

"That's possible."

Derrick was surprised that the tests couldn't provide information about the amount of gasoline spilled on the floor. It would be useful to know how much.

Clancy stood close to the witness with hands on his hips. "You certainly can't tell me where any of that gasoline residue came from."

"I cannot."

"Or that charred piece of red latex?"

"No."

"A store like the Senegalese Market contains many different kinds of flammable products?"

"I'm sure it does," Professor Moore said.

Clancy spun around and headed toward the jury. "The sample collected from the second-story bedroom contained acetone?"

"Yes."

"And that sample was collected near the open window?"

"I'm not sure."

"The window with access to the roof?"

"I'm unaware of the exact location."

"Acetone is an ingredient in nail polish remover?"

"It is."

"And we *all* know acetone is highly flammable?"

Professor Moore cocked his head as if trying to ascertain Clancy's angle. "I'm not sure if it's common knowledge, but acetone is categorized as an ignitable liquid."

Clancy clicked his tongue. "Perfect."

Derrick wondered why he was making such a big deal out of the nail polish remover spilled near the window. A flammable liquid. Why was it *perfect*?

"Excuse me?" Professor Moore said.

Clancy appeared startled for an instant, but his smile widened as he addressed the chemist. "Oh, *your tie* . . . it's just perfect. Do enjoy your weekend, Professor."

Derrick reconsidered Clancy's strategy. Customers were likely to track gasoline into a store near a gas station. A possibility. But, in case they didn't buy into that theory, the defense planted the seed that a mystery arsonist escaped out the second-story window and onto the roof. In addition, the window had nail polish remover spilled next to it. Derrick took off his glasses, breathed on the lenses, and rubbed them clean.

"Redirect?"

Marinelli rose. "Briefly, Your Honor."

Judge Killam nodded.

Marinelli walked near his podium. "How many samples were taken in the area where the dog alerted?"

"Three. Well, four if you count the piece of red latex."

"Okay. How many of those *different* samples tested positive for gasoline residue?"

"Why, all of them tested positive for gasoline residue."

Marinelli glanced at Derrick. "Why do you take several samples in a given area?"

Professor Moore sat forward and cleared his throat. "We can't specify the exact amounts of gasoline residue in a given sample. That's why a good arson investigator will take several samples in an area where the dog alerts."

"Did the comparison sample contain any traces of gasoline residue that could've been tracked in by customers or a stray pup?"

Sarah stood. "Objection. Leading question."

"Sustained." Judge Killam addressed Marinelli. "This is redirect examination, counselor. No leading questions."

"What is the purpose of taking a comparison sample in another part of the store?"

Professor Moore folded his hands and addressed the jury. "The comparison sample will provide us with the chemical composition for a base section of the store. It tells us the chemical makeup of the flooring, including varnishes, paints, cleaning products, et cetera. In this case, we didn't find any gasoline residue in the comparison sample. Not a scintilla." He raised his eyebrows at Clancy.

"No further questions."

Derrick watched Clancy get up from his seat to wheedle in the last word.

"You only tested one comparison sample?"

"Yes, but—"

"And it was small enough to fit into your tin can?"

"The sample represented a good cross section of that store."

"Ahhh." Clancy grinned. "Professor, professor. What if we cut one section of your bow tie which contained an exclamation point. Are we to assume that the tie is composed entirely of exclamation points? Would we automatically rule out the possibility that it may contain an equal number of question marks?"

Derrick peered around at the smiles in the jury box. He didn't even hear Professor Moore's response. Clancy scored big with that one. He continued watching the good ol' Irish lawyer after he resumed his seat next to Sarah and their client. Clancy was the true magician, a Houdini. He created smoke screens and used magic words, causing jurors to see things that might not even be there. He was right on point with that tie. They couldn't make assumptions. But, as foreperson, Derrick had to filter out the red magician's smoke and find the truth.

"I bet you're the first lawyer to base a cross-examination on a bow tie." Sarah grabbed the remaining legal pad from the defense table and stuffed it into her briefcase.

"Oh, it was great fun, great fun. That's why I love this place." Uncle Buddy spread his arms and walked in a small circle. "From the gallery to the jury box. This is where it's at." He released a long, satisfied sigh. "We're lucky we ended on that note. You see, the bow tie will remain in the jurors' heads all weekend, and they'll forget why Marinelli had 'ol Professor Moore up there in the first place. Called distract and conquer."

"With a bow tie." Sarah admired her uncle. He thrived at thinking outside the box.

"Speaking of cross, are you sure you want to handle Sergeant Brady on Monday? I'm happy to do it."

"Yes. I'll take Frank and you take Detective Callahan." This was something Sarah had to do to prove herself on the defense side. Cross-examining the lead investigator represented a rite of passage.

"I'll have a ball with Callahan, no doubt, but going against Frank will be more intense than any other witness. You used to be colleagues batting on the same team." Uncle Buddy stretched a galosh over his shoe.

"I know." Sarah realized she'd have to throw hand grenades at Frank's investigation to create reasonable doubt. "By the way, I saw Frank at the end of the lunch break, and he's stopping by the office later. I'd like to see what he knows about the Quincy fire that Amina mentioned. I bet the state police were involved." She knew this could be her last chance to grab information from Frank before he took the witness stand on Monday.

"Just be wary, that's all." He stretched. "I'm heading over to Locke-Ober's to see if I can grab anything on the governor from a few of the old cronies. Couple scotches and they'll start blabbing up a storm."

Sarah smiled, knowing he'd come up with something. Uncle Buddy always did.

23

"**I** noticed how you scheduled me in right at suppertime." Frank strolled into the reception area of Sarah's office.

"Hungry? Let's see . . . I might have a bag of half-eaten Doritos around someplace." Sarah stepped into the kitchenette and opened a cupboard. She noticed how good he looked in a pair of jeans and a dress shirt. Casual, yet it appeared like he took time to select his clothes. "Microwave popcorn? Extra butter?"

"No. I'm taking you out. Like Italian?"

A *real* dinner? Sarah hadn't had time to cook in over a month. Pizza, dried-out muffins, and salads had been her mainstays. "But that's crazy—"

Frank gestured toward the door. "Come on. I'll drive, or we can walk to the North End."

"Walk?"

"Why not? Last I checked it's right over the bridge."

"And risk being seen with me? What if one of the Boston cops spots us? Or, God forbid, a fireman. You keep forgetting I'm the enemy now. What will people think?"

"Have I ever cared about that?"

"No." And he didn't. She'd always admired Frank for that.

They crossed the bridge connecting Charlestown with the North End and cut over onto Prince Street. Frank stopped and inhaled. "I can smell the homemade sauce already."

"Where shall we eat?" Sarah watched Frank rubbing his hands together, putting thought into the decision.

She wondered why he'd never settled down. He had a romantic side and dated his share of women. She longed to scratch the surface and learn more about him. There was a quiet, mysterious side to Frank.

"They're all good. You pick," he said.

Sarah paused. "Let's see. Love the pumpkin ravioli at Giacomo's, but there's probably a line and I'm starving."

"Me too."

"How about Amaru's?" Sarah sidestepped around a cluster of foreign tourists.

"On Richmond Street?"

"That's the one."

They chose a corner table toward the back. Frank ordered a bottle of Beale red zinfandel and the calamari pasta salad to start.

Frank's cell phone rang. He excused himself and took the call outside.

"Am I going to have to deal with *that* all night?" Sarah pointed at his cell when he came back. "Typical cop." Sarah knew he didn't like being categorized with all the cops.

"There." Frank pressed the button on the side of his phone. "Silenced. But I'm leaving it on the table in case the office calls, okay?"

"Deal."

The waitress poured the wine and Frank raised his glass. "Here's to your career as a defense lawyer. I never thought I'd see the day."

"Thanks." Sarah clinked glasses with him and sipped her wine. It tasted full-bodied and jammy. The calamari was tender and sweet, complementing the garlic and balsamic vinaigrette on the pasta salad. Sarah glanced at the dinner menu. "It's all in Italian. The waitress'll have to translate. I'm sure you'll want to know the Italian word for hamburger."

"And hotdog." He winked. "Let's order and be surprised."

Sarah admired his spontaneity. She ordered *pollo* followed by a long line of Italian words. She knew *pollo* meant chicken. Frank ordered something with *pesce* and *gamberi*.

Sarah thought about delving right into the case. Her mind swam with questions regarding that old Quincy fire. Instead, she leaned back and enjoyed her wine. It felt good to relax and nibble on real food for a change. She watched Frank break off a piece of warm bread and dip it into the dish of herbed olive oil.

"Tell me, what've you been up to for the past four years?" she asked.

"Solving arsons."

"Besides work."

Frank shrugged.

"Girlfriends?"

"A few here and there."

Sarah knew she couldn't squeeze much out of him in that category. She helped herself to more calamari and passed the dish to Frank. "How's your family?"

"My parents are doing okay." He scraped the rest onto his plate. "They still live in West Roxbury and summer down in Falmouth."

"Do you have siblings in the area?"

"Not anymore." Frank ran his fingertips up and down the stem of his wine glass. "I had a younger sister. Kerry. She died."

Sarah noticed the sadness in Frank's eyes. "I'm sorry."

"Yeah." It came out like a long sigh.

"When?" Sarah pressed.

"She was eighteen."

So young. "What happened?"

"Kerry was born with a hole in her heart. She was

the kindest little girl . . ." His voice trailed off. "Her face and lips were purple-looking. Other kids made fun of her. She couldn't run like everyone else, excused from gym, you know, all that. People weren't as compassionate back then."

"No, they weren't. Especially other city kids. I remember." Sarah recalled the relentless name-calling when someone stood out as being different or handicapped or *had purple lips*. "Is that why?"

"Why what?" Frank chewed a forkful of calamari.

"You're the way you are. Sensitive, caring, but you have an edge about you. You're . . ."

"Cynical?" He smirked. "Kerry had a birthday party once. She was turning eight. I tried to tell my parents not to have it, but they were real into it, wouldn't listen. They invited her entire class, along with other kids from the block. They had all sorts of games, balloons, a matching paper tablecloth, plates, and napkins. I can see it now, Sleeping Beauty."

"What happened?"

"Only one kid showed up, a little boy. His mother made him come."

Sarah pictured a sad little girl with purple lips. No wonder Frank had a jaded perspective. "Something like that gets you deep down, doesn't it?" She smoothed the cloth napkin across her lap. "I sort of know the feeling."

"You do. As I mentioned before, life's not fair. That's why I told you about Kerry. I haven't shared that story with anyone."

Sarah sipped her wine in silence as she thought about John and the shooting, Frank's sister, and Amina. Life wasn't fair. It was random and she wanted so desperately to control it. Perhaps she should try the healing rhythm of the tama drum.

Frank touched her hand. "You'll work through it. Sometimes it takes longer than we expect. I'm not there yet either."

The waitress finally arrived with their dinners. Frank's turned out to be sautéed shrimp and fish in a garlic and white wine sauce served over lemon pepper fettuccine, and Sarah's chicken came smothered in steaming tomatoes, peppers, and fresh Italian spices.

"Share?" Frank motioned to his oversized portion.

Sarah gave him a generous serving of chicken, and he piled fettuccine, fish, and shrimp on her plate.

"I think we made excellent choices." He topped off their wine glasses.

"Thank you." Sarah decided it was time to question him about the old Quincy fire and the reporter who Amina feared was dead. "Remember what I mentioned earlier in court?"

"Yeah?"

She had to choose the right words. "I heard something about a fire in Quincy a few years back."

"We got plenty of those. Can you be more specific?"

"It had something to with a golf course and the LaSpada Development Company."

Frank looked down. He lifted a small mound of fettuccine with his fork. "The Quincy golf course project." He twirled the pasta into a ball. "Around six and a half years ago an antique barn blocked a major golf and condominium development project because it sat on the perfect parcel for the clubhouse. A Quincy neighborhood group fought like hell to save that barn and have it declared a historical landmark."

Sarah raised her eyebrows. "A multimillion-dollar project held up by an old barn? What happened?"

"The barn was privately owned. So the plan was to

have the city of Quincy take it from the owners by eminent domain. Then the city would turn around and sell it back to LaSpada, and they would bulldoze it down and build the clubhouse."

"Easy enough." Sarah took a bite of her chicken.

"Not quite. The neighborhood group went to court and stalled the eminent domain taking of that barn."

"And let me guess. The barn burned. Problem solved."

"Correct."

"LaSpada must've been on the hot seat." Sarah wished she could read Frank's mind.

"Yes, but they were investigated and came out clean." His voice sounded firm.

"And they moved forward with their golf course." Sarah used a mocking tone. "Arson carries a seven-year statute of limitations. How many years left?"

"At this point? Less than one."

"Not much time to solve it." She tapped her watch.

"If it turns out to be arson, we have all the time we need," Frank said, slowly.

"Why?"

"Unlimited for felony murder. Two homeless people were burned to death."

"Oh." Sarah swallowed. "That's awful."

"We couldn't identify the sex until the autopsy. Turned out to be an unidentified man and woman. They were huddled together."

Sarah visualized the charred bodies. "I don't recall reading about it."

"The article only made the second page of the *Patriot Ledger*. It was never even mentioned in the *Globe*."

Sarah recalled Danny's words from the other night: *nobody cares much about the homeless*. "Any evidence of arson?"

"We found gasoline, but in an area where the previous owner stored several tractors and a snowblower. A witness claimed he'd seen the homeless people smoking."

"Didn't all this business about LaSpada and the fire come up when they assigned Amina's case to you? It sounds like a conflict of interest."

"No, because that fire was determined to be caused by the careless use of cigarettes. It's a closed case." Frank swirled his wine. "But, if you have any information, I'll take it."

Sarah twisted the cloth napkin in her lap, and wondered whether Frank would pull the old file. Perhaps he already had. "Have you heard of a journalist named Donna Rapa?"

"Uhh . . . not that I recall." Frank's brow furrowed. "Why?"

Sarah detected hesitation. *Not that I recall* was a line used by cops all the time on the witness stand. And, almost always, it meant they knew the answer, but wouldn't say it. "Are you sure?"

"Yeah. Why?"

"She may've unearthed a connection between your Quincy fire and Amina's case."

"Now that's a stretch." Frank regarded her for a moment. "She's probably fishing for any kind of link. What'd she say?"

"I don't know. I can't find her." Sarah zeroed in on his eyes for a reaction. "Amina's worried she might be dead."

Frank stopped chewing.

"You know her." Sarah's voice came across firm, accusatory.

"No, I don't." He lifted his water glass, but maintained eye contact.

"Have you ever put an innocent person in jail, Frank?"

"I have." He drained the water until ice clinked against the glass. "And it's the worst feeling."

Sarah remained silent, watching him.

"I arrested a juvenile once for starting a brush fire based on a false witness statement. It was a mess. The kid who really did it was the son of a Boston cop. We eventually figured it all out, but, bottom line, I had an innocent kid in jail awaiting trial for sixty-five days."

"And you don't want it to happen again," Sarah said.

"Never."

"Finished?" the waitress asked. She smiled, cleared their plates, and gave them dessert menus.

"Excuse me a moment." Frank grabbed his cell from the table.

Sarah watched him walk out the door to the sidewalk and make a call. He was checking up on Donna, no question. Sarah figured the reporter had already been in touch with Frank. He obviously knew her and lied about it. What else did Frank know? Could he be withholding information pertinent to her case?

Sarah bottled her anger when he came back. Blowing up at him wouldn't get her anywhere.

"Would you like a cup of coffee or dessert?" Frank asked. "The lobster tails sound incredible. They're stuffed with whipped cream and ricotta. Split one with you?"

"Sure." Sarah forced herself to sound casual.

After placing the order, Frank got up and headed toward the restrooms in the back. Sarah stared at the stray crumbs on the tablecloth. Why had he lied like that? Her gaze lingered on his cell phone. Sarah glanced in the direction of the bathrooms and snatched up the phone. She clicked on the recent calls and saw D. Rapa. Sarah pressed the arrow for her contact information and memorized it.

24

On Saturday morning, Sarah parked next to the curb and double-checked the address for Donna Rapa. She knocked on the front door of the gray-shingled, Nantucket-style cottage, and a dog barked furiously in a low baritone. A slim blonde, who appeared to be in her late twenties, answered the door. She held a big Irish setter back by the collar.

"Donna?" Sarah had to speak up over the barking dog.

The woman stared for a moment. "You've got the wrong person." She shut the door, and the dog continued barking.

Sarah banged again. "I'm not leaving until I speak with Donna Rapa."

"Wrong house. I've never heard of anyone by that name."

"I know you're Donna." Maybe the woman really wasn't Donna, but Sarah wouldn't give in that easily.

"You're wrong." The voice sounded farther away.

"I'm not leaving until you speak with me," Sarah yelled.

"I'll call the police."

"Good. I can tell them you're withholding evidence in a criminal trial. Save me a phone call."

Hurried footsteps came from within and the door opened again. "What the hell are you talking about?"

"I'm Sarah Lynch and—"

"I know who you are." Her words came out rapid and venomous. "Don't threaten me with your lawyer bullshit either."

"You threatened me first with the police." The dog lunged and stuck its wet nose into Sarah's skirt.

Donna yanked him back. "How'd you find me?"

"I did some digging." Sarah felt a twinge of guilt for stealing the contact information from Frank. She did what she had to do, she reminded herself. The dog resumed barking and tugging against the collar.

"Rudy! Stop that." Donna held the door open with her shoulders and gripped the collar with both hands. "Listen, I can't help you. The whole thing's very complicated."

"My client's on trial for murder, and her case is very complicated too."

"You're in way over your head." Donna's knuckles turned white from pulling the dog's collar.

"Enlighten me, then." Sarah looked into her eyes. She had to get through to this woman.

Donna shook her head. "I'm meeting friends for breakfast."

"It'll only take a moment."

"I can't."

"Donna, I'm aware you're writing an article and don't want to be involved in this case. I respect your work product. I'd like to avoid hauling you into court, but I know Amina met with you several times. I need your help."

"I have nothing that will help your client."

"Please, Donna." Sarah clasped her hands together. "I'm just trying to do my job." She hoped Donna could provide her with some kind of explanation. *Anything.*

Donna looked down at her dog for a moment and appeared to be weighing her options. Sarah wondered how Uncle Buddy would sweet-talk this woman and win her trust. He had a knack for it. Sarah had decided against inviting him. She didn't want to tell him about grabbing Donna's information from Frank's cell.

"Great dog, beautiful." Sarah stroked Rudy's head with both hands. "My uncle has a golden named Rehnquist with a matching bow tie."

Donna looked up. "I can picture it."

"Are you rooting for us? For Amina?" Sarah scratched behind the dog's ears.

"Are you convinced she's innocent?"

The direct question caught Sarah by surprise. "I believe she is."

"Well, Frank Brady is convinced that Amina Diallo is guilty."

Sarah was surprised she mentioned Frank. "I know you've been in touch with Frank about this case and its connection to an old Quincy case."

"Frank." Donna's angry tone scared the dog, who started barking again. "*That's* how you got my address. I can't believe him."

"Don't blame Frank." Sarah sighed. She'd have to tell Donna the truth. "I saw your contact information on Frank's cell phone last night after he called you. He doesn't know I did that because he was in the men's room."

"Got something going with him?"

"With Frank? No."

Donna exhaled. "You better hope he doesn't find out."

"I know. I shouldn't have done that." Sarah regarded her. "But I'm desperate. I believe in Amina. I believe in her case. I've got that mortgage broker taking the stand against her this week."

"Mark LaSpada?"

"Yes. And he's smooth, good-looking, makes himself out to be an upstanding business man. It's him against an African immigrant who wears multicolored headscarves to court every day. He'll drive the final nail in Amina's coffin."

"How?"

"LaSpada will tell the jury that Amina stormed into his office, crazy over the pending foreclosure. The woman would do anything to save herself. You see?" Sarah raised her voice.

Donna folded her arms across her chest. "It's not my fault she barged into that office and picked a fight with Mark LaSpada."

Sarah noticed her folded arms, a defensive position. She wondered if Donna felt guilty about meeting with Amina and then hanging her out to dry.

"Donna, when you met with Amina, you enlightened her about your suspicions over all the foreclosures in the area. You fueled her passion. That's why she picked a fight with LaSpada."

"A fight she didn't stand a chance at winning," Donna said.

"Right." Sarah looked into her eyes. "That's why I'm begging for your help now."

"I hate that man." Donna exhaled and finally held the door open. "This has to be brief."

"Thank you." Sarah was making progress, which had seemed impossible when she first arrived. Mentioning Mark LaSpada hit a nerve with Donna. *Good*.

Sarah entered the modest home and smelled fragrant lilac incense. An array of original watercolors and pastels adorned the walls. "Nice artwork."

"They're mine." Donna let go of the dog, who immediately charged over to Sarah and jumped up, with his big paws on her shoulders. "Down, Rudy." She motioned to a floral couch. "Have a seat. Would you like a cup of coffee?"

"That would be wonderful, if you're having one."

Sarah sat down and the dog stuck his wet nose into her lap and stomach.

"Stop that, Rudy." Donna wagged a finger at the dog. "How do you take it?"

"Cream and two sugars. Thank you."

"I'll be right back." Donna left the room through a swinging door.

Sarah closed her eyes for a moment and stroked the dog's wavy auburn hair. She felt drained from a long night of tossing and turning. She wondered why Donna was so defensive and untrusting.

After a few minutes Donna set two cups of coffee on the glass table and sat in a chair across from the couch. Rudy circled once and lay down at her feet.

"Thank you for the coffee."

"Amina is a very passionate woman. I'm afraid meeting with her was a mistake," Donna said.

Sarah pictured the two of them discussing Mark LaSpada and his tactics. Amina would've been all riled up, talking with her hands flying in every direction.

"You're a lot alike. I can see your fighting spirit in the courtroom. Like the Olympics."

"Trial work is more exhilarating." Sarah lifted her cup and gently blew on the edge. "Especially when the stakes are so high."

"I bet." Donna leaned back in her chair. "You know, I felt sorry for Amina even after she stole the papers from my file." Donna sipped her coffee. "It's sad. All those people losing their homes."

"Foreclosures all over the country. Record numbers," Sarah said. "Immigrants like Amina have been hit especially hard."

"And the LaSpadas are taking advantage of the situation."

"Of course they are." Sarah sensed Donna's distaste. She had to play her cards just right, fuel the fire. "You always have those who profit from others' misfortune."

"Yes, but this—" Donna stopped in midsentence and ran her fingers through her hair.

"If we can expose a scandal?"

"The problem is, it's all legal. Those people were supposed to understand the risk when they signed the mortgage papers." Donna mimicked signing a document with her index finger.

"I know, but the practice is unethical," Sarah said.

"Since when does anyone care about ethics? You can preach about it from the rooftops, but you're not going to get your client off." Donna stared into her cup. "We both know that."

"You're right, but I'm not giving up. Amina was onto something when she confronted Mark LaSpada. She hit a nerve when she stormed into his office and spouted off all kinds of stuff from your notes. I think someone was worried she knew too much, so they burned her store. Don't you think Amina was targeted at the arraignment?" Sarah's left arm tingled when she thought about the shooting.

"You might be stretching it." Donna tossed a rawhide bone on the floor, and her dog attacked it with teeth and paws. "Frank thinks the shooter was a Boston fireman out for revenge, and somebody's covering for him."

"He said that?"

Donna nodded. "That's why I got in touch with him in the first place."

"*Frank.*" Sarah felt her anger at him rising higher. She wished he wasn't so single-minded. "Maybe there's something to that old fire in Quincy. Perhaps it wasn't accidental. The LaSpadas could've burned that barn and covered it up. I bet they pulled some strings back then and quashed the investigation." Sarah wished she could view the old file.

"I wouldn't put it past them." Donna watched the dog gnawing at the rawhide. "The LaSpada family is tight with everyone: cops, politicians, you name it." Donna grimaced. "We're swimming with sharks here."

"That means we're better off swimming together."

"Not my style." Donna waved her hand in dismissal.

"Then try something different. Amina's case can only enhance your story, and this one has the potential to be huge."

"I work alone." Donna rose from her chair. "And I should get ready for breakfast."

"Do you have anything I can use against Mark LaSpada?" Sarah had to keep pushing. "I'm running out of time."

Donna walked over to her dog and sat next to him on the floor. She appeared to be studying his teeth as he gnawed the bone.

"Anything?" Sarah asked again.

"Will you promise to leave me out of it? That means no subpoenas to testify in court, and no more surprise visits."

Sarah considered this. Would they need Donna to testify about her meetings with Amina? It could possibly hurt the case by supplying the jury with motive. She wished she could consult with Uncle Buddy.

Donna studied her. Sarah had to make the decision now. What did she have to lose? "I'll leave you alone. I promise."

"Okay." Donna left the room. Sarah recognized the scrape of a metal file cabinet drawer, and the low hum and shuffle of a copy machine. After a good fifteen minutes, she came back with a manila file folder.

"You can have these. They're all public records, mostly from the Registry of Deeds. I can't share my interviews and notes." Donna handed her the file.

"Thank you."

She nodded. "Try unraveling the tangled web of shell companies, limited partnerships, trusts . . . you name it. Maybe your uncle can make something out of it."

"He's got his Registry gals to help him."

"Good, because the records are confusing as hell."

Sarah fingered the smooth folder. "Amina also mentioned something about the governor?"

Donna appeared deep in thought, as if weighing her options again. "You know what you really need?"

"What?"

"A body."

"A body?"

"Yeah. You need to find out who shot you in court during Amina's arraignment and get him to flip."

Sarah stopped at Kelly's Roast Beef on Revere Beach for their famous fried clams with the bellies in honor of Quahog. She also needed to relieve stress by listening to the ocean. The swish of the gentle surf relaxed her mind.

It was low tide. Sarah opened the steaming Styrofoam box and took in the aroma of clams, french fries, and coleslaw. Seagulls circled and screeched overhead. The clams tasted crunchy and chewy and salty. Delicious.

Sarah wrapped her arms around her knees and stared out at the sea after inhaling the meal. She believed they were on course now. Sarah thought back to Amina's phone call from the religious fanatic protesting her blog. They had checked the phone records, but came up empty-handed. Was that theory a dead end? Amina had never heard from that man again. *Keep an open mind.*

Sarah's thoughts drifted. This time guilt surged through her. She shouldn't have taken that information from Frank's cell phone. He lied, she reminded herself, and that was her justification.

She hoped Donna wouldn't tell Frank how she went through his phone. He'd never trust her again. Why would Donna do that? She wouldn't. But, if she did, Sarah would accuse Frank of lying.

Sarah opened the manila file and flipped through the documents. They looked like a complicated jumble of real estate transactions, as Donna had described. Nothing jumped out at her. She'd save it for Uncle Buddy.

Sarah got up and brushed tiny shells from her nylons. How could she find the guy who shot her in court? *An impossible quest.* She gazed at the gray-black ocean, an immense expanse of the unknown. What was she up against? Sarah threw a piece of driftwood as hard as she could toward the horizon. She saw the white splash, but couldn't hear it. For a moment she visualized John and the way he would smile at her with just his eyes. God, how she loved him, her soulmate. Gone. She launched a larger piece of wood, throwing her legs into it, and sending it farther out. How could she find her shooter if she'd never found John's?

Cole watched her as he walked along the shore near the bubbling surf. They were pleased with his work that morning. The money was on its way.

25

Jeanette Giganti waited for the first witness to walk down the aisle. It was a crisp, yet sunny, Monday morning—a fine day for her early batch of daffodils. Perhaps they'd be in bloom after court. The yellow flowers carried her mind back again. Back to the old West End where her mother planted the bulbs in a neat line from the sidewalk to their front stoop. On Sunday she walked over to the spot where she thought Chambers Street might have been. The Longfellow Place high-rise covered all traces of her childhood street.

Jeanette dispelled the image and focused on a tall dapper man in a suit and tie. As he took the oath he towered over Clerk Kelly.

Marinelli positioned himself at the podium. "Good morning. Please introduce yourself to the ladies and gentlemen of the jury."

"Sergeant Frank Brady. I'm with the state police, assigned to the arson unit at the state fire marshal's office."

Jeanette listened to Sergeant Brady recite his education and sixteen years investigating fires and testifying as an expert. He had a deep, crisp voice and came across as a gentleman. Jeanette's eyes shifted into the gallery, where the Boston fire commissioner sat amongst throngs of firemen.

"What is your job as far as this case is concerned?" Marinelli asked.

"To find the origin and cause of the fire."

Jeanette watched Sarah taking notes. She looked particularly striking in her bright blue outfit, a perfect color for a redhead. Today Amina wore a mossy green dress with a subtle foliage pattern. Her headscarf matched the dress.

"Do you recall what happened on Thursday morning, July twentieth of last year?" Marinelli said in a smooth voice.

"At approximately 2:30 a.m. I responded to a fire scene at 107 Waldemar Ave., East Boston. I met with Boston Police Detective Michael Callahan and the deputy fire chief. I learned they were investigating the death of Boston Firefighter Jack Fogerty, and what they had accomplished up to that point. Next, I spoke with witnesses and performed a neighborhood canvas, which means I knocked on all doors with a line of sight to the fire. I also took exterior photographs."

Jeanette leaned forward and examined the photos that Sergeant Brady displayed on his easel. The firemen must have worked hard to extinguish that fire. Just doing their job. And one of them wouldn't make it home. Jeanette looked at the thin young widow.

"Did the fact that they were investigating the death of a Boston firefighter change your investigation?"

"No." Sergeant Brady appeared insulted by the question. "I follow the same protocols; doesn't change how I do my job at all."

Jeanette didn't buy it. Jack Fogerty's death must've changed everything. Of course they'd step up the investigation. A fireman got shot and killed, and the pressure was on.

Marinelli glanced at the jury. "At some point did you meet with the defendant?"

Sergeant Brady nodded. "At approximately 3:30 a.m., Detective Callahan and I interviewed Ms. Diallo in the command center. That's a trailer set up at the scene."

"What did she say?"

"Ms. Diallo gave us background about her grocery store and the pending foreclosure. She appeared angry that she was about to lose everything she had worked for. I also asked if she had insurance, and she told me she did. She didn't know the policy limits, which I found hard to believe."

Sarah and Clancy jumped up for an objection. Jeanette wouldn't know her own insurance policy limits; her husband handled that. Should Amina have known? Did she forget under pressure? Jeanette watched Sarah sitting on the edge of her seat, ready to pop up again and protect her client.

"What else did the defendant say?"

"Ms. Diallo said she went to bed a little before midnight and woke up to noises coming from downstairs in the store. The lights didn't work, but she went down to investigate and saw flames in the back left-hand corner. She ran over to the fire, panicked, and went back upstairs to get her son. It was dark and she couldn't find him in his bed. While she was looking, a fireman came and helped her. They found her son passed out in the living room and made it out of the building."

"What else did you inquire about?"

"I asked if she saw a college-aged man standing outside the store after the fire broke out. She didn't recall seeing *anybody*."

Jeanette wondered why Amina didn't mention the college student. She must've seen him. Did he catch her in the act as Marinelli implied?

"Did you make any observations about the defendant's demeanor?"

"She seemed very nervous, shifty eyes, moving her feet under the table, wringing her hands."

"What did that tell you as an experienced investigator?"

Clancy stood up. "Objection!"

"Overruled."

"Ms. Diallo's actions indicated she was hiding something, not being completely truthful with us."

Jeanette studied Amina. Had she looked guilty or nervous? What was a guilty person supposed to look like?

"What else did you note about the defendant?"

"We told her the firefighter didn't make it. Jack Fogerty. The one who rescued her and her unconscious son. She didn't appear upset at all. Showed no remorse whatsoever."

Sarah slapped her hands on the table. "Objection! Move to strike."

"Overruled."

Jeanette tried to imagine what it was like for Amina after the fire. Living hell. She and her son almost died; they'd barely made it out alive. Jeanette wondered if they'd received the proper medical treatment. Who could answer questions in that frame of mind? Did she have any idea that her every movement and facial expression would be judged? Had Amina asked for a lawyer? Was she read her rights?

"What did you do next?"

"We brought Sergeant Carol O'Brien and her dog, Milo, into the trailer. The dog immediately pointed to Ms. Diallo's slippers. Detective Callahan and I asked her to remove them, and we took them as evidence."

"Were you able to get in the building?"

"Yes, around 6:30 a.m. I proceeded with my investigation of the interior." Sergeant Brady faced the jury. "At first my job is to find the general location where the fire began. Once I do that, I can understand how the fire spread based on patterns of heat, flame, and smoke. These patterns will also indicate the specific area where heat ignited the first fuel. This spot is referred to as the point of origin."

Marinelli rubbed his chin between his thumb and index finger. "Where do you begin?"

"We practice a least-to-most-damage philosophy in fire investigation. The theory is where the fire burns longest and deepest is where the fire came from. So I started by examining the areas with the least damage and moved toward the location with the greatest damage."

"What were your observations?"

Sergeant Brady walked over to the giant easel and replaced the fire photos with enlarged diagrams of the first and second floors of the building. "I observed the lowest and heaviest fire damage to be in this corner." He tapped the back left-hand corner of the first-floor diagram with a pointer. "Right here."

"Can you be more specific about what you saw?"

"Heavy smoke and soot damage. If you stood there and looked up, you could see the sky. The fire had burned a hole right up through to the roof. Upon closer inspection, there appeared to be a lot of damage in the vicinity of the potato chip rack."

"How did you know where the potato chip rack was?"

"Based on conversations I had with the defendant and customers of the store. I also observed some metal melted down, which looked like pieces of rack."

"Did you notice anything else?"

He thought for a moment. "The electrical main to the building had been shut off before the fire started. Found that in the storage area."

Jeanette sat up. Someone flipped the main electrical switch off before the fire? It was definitely a planned arson. Jeanette studied Amina again. If *she* started the fire, why shut off the electricity? It would be that much harder to find her son and escape in the dark, unless she had a flashlight. If someone else did it . . .

"What did you do next?" Marinelli asked.

"Began a de-layering process."

Marinelli glanced at the jury. "What's that?"

"In a fire, things fall on top of the area of origin that don't belong there. We know the fire didn't come from the top and burn down; it came from the bottom and burned up. So stuff from up above falls down, like ceiling materials, light fixtures, roof shingles. For example, we removed a refrigerator and dishes that had fallen down from the upstairs kitchen."

"How long did it take you to de-layer?"

"Three to four hours. It's tedious work. We cleared a section at a time, starting with the locations of the least damage and worked our way to the area of origin. After that, we reconstructed the scene and brought the canine in."

Jeanette tuned out as he rehashed the part about the dog finding gasoline. She hadn't realized how meticulous a fire investigator had to be. She wondered how much the job stress affected his personal life. Despite the polished exterior, Sergeant Brady's eyes looked strained, and he didn't wear a wedding ring. She also caught him glancing over at Sarah on several occasions.

"Wouldn't that piece of latex have melted?" Marinelli asked.

Jeanette tuned in again. She had wondered the same thing about the balloon fragment.

"Under most fire conditions, the latex would've melted. In this particular case the latex was preserved when it somehow got lodged in the crack between the floorboards. It appears that a display of jarred pickles fell and broke on top of it. The pickle juice seeped into the crack, which aided in preserving that latex."

A *pickled balloon?* Jeanette wondered why the prosecution was making such a big deal out of the piece of red latex.

"Did you notice anything else?"

"Yes." He twisted toward the jury. "The first-floor ceiling had several exposed wooden beams running across, and there were four metal hooks screwed into one beam. We found that in the fire debris."

Marinelli introduced a section of the charred beam with the hooks into evidence. Jeanette was baffled. She hoped Sergeant Brady would tie it all in.

"What happened next?"

"I inspected rooms upstairs that were still intact on the right side of the building. In particular, Ms. Diallo had stated that she kept a gun for protection in the bureau next to her bed. She had experienced a problem with break-ins in the past. We checked her bedroom, but the gun wasn't there. Instead, we found a .380 handgun in a heavily charred metal desk drawer in the living room."

Wouldn't Amina know where her gun was? Jeanette wondered why Amina felt the need to keep a gun for protection. Why not have a security system installed? It seemed more dangerous having a gun around with a teenager in the house.

"What did you do when you recovered the weapon?"

"Detective Callahan made a phone call, and Captain Russo arrived from ballistics to recover the gun."

"Please describe the fire damage on the second floor."

Sergeant Brady pointed to the diagram. "I observed black soot and melting above the bedroom window located in the back right-hand corner of the building. I had to determine if the fire spread from the back left corner of the first floor to that back bedroom on right side of the second floor. You see, this hallway running through the center of the upstairs apartment acted as a fire wall."

"What do you mean?"

"It slowed the fire down, preventing it from spreading quickly to the right side. The fire in the second-floor bedroom appeared to be secondary. So I had to study the burn patterns to determine whether there was a connection to the fire on the first floor."

"Did you form any opinions as to the cause of the fire in the second-floor back bedroom?"

Sergeant Brady cleared his throat and looked at the jurors. "I determined that the fire spread from the left-hand corner of the first floor to this second-floor bedroom, despite the long hallway upstairs." He traced the path with his black pointer, made a circular motion, and tapped.

The tapping reminded Jeanette of her old piano teacher at the Peabody House, tapping out the beat with a ruler. Play it again. One more time. Jeanette forced herself to concentrate on the trial. She missed one of Marinelli's questions.

"There's a small bathroom downstairs on the right side of the store. The upstairs bathroom is directly above the downstairs bathroom, and the pipes are connected. The fire from the first floor spread up through those bathroom pipes. The bathroom is next to that back bedroom where we found evidence of the secondary fire."

Jeanette thought Sergeant Brady was overexplaining himself and had rehearsed the answer. It seemed very important that he specify how the fire traveled from down below to the upstairs back bedroom.

Marinelli moved closer to the jury box and raised his

voice. "Sergeant Brady, based on your entire investigation, training, and experience, do you have an opinion as to the cause of this fire?"

"I do."

"And what is your opinion?"

"Objection." Sarah and Clancy rose.

"Overruled," Judge Killam said. "Sergeant Brady is an expert in his field. He's entitled to state his opinion."

"After conducting my investigation and reviewing the lab reports with Professor Moore, there's no doubt this was a set fire. We have an open flame applied to existing combustible materials. Potato chips are highly flammable. In my opinion, an open flame was applied to ignite that potato chip display. Gasoline-filled latex balloons were hung from those metal hooks screwed into the exposed beam above the chips. The heat from the burning chips worked to pop the balloons and disperse gasoline throughout the area, which accelerated the fire."

"Did you rule out all accidental causes?"

"Absolutely. I didn't find any accidental heat source to get those potato chips going in the first place. There were no trash barrels or faulty electrical wiring in the area of origin."

"After determining the origin and cause of the fire, what did you do?"

"I focused on solving the crime, figuring out who had the motive and opportunity to set this fire."

"How'd you do that?"

"I consulted with Detective Callahan and compared all witness statements and reports of firefighters. I reviewed the accelerant testing on the defendant's slippers and other evidence taken from the scene and the defendant's car. I noted there was no evidence of forced entry into the building on the night of the fire. I spoke with the insurance adjuster and discovered information about Ms. Diallo's commercial insurance policy. The evidence showed that Ms. Diallo had both the motive and opportunity to intentionally set her store on fire, and that fire spread to her upstairs apartment."

"Did you make an arrest?"

"I arrested the woman sitting right over there for the crime of arson." Sergeant Brady extended his arm and pointed at Amina. "Specifically, I charged Amina Diallo with the intentional burning of a dwelling place in violation of Massachusetts General Laws, Chapter 266, Section 1."

Jeanette studied the beautiful woman in the green dress sitting beside Sarah. The evidence piled against Amina was staggering based on Sergeant Brady's meticulous investigation. How could they not convict? Why did Jeanette sympathize with her at that very moment? She should be angry, toss her in jail. After all, a fireman died.

Jeanette zeroed in on Sergeant Brady's pointed finger. People had been pointing at that woman for over a year. Pointing. *She did it.* Pointing. Pointing.

26

Sarah rose from her seat, ready to face off with Frank, the one who brought her lunch, and hand-picked flowers from his garden. He had helped foster her career at the DA's office, always singing her praises. If she needed evidence rushed through the state crime lab, Frank would make a phone call and take care of it.

Sarah met his gaze and stiffened. Frank had lied to her about Donna. *Aim right for the goal and shoot.* Uncle Buddy's words resonated. *Pretend he's a big defenseman, and you've gotta get around him to score. It's a tie game, sudden death.*

Sarah assumed center stage. "Sergeant Brady, you interrogated Amina inside a closed trailer?"

"We asked questions."

"You and Detective Callahan?"

"Yes."

"He a big man?"

His lips curled into a slight, but mischievous smile. "Not by NBA standards."

Quahog laughed.

Mocking. Sarah advanced. "You hauled Amina in at three thirty in the morning?"

Frank folded his hands on the witness stand. "She came voluntarily."

"I see. Where was her son at the time?" Sarah knew the answer but wanted to hear it from Frank.

"Mass General."

"The hospital?" Sarah looked at the jury. "The hospital. Amina's son, Malick, was unconscious after escaping the fire?"

"Malick was unconscious when Firefighter Jack Fogerty rescued him, and that would be right before he died from his gunshot wound."

Sarah noted how he managed to slip that in and glance at the jury as he did it. Score for Frank. One to nothing.

"Malick left the scene in an ambulance?"

"Of course."

Sarah placed her hands on her hips. "Let me get this straight. You interrogated Amina at three thirty in the morning, just hours after her store and home burned down, while her son was still in the hospital?"

Frank didn't flinch. "She was a suspect."

"Wow." Sarah had to push his buttons without getting her own pushed in return. *Keep the pressure on and remain calm.* "A suspect already? And you hadn't even entered the burned building?"

"We'd interviewed witnesses."

"No one witnessed Amina lighting her store on fire."

Frank smiled. "It's never that easy."

Quahog laughed again.

Damn him. "Did you interview a homeless man?"

"There weren't any homeless people around as far as I could see."

Sarah feigned a look of surprise. "Amina received medical treatment after the fire?"

"She was treated at the hospital and released."

"It's fair to say Amina had a rough night."

"I'd say so, getting arrested for murder and arson."

Sarah ignored his curt reply. "Did Amina appear tired at 3:30 a.m.?"

"We all were."

"Was she medicated?"

"Not that I recall. Nothing significant."

"You said she looked a bit nervous?"

"Real nervous. Wringing her hands, no eye contact. All the signs."

"You and Detective Callahan were carrying guns?"

"Yes."

"I see. Amina's a single mother?"

"Sure. There are many *law-abiding* single mothers in this city."

He was toying with her. Sarah glanced at the jury. The Italian grandmother gave her a nod of encouragement.

"Wouldn't any mother have been worried about her half-conscious son in the hospital?"

Frank shifted in his seat. "I'm sure she was. I didn't say Ms. Diallo wasn't worried about her son."

Sarah glided to the left and in toward the witness. Change directions, switch topics. "You didn't inspect the roof, did you."

"We had aerial photographs."

"But you didn't personally go up there."

"Too dangerous."

"Did you try accessing the roof from adjacent buildings?"

"Wasn't necessary."

"Oh really." Sarah raised her arms out to the side, a gesture she learned from Uncle Buddy. "It's possible you could've located additional evidence up there."

Frank folded his arms. "We had all the evidence we needed for a conviction, I mean, an arrest."

The jurors looked at Sarah for a comeback. She smiled. "Sergeant Brady, you may have found evidence up on that roof to *convict someone else*."

"I highly doubt that."

Sarah heard the conviction in his words. "There's a fire escape at the end of the row of buildings, right?"

"Exactly." Frank rubbed his fingers together as if he'd anxiously awaited the question. "However, no way anybody could've made it all the way from the roof of the Senegalese Market to that fire escape. Impossible. There's a gap between the buildings numbered 101 and 99 of at least twelve feet. Nobody could've jumped and made it unless he had wings."

Wings. Sarah recalled Danny's angel. She had to think of something fast—the jurors were looking at her again with expectation. "You didn't check that gap between the buildings on the night of the fire, did you?"

"Somebody would've noticed a board or something

bridging the two buildings, if that's where you're going with this."

"But you didn't personally check for a board, did you?"

"I didn't personally check. No."

Sarah caught a nod of encouragement from the foreperson. Perhaps he was rooting for her. "It's possible somebody could've been hiding in the storage room?"

"Possible, but I doubt it."

"In fact, the main electrical switch was located in that room?"

"Yes."

"And someone switched it off before the fire started?"

"It appears so."

"Did you check that switch for prints?"

"No, we couldn't due to the fire debris."

"The storage room is in close proximity to that potato chip display?"

"It is."

"Someone hiding in there could take a few steps over to the potato chip display and light that fire." Sarah raised her voice.

"Just as easily as your client could've done it from anywhere in the building."

"You didn't answer my question."

"I apologize." Frank drew a deep breath. "It's possible someone could've started the fire after hiding in the storage room."

"Someone hiding in the storage room wouldn't have to break into the store, would he?" Sarah had to counter the prosecution's evidence of no forced entry on the night of the fire, which was damaging to her client.

"No."

Sarah got her answer and decided to jump to her next topic. "The upstairs apartment had a long hallway which acted as a fire wall protecting the back bed-room?"

"Yes."

"The chair cushion and rug samples collected in that back bedroom contained an accelerant?"

"Fingernail polish remover."

"That accelerant had been spilled on a chair and part of the rug next to the window?"

"Yes, but—"

"That was the only window with access to the roof?" Frank shrugged. "It was."

"It's possible someone could've poured that liquid on the chair and rug to get a second fire going up there?"

"A bottle of nail polish remover is a common household item, which is often found in ladies' bed-rooms. My theory is that Ms. Diallo did her nails while sitting in that chair next to her window. The bottle of nail polish remover was probably sitting on the small stand adjacent to the chair. It may have melted and tipped over due to the heat of the fire, which caused the acetone to spill on the chair and rug."

"Sergeant Brady, your *theory* is that the acetone spilled accidentally. You have nothing concrete to back it."

"My years of training and experience and studying fire behavior back my theory. Amina Diallo set that fire on the first floor with gasoline-filled balloons, and the fire spread upstairs through the bathroom pipes."

Again, Sarah heard the conviction in Frank's words. There was nothing she could say to change his mind. She had to be careful not to challenge Frank in his area of expertise. Sarah would have her own fire expert tes-tify later on, which would support her theories.

"Sergeant, you simply failed to investigate the strong possibility that someone else lit the fire downstairs and had no choice but to start a second fire upstairs with matches and acetone and escape onto the roof. You didn't do your job."

Marinelli jumped up. "Objection!"

"Overruled."

"I did my job, counselor."

Sarah's instincts told her to fight, go for the jugular. *Now.* "Let's face it, Sergeant. This was a classic rush to judgment. You had to make this arrest to flaunt your superior skills in front of the Boston police and firemen. And with the governor following the case—"

"That's not true." Frank looked out into the gallery of firemen and back at Sarah.

Sarah folded her arms and stared at Frank.

"You don't know what you're talking about."

"Really?" Sarah felt the sting of his words.

"That's right."

"Ahh. I see." Sarah rubbed her chin. "You're repeating your mistake."

"What?"

"Objection," Marinelli said.

"Sustained. Put a question before the witness."

"Didn't you make a mistake under similar circumstances?"

"I'm not following you." Frank's eyes narrowed.

"Three years ago you arrested the wrong person?"

"Okay, I see where this is going." Frank gripped the sides of the witness stand; his fingers turned white. "I did, counselor."

"That's when you held an innocent juvenile in custody for sixty-five days."

"The witness against him recanted." Frank scanned the jury box. "We all learn from our mistakes."

"I see." Sarah gestured toward Amina. "It would be a

shame to make another mistake when the stakes are so high, wouldn't it, Sergeant?"

Frank held eye contact with her and folded his hands on the podium. "You're absolutely right."

"Thank you." Sarah smiled. "Nothing further."

27

Nick packed up his legal pads and trial materials. He savored the moment alone as the crowded gallery thinned out. The firemen and union officials would be waiting to make snide remarks about Frank in the hallway. They loved mimicking the bowlegged state police strut.

Sarah waltzed over in the slim electric blue suit that had distracted his male jurors all day; it accentuated her eyes. *She'd do anything to win.*

"Hey," she said.

"Why'd you get so personal with Frank?"

"I had to."

"No, you didn't. That's crossing the line."

"We're going to win."

He noticed the willpower in her voice and eyes. "You're so full of yourself."

"As I should be." Again Sarah looked determined. "Got a motion for you." She fluttered the stapled papers. At least the packet wasn't too thick for a regular staple.

"What do you want now?"

"We're amending our witness list." Sarah flicked her wrist and flung the document on his table like a Frisbee.

Nick scanned it. "This is bullshit. Who's Danny Sullivan?"

"The homeless guy. Gonna blow your case right out of the water."

"Not a chance. Callahan already spoke with him. This guy is nutso."

"Oh, really? Where's his witness statement? Are you holding back on us, Nick?" She placed her hands on her hips. "I'll have to ask for sanctions."

"We'll give you a report and it'll contain one word: incompetent. No way Killam's gonna let him take the stand."

"We'll see about that." Sarah swung her hips while walking down the corridor and turned abruptly as if she wanted to catch him watching her. "By the way, Nick, how come you didn't ask Sergeant Brady about . . . never mind."

"What?"

Sarah left Nick standing there. Did he really forget to ask something? He reviewed the testimony in his mind. With so much to cover, it was easy to leave out a question or two. That's why he made checklists. Lately his life resembled one big list of things to do. He dug through the crammed expandable file folder searching for the legal pad of the day.

After reviewing all the check marks, it dawned on him. Sarah was pulling his leg. He threw the pad down. He should've known better.

Nick jammed the pad back into his folder and looked across at the empty seats in the jury box. Who was on his side? The black foreperson seemed riveted by Sarah, as did the Dominican barber. They clung to her every word. The giant clam looked convinced Amina did it from the get-go. The liberal art teacher with the bangles worried him most. She had frowned throughout Frank's testimony. Liberals like her would sympathize with a poor, downtrodden single immigrant mother and hold the police to a higher standard. The grandmother from Revere had nodded at Sarah when Frank came up with his snide comments. Nick had advised him not to do that.

Nick carried a heavy file under each arm and headed toward the frenzy awaiting him in the hallway. He'd answer the inevitable questions and zip downstairs to the office. Mark LaSpada, the mortgage broker, was scheduled to testify the following morning. That guy was a son of a bitch, apt to say anything he pleased.

Nick pushed through the heavy courtroom doors. Frank led the attack. "What's her problem? Sarah raised it to a personal level, made me look incompetent, attacked my integrity. I told her about arresting the wrong guy in confidence, as a friend."

"Well, that was a big mistake." Nick shook his head. "You can't trust her anymore."

"Mr. Marinelli? Mr. Marinelli?"

Nick turned and stared into a news camera.

"Is it true you're having witness problems?" A pretty blond reporter stuck a microphone under his chin.

She caught him off guard. "What? Not that I'm aware of." He hesitated for a moment, sometimes the press knew more than he did. "I can't comment on the case."

"Sources say the police are looking for an accomplice? Did Amina Diallo act alone?"

"No comment."

"Is the defense team adding a witness?"

"Mr. Marinelli?" Nick spun in the opposite direction. It was the widow's voice. A union official stood guard by her side.

"How do you think it's going?" Maureen wrung her hands and looked into his eyes.

"Good, I guess." Nick cringed at his own words. Why did he say that? His voice had come across uncertain and dismissive.

The union guy stepped forward and leaned into his face. "That all you got to say to her?"

Nick felt light-headed. Maybe this guy would knock him out cold and put him out of his misery. When did he eat last? Did he have a hotdog for lunch? No, the hotdog was last week. "I'm sorry, Maureen, you're right. I—"

"Nick?"

He held up an index finger. It was his victim-witness advocate.

Nick placed a hand on Maureen's shoulder. "You can come down to my office, and we'll discuss the case in private. It's crazy out here. I can't even think straight."

"No." Maureen looked resigned.

"You sure?"

She nodded and walked away. The union guy placed an arm around her and glared over his shoulder. Beyond them, Nick spotted the Marinelli gang: his parents, grandparents, aunts, uncles, and cousins. They performed a synchronized wave and gestured him over.

Someone tapped him from behind. "Excuse me?"

Nick turned toward the unfamiliar voice, but his victim-witness advocate grabbed him by the elbow. "You have to come down to the office," she whispered. "It's real important. The governor wants you to brief him now. He can't wait because he'll be in a meeting all afternoon. Oh, I almost forgot, Mr. LaSpada is stuck in Sarasota."

"What?"

"Says it's impossible for him to be here tomorrow and wants to know if the judge will postpone the case a day or two."

"He has to be here. There's no choice."

"He can't."

Detective Callahan barged in between them. "Nick, you have to come with me right now. It's important."

Frank pushed his way in. "What is it?"

Callahan hesitated. "You can come too."

"*Oh, I can come.*" Frank scowled. "I have to have *your* permission now?"

Callahan smacked his lips. "You're in a bad mood because you just got spanked on the stand."

"F—"

Nick held out his hand and dropped one of the files. The elastic band snapped; papers scattered. "Don't fight out here." He lowered his voice. "There's a reporter." He could see it now, the two of them shouting expletives back and forth. Front-page news for the *Herald*.

"Nick! You have to call the governor," the victim-witness advocate said. "And what shall I tell LaSpada?"

"That he has to be here!" Nick closed his eyes. He didn't mean to snap at her. "Sorry. I'll deal with LaSpada. Can you have Captain Russo on standby for me just in case?"

"He's sick."

"Too bad."

"Throwing up sick."

"We'll place a bucket next to the witness stand."

Nick squatted and gathered the loose papers. His head throbbed.

Callahan handed him a pile with everything out of order and discombobulated. "Come on, Nick. Let's go. This can't wait."

"Whaaat?"

"The meeting."

. . .

Nick briefed the governor on his cell phone as he sat in the backseat of Callahan's unmarked cruiser amidst the empty Styrofoam coffee cups, old sports pages, and Big Red wrappers. He could barely hear over the bickering between Callahan and Frank up front.

"Why do they keep bringing my name up during the trial?" Noterman asked.

"I don't know." Nick hadn't noticed it happening that much. "You were there on the first day of the trial, and you've been vocal about the case in the news. That's probably why."

"Object next time." The governor yelled into the receiver and hung up. Now Nick hated politicians more than ever.

Callahan parked beneath a sign that read: LAW OF-FICE OF ALLEN CHASE, PERSONAL INJURY AND CRIMINAL DEFENSE. FREE CONSULTATIONS! A plastic Christmas wreath adorned the door even though it was almost spring.

Nick rested his head on the back of the seat. "Why are we *here*?"

Callahan looked around before getting out. "Just bear with me."

"God."

Ron Meehan scrambled up to the car. "What took you guys so long?"

Both Callahan and Frank pointed at Nick.

"What can I say? I'm only in the middle of the big-gest trial of my life, and I don't even know what's going on. Tomorrow's witness is stuck on a golf course in Florida. This better be good." Nick shook hands with the charismatic Ron Meehan, who knew everyone who was anyone across New England and beyond. He was a former law clerk, member of the coast guard, cop, private investigator, and currently headed up the state's Arson Watch Reward Program.

"You're not gonna believe it." Ron talked fast. "Attorney Chase called me this afternoon. He's got a client who witnessed something big."

Nick mulled it over. "Why'd he call you and not us?" The answer popped into his mind before Ron could respond. "Oh don't tell me. The client's looking for reward money and Allen Chase wants his third. I've heard it all now. They probably concocted this scheme together."

Frank laughed. "I have to side with Nick on this one."

Callahan ignored him. "Come on. Just hear what this guy has to say. I wouldn't bring you down here for nothing."

Ron nodded. "Yeah, it's interesting."

Nick rolled his eyes. "I've no doubt about that. Tell me, is this witness one of Chase's personal injury or criminal clients?" He didn't know which was worse.

"Both," Ron said.

"Wonderful. Anything else I should be aware of?"

"Right now he's out on bail for armed robbery."

Nick grimaced. What would Sarah think if he put this guy on the stand? An alcoholic, dysfunctional homeless man sounded better. "And I'm sure he was watching the trial on television."

Ron's eyes lit up. "Actually, he was, and that's how—"

Nick raised his hands. "Alright. Alright. Alright." He was afraid to ask any more questions. "I surrender."

28

"**Something's up with** Mark LaSpada being stuck down in Florida." Uncle Buddy sat next to Sarah at the defense table that morning and leaned over to remove his galoshes. "They're panicking."

"It'll give us more time to pore through the documents Donna gave me." Sarah didn't mind the extra time to prepare for the mortgage broker's cross.

"True." Uncle Buddy drummed his fingers on his lips. "From what I've deciphered so far, Mark LaSpada was working with his father's development company, targeting East Boston. We can connect them to multiple foreclosures in that area. But I'd like to know why."

"To take advantage of people, make money." *Wasn't that obvious?*

"But why stick to East Boston?" Uncle Buddy said.

"We may not have to answer that. If we can make LaSpada look slippery in front of the jury, they'll have more sympathy for Amina."

"It bothers me right here." Uncle Buddy patted his stomach. "Never ignore your gut."

"Ha. Uncle Buddy, you're just hungry again."

"My bus ran late. I didn't have time to stop for the lemon pastry."

"I knew it." Sarah had been analyzing her own gut feelings from the time she met with Donna. She knew there was so much more to the case that Donna hadn't revealed. Sarah had to figure out how to find her shooter. "I was up until two in the morning sifting through old newspaper articles on the Quincy fire and the neighborhood fight over that antique barn. I made a list of people to call."

"Bah humbug with the phone." Uncle Buddy swatted the air. "Let's take a drive down to Quincy after court. We'll walk around and talk to folks in person. I'll bring Rehnquist."

"Good idea." Rehnquist always won people over. "Hey, did your political cronies say anything about the governor?" Sarah forgot to ask him about his evening at Locke-Ober.

"Noterman's obsessed with his casino, and he's strongarming everybody on Beacon Hill to support him. That's the buzz."

"So Amina's case is all about publicity?"

Uncle Buddy's lips formed a sly grin. Sarah knew that look. "What are you scheming now?"

"If it's publicity he craves, let's give it to him."

"What do you mean?"

"We'll bring his name up during the trial whenever possible."

They both laughed.

A guard escorted Amina into court. She looked disheveled and exhausted, with dark circles below her eyes. The case, with its ups and downs, was grinding their client down. Amina had praised Sarah after her cross-examination of Frank, and she appeared hopeful for the first time. But now they were about to face the gun expert, who could tie Amina to shooting the fireman and seal her fate.

Sarah wished she could do more for her. She had to try everything both inside and outside the courtroom to arrive at the truth. *Keep an open mind. Examine all possibilities.*

"You look quite serious today, Sarah." Nick approached the defense table with a handful of papers and a smug grin.

"And good morning to you, Nick. Looks like you have something up your sleeve." Sarah braced herself.

"I do."

"Bring it on." Uncle Buddy adjusted his new bow tie, preparing for battle.

Nick fanned the papers across their table. "If you can add to your witness list, I can add to mine."

Sarah flipped to the second page. "Alex Kryuchkov? Who's that?"

"Nobody important. Just an eyewitness who caught your client filling those balloons with gasoline."

Amina gasped.

"All rise!" the clerk said.

Derrick sat in the foreperson's chair at 9:00 a.m. and glanced at Sarah. She appeared preoccupied with a packet of papers. Amina also seemed particularly distraught. On the other hand, Clancy came across more confident than ever.

"I wonder what they'll do with *that*?" Christine nudged him and pointed to a charred metal desk in front of the clerk's table.

"Wow." Derrick had been so focused on the defense table that he somehow missed it. "I can smell that thing from here." He recalled something about a desk when Sergeant Brady testified. What was it?

Marinelli stood behind his podium. "Please introduce yourself to the ladies and gentlemen of the jury."

"Captain James Russo, Boston Police."

Derrick could tell by the gruff voice and confident

demeanor that this guy was a veteran police investigator. He wondered how many more witnesses Marinelli had left to call. Going to court and running back every day to put out fires at his computer business had become a grind. His main tech guy attempted to manage the store but often sent customers into a tailspin. No one needed to know the minutiae behind a computer—how it worked or why it didn't. Derrick removed his glasses and rubbed his eyes. He longed for another cup of the burnt courthouse coffee.

"How long have you been employed with the Boston police?"

"Twenty-four years total. I've been assigned to the ballistics unit for eighteen years."

Derrick felt his stomach tighten. Captain Russo would've been a rookie back when Derrick witnessed that gang shooting years ago. Why had he been such a coward? Was it too late to come forward now? Derrick still remembered the name of the shooter.

"My training consists primarily of hands-on experience. I've attended armorer's school, conducted by various gun manufacturers, where we learn how weapons are manufactured and assembled. I've also trained at the FBI Academy."

"What are your duties and responsibilities?"

"I gather and preserve firearms and related evidence at crime scenes, attend autopsies, conduct test firings of weapons and microscopic examinations of recovered evidence."

"How many weapons have you examined or test fired?"

"Over two thousand."

"How many times have you testified as an expert in the field of firearms identification?"

"Over five hundred times."

"How many fatal-shooting investigations have you participated in?"

"North of seven hundred, including accidents and suicides. Approximately 125 of those would be homicides."

Derrick was impressed. This guy knew what he was doing. He imagined the all-nighters Captain Russo pulled over the course of his career. Most of it had to be gang-related violence.

"On July twentieth of last year, at approximately 3:45 a.m., what happened?"

"I proceeded to 107 Waldemar Avenue, East Boston, where Detective Michael Callahan and Sergeant Frank Brady brought me up to speed on the alleged shooting of Boston Firefighter Jack Fogerty during an early morning fire."

"What did you do after that?"

"I questioned the defendant, Amina Diallo, in the command center. I asked her if she owned any guns. She said she owned a .380 auto caliber handgun, which she routinely stored in a drawer near the cash register during business hours or in her bedside bureau at night. She denied firing the gun at any time during the previous twenty-four hours."

"On July twentieth of last year at approximately 6:00 a.m., what did you do?"

"I attended Jack Fogerty's autopsy at the morgue. I observed his wounds and received a projectile from the medical examiner."

Derrick leaned forward. He'd been waiting for more information about the shooting. He didn't know what to make of Andy Larson's testimony about seeing Amina squatting and pointing a gun through the thermal imaging screen.

"What were your initial observations at the autopsy?"

Marinelli grabbed his legal pad and moved closer to the jury box.

"First, I examined the victim's clothing. I observed one small hole in the front of the turnout coat, and another small hole in the front of the tee shirt."

"Did you bring that clothing with you to court today?"

"Yes." Captain Russo withdrew a black fireman's coat and white tee shirt from a clear plastic bag.

"Is that clothing in the same condition now as it was when you took it at the autopsy?"

"Yes."

Derrick watched Marinelli show the clothing to Clancy and Sarah and admit it into evidence. "What did you see next?"

"I viewed the victim with his clothes off and observed a small hole in his abdomen. It was in the shape of a concentric circle with red around the edges."

"What did that shape indicate to you?"

"The circular shape is consistent with an entrance wound caused by a projectile as it perforates the skin." Captain Russo looked at Derrick. "A projectile is a bullet."

"What did you do next?"

"I had the entrance wound photographed."

Marinelli introduced several enlarged photographs of the circular entrance wound into evidence. Derrick took note of the perfectly round shape. "What happened after that?"

"The medical examiner removed a projectile from the abdominal area and gave it to me. I maintained custody of that projectile and took it to the crime lab for further examination."

"Did you bring the projectile with you today?" Marinelli walked toward the witness.

"Yes."

"Is that projectile in the same condition now as it was when you took it at the autopsy?"

"It is."

Marinelli introduced the small bullet into evidence and handed it back to Captain Russo. "Did you examine this at the lab?"

"Yes, later in the day."

"What were your observations?"

"It weighs ninety-five grains and is a full-metal-jacketed projectile, which means the outer layer of the bullet is composed of a copper jacket surrounding a lead core. It's designed for complete penetration, the most common type of bullet."

"What else can you tell us about the bullet?"

Captain Russo displayed the bullet between his thumb and index finger and faced the jury. "I can tell you which type of weapon is most consistent with firing this projectile by examining its class characteristics. You see, when a gun is discharged, the expansion of the fired cartridge and pressure propelling the bullet through the barrel scrape or push it against the rifling."

Marinelli squinted. "What do you mean by *rifling*?"

"Rifling refers to the drilling process used to hollow out the barrel. Each manufacturer uses a somewhat different process to create small spiral grooves on the inside. The surfaces or ridges of these grooves are called lands. Therefore the bullet will bear the impressions of the lands and grooves along with other imperfections or striations within the barrel."

"What is the purpose of the rifling or grooves inside the barrel?"

"Spiral grooving within the barrel causes the projectile to spin when discharged, which stabilizes it during flight. Some manufacturers use spiral grooves to create a clockwise spin, which is also called a right-hand twist. Others utilize a counterclockwise spin or left-hand twist."

Derrick knew what was coming next. Captain Russo would inform them that Amina's gun fired the shot that killed Firefighter Jack Fogerty. That would bolster Andy Larson's sketchy testimony about witnessing Amina pointing the gun during the fire. He noticed the concentration amongst his fellow jurors. No one moved.

Marinelli made eye contact with Derrick. "When you studied the lands and grooves on the projectile recovered from Jack Fogerty, did you draw any conclusions?"

"Yes. I determined that this projectile is most consistent with being fired from a .380 auto caliber handgun with a rifling system of six lands and grooves with a right hand twist."

What a mouthful. Derrick jotted that down as fast as he could.

"Did you perform any other tests at the lab?"

"I tested the victim's clothes for gunshot residue."

"What were the results?"

"The test came out negative, which indicates that the muzzle of the weapon was a distance of three or more feet from the victim at the time of discharge."

"Did you go back to the crime scene?"

Captain Russo nodded. "After attending the autopsy, I brought evidence over to the lab and then went right out to the crime scene again at about 7:45 a.m."

"What did you do upon arrival?"

"I followed Detective Callahan and Sergeant Brady to the second-floor living room and observed a burned metal desk, which had a set of three drawers on each side. I opened the top right-hand drawer and saw a

.380 auto caliber semiautomatic pistol. I had photographs taken at that time."

"Did you bring that desk to court today?"

"Yes." Captain Russo pointed to the heavily charred desk next to the clerk's table, and Marinelli introduced it into evidence. Derrick looked forward to checking it out during deliberations.

"Did you bring the .380 auto caliber semiautomatic pistol to court with you today?"

"Yes." Captain Russo raised a clear evidence bag containing a small black handgun.

"Is that gun in the same condition now as it was when you found it in the desk drawer on July twentieth?"

"Yes it is."

Marinelli introduced the gun into evidence, and Derrick wondered if the jurors would be allowed to handle it.

"What further observations did you make?" Marinelli handed the gun to Captain Russo, who placed it gently on the witness stand.

"I observed a hole in the front of the desk drawer measuring approximately three-eighths of an inch wide." Captain Russo walked over to the desk and removed the charred top drawer. He turned it around and pointed out the hole to the jury. "The bevel of the metal on the outside is consistent with an exit hole; the entrance hole is from within the drawer. Gunshot residue was present on the interior of the drawer as well."

"Did you observe anything else?"

"Yes." He walked back to the witness stand and raised the handgun. "This is a .380 auto caliber semiautomatic pistol with a rifling system of six lands and grooves with a right-hand twist. I also noted a partially extracted cartridge case jammed in the ejection port;

the grips are off, and there are five melted cartridge cases in the magazine. There was no projectile in the barrel."

"What did your observations about the weapon and the condition of the desk drawer tell you?"

"That this weapon discharged inside the desk drawer due to excessive heat from the fire. There was a heat duct right under the desk. Heat from the fire traveled up through that duct and made the drawers real hot like an oven."

So the gun went off in the drawer. Derrick glanced over at Sarah, Clancy, and Amina. He remembered what Sarah had said in her opening statement: *keep an open mind*. She was right. This case was far from simple. In fact, it was very confusing. Were the others getting it?

"Did you examine the weapon later on at the lab?"

Captain Russo nodded. "I measured the width of the lands and grooves inside the barrel. I then compared them with the lands and grooves on the projectile recovered from Jack Fogerty's body."

"Did you draw any conclusions based upon your comparisons?"

"Yes. The projectile removed from Jack Fogerty's body shares the same class characteristics as the weapon recovered from the desk drawer. The widths are identical between the lands and grooves. Both reveal a rifling system of six lands and grooves with a right-hand twist."

Derrick scratched his head. Was this an accidental shooting? Did the gun go off by itself and kill the fireman? Why hadn't the murder charges against Amina been dismissed? It all boiled down to whether Andy Larson was a believable witness.

"Did you note anything else in your investigation?" Marinelli asked.

"I did. When the weapon discharged in the drawer,

the projectile went through the metal, which caused it to slow down and wobble in flight. If that projectile had traveled through the metal drawer and into the victim's body, the entrance hole in the body would've been irregular in shape due to the wobbling. However, the entrance hole that I observed in the victim's body was a clean, concentric circle. In my opinion, the projectile recovered from the victim's body was not fired when the weapon discharged in the drawer due to excessive heat."

Derrick exchanged an incredulous glance with Christine. So somebody shot Jack Fogerty, and *it wasn't accidental*. The bullet that went through the charred drawer apparently didn't strike the fireman. But where did the fatal bullet come from? The one that struck Fogerty in the stomach?

"Is it possible someone fired that weapon at Jack and then placed it in the drawer?" Marinelli must've read his mind.

Sarah jumped to her feet. "Objection! Leading."

"Overruled. This is expert testimony, counselor. Captain Russo may state his opinion."

Captain Russo appeared annoyed by the interruption. "It's possible someone could've fired this weapon, shot Fogerty, and placed it in the drawer. In that scenario, the entrance wound in the victim would appear like a concentric hole." He raised an enlarged photograph of Fogerty's gunshot wound before the jury. "Just like you see in this autopsy photograph."

"Were you able to trace the ownership of the weapon recovered from the drawer?"

"I traced the serial number, which was still intact. This weapon is registered to the defendant, Amina Diallo."

Marinelli paused and glared at Amina. "So you're telling us that the projectile recovered from Fogerty's body shares the same class characteristics as the weapon registered to Amina Diallo?"

"Yes."

"Did you have any further conversations with the defendant?"

"Ms. Diallo said she kept her gun in her bedside bureau, but we recovered it in the desk drawer in the living room." Captain Russo puffed his chest out.

"Did you confront Ms. Diallo with that information?"

"Yes and she suddenly remembered that she'd been doing paperwork at her living-room desk and forgot to put the gun in her bedroom bureau."

Marinelli cocked his head and gazed into the jury box. "No further questions."

Derrick nodded when Marinelli looked at him. The young prosecutor obviously wanted the jurors to make the connection that the bullet that killed Jack Fogerty came from the type of gun owned by Amina Diallo.

Derrick watched Clancy get up for cross-examination after the lunch break. He'd probably have a field day with this one. Derrick wondered if he got the new bow tie on sale at Target, since it was adorned with red circular target patterns.

"Captain Russo, how are you today?"

"Fine."

"Did you speak with the defendant?"

"Yes."

Clancy walked over to the clerk's table, removed the gun from its evidence bag, and held it in both hands.

Judge Killam leaned over the bench. "Keep that weapon pointed down, Clancy. We don't want any accidents, especially with all the targets on your bow tie." People in the gallery and jury box laughed. Captain Russo remained stoic.

"Of course, Your Honor. Best I could do with the tie." Clancy grinned at the jurors and faced Captain Russo. "Amina told you this was her gun?"

Captain Russo paused before answering. "She did."

"And that was before you traced the serial number?" Another pause. "Correct."

"She was up-front and cooperative when you spoke with her?"

"Yes."

"Your conversation occurred in that cramped trailer with Detective Callahan and Sergeant Brady present?"

"It did."

"Amina told you this is the only weapon she owns?" Clancy raised the handgun up and down as he spoke.

"Yes."

"And this is the only gun she's ever possessed in the store or upstairs apartment?"

"That's what *she* said."

"Amina told you she needed this .380 semiautomatic for protection? After all, she's a single mother?"

"Yes."

Derrick noticed how well Captain Russo maintained his cool. His answers were short and to the point, and he didn't volunteer any additional information. The veteran captain kept his eyes fixed on Clancy, listening carefully to each question. These two old-timers were pros. Derrick wondered how many times they'd faced off in court.

"Did you ask Amina where she routinely stores this weapon?"

Captain Russo nodded. "The defendant informed us that during the day she keeps the gun in a drawer near the cash register. After hours, she stores it in her bedside bureau."

"On the eve of the fire, Amina had been doing paperwork at this desk in the living room?"

"Paying bills."

"And she went to bed around midnight?"

"According to her statement . . . yes."

"Amina left the gun in that desk drawer in the living room?" Clancy pointed to the charred desk.

"The defendant told us she was tired and forgot to bring the weapon into the bedroom with her."

"Amina told you she kept five cartridges in the magazine and one in the chamber?"

Captain Russo considered the question. "The defendant's exact words were that she *believed* there were five cartridges in the magazine and one in the chamber." His words came out measured, calculated.

"Five." Clancy held the gun in his left hand and raised five fingers. "One projectile was discharged from the chamber due to excessive heat from the fire?"

"The weapon discharged in that drawer."

"*One* bullet was discharged in the drawer?"

"That's what the evidence suggests."

"If there were six cartridges altogether in this gun and one was fired due to excessive heat, that leaves you with five cartridges left in the gun."

"Correct."

"How many cartridges did you find in this gun after you recovered it in the drawer?"

"Five."

"Did you test fire the gun?"

"The weapon was rendered inoperable due to melting."

"So you couldn't test fire this gun."

"No."

"Did you take a casting of this weapon to match striations or other individual marks within the barrel?"

"I attempted to, but those types of individual characteristics were insufficient for identification due to excessive heat and melting."

Derrick watched Clancy grab the bullet from the clerk's table and roll it between two fingers in his right hand, while holding the weapon with his left. "When this weapon discharged in the drawer, it would've created an irregular entrance wound in the victim because it passed through the metal drawer."

"Correct."

"But you observed a concentric circle in the victim caused by this projectile entering the abdominal area." Clancy raised the bullet and walked the length of the jury box.

"Yes."

"Therefore, this bullet did not come from this gun when it discharged in the drawer."

"It did not."

"You have no direct proof that the defendant's gun fired any projectiles besides the one discharged through the drawer."

"That's right."

"And we know this one projectile that discharged in the drawer was not the one that entered Fogerty's body."

"That is my opinion."

"A .380 auto caliber semiautomatic pistol is a very common handgun?"

"Yes."

He raised the gun in the air and waved it from side to side. "So this weapon in my hand is very common?"

"Yes."

Clancy looked at the bullet and into the jury box, making eye contact with Derrick. "Captain Russo, is it possible that someone else could've shot Jack Fogerty with a .380 auto caliber semiautomatic pistol and escaped across the roof?"

Marinelli pounded his fist on the table. "Objection! Calls for speculation."

"Overruled."

"It's possible." Captain Russo kept his eyes fixed on Clancy.

"Thank you, Captain. No further questions." Clancy replaced the evidence on the clerk's table.

"Redirect?"

Marinelli rounded his table before Clancy had the chance to sit down. "If I may, Your Honor."

"Proceed."

Marinelli picked up the handgun and held it out before him. "Captain Russo, how many cartridges is this handgun capable of holding when it's fully loaded?"

"Seven altogether. Six in the magazine and one in the chamber."

"It's possible that two shots could've been fired from this gun?" Marinelli raised two fingers.

Sarah rose. "Objection, leading."

"Sustained. This is redirect examination."

"How many cartridges did you recover from this weapon?"

"Five."

"If this gun had been fully loaded, how many shots could've been fired?"

"Two."

"Nothing further." Marinelli kept his two fingers raised as he walked in front of the jury box and replaced the gun on the clerk's table.

Judge Killam checked his watch and eyed Clancy. "Recross?"

"I'll make it quick."

Judge Killam grunted. "I've heard that one before."

Clancy rubbed his lower back. "Captain, you didn't recover any missing cartridge cases?"

"No."

"Was there any gunshot residue on Amina's hands?"

"No, but she had been treated at the hospital before we had the chance to test her hands."

"The defendant's clothing tested negative for gunshot residue as well?"

"It did."

Clancy walked over to the clerk's table and took the gun. He positioned himself in front of the jury box and turned the weapon over and over in his hands without saying a word.

Judge Killam sighed. "Counselor?"

"Captain, you have no evidence whatsoever that this gun fired any bullets besides the one that accidentally discharged through the drawer." Clancy's voice boomed and reverberated throughout the courtroom.

"Correct."

Clancy smiled. "Thank you once again, Captain Russo, for your most helpful testimony."

Derrick studied the defendant as she sat next to Sarah. Would Amina have shot the fireman and placed the gun back in the drawer during the fire? How could she see in the dark? Why not throw the gun into the kitchen, which was probably burning pretty good by then? Perhaps she was standing near the desk when she shot the fireman, panicked, and stuck it back in the drawer out of habit.

He wished he could hear Andy Larson's testimony again. Did he really see Amina pointing that gun through the thermal imaging screen?

Derrick found it difficult to concentrate on the next

witness, an assistant medical examiner for Suffolk County. The mundane doctor described the autopsy with too much detail. *A forensic overload.* Christine appeared to take interest in the medical jargon due to her occupation as a pediatric nurse. Derrick knew the cause of death was important to remember: a bullet wound to the outer capsule of the spleen.

The pain must've been excruciating.

29

Out of the corner of her eye, Sarah could see Frank hovering at the entrance to the attorneys' bar with his arms crossed. The people in the spectators' gallery had cleared out for the day, including Nick.

"What's he want? Still mad about your cross?" Uncle Buddy whispered.

"I'm about to find out." Sarah hoped it wasn't about her taking the information from his phone. If so, why would Donna tell him?

"Good luck."

"Thanks, judging by the look on his face, I'm going to need it." Sarah rose and pretended to be organizing papers.

"I'll step out for a moment. Remember, we have to grab Rehnquist and head down to Quincy."

"I'll join you by the elevators in a minute." Sarah waited until Uncle Buddy left and they were alone. "Hi," she said.

Frank walked up to her table and sat on the edge. "Is that all you have to say?"

"If this is about my cross-examination of you . . . I did what I had to do. No hard feelings, okay?"

"No hard feelings?" Frank crossed his arms. "The other night at dinner, we went out as friends." He gazed into her eyes. "Old friends. I even told you about my sister."

"Frank—" Sarah slumped back down in her chair. *His sister. Kerry, with the purple lips.*

"The part about me putting an innocent guy in jail? That was personal, something I'm not proud of. Why did you use it against me?"

"I could've dug that information up on my own." Her voice sounded feeble.

"But you didn't."

Sarah sighed. *He was right.*

"And there's more."

"What's up?" Sarah replied, without enthusiasm. She couldn't maintain eye contact. Donna must've told him.

"What's up?" Frank tapped his foot. "You tell me what's up."

Sarah wished he would come right out and tell her. Get it over with. Couldn't he yell and lose his temper like most men? But Frank was different. He wanted her to fess up. Sarah turned her pen upside down and repeatedly clicked the silver release button against the table.

Frank didn't say a word. He waited.

"Is this about the journalist?" She continued clicking the pen.

"Keep going."

"I had to speak with her."

"And you found Donna's information where?"

"You obviously know, Frank."

"I want to hear it from you."

"Okay. I happened to see Donna's number on your cell phone and looked at her contact information."

"You just happened to see it?" Frank maintained an even tone.

"I know. It was—"

"When did you do this?"

"While you were in the bathroom." Sarah lowered her voice and focused on the pen.

Frank stood and leaned against the table with his weight on both hands. "You used me, Sarah. I should arrest you for larceny and have you disbarred. This is unforgivable."

"I didn't steal anything."

"You stole information."

"Frank, you lied about knowing Donna. I had no choice," Sarah yelled. "After speaking with her, I'm convinced Amina is innocent. What kills me is you knew about Amina's confrontation with Mark LaSpada, and the chain of events that followed, and you're continuing with the case. It should be dismissed."

"No way." Frank's voice remained steady. "Your client is a loose cannon. Donna's investigation into the foreclosures fueled Amina's fire. Her words and actions demonstrate she had the motive to torch her place for insurance money. She got caught. End of story. So don't try turning this around with your legal bullshit. You're a thief."

Sarah felt the sting in his words. "I feel guilty about taking the contact information, but—"

"Ha." Frank snickered. "*A lawyer* actually capable of feeling guilty? I don't buy it."

"You could've helped me, but it's always all about you."

"How, Sarah? By volunteering an informant's phone

number and address? I took an oath as a state trooper to protect the public."

"Now Donna's an informant? Gimme a break. I did what I had to do. You could've somehow pointed me in the right direction. *If you cared.*"

"If I cared." Frank's face turned red. "I cared about Donna and her story. She's one hell of a woman. You could learn a lot from her. Donna's not afraid to put herself out there in search of the truth. You're all about winning the game and collecting a check. A sellout. You don't care how many lives are on the line."

This was a personal assault. Sarah felt cornered. Her hockey training kicked in. Fight back, play dirty. "You sleeping with her, Frank? That why you're so upset?"

"Sleeping with Donna? Is that the best you can do? Pathetic, Sarah."

"I wouldn't put it past you."

Frank stared at her for a moment. "As a result of your stupidity, Donna's gone now. But you don't care because you got what you wanted."

"Gone?" Sarah said. "What do you mean by that?"

"Cleared out." Frank marched toward the door. "I've had enough."

Sarah rested her head in her hands. She held her breath to stop herself from crying.

"Know what burns me the most?"

Sarah turned around to see Frank facing her from the back of the spectators' gallery.

"You never apologized."

Cole ordered extra olives in his large Greek salad at Maria's, and sat in an orange booth near the window where he could see the harbor. He cut the greens and feta chunks into tiny pieces. Red onions topped the salad.

They were perfect rings, from large to small. Fitting to-gether. Circling toward dead center: closing in, choking, killing.

The place had been emptied out, a professional job. He cherry-picked the olives one by one.

Cole's thoughts drifted to that day's testimony on tele-vision. It was interesting how her gun had gone off in the desk drawer. *Not what killed the fireman.* He swirled the Greek dressing over the salad and stirred vigorously. Would the lawyer figure it out? She was a fighter. The women always gave him trouble; that's why he never married. He had his mother. That's all he needed.

Cole shoved two large forkfuls of salad into his mouth and chewed and chewed. It tasted good, but he spit it into his napkin. His stomach couldn't handle it. He tore off a piece of pita bread and swallowed that instead.

Her place was next. It would be an easy job.

30

Sarah slid into the passenger seat of Uncle Buddy's car and placed a warm bag containing three chicken parmesan subs on her lap. Rehnquist leaned over her shoulder, stuck his snout all the way into the bag, and fished around.

"Hey." She pulled the bag away and placed her palm under his chin. "Where're your manners?"

"He's hungry for his sub and so am I. Let's eat." Un-cle Buddy reached across for the bag, and took a sharp left turn onto Rutherford Avenue. His tires squealed as Sarah and Rehnquist slid across the seat.

"Whoa." Sarah grabbed the dashboard. "Keep your eyes on the road, Uncle Buddy. I'll get it for you." She buckled her seat belt. "The two of you. It's not even five o'clock. What's the big rush?" Sarah fed Rehnquist part of his sub and unwrapped another one for Uncle Buddy.

"Thanks," Uncle Buddy said, in between bites. "Did you get chips?"

"Here." Sarah opened a small bag of potato chips and placed it on his lap, along with a napkin. "Keep one hand on the wheel."

"But I'm skilled at driving with my knee."

"Rehnquist and I would rather make it to Quincy in one piece."

"Worrywart. Just like your Aunt Margaret." He turned sideways. "Aren't you having yours?"

"Eyes on the road, Uncle Buddy." Sarah sighed. "I'm not even close to being hungry."

"Why, what's the matter?"

"Frank's mad at me." Sarah had played their conversation over and over in her mind. *Maybe* she had been wrong. *Only a little.*

"Oh, come on." Uncle Buddy spoke with his mouth full. "Still?"

"We just had a big blowout in the courtroom."

"I figured that by the look on your face. So, spill it. What's his deal?"

"I didn't tell you before, but he told me about arresting the wrong guy over dinner, as a friend. I used it against him on cross."

Uncle Buddy nodded while he chewed.

"I also took Donna's number from his cell."

He swallowed. "You *took* it? I figured Frank gave it to you."

"He didn't." Sarah fed Rehnquist another piece of

sub. "I peeked in his cell phone when he went to the restroom."

"Peeked? You peeked?" Uncle Buddy's shoulders sagged. "Aw hell, Sarah, I like Frank."

"Me too." She leaned back against the headrest. Rehnquist licked her ear. "Donna cleared out after I left on Saturday."

"What? I don't like the sound of that." Uncle Buddy zigzagged onto the expressway, heading south. Someone honked at him for cutting in too close. "What else did Frank say?"

Sarah relayed their conversation.

"He's still convinced Amina's guilty?"

"Of course."

"There's gotta be more to this." Uncle Buddy started on the other half of his sub, chewing at a record pace.

"It's all so complicated." Sarah focused on the blur of red brake lights in the rush hour traffic ahead.

"When a case gets too complicated, it raises more reasonable doubt, which is good for us. If we find a link to this old Quincy fire, we'll have to make amends with Frank."

"Impossible."

Uncle Buddy raised his chip bag. "Tears."

"What?"

"Say you're sorry and start crying. It's worth a try."

"Go ahead and ring the bell. We'll wait here." Uncle Buddy straightened Rehnquist's plaid bow tie.

Sarah strained to keep her eyes open as she rang Mrs. Donahue's lighted doorbell. They'd spent three hours canvassing the old Quincy neighborhood, which abutted the new cookie-cutter golf course community. How many more long stories would they have to listen to?

Everyone remembered the fire. Most were convinced it was arson, but no one came up with anything concrete. The elderly woman who had owned the barn died a year ago. Sarah felt like they were spinning wheels in the mud, getting nowhere, wasting time. On the other hand, Uncle Buddy and Rehnquist enjoyed kibitzing over tea, gingersnaps, and dog biscuits. Sarah was convinced they could do it all night long.

A woman in her sixties answered the door wearing baggy sweatpants and a faded New England Patriots sweatshirt. "You must be Sarah." She extended a hand. "Mary Donahue. Leslie Lonergan just rang and told me you'd be coming." She waved at Uncle Buddy, who tipped his hat in return. "Come on in and bring your friend there with the bow tie."

Mrs. Donahue seated them around the kitchen table, serving fresh banana bread, dog treats, and more tea. "My dear, you look exhausted," she said to Sarah.

"I am." Sarah bobbed her Lemon Zinger herbal tea bag up and down in the steaming water. What she'd give to sink down into a hot bath. "It's been a long day."

"I'll say. That trial must be taking a toll on you. I've been glued to it on TV."

"And what do you think so far?" Uncle Buddy helped himself to a second piece of banana bread.

"That your client's guilty. If she didn't do it, why was she arrested?" She tossed Rehnquist another doggie treat. "You're both doing a great job with what you have and all. Seriously. But it's a dog of a case the way I see it. Your Arab just looks guilty to me. The way she hides behind those colored headscarves? Everyone thinks so." She took a sip of tea. "No offense, but I'm with the firemen on this one."

Amina's not an Arab. She's African, Sarah wanted to say. But tonight she just didn't have the energy. She reminded herself to stay positive and focus. Why had Uncle Buddy asked for this woman's opinion anyway?

"Tell us what you know about the barn fire where the homeless people died?" Sarah asked.

Mrs. Donahue started her story from the beginning, veering off on tangents, just like everyone else. Sarah forced herself to nod and remain polite. Uncle Buddy appeared relaxed and in his element, while Rehnquist stared at the jar of dog biscuits.

"What do you know about the Quincy city councillor who took your side in the fight to save the barn?" Uncle Buddy asked.

"Grease Gordon." She rubbed her thumb and fingers together. "That's what everybody called him. Or just plain Grease. If you wanted to get something done back then, you had to grease Bob Gordon."

Uncle Buddy laughed. "The developers must've greased him good to get their permits."

"Sure did." She grinned. "Yup, all the time."

"What was his relationship with the LaSpada family?" Sarah had perked up. The city councillor's nickname intrigued her. *Grease.*

"I'm willing to bet they had a falling out somewhere along the road because Grease sided with us over the barn instead of the developer, which was unusual. None of us could afford him."

"Maybe the LaSpadas stopped greasing him," Uncle Buddy said.

"Come to think of it . . ." Mrs. Donahue wagged a half-eaten slice of banana bread at him. "Not long after that fire, the feds arrested Grease for extortion or accepting bribes . . . something like that."

"Where is Grease now?" Sarah couldn't wait to find him. She hoped to get more dirt on the LaSpada family.

"He resigned from office, and I'm not sure what

happened to his case. I didn't hear whether he went to jail or not." She shrugged. "They're all crooks if you ask me. Especially the LaSpadas. We all know they burned that barn. Shame about those homeless people who got stuck in there. I guess somebody saw them smoking in the barn before the fire. But I don't know about that. Have my doubts."

"What do you mean?" Sarah inched to the edge of her seat.

"We all know each other's business around here, and none of us can figure out who it was who saw them smoking."

31

Amina was the first to arrive in the courtroom that morning. The guard left her handcuffs on as they waited for her lawyers. She felt woozy. She hadn't eaten dinner last night or breakfast due to her fasting. They were supposed to provide her with something to eat after sundown but had forgotten again. Amina didn't have the energy to protest. She had stayed up all night too, tossing on the hard mattress, while her mind jumped from the gun testimony to Malick to today's surprise witness and back to Malick.

"Good morning." Sarah walked in and set her briefcase on the table. "You look exhausted. Are you getting any sleep?"

"Not much." Amina stretched her arms out as the guard unlocked her cuffs. "My family is making arrangements for Malick to go back. Lamine is flying his brother over at the end of the week to fetch him."

"This week? Why not hold off until the trial ends?" Sarah unlatched her briefcase but maintained eye contact.

"Lamine decided it is best for Malick to leave immediately. When . . . if I am found guilty, Malick must be with family. He has to move on and forget about me . . . carry on as if I am dead." A lump lodged in the back of her throat. "Lamine has been in contact with the social workers over here, and they agree. Malick must return to Senegal."

"Amina, I haven't given up yet. We've been working hard, making progress. We went to Quincy last night and dug up information on that old fire you told us about, and I'm following up after court. It may help."

"I have a bad feeling." Amina felt the panic setting in; her heart raced. "This whole thing with Malick, I can't, I can't, I just can't think."

"Amina." Sarah's voice was soft, but firm. "Take a deep breath and let's focus on your case. This is important, okay? Remember when you barged into Mark LaSpada's office and read names from Donna's notes? You mentioned a guy with a nickname?"

Amina dabbed at her eyes with her headscarf. *Mark LaSpada's office. Don't take me back there.*

"Does the name Bob Gordon ring a bell? Grease Gordon?"

Grease. She pictured the name as it appeared in Donna's handwriting, and recalled thinking about how strange it was. "Yes. Grease. That was definitely one of the names."

"Good." Sarah appeared pensive. "I'm going to try and meet with him after court."

The heavy doors banged open, and Mr. Clancy ran down the aisle. He tossed his briefcase and a white pastry bag on the table. Several reports fluttered off the edge.

"Good morning, my dear." He was out of breath, but managed a smile for Amina. "You look lovely."

"Thank you." Amina knew she looked drawn and haggard, but she always appreciated his compliments.

"Rehnquist and I are going to the Registry of Deeds after court to see if we can dig up more dirt with those documents from your reporter."

Sarah gathered the reports that had fallen off the table. "I hope you bought some candy."

"Whole case of rocky roads."

"What are those?" At this point, Amina was quite familiar with Mr. Clancy's sweet tooth.

"Famous bars from Phillips Candy House in Dorchester. They're made of chocolate, caramel, peanuts, and little marshmallows."

Sarah arranged her legal pads. "They're for all the old ladies at the Registry of Deeds who'll be doing Uncle Buddy's legwork this afternoon. He has it made over there. They fawn all over Rehnquist too."

Mr. Clancy unbuttoned his overcoat. "I'd like to see Mark LaSpada squirm tomorrow when he takes the stand. It's a crucial cross-examination." He hung the coat on the back of his chair and removed his hat. "But in the meantime, I can't wait for the next witness. Nick's making a big mistake by putting him on the stand." He walked in front of the table, spread his arms, and turned around. "Like my tie?"

Amina leaned forward. What on earth? Were those . . .

"Are those mice, Uncle Buddy? Why do you have—"

"All rise!"

. . .

Nick wondered what the oath really meant to this large-framed Russian with a Fu Manchu mustache and shoulder-length brown hair. He wore a black dress shirt that looked two sizes too big and baggy brown pants with huge pockets on the legs.

"Please introduce yourself to the ladies and gentlemen of the jury."

"Alex Kryuchkov."

"How old are you?"

"Twenty-two."

"Are you employed?"

"Nope."

"Do you have a criminal record?" Nick had to expose the bad stuff to lessen the impact of cross-examination by the defense.

The Russian shrugged. "Grew up in a St. Petersburg orphanage, so I been in some trouble. Yeah."

"Can you describe your record?"

"Uhh . . . assault and battery, dangerous weapon. Two of those, I think. Got in some fights, you know? Had two OUIs, coke possession, a B&E or two."

Nick glanced sideways at the jury to gauge their reaction. Several women appeared confused that he was bringing up a criminal record. The guy who called himself Quahog sat with his arms crossed and a smug look on his face.

"Do you recall Wednesday, July nineteenth of last year?" Nick decided to cut to the chase.

"Yeah."

"What were you doing at approximately 2:30 a.m?"

"Sitting in my car outside the Mobil Mart on Shelby Street."

"What were you doing there?" Nick had to bite his tongue; the answer was comical.

"Casing out the place. Me and my friend planned to rob it."

Nick saw the surprised faces in the jury box. Quahog laughed out loud.

"How long had you been casing the Mobil Mart?"

"That night? Little over two hours." The Russian answered as if a stakeout was nothing out of the ordinary.

"What happened?"

"Saw this white car pull up to the pumps. A lady with a black scarf wrapped around her head, like the Arabs wear, got out and grabbed a cardboard box from the back. Somebody else went in and paid."

"Can you further describe the woman who wore the headscarf?" Nick glanced at Amina in her dark brown scarf. *Perfect.* Hers was almost black, and from a distance it might appear black. Maybe the jurors would think it *was* black. *Great timing.*

"The one with the scarf looked a lot like the lady sitting over there." The Russian pointed to Amina Diallo.

Good job. "Can you describe the person who went inside the Mobil Mart?"

"I was paying more attention to the lady with the scarf. Not sure if the other one was a man or a woman, but if I had to guess—"

"We don't want you to guess. Just do the best you can." Nick wondered who the second person was. Could it have been her son?

The Russian shrugged. "The other one had jeans, baseball cap, short black hair."

Sarah rose halfway to object but then sat back down.

"Please describe the car to the best of your ability."

"It was a white two-door Japanese car, like a Toyota or something. Probably over ten years old."

"How close were you to the white car?"

"About fifteen, twenty yards away."

"Did you have a clear, unobstructed view?"

Sarah stood. "Objection, leading."

"Sustained."

"Please describe your view of the car."

"I could see good enough. Nothing in the way."

"Can you describe the lighting?"

"Had them orange lights near the pumps. My car wasn't parked under one—with what I was doing." Nick heard Quahog laugh again.

Nick wished the security cameras at the Mobil Mart had been working properly. The assistant district attorney who handled the Russian's armed robbery case had provided Nick with a copy of the thirty-six-hour tape. The video taken around the gas pumps revealed white static. The camera behind the counter worked better, but the lady with the black headscarf never went inside. He hadn't seen anyone who resembled her son either.

Nick checked his legal pad. "What did you observe next?"

"The lady with the scarf got a couple gas cans and a cardboard box out of the back and set them down next to the pumps."

"Did it look like she grabbed the items from the floor of the car or the seat?"

"Objection." Sarah got up. "Leading."

"Sustained."

"What part of the car did the lady appear to take the box from?"

"The floor in back."

Good, the kid remembered. Nick thought it was interesting that the back floor mat had tested positive for gasoline. He wondered what happened to the box and gas cans. They would be nice to have.

"Can you describe the box?" Nick looked at the jurors. The Italian grandmother at the end of the second row smiled at him. Nick wondered if she was connecting the part about the floor mat.

"The box was brown, about this big." The Russian demonstrated with his hands, holding them about two and a half feet wide and six inches deep.

"What happened next?"

"The one with the baseball hat came back outside and bent over the box with his back to the gas station like he was trying to block the clerk's view. The lady with the scarf put the gas nozzle in the box. I thought that was kind of weird."

"So, what did you do?"

"I wondered what she was filling up in the box. Couldn't see from inside the car. So, I climbed up on the door frame and leaned over the roof for a better view."

"What did you see?"

"She had a balloon stretched around the gas nozzle. It looked like she was filling balloons with gas, like you make water balloons."

"Did you see more than one balloon?"

"There was a bunch in the box."

"How many?"

"I don't know . . . a dozen maybe."

"What color were the balloons?"

"Red."

"What else did you observe about the lady as she filled the balloons with gasoline?" Nick raised his hands chest high and spread his fingers. *Come on, don't forget.*

The Russian looked at him and paused. "Oh. The gloves. She was wearing black leather gloves."

Nick nodded. "How long did you watch the lady filling balloons with gasoline?"

"Not long, less than a minute. They were looking around, and I didn't want them to notice me."

"How long were they there?"

"Several minutes, that's it. It looked like she pumped the gas and the other one bent down and helped. He may've tied the balloons."

"Objection." Sarah rose. "Move to strike the last sentence as speculative."

"Sustained. The last sentence is stricken from the record." Judge Killam turned to the jury. "Please disregard."

"Did you report this incident to the police?"

The Russian contorted his face. "Tell the cops? Hell no. If I'd said anything, cops would've asked me what I was doing there too. I didn't think much about it at the time. Should've figured they were up to no good at two thirty in the morning."

Sarah rose. "Objection, move to strike the last two sentences as unresponsive."

"Sustained."

"Did you come back to that Mobil Mart?"

"Robbed it the next week."

Nick heard Quahog laughing again. "Were you arrested for that robbery?"

"Yup."

"When?"

"Several days after we did it."

"What happened with your case?"

"Made bail. Just waiting for my trial to come up."

Nick wondered how this guy made bail. He probably had the easy superior court judge who reduced everything.

"What happened recently?"

"I was flipping through channels on TV and started watching a little of this case. Happened to see the part where the lab guy talked about finding gas on the balloon, so I got my calendar out. It was only a day before the fire that I was there, and I know the Mobil Mart isn't too far from the store that burned."

"What did you do?"

"I told my lawyer, Allen Chase, and we worked out a plea bargain with the prosecutor if I would testify about what I saw."

"Did you make any other arrangements?"

"If I testify in this case, they're going to give me money from some sort of arson program because I came forward. A good-citizen reward."

"No further questions." Nick sat down and gazed at the defense table. Amina cowered beneath her black/brown headscarf, looking guiltier than ever. Sarah appeared angry, as if she'd been caught off guard. And Clancy? He was preoccupied adjusting a new bow tie.

"Cross?" Judge Killam said.

"One moment, Your Honor." Clancy grinned with both hands on his tie and walked around the table.

Nick wondered why anyone would wear a tie with two big mice on it. Where did Clancy—it dawned on him. "Objection!" Nick popped up. "Sidebar, Your Honor."

Clancy turned toward Nick and stretched out his hands. "Why, I haven't even said anything yet, Mr. Marinelli."

"Sidebar, Your Honor." Nick marched past Clancy.

"What's your objection?" All three attorneys huddled at sidebar and Judge Killam eyed Nick.

"I'm objecting to the tie." Nick gestured at Clancy. "Those are rats."

"What?" Judge Killam leaned over and examined the bow tie.

"It's inflammatory, Your Honor. Attorney Clancy wore

a rat tie to mock the witness, insinuating that he ratted out his friend on that robbery."

"Your Honor." Sarah raised a finger. "My cocounsel has the First Amendment right to freedom of expression. It's just a tie with cute little mice on it."

Judge Killam closed his eyes and rubbed his brow. "Ms. Lynch, I've known your uncle for many years. We practiced law in the same courts, ran with the same crowds. He does everything for a reason, nothing's happenstance. From his Big Dig excuse on the first day of the trial to the all-purpose, multicolored bow ties." He addressed Nick. "What are you asking me to do?"

"I'm making a motion to exclude Attorney Clancy's bow tie."

"This is a first." Judge Killam studied the tie again. "Motion granted."

"What?" Clancy's eyes widened. "You're making me take off the tie? *My wife* made it for me. She drove all the way up to Zimman's in Lynn for the material."

"The tie goes, Clancy." Judge Killam's face puffed and he banged the gavel. "That is my ruling."

"Note my objection for the record." Clancy huffed. "Oh, and also for the record, I *did* get lost with the Big Dig."

"So noted." Judge Killam pursed his lips. "Don't make a huge production out of taking the tie off. I'm watching every move you make."

Nick smiled, basking in his minivictory. "Thank you, Your Honor."

Quahog watched Clancy sit back down with Miss Hockey at the defense table. She appeared lost in thought. What was Clancy fiddling with? He sat forward in his chair and leaned over the jury box for a better view. Taking off his tie? Is that what the commotion was over? Marinelli didn't like the mouse tie? Quahog glanced up at the judge, who was staring down at the defense table like a hawk.

Clancy rose and walked over to the jury box. "I apologize for the slight delay." Quahog noticed he had replaced the mouse tie with the target tie again.

Clancy faced the Ruskie. "So, how'd that armed robbery go?" Quahog laughed to himself. Clancy liked to dive right in.

"Good. 'Til we got caught."

"Too bad for you." Clancy smiled. "Have a good defense lawyer?"

The Ruskie shrugged. Clancy was shilling for business.

"Get some good loot, did you?" Clancy said it with such enthusiasm that Quahog laughed again. *Loot.* Nobody used that word anymore.

The Ruskie paused. "Not as much as we thought."

"You robbed the place at gunpoint?" Clancy walked forward and held his index finger out like a gun. Maybe the target tie was appropriate. Quahog scratched his head. Why did he have to remove the mouse tie?

"My friend held the gun."

"And you were standing next to him."

"Right."

"The police charged you with armed robbery too?"

"Yeah."

"Armed robbery carries a maximum penalty of life in the can?"

The can. Quahog grinned. Another Clancy expression. *The can.* He missed the Ruskie's answer.

"Mmmmm." Clancy pursed his lips and looked at the jury. "Life. That's a long time. But *you're* not getting a life sentence, right?"

"No."

"Matter a fact, you might not be facing jail time at all."

The Ruskie nodded. "Credit for time served and a suspended sentence."

"Wow!" Clancy raised his fist in the air like a cheerleader. "What a deal! Your lawyer must be proud. Does he have it up on his website?"

"I don't know."

Quahog chortled. He knew drunk drivers who served longer. Why'd this kid get off so easy? He caught a glimpse of a smile on the Ruskie's lips. Cocky little prick.

"It was dark out when you were casing the Mobil Mart?" Clancy was on the move again.

"Two thirty in the morning. *I'd say so.*" He sneered at Clancy.

That was a mistake, Quahog thought. Cop an attitude with Clancy and you're done.

"You were watching the place for over two hours?"

"Yeah."

"How many cars pulled up to those pumps while you were there?"

"I didn't count."

"Over thirty?"

"Maybe."

"You were parked twenty yards away?"

"About."

"That's sixty feet?"

The Ruskie paused and cocked his head. "About."

"You never left your car?"

"Nope."

Quahog wondered how much money they got. Convenience stores didn't keep as much in the cash registers anymore. Everyone knew that. Maybe the guy behind the counter was in on it. Russian mob. They were the ones to watch out for these days. Ruskies and towel-heads.

Quahog missed a question and answer.

"Someone else grabbed a box out of the backseat?" Clancy circled toward the witness stand.

"A cardboard box with balloons."

Clancy halted and scanned the jury box. Quahog could tell by the way Clancy looked at them that something was off with the Ruskie's answer.

"The one with the box squatted between the car and the gas pumps?"

"Right."

"His or her face was bent toward the box?"

"Her. Was a woman."

"You didn't see the anatomy."

Quahog wondered what Clancy expected. The towel-heads never showed any skin.

"She wore a headscarf."

"A man can wear a headscarf. It's not against the law, right?"

He shrugged.

"Might be a good thing to wear if you're doing something criminal? Hey, maybe you should try it next time!"

The Ruskie glared and Quahog laughed along with several others.

"Objection!"

Quahog was still laughing.

"Sustained." Judge Killam looked at Quahog and banged the gavel.

Quahog forced himself to stop laughing and mouthed an apology to the judge. It really wasn't his fault. Clancy was full of it today. *Try wearing a scarf next time.* Good one.

"Could you see the color of the hair?" he asked.

"No."

"Type of shoes?"

"No."

"This person wasn't wearing a nice-lookin' dress like my niece has on over there?" Quahog watched Miss Hockey blush. She did wear hot-looking dresses. Great legs.

"I think it was jeans or black pants."

Clancy stepped toward the Ruskie. "The other one was a man?"

"Think so."

"Was he wearing gloves?"

"I don't remember."

"Did he have dark hair?"

"Yeah."

"You couldn't hear what was being said between the two?"

"No."

"The passenger's side of your car was parked against the curb on Shelby Ave.?"

"Yeah."

"Which side were you sitting on?"

"Driver's side."

"So you slid over to the passenger's side when you wanted to see what was in the box?"

The Ruskie nodded. "Because the window was down on that side."

"I see. You had the driver's side window up so others couldn't see in due to the glare of the orange lights?"

"Right."

"Ahh. Armed robbery 101."

Quahog laughed again.

Marinelli rose. "Objection, Your Honor. Attorney Clancy's mocking the witness."

"Sustained. Enough with the comedy act."

Too bad. Quahog was enjoying the sideshow. What did Marinelli expect anyway? He's the one who put an armed robber on the stand.

Clancy cocked his head. "You stood on the driver's side door frame?"

"Yeah."

"That way you could see over the roof of your car?"

"That's right."

"You certainly didn't want to attract attention to yourself."

"No."

"I bet you couldn't stand in that awkward position for long."

"No."

"A second or two?"

"Little more, maybe five to ten seconds."

"Hmmm." Clancy rubbed his chin, appearing skeptical. "If you hadn't been arrested for the armed robbery, you wouldn't be here today."

The Ruskie opened his mouth. He was obviously not prepared for that question. Quahog leaned forward, waiting for the answer.

Clancy looked at the jurors and nodded several times. "And now you're up for a good-citizen reward?"

"What?"

"After testifying here today you'll get a reward sponsored by the Massachusetts Arson Watch Reward Program."

"Oh that." The Ruskie grinned. "Yeah."

"Of course, your lawyer's cut will be a third of that reward?"

"Yup."

"A win-win situation for both of you."

"Objection." Nick stood. "As to the form of the question."

"Sustained."

"Well, everyone wins except for one person, right?" Clancy hooked his thumbs behind his suspenders.

The Ruskie glanced at Amina Diallo. "I don't understand."

"*Your friend.*" Quahog watched Clancy close in on the witness. "Your friend's on vacation in Walpole as we speak?"

"I wouldn't call it vacation."

"He's doing ten years in the pen at Cedar Junction, right?"

"Right."

"That's because you *ratted* him out on the armed robbery."

Quahog practically jumped right out of his seat. My God, he finally got it. Son of a bitch. Those were rats, not mice, on Clancy's tie. The Russian was a lowlife rat, a snitch. A commie. Ha. Clancy said it all with that tie. Why should Quahog or anyone else believe a rat?

Quahog watched Clancy take a seat next to Miss Hockey. He remembered from the first day of jury selection that their law firm was in Charlestown. No doubt Clancy knew all about life on the streets and what it meant to be a rat.

Quahog barely paid attention to Marinelli's next witness, an insurance company stiff with slicked back hair and a starched suit. His mind wandered back to Clancy's tie. He looked around at his fellow jurors. Did they get it? He was dying to take a poll. The Ruskie probably watched the trial on TV and came up with the balloon idea on his own or maybe his lawyer helped him. Dumb to do it at the gas pumps anyway. Quahog would've used a gas can and filled the balloons later.

"The court will take a fifteen-minute recess."

"All rise!"

Quahog caught up with Antiliano in the hallway and lowered his voice. "Hey, did you get the part about Clancy's tie?"

Antiliano grinned. "The one he had to take off?"

"Yeah."

"Not at first, but—"

"Rats," Quahog blurted it out; he couldn't help himself.

"Some friend, huh?"

"Ten years." Quahog wondered how bad the prison food was. "Hey, is that insurance guy coming back on?"

"I think he's all done."

"Oh. I was thinking about the rat tie and missed the whole thing."

"Don't worry about it." Antiliano flicked his wrist. "All you need is the policy amount. You know, how much she could collect for insurance from the fire?"

"How much was it?"

"A million."

"Holy shit. Got any Sox tickets?"

32

Cole snapped his cell phone shut with both hands. They didn't like the Russian's testimony. *His fault again.* No money today. It wasn't fair. He shoved an olive into his mouth.

Now Cole had to watch, watch, watch. He couldn't go home. His stomach burned. The lobster pot was half-filled in the passenger seat. His mother needed him, but he had to stay out. Specific orders.

He spit another pit out the window. They were protecting someone. Cole would get them what they wanted, but this time he'd add to his private collection.

Sarah checked the digital alarm clock: 1:45 a.m. The last time it read 1:28. Tomorrow, Nick would be calling Mark LaSpada, and Sarah would be handling the cross. Uncle Buddy, Rehnquist, and she had stayed up until midnight around her kitchen table with milk and chocolate chip cookies, sifting through the registry documents, connecting the dots. She recalled his pep talk: *Pretend you're in a hockey game and LaSpada's playing dirty. Get him all riled up, forecheck him good, and then hit him over the head with your hockey stick.* Sarah smiled to herself as she pictured her hockey stick in court. Quahog would like that.

This is our big chance to portray Amina as the underdog, and don't forget to throw the governor's name into the mix, Uncle Buddy had said. *Let's stir up the pot real good.* Remember that tomorrow. Associate LaSpada with the governor. Sarah willed herself to fall asleep; she had to be on her game in the morning.

Sarah closed her eyes, but her mind drifted back to her failed attempts at meeting with Bob "Grease" Gordon. Her research showed that he plea bargained his bribery case with the feds and currently worked for the Massachusetts Department of Public Safety and Security in the area of building regulations. After court, Sarah found his office at One Ashburton Place, but his assistant said he was in a closed-door meeting, and suggested she come back at five thirty. Sarah had arrived at five twenty, and he was gone for the day. The assistant refused to provide her with a phone number. She left him a note but wondered if Grease was avoiding her. She would have to camp out at his office.

Sarah tried not to think about it. It was now 2:00 a.m. She had to get some sleep.

Frank popped into her head. She had to make up with him before court. Get it over with. She'd like to discover what Frank knew about Grease Gordon. The wind whistled at the window. Sarah got up, flipped the lock, and flopped back into bed.

Glass shattered downstairs. Sarah jumped and then grimaced. She'd left the kitchen window open to air out the stench from the moldy sour cream container in the refrigerator. Something must've been knocked out of the dish drainer by the wind. She hoped it wasn't one of her good Deb Schlueter wine glasses with the colorful glass beads. Dammit. She didn't feel like getting up again.

The wind gusted against her bedroom window and something else fell downstairs. It didn't sound like glass, more like a clang. Sarah forced herself up. If she didn't shut that window now, she'd be up all night guessing which kitchen items remained intact.

Sarah bounded down the stairs in the dark. Get it over with and go back to sleep. Would he accept an apology now? Stop thinking about Frank.

Sarah reached the bottom step and froze. Someone with a flashlight was dumping out her pocketbook. It looked like her briefcase had been ransacked first. A bright light shined in her face less than ten feet away.

"Stay there," a man said. The light traveled slowly from her face down to her tee shirt. It ran the full length of her bare legs and back up. "Got a gun."

Sarah gripped the banister. *Oh my God.* What would he do to her? She felt vulnerable. Scream? Fight? Do nothing?

The man shifted, but remained squatting. His free

hand shuffled through the spilled contents of the pocketbook. The light oscillated between the pile of receipts, makeup, and loose change, and Sarah's half-exposed body.

Sarah felt her kneecaps shaking. If the flashlight was in one hand and the other was feeling around for something on the floor, where was the gun? Maybe there wasn't one. Start talking.

"What do you want?" Her voice sounded feeble.

"Shut up." He shined the light in her eyes. When he took it away she saw nothing but large purple spots. Sarah heard the wind blow through the kitchen window. That's how he got in.

The man zipped her wallet into a pouch belted to his waist. He rose and walked forward, closing the gap between them. The light flickered on her upper thighs. *No.* Sarah had nothing to defend herself with. She turned and fled back up the stairs. He followed. When Sarah reached the top step, he grabbed the back of her tee shirt, which snapped her neck back. Sarah twisted and elbowed him in the temple as hard as she could. He released the shirt and stumbled sideways against the banister. The flashlight bounced down the stairs.

Sarah ran into the bathroom and locked the door. He jiggled the handle. *Shit.* The button lock wasn't that strong. She flipped on the light, searching for something to defend herself with just in case. He kicked the door. Toothbrushes. Another kick. Plunger? Not strong enough.

"I'm calling the police!" Sarah pulled open drawers. "I have my cell." Scissors? Only fingernail size. Nail file? He probably saw the pink cell phone when he dumped her pocketbook. *If that's where it was.*

He kicked again and again.

"They're on the way!" The door wouldn't take much more. Sarah grabbed the scale and lifted it above her head. *No.* He was a few inches taller. She flipped the Bruins garbage can upside down, balanced on top, and waited. There was barely enough room for her feet. How long could she hold the position before toppling over? Her wrists and forearms hurt from holding the scale up.

Something heavy banged against the door. His body? Another thud and the lock gave. The man burst into the room. Sarah slammed the scale down on his head.

At 2:55 a.m., Frank tossed and turned, thinking about the confrontation with Sarah. He was completely in the right, so why did he feel guilty? Sarah broke his trust. She'd taken on too much with this case. Did she think before acting and taking that number from his cell? Or cross-examining him about arresting the wrong guy? Why had she done that? There was no excuse for it. He was under no obligation to tell her about Donna Rapa. Maybe he shouldn't have lied. He closed his eyes and tried not to think about Sarah.

His cell phone rang ten minutes later. A Charlestown number. Sarah? *Don't pick up.* He stared at the number and pressed the talk button before it passed into voice mail.

"Frank, I need to speak with you." Sarah spoke rapidly as if she expected him to hang up.

"It's after three in the morning." Frank made his voice sound hoarse, like he'd been in a deep sleep.

"Can you come over?"

"What?" Had she lost her mind? "You mean now?"

Sarah paused. "Yes."

"I'm sleeping."

"*Please.*"

"If you're calling to apologize, you can do it in the morning."

"Somebody just broke in."

"Where?"

"My apartment." Sarah's voice cracked. It sounded like she was about to cry.

"Did you call 9-1-1?"

"The police came already. I'm alone."

Frank paused. "Are you okay?"

She didn't respond. Of course she wasn't okay, probably scared to death. Sarah needed him now.

"Sarah, you there?"

"Just come over." Her words were barely audible. "Please."

It took Frank less than twenty minutes to arrive at Sarah's apartment in Charlestown from West Roxbury. He was still angry, but this was the right thing to do.

Frank rang the buzzer and Sarah opened the door, wearing a long tee shirt and sweatpants. Her eyes and cheeks were red. She looked upset, disheveled . . . and beautiful.

"Thanks for coming." Sarah wrapped her arms around him, squeezing hard. After a moment he pulled away and brushed tears from her cheek with his thumb.

"No problem." Frank felt a rush of nervous energy, not knowing what to do or say. He was out of his comfort zone; this was not a case for the methodical investigator. Figuring Sarah out represented a challenge several hundred times harder than any of his arsons. Frank procrastinated. He circled around the living room and examined several black-and-white photographs of the Green Monster. There were no run-of-the-mill landscapes on the wall. Her place was covered with sports memorabilia.

"Is that a seat from the old Boston Garden?" He pointed to a worn green metal chair in the corner.

"Yes, it was my grandfather's, section 44, row G, seat 12."

"Wow!" Frank almost tripped over a pair of running sneakers. "How'd you get the Ted Williams uniform? And it's autographed?"

"My grandfather again." Sarah joined him next to the framed number nine jersey. "It's dated too. See?"

"No kidding." Frank touched the glass in disbelief. "1941. The year he batted 406."

"You got it."

After admiring the jersey, Frank removed two women's suit jackets, a pair of nylons, and last Sunday's *Globe* from the couch. Sarah wasn't exactly neat. He sat down and she curled up next to him. "Okay, tell me what happened."

Sarah lifted her head and looked into his eyes. "I was awake, thinking about you, before the man broke in." She sniffled. "I'd been up all night figuring out how to . . ." Her voice trailed off. "Frank, I'm sorry about taking the information from your phone. I was wrong. And about my cross-examination. I shouldn't have brought up your story about arresting the wrong guy. I'm sorry."

He placed his arm around Sarah's shoulders. "I appreciate the apology." It felt good to hold her. Neither issue seemed important anymore. He knew he should still be mad and hold it over her head longer, but Sarah had apologized. Her words came from the heart. "Sarah, I know you did it because you care so much about Amina and finding the truth. Sometimes your passion just boils over and you act on instinct without thinking things through."

"That's exactly what happened four years ago when John got shot. I don't consider the consequences. I can't be like that anymore."

"But your passion is part of who you are. It's what I love about you. You'll have to learn to work with it, that's all." Frank smiled at her. "If you really want to make it up to me, I'll settle for that Ted Williams jersey."

Sarah smiled. "Not a chance."

Frank didn't tell her that he'd been up half the night dwelling on their fight too. He kept his arm around her as she told him about the man with the flashlight.

"You hit him with the scale?"

"Gave his head quite a crack."

"Good move. Break it open?"

"No, but I broke the scale, which isn't a bad thing. Too accurate."

"You mean the scale?"

"Yeah, I prefer a few pounds under."

"You don't have to worry about that." Frank knew every woman liked that line. "So what happened to the guy?"

"He fell on his face. I ran outside to my friend's apartment up the block, and we called the police."

"They catch him?"

"No, and he made off with my wallet. Credit cards, license, everything."

"At least he didn't steal Ted Williams." Frank pointed at the framed jersey. "How'd he get in?"

Sarah sighed. "I left the kitchen window unlocked. Looks like he pried it up with a screwdriver and knocked the screen out. He broke a wine glass in the process. That's why I came down."

"Thank God you're okay." Frank squeezed her shoulders.

Sarah shivered, and another tear rolled down her cheek. "I knew right away what he wanted from me. It's a helpless feeling."

"I can't imagine." Frank combed his fingers through her hair and neither spoke for several minutes. "Sarah, do you think the break-in could be related to your case?"

"It looked like he was after money." She paused. "And me."

"Anything else missing?" Frank was skeptical.

"The guy dumped my briefcase, papers everywhere."

"I'd double-check. You never know."

Sarah made no effort to get up. "Have you heard from Donna?"

"I've left messages on her cell, but haven't heard back."

"Me too." Sarah shook her head. "I hope she's okay."

That thought had crossed Frank's mind too. "I've often wondered what her deal is." He felt that something wasn't making sense about Donna.

"What do you mean?" Sarah asked.

"It's just a feeling I have. Donna seemed to know an awful lot about my old Quincy case, more than your average reporter."

"Maybe she's above average," Sarah said.

He shrugged. "I couldn't find any articles she's allegedly written as a reporter."

"Donna probably writes under a pen name." Sarah chewed on a hangnail. "Have you heard of a guy called Bob 'Grease' Gordon?"

Frank cocked his head. All roads led to his old Quincy fire investigation. Maybe this really wasn't a burglary, only a persistent redhead digging for more information. "Is that why you called me over here after 3:00 a.m.?"

"And staged a break-in? Hadn't thought of that, but I'll keep it in mind for next time." She elbowed him.

"Just checking." He mussed her hair. "Grease Gordon is the Quincy city councillor who sided with the neighborhood group over that antique barn. Why?"

"Amina blurted his name to Mark LaSpada when she barged into his office. She got it from Donna's notes."

"Really." Frank wondered about that. Donna hadn't

mentioned anything about Grease Gordon during her prior inquiries. *Odd.* "Grease took kickbacks from the developers. He pushed a number of projects through in Quincy, but eventually got nailed by the feds."

"And now he has a cushy job with the state."

"Figures." Frank rolled his eyes. "Grease must've weaseled out of it, and now he's clawing his way back up. Politicians tend to do that."

"You got that right. My uncle has represented some along the way." She yawned.

Frank made a mental note to place another call to Donna. Was she really working on an article? Why and how did she clear out of her apartment so fast? If she wasn't a reporter, what was she doing? Whom did she work for? And what about this Grease Gordon? Frank needed to get in touch with him too.

"I'm tired." Sarah leaned her head against his chest and closed her eyes. He rubbed her head and let her fall asleep.

At 7:00 a.m., Sarah woke up nestled in Frank's arms on the couch. She stretched and he smiled at her.

"I'll put some coffee on." She walked into the kitchen, scooped the grounds, and filled the machine with water. Sarah considered the arduous morning that loomed ahead when she'd face off against LaSpada. She gazed at the piles of registry documents arranged and labeled around her table. Something appeared off. Sarah recalled making six piles yesterday with Uncle Buddy. Six. Now there were only five.

33

The man's polished shoes and crisp black suit reminded Jeanette of her undertaker from Revere. She wondered what her fellow jurors thought. Most appeared a bit dazed that morning.

"Please introduce yourself to the jury," Marinelli said.

"Mark LaSpada." His voice sounded sugary, just like the undertaker when he comforted the old widows.

"Where are you from?"

"I live in Norwell with my wife and two children."

Upscale town. Jeanette's cousin lived there.

"What do you do for work?"

"I'm president of Ameritrust Mortgage Corporation."

The mortgage broker. It figures. Jeanette reminded herself to keep an open mind and listen to what this man had to say.

"Approximately three years ago, did you meet the defendant, Amina Diallo?"

"I used to have lunch at her deli. I loved her lamb kebabs and the marinated olives." He smiled with his lips pressed together.

"Did you have any conversations with her?"

"Sure." He nodded toward the defense table. "We talked about her situation. You see, the building where she worked and lived had been placed on the market by her landlord. Amina worried that someone would buy it and evict her or jack up the rent. She had concerns about relocating her business and feared losing customers."

"Did you try and help her?" Marinelli asked.

"I analyzed her financial situation and suggested she buy the building herself. I negotiated a fair price and set her up with a mortgage. She was thrilled at the prospect of being a property owner, and I was happy to be of help."

"Did you explain the transaction to Amina?"

"Absolutely. I explained what her down payment, closing costs, and monthly mortgage payments would be. I also discussed the risks of foreclosure if she failed to pay her mortgage."

"Did Amina say anything at the time?"

"She told me she understood everything, including the payment schedule. After the closing, Amina thanked me over and over and insisted on treating me to lunch at her deli." LaSpada turned toward Jeanette and flashed that tight smile again.

"Approximately four years later, did you see Amina?"

"That's when she barged into my office." LaSpada shook his head. "After all I did for her, what does she do? Insults my family, yells obscenities, accuses me of lying."

"Amina accused you of lying about what?" Marinelli appeared incredulous.

"Her mortgage. She said she couldn't afford it anymore because her business was failing. Like that was my fault?" LaSpada grasped his chest.

"Did Amina say anything else?"

"Yeah." LaSpada leaned forward and raised his voice. "Amina said she'd destroy the place herself before she'd let the foreclosure go through. Those were her exact words, *destroy the place herself.*" He turned to the jury. "And look what happened."

Sarah sprang to her feet. "Objection! Move to strike the last sentence."

"Sustained! Mr. LaSpada, please do not offer your

opinions. The last sentence is stricken." Judge Killam looked at the jury. "You must disregard it."

"What else happened?"

"I tried to calm her down. I told Amina she didn't mean what she said. I suggested borrowing money from her family." LaSpada made eye contact with Jeanette. "You know, these are tough times for everyone."

"How did Amina respond?"

"She grabbed a picture of my family and threw it at me. She missed, but it shattered. I had to call the police, and they arrested her on destruction of property charges."

"Did you hear from her after that?"

"No, but I know the lender continued with its fore-closure proceedings, and the fire occurred exactly nine days after she threw the picture at me. Nine days."

Marinelli nodded. "Nothing further."

Jeanette studied Amina. She could imagine the emotion brewing beneath that maroon headscarf. Her business was about to go under and she couldn't afford the mortgage. She had to do something. The million-dollar insurance policy would've been appealing. Desperate times, desperate measures.

Jeanette watched Sarah rise and wondered how she'd fare against this plastic-looking business man with all the answers.

"Good afternoon, Mr. LaSpada." Sarah fixed her gaze on the mortgage broker. "Amina worked hard to build her business?"

"I wasn't a witness to that."

"That's what she told you?"

"She *said* lots of things."

Sarah stepped behind Amina and placed both hands on the back of her chair. "Amina wanted to live the American dream."

"We all do."

"Did you know Amina never missed a rental payment in the fifteen years she ran her business and lived in that building?"

"Good for her."

Jeanette caught the sarcasm in LaSpada's voice.

"*You are a predator.*" Sarah emphasized each word and marched into center court.

"Objection!" Marinelli bolted up. "That's not a question."

"Sustained."

"I'll rephrase. Are you a predator?"

"I'm a savior, Ms. Lynch." LaSpada leaned back and folded his hands on the podium. "I gave Amina the *opportunity* to live the American dream."

"You?" Sarah's eyes lit up. "You provided Amina with a high-interest, high-fee, subprime mortgage. A mortgage that would more than triple her monthly payments after three years. A mortgage you knew she couldn't afford."

"It's all she qualified for."

"Really?" Sarah grabbed a sheath of papers from her table. "According to these figures, Amina qualified for a 5½ percent, fixed-rate, thirty-year mortgage. Would you care to review them?"

He shrugged. "I gave her the best possible deal at the time."

"You gave her the best deal for *you*, Mr. LaSpada."

"That's not true."

"Come on. You pocketed a much larger fee by pushing Amina into this subprime loan."

"Her fee was standard. Everyone charged those fees."

"And *everyone* got rich at the expense of people like Amina."

"No. Those loans were risky. That's why the fees were higher."

"*Risky*. So you're admitting you manipulated Amina into a riskier loan."

"I explained all the options." He cleared his throat. "She wanted it."

LaSpada's line reminded Jeanette of what a rapist would say about his victim. *She wanted it*.

"Did you explain that you also received a kickback from the lender for landing the higher interest, sub-prime loan?"

"It wasn't a kickback."

"Oh, I'm sorry. I meant to say *bribe*."

"Objection."

"Overruled."

"I didn't take any kickbacks or bribes."

"You were paid an additional fee after closing?"

"Yes."

"Sooo." Sarah puckered her lips. "You'd call that a bonus?"

"Part of the closing costs."

"Oh, yes. The exorbitant closing costs that came out of Amina's pocket?"

"I wouldn't use the word *exorbitant*, but she paid them."

"In essence, Amina paid you two fees." Sarah raised two fingers. "And one was hidden somewhere in the closing costs."

"Standard practice at the time." LaSpada shrugged. "No one predicted the housing market would crash."

Jeanette didn't like LaSpada's sarcasm. She concentrated on Sarah. *Don't get riled. He's trying to bait you.*

"Why, I'm surprised, Mr. LaSpada. Didn't the market crash because of predators like you?"

Jeanette loved that one. It was true.

"Objection!"

"Overruled."

"I resent that." LaSpada's face reddened. He appeared to be struggling to cap his anger. "I tried to make owning a home a reality for people and this is what I get? It's her fault she didn't pay the mortgage. Right over there." He pointed at Amina. "Her fault. I explained everything."

"Everything?"

"Everything." LaSpada rolled his knuckles in his hand.

"Then you must've explained how the lending company you picked to finance Amina's subprime loan was in fact an affiliate of your father's conglomerate, LaSpada Development?"

Jeanette had seen the billboards advertising LaSpada Development Company. They'd been hired on the Big Dig too. Probably corrupt. No, *definitely corrupt.* She waited for a response. LaSpada's eyes narrowed, forming slits. It looked like he wasn't sure how to answer that one. Sarah had him cornered.

"Mr. LaSpada?" Sarah placed her hands on her hips. Still nothing.

"Your Honor? Will you please instruct Mr. LaSpada to answer the question?"

"Please answer the question before you, sir."

"Fine. The lender was loosely affiliated with my family's company, but I didn't work there at the time."

"Still, that's a conflict of interest?"

"No, because . . . because I disclosed it. I told Amina that the lender was associated with LaSpada Development. It was better for her. I knew people there and they gave me, I mean, *her*, a better deal."

"A better deal. I see." Sarah sounded sarcastic this time. "Your father's colossal company, LaSpada Development, is affiliated with three additional lending companies, each with a different name?"

"I'd have to double-check on that."

"You don't know? Didn't you use all four LaSpada-affiliated lending companies to obtain hundreds of sub-prime loans?" Sarah grabbed a thick pile of documents from her table.

"I used many different lenders."

"In fact, you sold over a thousand subprime mortgages throughout the city?"

"Over the course of several years."

"You targeted East Boston?"

"I didn't target any area in particular."

"Really? Do you recall financing a subprime mortgage for Pei Yee Choong's Laundromat, two doors down from Amina's store?"

"Sounds familiar."

"What happened to Mrs. Choong?"

"I don't know."

"The lender foreclosed, didn't it?"

"Probably."

"That lender was also affiliated with LaSpada Development?"

"I'm not sure."

"Mrs. Choong's property was recently purchased, correct?"

"I don't know."

"Come on, you're under oath, Mr. LaSpada."

"I said, I don't know."

"According to the Registry of Deeds, Mrs. Choong's old building was purchased for $215,000, well below its appraised value, by LaSpada Development Company. You must be aware of that?"

"No."

Jeanette didn't believe him.

"What about Jorge Cardoza?"

"Who?"

"Didn't you provide him with a subprime loan for the double-decker at the end of the block?"

"I don't recall."

Jeanette listened as Sarah questioned LaSpada about dozens of people from the East Boston area who were victims of his subprime loan scam. And, in most cases, LaSpada Development Company gobbled up the properties at cheap foreclosure sales.

Jeanette wanted to wring this guy's neck. Neighborhoods were being stolen out from under folks with all the foreclosures. Lenders pulled the carpet and people scattered in the wind.

"This isn't fair!" LaSpada pounded the witness stand. "My father's company has revitalized Boston's slums." He nodded at the black foreperson, Derrick. Jeanette thought that was a bit over-the-top. "LaSpada Development will breathe new life into East Boston. Right now, it's run-down and dilapidated. Blighted."

Jeanette recalled those famous last words used to describe the West End before the city took it by eminent domain in the sixties. They stopped collecting the garbage. Jeanette recalled the stench. The politicians wanted to make her neighborhood look like a slum so they could justify their actions. *Here we go again.*

LaSpada raised a finger. "In fact, my father's company has provided more affordable housing statewide than any other developer. And they give more to charity."

"Speaking of *giving*." Sarah grinned and glanced at her uncle, who was also grinning. "LaSpada Development, along with members of the LaSpada family, top the governor's list for campaign donations?"

"Objection!" Marinelli popped up. "Relevance?"

"Overruled."

"I'm not aware of that."

"*Really?* You and your father attended scores of Governor Noterman's political fundraisers."

"We like the man."

"That's been well documented." Sarah looked at Jeanette. "You personally donated funds to support his campaign?"

"Only five hundred dollars. That's the cap."

"Your wife also gave five hundred?"

"I believe so."

"Each of your children gave five hundred?"

"I don't know."

"Your employees donated five hundred each?"

"Some did."

"LaSpada Development also made a corporate donation of five thousand dollars?"

"Absolutely. The governor's done a lot for this state." He sounded defensive.

"And LaSpada Development's done well by the governor."

Good for her, Jeanette thought. If there were rules, the LaSpadas knew how to bend them. Sarah hinted he got around the five-hundred-dollar cap by donating funds in other people's names. Of course, LaSpada presented the governor with a private donor list, along with a wink and a nod. So much happened beneath the political radar. You had to play the game.

"Ever since Governor Noterman was elected into office, your family business has boomed." Sarah stretched her arms and stressed the word *boomed*.

"Objection!" Nick jumped up again.

"Overruled."

"There are many economic factors involved when it comes down to my family's business."

LaSpada's words sounded tight and sarcastic. Jeanette

glanced at the other jurors. Some were shaking their heads.

"Fair enough." Sarah sidestepped toward the jury box. "Let's talk about other LaSpada projects across the state." Her tone sounded lighter. "How about that beautiful golf course and luxury condominium project in Quincy?"

"What about it?" LaSpada crossed his arms.

"The governor and the city of Quincy displaced a number of residents using eminent domain for your family's golf course?"

LaSpada gripped the podium. "What does a golf course in Quincy have to do with this case?"

Judge Killam peered down at the witness. "Answer the question, sir."

"Fine." He huffed. "The state and the city took several properties by eminent domain. It's a lovely semi-private course that benefits the community as a whole."

"Quincy residents wanted to save an antique barn from the LaSpada bulldozers?" Sarah snaked toward the witness stand.

"It was just an old barn." LaSpada scowled at Amina and raised his voice. "You always have the few who like to *fight*."

"Rather strange how that antique barn was mysteriously destroyed in a fire?"

LaSpada's face reddened.

"Objection, Your Honor!" Nick spread his arms. "Relevancy to this case?"

"Overruled. This is cross-examination."

LaSpada slurped a mouthful of water. "So the barn burned down." He shrugged. "The fire was ruled accidental. It was caused by cigarette smoking."

Sarah glared at him for a moment before speaking. "You may shrug your shoulders, Mr. LaSpada, but two homeless people were burned to death in that fire."

"Objection!" Marinelli slapped his table. "Sidebar, Your Honor?"

Jeanette watched the lawyers parade up to the bench. Marinelli's arms flailed so much that he almost hit Sarah and her uncle. Judge Killam stood and motioned for him to calm down. Marinelli was obviously upset that Sarah brought up the Quincy fire where two people died. Jeanette looked at LaSpada, whose face remained red and puffy. It would've been much easier to burn the antique barn than fight with a neighborhood preservation group. If it was done successfully once, why not try again?

Judge Killam addressed the jury when the lawyers returned from sidebar. "The objection is sustained."

Jeanette wasn't certain what they were supposed to disregard. Was it the Quincy fire altogether or just the part about the homeless people getting burned to death? She shuddered at the thought.

"Directing your attention to that day when Amina came to your office." Sarah faced LaSpada again.

"When she threw the picture at me?"

"That day, Amina told you she received damaging information about you, LaSpada Development Company, and the governor from an investigative reporter?"

"What?" LaSpada scrunched his face.

"Amina threatened to expose you for your fraudulent mortgage scams. She discovered how you and your family swindle innocent people out of their property, ruin lives, and destroy dreams. She'd uncovered the truth."

"No. She was yelling like a raging lunatic." He pointed an elbow at Amina. "I didn't believe anything that woman said about the reporter writing an article. It was all bullshit."

Judge Killam pounded his gavel. "You'll refrain from using that language in my courtroom."

"Mr. LaSpada, you had the *motive* to burn down my client's store. You were afraid Amina knew too much!"

"Objection!"

"Overruled."

LaSpada jumped up, knocking his chair over backward. "You're implying I had something to do with that fire? Or my family? And, and the governor? That's absurd! You think we'd be ass enough to set a termite-infested Arab . . . African or whatever the hell store it was on fire?"

"Mr. LaSpada! Watch your language!"

LaSpada glanced up at the judge and addressed Sarah again. "And ruin our good name? It's not fair. My family business winds up with a black eye on TV." He gestured at the camera. "I'm suing you and your client for loss of reputation and slander." He righted the chair, sat back down, and got up again. "She set that fire and killed a fireman. Everybody knows it." He extended both hands toward Amina. "Those Arabs are capable of anything. All a bunch of whackos if you ask me."

"Thank you, Mr. LaSpada." Sarah's voice sounded smooth. "Nothing further."

34

"**M**s. Lynch! Ms. Lynch!"

"Excuse me." Sarah faked right and skirted left.

"What else can you tell us about the governor and his ties with LaSpada Development?"

"No comment." She zigzagged up the middle. The

hockey training came in handy in a hallway jammed with reporters.

"Will you subpoena the governor as a witness?"

She liked that one. "We're looking into it."

"Can you tell us more about that fire in Quincy? Is it related to this case?"

"No comment."

"Were the homeless people murdered?"

Sarah had created a firestorm. *Good.* She spotted Uncle Buddy exiting the courtroom. He'd have a field day with these questions, and she was on a mission to find Grease Gordon. "My uncle will take your questions; he's right over there." She pointed and they scrambled.

When Sarah arrived at Grease Gordon's building, she avoided his secretary and waited by the elevators on the ninth floor, hoping to catch him on his way out for the day. She knew what he looked like from all her Internet research: a tall dark-haired man with a long, thin face and gray sideburns. After twenty minutes, she spotted him heading her way with another man. She had hoped to catch the infamous Grease Gordon alone.

"Excuse me, Mr. Gordon, I'm Sarah Lynch." She extended her hand. "I have an urgent matter to discuss with you."

He shook hands with three fingers and pulled away. "I'm going out. Heading to a meeting. Over dinner, and it's important."

"You'll want to speak with me before the police come." Sarah had rehearsed this. She had to play hardball.

"What? I didn't do anything—"

"It's about your connection to a fire in Quincy where two homeless people were killed."

"That was years ago."

"Hey Bob, she's the lawyer for that Arab who killed the fireman," the other man said. "Watch what you say."

"I know who she is." Gordon curled his lips over his teeth. "Go ahead, Jerry, I'll catch up with you at the restaurant." He waited for the elevator doors to close. "What the hell do you want with me?"

"I need to know what happened in Quincy with the LaSpadas and that fire."

"Why are the police involved now?" he asked.

Sarah had to stretch the truth a little. "Because they're investigating that fire again and your name came up. *Multiple times.*"

"Who exactly is investigating?"

"I can't say. But tell me, why did you side with the neighborhood group against the LaSpadas? I know the LaSpada family got you elected." Sarah rubbed her thumb and two fingers together. "So why did you turn against them?"

"The LaSpada . . ." Gordon stopped talking as three women approached the elevators. He stepped away and Sarah followed. "Why should I tell you anything?"

"Right after the Quincy fire, you were arrested for bribery. Coincidence? I don't think so."

"You have no idea." Gordon snickered. "Way off track."

"I bet the LaSpada family did you in."

"Get the hell away from me." He turned his back on her and beelined toward his office.

"I'm going to expose you," Sarah yelled.

He spun around. "Watch your back."

Cole bit into an olive and leaned against the brick wall near the end of the long, narrow alley. *They couldn't take any chances now.*

It was dark, a place where the streetlights never shined. He stood between the television without a plug and the birdcage without a bird. What could one watch on an empty screen? An empty life? Mistakes of the past? He set the olive tub on top of the birdcage and held the long black scarf in his left hand.

The dumpster blocking the alley smelled like vomit and the sunken couch reeked of urine. Is this how it would be in the end?

Cole grasped four olives; one slipped and rolled into a crack. Could his fingers fit in there? Hell, let the rats have it. His mouth watered; he craved the salt. He sucked the first three before biting down into the flesh.

Cole worked his tongue and stripped all three olives down to the pit. It paid to be alert. His mother taught him that. The blue coffee can? He dumped the water, placed it at his feet, and spit. Ting. Ting. Ting. More olives.

Time passed as it always did. Not much time left. A pocket of burning air lurched up from his stomach. *Keep it down.* He concentrated on the singed Senegalese Market across the street. Another project. Another life. Another olive. Chew. Spit. Ting.

He fingered the double knot tied in the center of the scarf. The method had been used for centuries. Other options were too bloody. Move fast, wrap the scarf around the neck, cross the ends, and yank hard with the knot at his throat. One, two, three, four . . . only nine more olives left. He spit the remaining pits back in the plastic tub, swirled them in the oil at the bottom, and sucked them one by one.

He found the perfect bridge; the weights were in place. They'd like it that way.

35

Derrick gazed at Sarah as he entered the courtroom that morning. She wore her red hair pulled up in a tight twist. So put together, so passionate about her case. Sarah had created monsters out of Mark LaSpada and his father's development company. Derrick had seen the red LaSpada billboards. What a scam with all the foreclosures! Sarah hit the nail on the head. Developers like LaSpada were gobbling up the city piece by piece. They came into neighborhoods like his in Roxbury pretending to be champions of the poor. When LaSpada said the word *slums*, he had looked right at Derrick.

Clear out those slums. Derrick recalled learning that urban renewal had once been called negro removal. Now, the people were shoved out and the slumlords were back again. Thursdays were designated *eviction day* at the housing court. He'd wasted two Thursdays with his sister a few months back. She lost her case.

Derrick admired Sarah for her attack against LaSpada, but wondered why she had dragged the governor into it. The media had a field day with that one. He remembered the governor sitting in court with the fireman's family on the first day of the trial. Had that reporter turned up something connecting LaSpada and the governor? Is that what set Amina off, and motivated her to burn her store? He cleaned his glasses. Too many unanswered questions. Would the investigative reporter testify?

Derrick watched Detective Callahan parading down the aisle in a navy blue suit and yellow tie. After getting sworn in by Clerk Kelly, he nodded at the judge and jurors. This should be Marinelli's final witness, where he'd wrap it all up with the homicide detective. Then it would be Sarah and her uncle's turn to present their case, and Derrick couldn't wait.

"Good afternoon." Marinelli placed his pad on the podium. "Please introduce yourself to the jury."

"Michael J. Callahan."

"How are you employed?"

"I'm a sergeant detective with the Boston Police Department's homicide unit."

"What happened on Friday, July twentieth of last year around 2:00 a.m.?" Marinelli stepped out from the podium.

"I responded to 107 Waldemar Ave. in East Boston to investigate the alleged homicide of Boston Firefighter Jack Fogerty."

"Please describe your role in the investigation."

"As the lead homicide detective, I'm the quarterback of the team. It's my job to coordinate the efforts of each expert, interview witnesses, and piece the case together." Callahan spoke with authority.

Derrick tried his best to concentrate as Detective Callahan took them through the meticulous steps of his investigation. Callahan was a seasoned detective, but did he have it right this time? How did he feel about this one? Deep down?

He studied Amina. What really happened during that fire?

"Did you make any observations about the defendant's demeanor when you and Sergeant Brady interviewed her after the fire?"

"Ms. Diallo came across nervous, defensive, jittery. Failed to maintain eye contact with us." Callahan scanned the jury box. "She didn't show any remorse for the fire-fighter who died rescuing her son."

Derrick studied Amina again. If she did it, was she sorry? Even if she didn't do it, did she feel any remorse for the victim and his family? He had tried to read her feelings throughout the trial, but her face was often hidden by the veil.

"Did Ms. Diallo make any statements about her mortgage broker, Mark LaSpada?" Marinelli gestured toward Amina.

"Objection!" Clancy and Sarah both rose. "Leading."

"Sustained."

"What else did the defendant say?"

"Ms. Diallo rambled on and on about her son, whether he was a suspect. She denied starting the fire and shooting Jack Fogerty, so I asked if she suspected anyone else. She couldn't think of anyone." Callahan turned toward the jury. "I asked if she had any enemies or knew of anyone with the motive to burn down her store. Ms. Diallo said she had no idea who could do something like this."

"Did Ms. Diallo ever mention speaking with an investigative reporter?"

"Objection, leading."

"Sustained."

Derrick observed Detective Callahan's facial expressions. It was clear Amina had never mentioned anything about the LaSpadas and their subprime mortgage scam or an alleged investigative reporter. Why not? Was Amina afraid? At that point she had nothing to lose. Derrick studied Sarah and her uncle. Were they vilifying the developer and creating sympathy for Amina? It was a crafty strategy with a jury of Bostonians. The foreclosure angle would likely strike a chord with someone. Derrick looked around. Who would it be? Antiliano? Linda, the liberal who wore the wild jewelry? Perhaps the Asian research librarian. After all, LaSpada had scammed a Chinese lady too.

"What else did you inquire about?" Marinelli placed a thumb on his legal pad.

"Whether Ms. Diallo heard any gunshots. She hesitated for a moment and then said that she hadn't. She added that the noises from the fire were loud, such as glass breaking, the fire alarm blaring."

Derrick glanced at Amina as she whispered something to Sarah. She would've heard a gunshot, no doubt about it. *If* someone else did it.

Marinelli played the videotape of the fire investigation and recovery of the handgun from the desk drawer. Derrick wondered what the other jurors thought about the ballistics evidence. Clancy and Sarah had done a nice job raising questions.

"Based upon your entire investigation, did you form any opinions?"

"Yes." Callahan cleared his throat. "I formed the opinion that the defendant, Amina Diallo, shot and killed Boston Firefighter Jack Fogerty with her .380 auto caliber semiautomatic weapon on July twentieth of last year."

"What did you do after forming the opinion that Amina Diallo killed Boston Firefighter Jack Fogerty?" Marinelli looked at the jury and enunciated each word.

"I arrested her for murder."

"I'm surprised." Clancy got up and rubbed his back.

Callahan drew a deep breath as he watched Clancy adjusting his New England Patriots bow tie. He'd successfully reviewed the evidence and outlined the prosecution's case. He finished on a high note, just what the lead homicide investigator was supposed to do. Callahan took one look at Clancy and thought of the story of the three little pigs and the big bad wolf. *He huffed and he puffed and he blew the house down.* Callahan only hoped the house he built was made of brick.

"You're surprised about what?" Callahan responded as natural as he could. He wouldn't allow himself to get riled this time, no matter what the accusations were. He and Clancy had a sordid past. Callahan lost his cool in the last murder trial against Clancy.

"Twenty-two years on the force, fourteen with homicide." Clancy placed a hand on his hip. "That right?"

"Yes." The windup and the pitch. It was coming.

"Have you been feeling alright lately?" Clancy cocked his head, feigning concern.

"Just fine." Callahan curled his toes; nobody could see that.

"Long nights on the job?"

"That's right." Keep the answers short, Callahan reminded himself.

"The city's homicide numbers are up this year?"

"Yes."

Clancy nodded and lowered his voice. "Pressure getting to you, Detective?"

Trick question. "Sometimes." Callahan closed his mouth and smiled at the jurors. Everyone had to deal with pressure.

Clancy clicked his tongue. "I guess that explains it then."

"Objection as to form," Marinelli said.

"Sustained." Judge Killam eyed Clancy. "Put a question before the witness, counselor."

"I'm quite surprised, Detective." Clancy scrunched up

his face. "*You're* the one who arrested this woman on murder charges, not some anxious rookie?"

"I arrested Amina Diallo for murder based on all the evidence." Callahan deliberately slowed his speech. *Don't let Buddy Clancy get under your skin*.

"Hmmm." Clancy yanked at his suspenders. "This time it appears you've ignored gaping holes in your case. How'd you let that happen, Detective?"

"There are no holes in my case." Callahan looked Clancy right in the eyes.

"Oh really?"

"That's right, and I'll stand by it." Callahan spoke with as much conviction as he could muster.

"The way I see it, Detective, you picked your suspect, made the arrest, and then piled whatever bogus evidence you could find to fluff it up." Clancy raised his voice an octave and made fluffing motions with his fingers.

"Objection again, Your Honor." Nick knocked his knuckles against the table. "Attorney Clancy's making blanket statements. He's preaching."

"I agree. Sustained."

"Okay, let's take this step-by-step. You made the arrest based on witness statements?"

"Partially."

"That BU student certainly didn't see Amina committing any crimes, did he?"

"No, but—"

"You interviewed Andy Larson, Jack's partner, at the fire scene?"

"I did."

Clancy raised a finger. "Andy never told you he saw Amina pointing a gun."

"The man was a mess. He just found out he lost his partner." Callahan knew this was coming. Everyone had been surprised about Andy's revelation on the stand.

"In fact, Andy's report, which was prepared *before* he knew what happened to his partner, helps *our case*."

"I don't see it that way."

"Andy said he saw someone running away down the hall." Clancy raised his chin.

"Correct."

"That hallway leads to a back bedroom with access to the roof, where someone could've escaped?"

"It also leads to the second living room entrance where we recovered the gun in the desk and where Jack found *your client*." Callahan leaned back and made eye contact with each juror.

"Detective, as quarterback of the team, it's your job to huddle in the hallway with witnesses while they're waiting to testify?"

Where was this going? "It's not necessarily my job, but I do it."

"Did you *huddle* with Andy Larson?" Clancy mimicked a football huddle—hence the New England Patriots bow tie.

"I just sat with him. We didn't talk about the trial."

"Really?" Clancy protruded his lower lip. "Were you present when Marinelli prepped Andy for trial?"

Callahan waited for Nick to object, but it didn't happen. He had to come up with something clever. "I was there for some of it." Callahan decided to use the old standby. "Mr. Marinelli told Andy to get up there and tell the truth."

"And that's all Marinelli said?"

"Objection!"

"Sustained."

Clancy cocked his head. "My client told you she heard popping noises, ran downstairs to the fire, and then back up to rescue her son, correct?"

"That's what she said."

"The gasoline residue was on the *bottom* of her slippers?"

"Right."

"That's consistent with Amina's version of what happened. She stepped in gas after someone else started that fire."

"No." Callahan leaned forward. "Ms. Diallo stepped in gasoline when she hung those balloons on hooks before *she* started the fire."

"Guesswork again." Clancy raised his voice an octave. "Let's see what else we can *speculate* about. Oh, the driving gloves. Don't most folks keep their gloves on when pumping gas in the cold weather?"

"The fire occurred in July." Callahan glanced at the jurors. They all looked stoic.

"Ahh. But winter gloves stored in the glove box would still contain gasoline residue?"

"I don't know." *Of course they would.*

"When you pump your own gas, you're liable to track it in on the mat too?"

"Not in the back."

"Haven't you ever set a pair of boots down in the back, Detective? Or had a passenger ride in the backseat?"

"I don't recall."

"Mmmm." Clancy rolled his eyes. "You have no proof that my client's gun fired the shot that killed Jack Fogerty."

Callahan had to be careful with this one. Clancy didn't give him much wiggle room. "The circumstantial evidence—"

"Oh, Detective, Detective." Clancy clapped his hands together. "We've reviewed what little *circumstantial* and *speculative* evidence you piled on to bolster your arrest. Now let's go over what you *don't* have."

"Objection." Nick rose. "The form of the question again, Your Honor."

"Sustained." Judge Killam struck his gavel.

"Did you find any gunshot residue on Amina's hands?"

"No."

"Any gunshot residue on her clothing?"

"No."

"What about her slippers?"

"No."

"Did you ever go up to the roof of the Senegalese Market?"

"I did."

"Seriously?" Clancy's eyes widened, reminding Callahan of those white-headed owls.

"It was too dangerous the day after the fire." Callahan wished he had dangled from a helicopter that day and checked the roof so he could give Clancy one less thing to hound him about. "I went up later on and didn't find anything significant."

Clancy scratched his head and looked at the jurors. "When?"

Callahan shrugged. "About a week or so after the fire."

"Did you *forget* to put that in your report?"

"I had turned in my report by then."

"You didn't prepare a supplemental report?"

"No, because there was nothing to report. I didn't find anything up there."

"Hmmm." Clancy clasped his hands behind his back and paced back and forth. "Detective, did you go up to the roof a week or so after you arrested my client because something bothered you deep down about this case?"

"Not at all."

"Perhaps you were a bit *unsure* of yourself on this one?"

"I knew you'd ask me about the roof on cross. That's why I went up there." Several jurors laughed. "I arrested your client for murder based on all the evidence against her."

Clancy stared at him for a moment. Callahan returned his gaze.

"What about the homeless man who hung out across the street?" Clancy asked. "Did you interview him?"

"Yes."

"That's right. You did that last week. For the first time."

"The homeless man didn't add anything of value." Those were the wrong words, but it was too late now.

"He didn't add any value to *your case* because you didn't like what he had to say. What if he saw someone escaping across the roof?"

"He didn't."

"Sure about that?" Clancy blinked several times.

"Positive."

"Did you thoroughly investigate all the others who had a motive to burn the store and get rid of Amina?"

"Yes and they were ruled out."

Clancy jumped as if he'd stepped on a live wire. "So you're admitting there are people out there with the motive to burn the store and kill Amina?"

Callahan gripped the witness stand. "I'm saying we looked into anyone with a possible motive, put them under a magnifying glass, and ruled them out." Clancy had a knack for twisting words around to fit his case. Callahan glanced at Sarah in her attractive green suit. He hoped she wouldn't end up like her uncle. Sarah had such an endearing side to her.

"Now let's examine the largest gap in your investigation. What was that mortgage broker, Mark LaSpada, doing within the twenty-four hours prior to the fire?"

"He wasn't a suspect at the time."

"Wow." Clancy looked at the jury. "Did you at least execute a search warrant for Mark LaSpada's home and vehicles?"

"No." Callahan wished Nick would object. Clancy was dangling bait before the jury, hoping someone would bite. The judge emphasized that lawyers' questions weren't evidence. Didn't matter. Many times jurors focused on the questions more than the evidence.

"Were you ill for a while during this investigation?"

"No."

"I can't believe you missed so much."

"Objection!"

"Sustained."

"Did you investigate the private lending institution that was about to foreclose on Amina's store and home?"

"I looked into the history of Ms. Diallo's loan."

"So you must've discovered that the lender was affiliated with LaSpada Development Company?"

"That was not the focus of my investigation."

"Are you telling me you didn't even notice that the LaSpadas were stealing people's properties through foreclosure and buying them back later at ridiculous prices?"

"Again, that was not the focus of my investigation." Callahan clenched his jaw.

"Did you interview the investigative reporter who met with Amina?"

"I have doubts as to whether that woman exists."

"I see. Do you think somebody killed her like they tried to kill my client?"

"No." Callahan locked eyes with Clancy. "Now you're exaggerating and misleading this jury."

"Exaggerating? Misleading?" Clancy's mouth dropped

open. "How can you possibly say that, Detective?" He stretched an arm toward his client. "Somebody took a shot at Amina during her arraignment. The bullet struck my niece." The courtroom was eerily quiet.

"Objection!" Marinelli jumped up, jarring his table. "Sidebar?"

Callahan heard the lawyers arguing in hushed tones on the other side of the judge's bench. He could hear Marinelli saying that the courthouse shooting prejudiced his case. It sounded like he had filed a previous motion excluding any mention of the shooting. Clancy and Sarah claimed it was relevant regarding motive and the theory of their case. Somebody was out to get Amina from the very beginning. Callahan wondered how Judge Killam would rule. It was a tough one.

"Objection overruled." Judge Killam announced his decision as the lawyers left the bench.

Clancy marched back into center court. "Detective, someone fired a shot at Amina during her arraignment?"

"It's unclear who the intended target was. Your niece, Sarah, got shot." Callahan looked at Sarah. He hated to do this to her, but her uncle had cornered him. "The shooter could've been after Sarah due to her previous history of prosecuting gang members, especially the last case she was involved in where her partner was killed due to her mistake in judgment."

"Since you're speculating again, Detective, perhaps someone wanted Amina dead because he was afraid of what would come out during the course of this trial?"

"We don't know at this point."

"Perhaps that *someone* was Mark LaSpada?"

"Not to my knowledge."

"Or, perhaps, it was the *governor* who had so much to lose here?" Clancy rubbed his hands together.

"Objection!" Nick bolted out of his seat.

"Sustained."

Callahan was relieved he didn't have to answer.

"Detective Callahan, the Boston Police never caught the shooter. I'd like to know how hard you tried?"

"We're still investigating."

"Are you afraid if you caught the shooter, this case would blow up? *You know what* would hit the fan down at headquarters."

"Objection!"

"Sustained."

Callahan ignored the objection and shot to his feet. "How dare you attack my integrity or the integrity of the Boston Police Department. You'll say anything to get your client off."

"Order!" Judge Killam banged the gavel.

Callahan faced the judge. "He pulls this every time." He gestured toward the jury box. "They should know about it!"

"Sit down right now or I'll find you in contempt. I sustained Mr. Marinelli's objection. You know you're not supposed to talk."

Callahan sat down; his heart raced. He had worked this case to the bone with very little sleep. He let the widow cry on his shoulder and explained the legal system to her. Callahan interviewed more witnesses than he could count. Why? *Because he cared*. What was the end result? Getting slapped on the witness stand. Callahan glanced at the jurors. They were all staring at him.

"It's fair to say you've got many unanswered questions here?"

"My investigation is solid. Jack Fogerty was shot down in the line of duty by your client."

Clancy looked at him with sad eyes, like a father

disappointed in his son. "I have one last question for you, Detective." He paused, looked at the jurors and back at Callahan. "When did you start arresting people based on guesswork instead of proof?"

Callahan stared at him. *Don't answer.*

"Ahh. Just as I thought." Clancy nodded. "Thank you, Detective. Nothing further."

36

"**W**e're gaining momentum here." Buddy stepped on the gas pedal. "I believe we can win this one."

"Slow down, Uncle Buddy." Sarah sat in the passenger seat with Rehnquist panting over her shoulder. "You're going to get pulled over, and after your cross of Callahan today, they'll double the ticket."

"I'd say triple." He still felt that burst of energy that came with a good cross-examination.

"If we're lucky, they'll take your license away. There's a stop sign up there, you know."

"I see it. You sound like your Aunt Margaret."

Sarah shook her head. "I came on way too strong with Grease Gordon. I cornered him like the rat that he is and we lost him."

"Don't be a Monday morning quarterback." Buddy wished Sarah wasn't so critical of herself. "Give him time. He'll come around."

"No way. And, we don't have *time*, Uncle Buddy." Sarah sounded exasperated with him. "The trial will be over."

"Stop watching the clock and slow down." Buddy knew that the word *patience* could not be found in her aggressive, competitive dictionary. Sarah was born running. "Remember when we would go fishing together years ago?"

She cocked her head.

"Come on. What did I tell you after your hundredth cast and no fish?"

"Try a different lure."

"And what else?"

"Be patient."

"Exactly." Buddy parked in front of the burned-out Senegalese Market. "Now trust me. Grease Gordon will come around due to his own self-interest, whatever that may be. We have to give him a chance." He reached back and stroked Rehnquist. "We also have to tread lightly with Danny tonight. Guys like him hate court."

"But we need Danny on the witness stand tomorrow morning, and we have to prepare him."

"We've got loads of time. I've scraped around for witnesses five minutes before court." Buddy walked around the car with a flashlight under his arm and a black coffee for Danny. Sarah and Rehnquist hopped out of the passenger side.

"Windy out here tonight." Sarah clutched her skirt in one hand and Rehnquist's leash in the other. Strands of her long red hair dislodged from the twist on her head and whipped sideways.

"Danny?" Buddy placed a hand against the rough brick building and peered down the narrow alley. He smelled vomit; they were downwind of the Dumpster. The television set had been knocked on its side, and the lava lamp smashed to pieces. "Keep Rehnquist back. There's broken glass in here." Buddy had a bad feeling—maybe they were too late. Maybe they had waited too long.

"What's that?" Sarah held Rehnquist by the collar and pointed to several dark brown stains on the couch. "Blood?"

Buddy squatted and shined his light down for a better look. "Can't tell. Could be anything."

"Lookin' for me?" Danny squeezed around the Dumpster.

Buddy sighed with relief. "Yes, we were getting worried." He shook hands with Danny and extended a pack of cigarettes. "Smoke?"

Danny nodded and Buddy cupped his hand against the wind and lit a cigarette. It glowed orange as Danny inhaled hard. He patted Rehnquist with his cut-off tan gloves.

"Are you okay?" Sarah said.

"I learned how to take care of myself." Danny kicked a piece of the lava lamp with his work boot. "But they just can't leave me alone out here."

"If you don't mind holding Rehnquist," Sarah said, handing him the leash, "we'll clean up for you." She righted the three-legged stool. "Got a broom and dustpan?"

"I make do with a newspaper and my hand."

Buddy helped Sarah tidy up the alley while Danny smoked and fed Rehnquist a muffin. The homeless made do day after day until they reached the end of their rope. Sometimes others cut that rope for them. He thought about the folks who had died in the Quincy barn fire. What were their stories? Had they been murdered?

"Danny, what happened in here?" Sarah picked up several large shards of orange glass and tossed them into the Dumpster.

"The devil. When he shows up with the black noose, I gotta be prepared. Learned that back in Khe Sanh."

"What did the devil try and do?" Buddy helped Sarah balance the television back on the inverted plant stand. The screen had cracked, but it was no less functional than before.

"Tied me up tight around the neck with his noose and tried to take me down. Wasn't my time." Danny released a long stream of smoke from his nostrils and sucked on the cigarette again.

"What did the devil look like?" Sarah gathered the last two large pieces of broken glass and threw them into the Dumpster.

"It was dark." Danny coughed and spit the phlegm into his blue coffee can. "He had the eyes of fire. Seen them before."

"Where?" Buddy wondered whether this mess was the work of vandals or if it could be connected to their case.

"During the siege we all saw the eyes of fire." Danny puffed on the cigarette.

"Do you have any bruises?" Buddy asked. Perhaps Danny was delusional. Did he think the devil was after him and damage the place himself? Maybe night terrors dominated his sleep like many of the veterans who'd experienced combat.

"Right here." Danny rolled his soiled turtleneck down. "My neck."

Buddy observed the deep purple and black bruise.

"That looks awful." Sarah grimaced. "Can we treat you to dinner?"

"Never turned down a free meal." Danny coughed and spit again.

"Come on then." She rose. "I've gotta talk to you about your testimony."

Danny stopped smoking. He scratched at his bearded chin and appeared dumbfounded.

Buddy wished Sarah hadn't used the word *testimony*. "Danny, remember when Amina's store burned?"

He resumed smoking.

"We'd like to ask you a few questions about the fire, that's all."

"Not me." Danny carefully snuffed out the butt and set it in a chipped SpongeBob soap holder to smoke later.

"It won't take long. We promise," Sarah said.

"I'm not going to court." Danny raised his voice.

Buddy lit another cigarette and handed it to him. "Here, take the pack, Danny."

"God bless." Danny kneeled next to Rehnquist and buried his face in the dog's fur.

"You know that's why he came, don't you?" Sarah scratched Rehnquist under the chin and softened her voice.

"Who?" Danny asked.

"The devil. He doesn't want you to tell anyone about the miracle. Remember the angel you saw flying across the roof during the fire? The messenger of God?"

"I'll never forget."

"The devil wants to keep you from spreading that message." Sarah squatted next to him.

"You can't beat the devil."

"Yes you can," Sarah said, with conviction. "Remember all the delicious hot meals Amina made for you?"

He nodded.

"Look, Danny, Amina really needs your help now." Sarah motioned toward the burned market.

"The devil burned her place." He lit another cigarette. "Can't beat the devil."

Buddy gathered several dried olive pits and tossed them. "You like olives, Danny?"

"Hate 'em." He exhaled a long stream of smoke. "S'what makes him sick."

Buddy considered his comments for a moment. If Danny hated olives, whose pits were these? Vandals would just trash the place, but the pits may indicate that somebody waited here for a period of time and ate olives. "Do you know who ate the olives?"

"Had to be him. The devil."

"You think he's sick?" Buddy had to decipher Danny's code of half-truths. "What's wrong with him?"

"The innards." Danny gripped his stomach. "Like black sludge. It's one way of knowing."

"Knowing what?" Sarah asked.

"That he is the devil."

Sarah nodded. "Come on, we'll talk more over dinner, and then you can sleep in a hotel room tonight."

Danny took Rehnquist's leash and followed Sarah without saying a word. Buddy wondered what other delusions they would uncover. Sarah was right—it would take a lot of work to get him prepared for court. He hoped Danny wouldn't rant too much on the stand. Marinelli would have him disqualified.

Danny's beard blew straight up as he walked Rehnquist ahead of them up the street. He looked like he was talking to the dog and shaking his head.

"See that building?" Danny turned around and pointed down the block. "That's where the angel went up."

"Or down," Buddy mumbled to Sarah. "Hold on." He jogged around to the back. The building Danny pointed out had a small balcony off the second floor. Someone could possibly hang down from the roof, and the drop to the balcony would be about six feet. It tied in with their theory that someone other than Amina set the fire and escaped across the roof. He wondered who lived there at the time of the fire.

"Why did you go back behind the buildings, Uncle Buddy?" Sarah asked, when he rejoined them near the car.

"Searching for that angel to supplement our witness list." He smiled.

"Not a good idea," Danny said. "Angels don't like court much." Danny addressed Buddy. "After supper I'll have time to come back here and collect my cans?"

"My niece will be happy to help you." Buddy nudged Sarah. "Got another shopping cart, Danny?"

"I know where we can get one." Danny winked at Sarah. "God bless."

"You can help too," Sarah whispered.

Buddy knew that was coming. "I have an errand."

"And what's that?" She placed her hands on her hips.

"I'm running home and grabbing my camera for this one." He grinned. "My sophisticated niece collecting cans like a scrappy street lawyer. Priceless."

"Priceless my ass. You're helping."

37

Amina felt nervous that morning as she rose for the judge. It was their turn now. Sarah and Mr. Clancy would present Amina's side of the story. This would be her only chance. And if they failed? Amina would spend the rest of her life in prison. But worse, she would lose her son.

"Mr. Marinelli, do you wish to be heard before we bring the jury in?" Judge Killam poured himself a glass of water.

"Yes, Your Honor. The Commonwealth rests, but I reserve the right to call witnesses for purposes of rebuttal."

"So noted." Judge Killam peered at Amina and her lawyers.

"Good morning, Your Honor." Mr. Clancy rose. "The evidence presented by the prosecution lacks the necessary proof to support arson and first-degree-murder indictments against Amina Diallo. We're making a motion for a required finding of not guilty on both counts."

"I'll hear you, counselor."

A finding of not guilty? Amina felt a surge of hope, and tugged Sarah's sleeve. "Can it all end right here?"

"Real tough," Sarah whispered. "This is a standard defense motion to dismiss. It's always argued after the commonwealth rests, and again at the close of all the evidence. In your case, Nick has presented enough evidence in support of the charges against you. For us to win this, Judge Killam would have to rule that the evidence against you is insufficient as a matter of law. He'd be taking the case away from the jury, and that doesn't happen very often."

"So why do you bother?" Amina felt deflated again. She hated the highs and lows of the trial.

"To cover all the bases."

"Your Honor." Marinelli rose again when Mr. Clancy had finished pointing out the weaknesses in the Commonwealth's case. "In the light most favorable to the Commonwealth, each element of the offenses has been proven."

Amina watched Sarah taking notes as Marinelli high-lighted his evidence and witness testimony. He was flawless.

"The defendant's motion for a required finding of not guilty on both counts is denied." Judge Killam struck the gavel. "Are there any other matters to be addressed before we bring the jury in?"

Nick remained standing. "I'm requesting a hearing to determine the competency of the defendant's first witness."

Amina held her breath. He was talking about Danny.

"Basis?" Judge Killam asked.

"Detective Callahan interviewed Daniel Sullivan and found him to be mentally unstable and delusional. He's an alcoholic who lives on the streets."

Judge Killam furrowed his brow and eyed Sarah and Mr. Clancy. "Bring him in."

Sarah scurried out to get Danny. Amina knew they had taken hours convincing him to testify, and even longer preparing him for trial. She worried he'd take the stand and freeze, or, worse, rant and rave.

Danny mumbled to himself as he walked down the aisle. His complexion paled as Sarah left his side and the court officer escorted him to the witness stand. Mr. Clancy had purchased him a new pair of pants, blue V-neck sweater, and white dress shirt for court. Danny wore the shirt buttoned all the way up. Amina said a quick prayer.

"Mr. Sullivan." Judge Killam's voice boomed and startled Danny. "Do you know why you're here to-day?"

Danny stared at his feet without saying anything. Amina held her breath.

The judge raised an eyebrow and repeated his question.

Danny scanned the spectators' gallery. "To tell the truth about what I saw."

Amina breathed a sigh of relief. She knew they had practiced over and over for that one.

"Do you know what it means to tell the truth?" Judge Killam gripped the side of his bench.

Danny nodded. "To say exactly what happened."

"Are you under the influence of any intoxicating drugs or liquor?"

"No."

"Thank you, sir."

Danny looked up at the judge. "God bless."

Amina's heart ached for him. God bless *you*, Danny. At that moment, he reminded Amina of the man who came every morning to collect the cows in Khombole. He wasn't all there, mentally, yet he was simple and kind to the animals. All the cows would follow him over two miles every day, to and from the pastures. He never used any ropes or leads. Amina and the others referred to him as the *sambi* because in Wolof it meant "to look after." He looked after the cows, but the people of Khombole looked after him in return. Danny had no one.

"I find this witness competent to testify. He has sufficient understanding of the proceedings," Judge Killam said.

Marinelli rose. "Your Honor, may I question the witness?"

"When it's your turn for cross-examination. Court Officer, we're ready for the jury."

"I'm not sure about this," Amina whispered to Mr. Clancy. "What if it's too much for Danny?"

"He'll be alright. Sarah will make him feel comfortable, and gain the sympathy of the jury. After all, he's a homeless veteran."

"It is nice that Danny does this for me."

"You were good to him." Sarah rose and smoothed the back of her suit jacket.

"He's lonely." Amina watched Danny gnawing at his fingernails. "People don't understand."

"They don't take the time." Mr. Clancy leaned back and crossed his legs. "Except you. You're the only one who cared."

Sarah watched the jurors take their seats. Judge Killam explained that the commonwealth had rested its case but continued to bear the burden of proof. She thought Nick appeared more relaxed now that he'd finished his case-in-chief.

Judge Killam also reminded the jurors that Amina did not have to present any witnesses or evidence in her own defense. No matter how many times he stressed that point, they always expected a case from the defense. She could see the anticipation in their eyes.

Now it was Sarah's turn to stand quietly near the podium at the end of the jury box and ask open-ended questions during direct examination. The focus was supposed to be on the witness, not the lawyer.

"Please introduce yourself to the jury." Sarah watched Danny gazing up at the ceiling. What was he looking at? She hoped it wasn't another angel.

"Danny Sullivan." His voice sounded gruff.

"How do you describe yourself?" It was an odd question, but one that Sarah knew Danny understood.

"One of the homeless nobody cares about." His words came out loud and carried an edge.

Good, Sarah thought. Maybe it would go more smoothly than she'd anticipated. "Did you serve your country, Mr. Sullivan?"

"I served in the First Battalion, Twenty-sixth Marines."

"You're a Vietnam veteran?"

"How'd you think I got like this? I'd be sitting over there if it wasn't for that goddamn, useless war." Danny pointed at the jury box.

"Thank you for your service." Sarah needed to move off Vietnam before he grew too animated. Danny blamed his present situation entirely on the war. "Do you recall seeing a fire last summer?"

Nick rose. "Objection, leading question."

"Sustained." Judge Killam looked down at Danny. "Don't answer, sir."

Sarah had to rephrase her question. "In July of last year, did anything unusual happen?"

"Unusual . . ." Danny scratched his head with ten fingers. "Saw sewer rats this big." He stretched his hands about a foot apart.

That wasn't the answer she wanted. Sarah noticed several jurors smiling; they knew it too.

"Danny, did you witness something last summer?"

"I see strange things happening every day on the streets. Like what?"

Like a fire? Sarah couldn't ask another leading question. She'd have to approach it a different way. She paused and flipped a page in her pad. The jurors were watching her.

"Can you describe your home?" Now the jurors were giving her strange looks. She had just established that Danny was homeless.

"My place has a TV, couch, table to take my meals, and a birdcage for my birds."

"Your Honor, may I approach the witness?"

"You may."

Luckily, Sarah had taken a picture inside the alley.

She showed the picture to Nick and handed it to Danny. "Do you recognize this?"

"I do."

"Is that what your home looks like?"

Danny nodded and fidgeted with a button on his shirt cuff.

"It's located outside in an alley?"

"Yup."

Sarah introduced the photograph into evidence. "Danny, what building is across from your home in the alley?"

"The dungeon of darkness."

Sarah hadn't heard him say that before. "What used to be located across from your apartment in the alley?"

"The African market."

Sarah breathed a sigh of relief. "Are you referring to the Senegalese Market?"

"Uh huh."

"What happened to the Senegalese Market last summer?" Sarah wanted to cross her fingers, but couldn't do it in front of the jury.

"It burned."

Good. Sarah had to take the scenic route, but she got her answer. "Did you witness the fire?"

"Quite a sight."

"Can you describe what you saw?" Sarah watched the jurors. The Red Sox barber appeared skeptical.

"The black smoke and flames."

"Do you recognize the woman seated over there in the turquoise dress?" Sarah watched Amina give Danny a tiny smile.

Danny stared back at her for a moment. "She's the one who gave me a dinner every Wednesday night."

"Why Wednesdays?"

"Because I'm always there collecting cans on Wednesdays."

"Can you describe the meals Amina made for you?" Sarah noticed the older Italian woman looking at Amina. There was a particular softness to this juror; Sarah could sense it.

"Her meals." Danny licked his lips. "Always good and hot, like my mother used to make. A big bowl of food."

"How long has Amina made meals for you?"

"Eight, nine years. Every Wednesday." He paused. "You see, folks don't care much for my kind. They pass us on the street and look away like we got some disease or we'll up and attack 'em." He nodded at Amina. "Not her."

"When was the last time you had one of Amina's meals?"

"Night of the fire."

"When?"

"Not long after she closed up the store."

"What time does the store close?"

"Around six or so."

"Do you recognize this?" Sarah handed him Amina's dinner bowl decorated with the red African tulips.

"That's it." He held the bowl eye level and rotated it. "What she used for the meals."

"Was this bowl used to serve your last meal?"

"Yup. I washed and saved it for her." Danny regarded Sarah. "Gave it to you."

Sarah introduced the bowl into evidence. She hoped the jurors would hold and reflect upon it during deliberations.

"Danny, did you make any observations about the roof of the Senegalese Market on the night of the fire?"

"Is this where you want me to tell them about the angel?"

"Please describe what you saw." Sarah closed her mouth and forced a smile. She noticed Nick taking notes at his table.

"The Angel of Death appeared out of the flames and flew right across the roof." Danny spread his arms and slowly raised his palms. Sarah saw Quahog lean back and roll his eyes.

"Where was this angel when you first saw it?"

"Hovering above the African market. It just rose up out of the black smoke."

"As you were facing the market, which direction did it go? To your right or left?"

"It flew to my left across the row of buildings and disappeared."

"When did you see the angel?"

"Some point after the firemen went in." Danny addressed the jury for the first time. "Angels are messengers of the truth. I learned that back in Khe Sanh. Came home and nobody believes. They all think I'm crazy."

"No further questions." Sarah checked the clock—1:07 p.m. Perfect timing. The lunch break would enable her to prepare Danny for Nick's questions.

Quahog had heard it all now. An angel? Is that all they could find for their side? A bum who was probably on something or drunk out of his mind at the time of the fire? Strike one for the defense. Quahog looked at the guilty Arab. What would *she* say happened during the fire? They were probably saving her for last.

"Good afternoon, sir." Marinelli got up without a legal pad this time. Quahog wondered if he'd be as good as Miss Hockey and Clancy at cross-examination.

"How'd you get to court this morning?" Marinelli positioned himself in full view of the jury.

"Sarah and her uncle took me here."

"Where'd they pick you up from?" Marinelli asked.

"My hotel room."

"Did they put you up in a hotel?" Marinelli pointed at the defense table and paced to the left.

"The Holiday Inn."

"Downtown?"

The bum nodded with his gaze fixed on Marinelli as he moved about. Quahog noticed the lawyers seemed to dance around more during cross-examination, like they had ants in their pants. Lawyers were a strange breed.

Marinelli whistled. "Did Sarah and her uncle take you out to dinner?"

"Yup. I had a big steak, mashed potatoes, and a Boston cream pie."

"Did they also buy you new clothes to wear to court this morning?"

"Yessir and a carton of cigarettes."

"That was nice of them." Marinelli smiled and looked at Miss Hockey. Quahog noticed her face was red. "Did you discuss your testimony over dinner?"

Miss Hockey rose. "Objection."

"Overruled."

"That's all we talked about."

"I see." Marinelli rubbed his chin. "Did they tell you what to say?"

"Yup."

Marinelli gazed into the jury box with a look of disbelief. "Do you remember talking to Detective Michael Callahan about the fire?"

"He came around last week."

Something about Detective Callahan bugged Quahog. The guy was too sure of himself, cocky. Quahog hadn't believed he checked the roof after the fire. Callahan had all the right answers—in his own mind. Clancy's cross had gotten under his skin.

"Did you mention seeing an angel to Detective Callahan?" Marinelli stepped closer to the witness.

"No, but I didn't tell the other one either, with the devil's eyes, who attacked me."

"You told Detective Callahan about the first fire truck to arrive on scene?"

"The one that fell from the sky?"

"Exactly." Marinelli raised a finger. "Tell us about that fire truck falling out of the sky."

"It was a miracle. The truck fell right out of the sky. I think a choir of angels flew up and dropped it there so they could put out the fire."

"Did you see those angels too?"

He scratched his head. "I missed the choir. Would've been something to behold."

"I'll say." Marinelli raised his eyebrows. "You mentioned to Detective Callahan that you were drinking from your bottle of Jack Daniel's that night?"

"Was I?" He pulled his beard. "Okay."

"You said on direct that you see strange things happening every day on the streets?"

"That's right."

"What are some of the other strange things you've seen?"

"Saw elephants dancing on that new big blue bridge." He waved his arms in a semicircle. "In the middle of winter there were two hundred Santa Clauses running downtown in their underwear."

Quahog laughed. This guy had lost his marbles.

"Anything else?"

"Oh, one thing was very unusual. Not too far from where I live, the baseball team won a World Series. Twice."

Quahog loved that one, and it was true. A real miracle. He wondered if the Sox would close the deal on that pitcher before opening day. He missed a few questions and answers thinking about it.

Quahog watched Miss Hockey get up and walk around her table. Why had she and Clancy bothered with this guy in the first place? They certainly hadn't told him what to say. Otherwise, he would've testified that he saw an arsonist escape from the burning building and run across the roof. But an angel? Maybe the bum forgot his lines and the whole thing backfired on them.

"When did you tell me about the angel?" Sarah questioned him in a gentle voice.

"Last week when we met."

"Did you hear a siren when the first fire truck arrived on scene?"

"No."

"The truck suddenly appeared at the fire scene?"

"Objection." Marinelli rose. "Leading. This is redirect."

"Sustained."

Quahog knew what Sarah was trying to do. Why not ask him whether he actually saw the fire truck drop from the sky? Maybe she was afraid of the answer.

"When we came to see you yesterday, what condition was your home in?"

"It was all messed up."

Just like him, Quahog thought.

"Can you describe what it looked like?"

"A lamp was broken to pieces, my television knocked over."

He had a TV? Quahog wondered how he got cable hooked up out there in an alley.

"What happened, Mr. Sullivan?"

"The devil attacked me. He didn't want me to be here today and say what happened."

"Is that why we suggested a hotel room?"

Marinelli jumped up. "Objection, leading again."

"Sustained."

"How did you get attacked?" Sarah made eye contact with Quahog. She appeared concerned for the bum.

"I came home and the devil was waiting for me in the dark behind the birdcage. Jumped me and wrapped a noose around my neck. Lost my breath for a bit. But I fought back and chased him off. They taught me how to survive back in Khe Sanh. Not even the devil himself can take me down."

"Do you have any bruises from the attack?"

"Right here." He unbuttoned the top two buttons and pulled his shirt collar back. "Got a purple necklace to go with my Purple Heart."

Quahog could see the dark purple ring around the lower part of the bum's neck. It looked like somebody tried to choke him. Were they really attempting to stop him from testifying? It didn't make sense. Why would anyone be threatened because the guy saw an angel? Quahog shrugged. Street people got into brawls all the time.

"Did you receive a Purple Heart?" Sarah looked surprised.

"I did." He sighed. "I pawned it last year."

"Nothing further." Sarah walked back to her table and sat down next to the Arab.

"Recross?"

Marinelli rose. "No, Your Honor."

"Very well." Judge Killam smiled. "You may step down, sir."

"God bless."

Quahog saw the judge nod back. A court officer grabbed the bum by the elbow and escorted him into the hallway. Where would he go now that the defense didn't need him anymore? Back to that alley where he'd eventually die on the streets. No more fancy hotel rooms. Quahog's father was a World War II veteran, and he had managed just fine.

Quahog glanced sideways at Liberal Linda, who appeared sorry for the bum. All she needed was green hair to go with the weird brown dress and she'd look like a giant oak tree. *A tree hugger.* Linda shouldn't be on this jury. She probably took up every left-wing, liberal cause she could get her hands on. She had acted appalled when that mortgage broker was testifying. Quahog's father always paid his mortgage on time, and his house had been paid off for years. He was a hardworking American and so was Quahog. He watched the Arab slouching beneath that damn bluish headscarf. The immigrants and minorities nowadays had no sense of responsibility. If they didn't feel like paying anymore, they simply stopped, and got away with it. Quahog had no sympathy; a fireman got killed. He looked at Liberal Linda again with her dangly earrings, which almost touched her shoulders. She'd probably side with the Arab.

Cole hiked over the jagged rocks to the end of the jetty near the Scituate Lighthouse and cast his line. The stripers had been hitting all week.

His mind drifted back to the trial. An angel flying across the roof? Who'd believe that? If he'd known the guy was such a whacko, he wouldn't have bothered with him in the first place. But, he had no choice. They would take care of her. He picked an olive from his Greek salad and held it to his puckered lips. His fingers smelled fishy from the bait. He popped the olive in his mouth and bit down hard on the pit. Focus on the line, keep it straight. His mother used to tell him to think about something else when he'd get his shots. Anything to remove his mind from the real pain.

Cole remembered his mother's pot of boiling beans. The lid rattled and rattled until the white froth seeped over the sides of the pot, sizzling on the hot burner. He could hear it now. In this case, he had to hold the cover down. The froth had begun to seep.

38

Sarah stuffed her helmet, shin guards, and skates into her large canvas hockey bag in the women's locker room. It had been a satisfying night: two goals, one assist, and a win.

Sometimes it was tough being the only woman in a male hockey league. A large puckhead on the other team came up from behind, gave her a hard cross-check, and banged her down to the ice. The ref never called the penalty. Several minutes later, Sarah forechecked the guy, knocked him off the puck, and took it in for the score. His teammates would give him a hard time over beers at Sully's. Sarah smiled to herself. Sometimes it was great being the only woman.

A hard-fought game on the ice was what Sarah needed to take her mind off the trial. She swung the heavy bag over her shoulder and pushed through the locker-room door. The smell of stale popcorn oil and brittle snack bar pizza accosted her.

"Comin' to Sully's, Red?" Sean Farley, their goalie, had to yell over the rumble of the Zamboni as it cleaned the ice.

Sarah glanced at her watch. "It's quarter of twelve, Farls. I—"

"Come on, just a quickie. You played like a man tonight."

"I only have a few trial days left." The cold beer was tempting, but Sarah had to refrain. "Next week. Promise."

"Okay, I'll hold you to it. What do you think the jury'll do?" he asked.

"No clue." Sarah hated that question.

"Sorry Red, but I'm rooting for the other side. Can't get by the fact that your client shot a fireman." He waved and rushed toward the exit. "See ya."

"Later." Sarah's heart sank. People watching the trial on TV usually rooted for the other side for the same reason. *A fireman died in the line of duty.* Would the jury arrive at a verdict based on emotion no matter how well they scored on defense?

Think positive, Sarah reminded herself. *We're still the underdog.* She shoved the door so hard that it smacked against the cement wall of the building. The outside air blew against her face; it felt heavy and misty. Sarah hoped to make it home before it started raining. She picked up her pace as she cut across the dark parking lot toward Rutherford Avenue.

"Ms. Lynch?"

The man's voice startled her. Sarah turned to see a tall figure slide out from behind a pickup truck. Shadows from the orange street lights made it difficult to see. She felt unsettled. "Who are you?"

"Don't you recognize me?"

A heavy Boston accent. Grease Gordon. What was he doing here at midnight? Sarah swung the hockey bag from her shoulder and set it on the pavement in case she had to run. She zoned in on his empty hands and then glanced around the lot to see whether anyone was in shouting distance. Farls must've bolted out. *Not a soul left.* She took a step backward and wished she had a can of mace.

"Don't worry. I'm not about to attack you, if that's what you're thinking. I'm here as a friend," he said.

"But it's midnight and we're in an empty parking lot."

"I know. I'm sorry, but I'd rather not be seen with you right now, for reasons I can't get into."

"O-kay." Sarah hesitated. This guy sounded sincere, but she didn't trust him, especially after their last encounter when he told her to watch her back. She retreated another step.

"You can trust me."

Sarah had her doubts. What should she do? Perhaps Uncle Buddy had been right when he predicted Gordon would come around for his own reasons. *Here he was.* She decided to test the waters and take a different tack. "I'm sorry if I came on too strong the other day."

He extended his palms as if to say he understood. "I can't help but admire your tenacity. You're a fighter all the way. From the rink to the courtroom."

"It's what I'm trained for." Sarah maintained her guard as her mind raced ahead.

"You went in for the kill against Mark LaSpada. I enjoyed it so much I watched it twice already on TiVo."

"So, you don't care for the LaSpada family?" Sarah kept her voice even.

"I despise them."

Her hunch had been right on. "I figured that since you sided with the neighborhood group in their fight to save the barn. How come?"

"You're the lawyer. What does everybody fight over?"

"Money." Sarah had assumed it was over money. What else would it be? "But the LaSpada family gave generously to your campaign?"

"They'll throw money at anyone who breathes."

"As long as you give them what they want in return."

"Bingo."

Sarah wondered if Gordon had asked for money under the table when the barn became an issue. Perhaps the LaSpadas had told him to go pound sand instead. "What really happened to that barn? Was it arson?"

"For the record, I had nothing to do with the barn fire. I was against the LaSpadas throughout the whole fight."

"Did you know something?"

"About the fire? No."

"I noticed the FBI arrested you for bribery shortly after the barn burned." Sarah watched him flinch. "A coincidence?"

"A setup."

"By whom?"

He apprised her for a moment. "Who do you think?"

"The LaSpada family. But I'd like to know why."

"Because I had the nerve to go against them in the first place. Because I may have been too vocal after the barn burned. Because I knew they paid somebody to do the job."

"Arson for hire, but you don't have any proof."

"Nope. No proof."

Back to square one. Sarah felt large raindrops falling on her head; the sky would let loose any moment. *Keep him talking.* "Why did Donna Rapa, the reporter, contact you?"

He shrugged. "My name must've come up because I was involved with the barn fight. I didn't have much information for her to go on."

Sarah suspected more to the story. "I know she investigated the LaSpadas. If you've been following the trial, Amina burst into Mark LaSpada's office and read from Donna's notes about the Quincy barn fire and all the recent foreclosures in East Boston. She mentioned several names, including yours and the governor's."

He shrugged. "So what?"

"Donna knows what's going on beneath the surface, but I can't get through to her. Can't find her. Time's running out." Sarah stepped toward Gordon. "Would you like to know Donna's parting words to me?"

He cocked his head.

"That I need to find the guy who shot me and get him to flip."

"She said that?"

Sarah nodded. The rain came down harder.

"Hmmm." He folded his arms. "You think I know him? Is that why you've been stalking me?"

"Maybe. I believe you know something. Otherwise, you wouldn't be standing out here in the rain at midnight." Sarah decided to be direct. "Help me find this guy."

"That's a tall order."

"I have to find him." Sarah felt the edge in her words. "Will you help me?"

He appeared to be weighing his options as he concentrated on her. "See what I can do."

Sarah wanted to ask what was in it for him but decided not to ask the right question at the wrong time. Uncle Buddy would be proud of her.

39

Amina had been dreading this moment from the time the trial began. She had to keep her son safe and off the witness stand. "Malick passed out during the fire. You don't need him."

"Amina," Sarah said, "he has to do this. Malick wants to testify, and he may tip the scales just enough in your favor. He'll provide the sympathy factor, which is crucial since you're not taking the stand in your own defense." Sarah sat sideways in her chair pleading with Amina at the defense table. Mr. Clancy remained in the hallway with Malick.

"I can't testify." Amina had been adamant since the beginning. *No way.*

"We agree, it's too risky for you, but Malick—"

"It's not worth it."

"But if he can say someone else was there during the fire?"

"What if Marinelli tricks him into saying the wrong thing?" Amina pictured her son cowering on the stand before a relentless prosecutor.

"Malick can handle the cross. We've gone over what to expect."

"I've kept him safe through this whole thing, and I have a bad feeling about him testifying now." Amina had been waking up at night with a recurring nightmare about Malick drowning at sea. She cracked her knuckles. "He'll be flying back to Senegal any day now. They're coming soon."

Sarah leaned forward and cupped her hands over her

nose and mouth. She looked like she was about to get sick.

"Sarah?"

"Amina, I really hate to put it this way, but if we lose here, Malick will spend the rest of his life wondering what he could have done to save his mother."

Save me? Amina froze. She hadn't thought of it that way before. *Save me. All he wants to do is save me. The rest of his life would be a long time. Let him do this.*

Amina experienced a surge of emotions as she watched Malick take the stand and begin testifying. He wore a charcoal gray suit . . . so tall and handsome like his father. Amina placed her hands over her heart as she listened. He was articulate, well spoken . . . so smart. Amina looked on with pride as Sarah highlighted his grades and honors courses at Boston Latin. She had raised him well, and now it was time to let him go. At that moment she knew he would be okay. *She could let him go. She could . . .*

"Before the fire, I worked a lot too." Malick made eye contact with the jurors. "At the market."

"What did you do?" Sarah asked.

"Stocked, cleaned up, manned the cash register. Whatever needed to be done."

He was trying so hard, Amina noticed. *So hard.*

"How would you describe the relationship between you and your mother?" Sarah gestured toward Amina.

Malick's gaze rested on his mother. Amina wished those large brown eyes could just swallow her whole. She had stared into them when he was a newborn. He's mine, she remembered thinking. *My son.*

"We only have each other." Malick paused. His lips

trembled and his eyes welled with tears. "Without my dad, it was—"

"Take your time." Sarah waited while he composed himself. Amina wiped her eyes and nodded at him for encouragement.

"All her life she worked for me at the store, and sometimes she braided hair for extra money. My mom did all that. I know I took her for granted, but—" Malick's gaze shifted to the jury box. "She never had time to make friends really, because she always worked. Oh, except Danny, our homeless friend, she took time out for him."

"What happened to your father?"

Malick stared off into the gallery, but Amina knew he wasn't focusing on the people. "My dad bought me a brand-new two-wheeler for my sixth birthday . . ." Amina witnessed sympathy in the eyes of the jurors as Malick told them how he'd been knocked right off that blue and silver bike. "And my dad just tried to get it back, but they jumped him, and so my dad ended up in jail, not them." Malick's words came out in rapid succession as if he was still on that bike, riding faster and faster, trying to get away. Amina always suspected he felt guilty for not getting away. What if those boys hadn't caught him? ". . . and my dad got kicked out of the country, deported." Malick's shoulders sagged. "That was the last time I saw my dad. Nine years ago."

"Did you notice any changes in your mother recently?" Sarah asked.

Malick nodded. "When they were going to foreclose. You know, take our store and home away. My mom got wicked scared. Like, she didn't know what to do. She thought they cheated her."

"Objection." Nick rose. "Move to strike the last sentence. The witness is speculating about what his mother thought."

"Sustained. The last sentence is stricken."

"Did your mom express any of her fears or concerns with you?"

"To me she didn't. But, I heard her yelling into the phone, things like . . . you know, 'I can't do this anymore. What's going to happen?'" Malick bit his lower lip. "Mom just started looking scared all the time, you know? She tried to hide it from me, but when I asked she always said everything would be okay. I didn't believe her. I knew something bad would happen."

And he was right.

"Did you hear your mother speaking with anyone about her fears at the store?"

"She met with this blond lady a bunch of times and got papers and stuff from her."

"Did you observe your mom's demeanor after meeting with the lady?"

"Yeah, she was really upset each time. I think the lady told her—"

"Objection," Marinelli said. "Hearsay."

"Sustained."

"Do you recall Tuesday, July eighteenth of last year?"

Amina remembered that was the night when the Russian witness claimed to have seen her and a man filling balloons with gas at the Mobil Mart.

"Yeah. Me and my mom had a delivery late in the afternoon, so we stocked shelves that night. I remember because it was real hot and we made ice cream sundaes after the store closed. It was the last time we had fun together."

Amina remembered Malick taking the canister of whipped cream and filling up his mouth. Amina did it too, and they had doubled over laughing. What she'd give to relive that moment.

"What time did you and your mom go to bed?"

"Around midnight."

"Can you tell me about the door to your mother's room?" Sarah mimicked opening a door.

"It sticks when it's hot out and the hinges squeak. I could always tell if she left the room at night. The noise would wake me up."

"What does your mom routinely do with her door after she goes to bed?"

"Shuts it."

"Did you hear any noises from your mom's door after you went to bed?"

"No." Malick raised his voice. "My mom never left her room. I would've heard it. That Russian mob guy lied about seeing her fill those balloons." Malick faced the jury. "He lied for the money."

Nick jumped to his feet. "Objection, move to strike the last two sentences as nonresponsive."

"Sustained." Judge Killam said. "Please disregard the last sentences referring to the Russian."

Amina wondered if the jurors bought Malick's squeaky hinge story. The businesswoman who sat in the second row grimaced.

"Do you recall what time you went to bed on Wednesday, July nineteenth? The night of the fire?"

"Around eleven."

"Did you wake up at some point during the night?"

"Yeah, because I heard somebody running."

Amina tensed.

"Do you know what time that was?"

"No."

Sarah paused and looked at the jury. "What happened next?"

"I ran out of my bedroom and called for my mom. The lights didn't work. I couldn't see, it was smoky. Then somebody ran near me, and I could tell it wasn't my mom."

"How?"

"Um. I don't know . . . I'm not sure. I just know it wasn't her."

"What did you do after that?"

"After that? Uhh, I remember panicking. It was wicked dark. I think I checked in the kitchen, but I don't really remember. There was tons of smoke. I remember my eyes stinging. Then, I thought I heard my mom's voice coming from the living room, so I headed that way and . . ." Malick paused and locked eyes with Amina.

Amina could hear her own voice screaming. *Malick!*

"You headed toward the living room and what happened?" Sarah raised her voice.

Malick didn't answer, he continued staring at Amina. She wished she could run to the witness stand and hold him, protect him, take him away.

Sarah stepped forward. "Malick?"

His gaze shifted to Sarah. "I—"

Amina held her breath.

"—don't remember anything after that."

"What's the next thing you remember?" Sarah pinched her lower lip; she appeared pensive.

"Waking up in the ambulance."

Amina exhaled.

"At some point do you remember speaking with Detective Michael Callahan?"

"Yeah, he asked me what happened during the fire."

"Where were you at the time?"

"In my hospital room."

"What did you tell Detective Callahan?"

"Everything I just mentioned except for the part about hearing somebody running by me during the fire."

"Why did you leave it out?" Sarah clasped her hands.

"There was so much going on. I was worried for my mom. I . . . I forgot."

Sarah nodded. "Nothing further."

40

Jeanette felt for Malick and sensed his fear of the unknown. The boy's eyes widened as Marinelli approached for cross-examination. Sarah had guided him through the ordeal of testifying with that soothing voice of hers. Amina looked like she had agonized over watching her son. How could any mother endure it?

"Good morning." Marinelli sounded overconfident.

Malick mumbled an inaudible reply.

"You've been planning to testify since the beginning of this case, right?"

Malick nodded.

"Please provide a verbal answer."

"Yes."

Jeanette thought Marinelli sounded a bit harsh. *Give the kid a break.*

"You're a sequestered witness?"

"Uh huh."

"That means you are not supposed to listen to the testimony of other witnesses?" Marinelli cocked his head.

"I haven't been in court. I didn't watch the trial."

"You didn't see it live on cable TV?" He extended an arm toward the television camera.

Jeanette watched Malick freeze. Of course he tuned in to his mother's trial. *Just admit it.* Jeanette felt her body stiffen as Malick peered over at Sarah with a blank expression.

"Did you watch the trial on TV?" Marinelli stepped toward the witness. "You have to answer yes or no."

"No."

Marinelli raised his eyebrows and looked at the jury with surprise. Jeanette wished Malick had told the truth. She wouldn't hold it against him if he'd admitted watching the trial on TV. Who could blame him?

"Do you recall Detective Callahan recording your statement in the hospital?"

"Yeah."

"I'm going to play a portion of that tape for you."

Malick nodded once.

Jeanette watched Marinelli press the play button on a cassette player which was connected to a large speaker on the clerk's table. She listened as Detective Callahan explained his role to Malick on the tape. Jeanette closed her eyes and pictured Malick wearing a johnny in his hospital bed. Had the boy known they were about to arrest his mother for murder and arson?

"*What happened after you went to bed last night, Malick?*" Jeanette recognized Detective Callahan's voice on the tape. She thought he sounded too smooth, like he'd been trying to sugarcoat the events surrounding the fire.

"*I woke up and smelled smoke. I ran into the hallway to look for my mom. All I remember is that it was dark and smoky. I must've passed out right away.*"

"*Do you remember hearing any noises after waking up?*"

"*No.*"

"*Did you see anyone in the house?*"

"*No.*"

"*Are you aware that a fireman found you passed out in the living room?*"

"*That's what I heard.*"

"*Do you have any idea how you got there?*"

"*I must've run across the hall from my room and passed out—that's where the living room is.*"

"*Do you remember anything significant at all that happened from the time you woke up and smelled smoke?*"

"*No.*"

"*Okay. If you can recall anything, Malick, no matter how insignificant it may seem to you, it's very important to bring it up now.*"

"*I don't remember anything.*"

Marinelli pressed the stop button and looked at the jury with disbelief. Jeanette wondered why Malick added more to his story in court when he knew about the tape recording. The poor kid would do anything to help his mother. Why did Sarah and Clancy put him on the witness stand?

Marinelli resumed his position in front of the jury box. "Was that your voice on the tape, Malick?"

"Yes."

"You never told Detective Callahan about somebody running near you during the fire."

"I forgot about that when he asked."

"I see." Marinelli rubbed his chin. "So it wasn't until later on that you remembered seeing somebody running?"

"Right."

Marinelli raised his hands. "Don't you think that was an important detail to leave out?"

"I was scared of Detective Callahan."

Jeanette didn't buy it. Detective Callahan had not sounded the least bit intimidating on that tape. Maybe Malick had something to hide, maybe he had witnessed something else. There had to be an explanation.

"You never told Detective Callahan because you were scared of him?" Marinelli blinked several times.

"Right, but I told Ms. Lynch."

"Did you tell Ms. Lynch during this trial?"

"The fireman remembered stuff later on. How come he can tell about it, but not me?" Malick's voice sounded whiney to Jeanette.

"You mean, Andy Larson?"

"Yeah, that's him."

"You watched Andy Larson's testimony?"

Malick hesitated. "If your mother was on trial for murder, you would too."

"Now you're admitting you watched the trial on TV?"

"A little bit."

"You lied to this jury a few minutes ago."

Malick lowered his gaze to the floor. "I'm sorry."

"Do you know what it means when you take the oath and swear to tell the truth?" Marinelli stepped in and raised his voice.

"Yes."

"Let me get this straight. You just raised your right hand, swore to tell the truth to this jury, and lied?"

"Objection!" Sarah rose. "Asked and answered."

"Sustained."

"You also watched the testimony of the Russian witness, Alex Kryuchkov?"

"Yeah, and he lied about seeing my mom at the gas station. He watched on TV too."

"Is that when you came up with the squeaky hinge idea? After you heard his testimony?"

Malick paused. "No, it's true. My mom's door sticks and the hinges squeak."

"I see. Are we to assume you're telling the truth now or not?" Marinelli gestured toward the jury.

"I'm telling the truth." He sounded panicky.

Jeanette wondered about that. Didn't most mothers sleep with their bedroom door open? Especially a single mother? Jeanette had always left her door open when her children were young.

"Shall I remind you that you're still under oath?"

"I'm telling the truth this time."

"*This time.*" Marinelli smirked. "No further questions."

"Redirect?"

"Yes, Your Honor." Sarah rose and smiled at the judge. Jeanette gave her credit for smiling. Malick certainly didn't do much to help her case.

"Malick, can you please explain what your state of mind was the day following the fire?"

"When I was in the hospital?"

"Yes."

"Scared and . . . because . . . because—" Malick looked at his mother. "My mom told me not to—" He looked over at the jury and back at Sarah. "I shot the fireman."

Jeanette gasped along with everyone else in the courtroom. She couldn't believe her ears.

Sarah's mouth dropped open. "I'm requesting a recess, Your Honor."

Judge Killam banged his gavel. "The court will take a recess. Do not discuss the case."

"All rise!"

Jeanette watched Amina shaking her head and speaking rapidly to Clancy. She wondered what would happen next as she filed out of the courtroom with her fellow jurors. Would Malick confess to everything? Who started the fire? Had he helped his mother fill the balloons with gas? Were they both guilty?

"Malick, do you realize what you just said?" Sarah paced the length of the conference room and paused in front of Malick, who sat with his forehead against the table and hands interlaced on top of his head. Judge Killam had appointed him legal counsel to advise him of his rights. The young male defense attorney sat beside him.

Uncle Buddy sat with his legs crossed in a chair opposite Malick and his lawyer. He looked relaxed. Sarah wondered whether anything fazed her uncle anymore.

"My mom can't go to jail for her whole life. She'll die in there."

Sarah placed her palms on the table and leaned toward Malick with her weight on her arms. *What a mess.* She wished she hadn't asked any questions on redirect. Perhaps Amina had been right all along; he shouldn't have testified.

Malick looked at his lawyer. Sarah saw the tearstains on his face. Amina had cried too. She had insisted over and over that her son was innocent as the court officers escorted her out of the courtroom. Sarah had promised to get everything straightened out.

"Would you like another moment alone with me?" the lawyer asked.

"Is it true they'd let me out of jail when I turn eighteen?"

The lawyer shook his head. "I'm sure the prosecutor will request a hearing and get you transferred into adult court on this one. You'd be tried as an adult, Malick, not a juvenile."

"That's not what my friend said."

"Well, your friend's wrong, and I bet he or she isn't a lawyer."

Sarah raised a finger. "Do you mind if I ask him something?"

The lawyer nodded. "I may instruct him not to answer, but go ahead."

"Malick, I understand you don't want your mom to go to jail." Sarah looked into his eyes. "Did you say you shot the fireman because you thought you'd only serve three years and, if convicted, your mom would serve a life sentence?"

"You don't believe I shot the fireman?"

Sarah rubbed her eyes. "No."

"I think you're trying to protect your mom," Uncle Buddy said, in a gentle voice. "Come on, Sarah, let's step out so he can speak with his lawyer again."

Sarah patted Malick's shoulder. "Take your time and think about it."

"Will the jury let my mom off? What do you think so far?"

"I don't know." Sarah wiped her brow. Some jurors appeared open minded as they followed the testimony, while others looked like they had their mind set on a conviction from the beginning.

"But you gotta have an idea by now." Malick looked from Sarah to Uncle Buddy. Sarah heard the desperation in his words.

"Look, Malick. I've been doing this a long time." Uncle Buddy smacked his lips together. "I can barely remember what life was like as a layman. I'll tell you from experience: no one can predict what a jury'll do, no matter how strong or weak the evidence is. They often decide cases on pure emotion."

Sarah watched Malick take the witness stand again. Court had been delayed for thirty-five minutes while Malick consulted with his lawyer.

"Malick, did you mean what you said last on the witness stand about shooting the fireman?"

"No." Malick looked at his mother. "I didn't shoot the fireman."

"Why did you say that you did?"

"Because I don't want my mom to go to jail." Malick faced the jury. "I'd rather go myself. I know she didn't do it. She would never kill anybody or light the store on fire while I slept upstairs. No way." Malick covered his face with his fingers to hide the tears. "She loves me too much."

"Nothing further."

"Recross?"

"Yes, Your Honor." Marinelli marched back to his spot before the jury.

"Malick, it's fair to say you'd do anything to help your mom."

He nodded. "We stick together."

"Thank you."

Sarah watched Malick walk back down the aisle with head hung low. She studied the jurors. Would they believe any part of his story? Would they take it out on Uncle Buddy and her for making him testify?

41

"**A**re we wasting our time out here, Uncle Buddy?" Sarah paced the length of the cramped conference room provided by one of her uncle's lawyer friends in Cambridge. Grease Gordon didn't want to risk being seen in their Charlestown office.

"It's all part of the process. Gordon knows quite a few unsavory characters, and he's willing to work with us. Worth a shot."

"I don't know about this, Uncle Buddy. I don't trust the guy. Why all the secrecy? And why's he so willing to help us?"

"Grease Gordon has an agenda." Uncle Buddy retrieved the surveillance video taken from inside the Mobile Mart during the time the Russian claimed to see someone filling balloons with gas.

"And what's his agenda?" Sarah wished she had more answers.

"Revenge possibly? But let's not waste time monkeying with that. We'll figure it out eventually."

"What if he's working for the other side?"

"You've been watching too many Bond movies. Let's see what he has to say and not give up too much in return."

Sarah couldn't help feeling leery about a guy with the nickname *Grease*. He also worked for the governor, whose name kept popping up.

"I've got a good one for you." Uncle Buddy reached into his coat pocket and pulled out a set of keys. "I lost these in the house last week. Aunt Margaret and I turned the place upside down and searched for hours until we had to stop. She kept telling me to pray to St. Anthony and they'd turn up." He rolled his eyes. "Like they'd suddenly appear out of thin air? *Right.*"

Sarah sighed. "So, where were the keys?"

"Two days later I found them jammed into the toe of my Sunday shoes."

Sarah was quite familiar with the polished black shoes her uncle wore to church. "Am I to assume your Sunday shoes are related to our case? Did you find a clue inside?"

Uncle Buddy raised a finger. "No, but things have a funny way of turning up. I'll tell you another one. About three years ago—"

Someone knocked on the conference room door. *Saved by a knock.* Sarah had been spared another story.

"Mr. Gordon's here. Ready for him?" the lawyer said.

"Send him right on in." Uncle Buddy waved his hand. "Thanks, Kevin."

Sarah exchanged a brief handshake with Gordon, while Uncle Buddy started right in with his typical kibitzing and name-dropping. She was surprised at how many people her uncle knew from Quincy. This could take all night if she didn't rein them in.

"I can start this videotape anytime." Sarah walked over to the television and placed her finger on the VCR's play button.

"Go ahead." Gordon scratched his sideburn. "Again, no guarantees I'll recognize anyone."

Sarah nodded. "The quality isn't very good, so you'll have to move your chair a bit closer."

He scooted his chair toward the TV and leaned forward. Sarah pressed play, and, after a few seconds, the counter of the Mobil Mart came into view. They watched over a period of time as several lone customers entered and paid for various items, including gas.

"What about that guy?" Uncle Buddy pointed at the screen. "Sarah, rewind the tape. I don't think we need to monkey with the rest of it."

Sarah pressed the rewind button until she located the thin, dark-clad figure wearing a baseball cap.

"Okay, let's play this part over a few times." Uncle Buddy turned to Gordon. "See if you can recognize anything about this man. The way he walks? His posture? His hands? Anything at all."

"Is this the guy who paid while she, I mean, the other one wearing the headscarf, filled the balloons with gas?" Gordon asked.

"Allegedly." Sarah's stomach muscles tensed. Why was he glued to their trial? What was his agenda? "I don't believe a word the Russian said anyway." Sarah wanted to make that point loud and clear.

"So, why are we bothering with this at all?" Gordon asked.

Uncle Buddy nodded. "We have to keep an open mind and explore all possibilities, even if we don't want to believe in them. I've learned the hard way over the years." He winked at Sarah. "Playing the devil's advocate, if we believe any of the Russian's testimony, this may have been the man who paid for the gas inside. The timing's about right."

"You know . . ." Gordon raised his index finger. "I watched the Russian guy testify. Looked like he wanted to collect the reward money and cop a good plea for himself on the armed robbery. He screwed his friend. Speaking of that, I figured out the meaning of your tie that day."

"Yes, the two rats, but the judge made me take it off." Uncle Buddy looked disappointed, but Sarah knew that whole charade drew attention to the tie.

"Was the Russian arrested by the feds?" Gordon

asked. "They're always working deals, getting people to rat out."

"The feds weren't involved because the Boston Police had the case." Uncle Buddy paused. Sarah knew what he was thinking—Gordon had experience dealing with the feds on his own bribery case. She wondered how he got them to sweep it under the carpet.

"Show that part over." Gordon moved closer to the television and squinted as they watched the man enter and pay again. "It's tough to see what the guy looks like beneath the cap. Can't you make the image clearer?"

"No, it's an outdated security system. Terrible quality," Uncle Buddy said.

"What's his cap say?" Gordon addressed Sarah.

"Cast It." Sarah had noticed that before. "Whatever that means."

"Refers to fishing, I bet." Uncle Buddy put his hands together and made a throwing motion. "Like casting out a line."

"You're probably right." Gordon studied the grainy image of the man on the screen once more and shook his head. "I can't help you here. Sorry."

"No problem, we appreciate your time." Uncle Buddy ejected the tape. "More food for thought: the guy we're looking for may have some sort of illness and possibly likes olives."

Sarah hoped her uncle wasn't giving up too much information.

"Olives?" Gordon asked.

"We found some pits."

"Hmmm. Maybe I should take a look at the original state police file on the Quincy fire case," Gordon said.

"You can't." Sarah wondered about that. He had to be on a fishing expedition. Someone out there must have paid him to gather information. "That's impossible."

"Why not?" Uncle Buddy shrugged and addressed Sarah. "Why don't you go ask Frank?"

42

Derrick watched a good-looking, gray-haired man take the witness stand. He wondered how many more witnesses the defense would call. That morning, several jurors expressed a desire to get on with deliberations, especially Quahog. Derrick felt obligated as foreperson to remind them all that they had to refrain from discussing the case.

"Please introduce yourself to the jury." Sarah stood behind the podium with her legal pad. Derrick admired her poise. She had such a tough go-around with Amina's son. Derrick felt sorry for the boy, especially after hearing the story about his father. He wondered what would happen to Malick if they convicted his mother. He shouldn't have testified.

"Good afternoon." The witness smiled at the jury. "My name is Paul Antico."

"How are you employed?" Sarah asked.

"I'm the founding president of Origin & Cause, Inc. My company provides nationwide consulting services in the fields of fire and explosive investigation."

"What experience do you have with fire investigation?"

"I'm a retired lieutenant commander for the Massachusetts State Police. I spent nineteen of my twenty-five years in the fire and explosion investigation unit operating out of the state fire marshal's office. Before retirement, I commanded the unit for seven years."

Derrick listened to Paul Antico describe his years of specialized training and experience. The certifications this man had earned were quite impressive. He lectured at the National Fire Academy and elsewhere around the world, and published books and articles on advanced fire investigation techniques.

"How many times have you offered expert testimony in the field of fire investigation?" Sarah looked up from her pad.

"Hundreds of times in both state and federal court. I've testified as an expert primarily for the commonwealth and only twice for the defense in a criminal case." He smiled and looked at the defense table. "I've also endured several of Attorney Clancy's cross-examinations and lived to tell about it."

Derrick laughed along with the rest of the courtroom. He saw the wide grin on Clancy's face.

"When were you first consulted in this case?" Sarah eased away from the podium.

"On July twenty-fifth of last year."

"What were you asked to do?"

"Perform a preliminary review of the case, which included reading all police and fire reports and lab results. I also examined the fire scene."

"How are you paid for your work?"

"I'm paid an hourly rate of $215 plus expenses. I receive $350 per hour for court appearances."

Derrick wondered how Amina came up with the money for her defense. Malick's college fund? Her retirement savings? No wonder this guy took so long reciting his credentials—he was on the clock. Now he made the big bucks testifying as an expert witness. Derrick removed his glasses and rubbed them clean.

"After your preliminary review of the case, what did you do?"

"I conducted my own detailed fire investigation."

Derrick forced himself to take notes as Antico described his exterior and interior investigation of the burned building. He employed the same basic techniques as Sergeant Brady and collected his own fire debris samples. It had been interesting and informative the first time around, but now the afternoon dragged. He caught several jurors focusing on the clock. Derrick watched Sarah introduce dozens of photographs of the charred first and second floors. Derrick imagined the pile of pictures they'd have to sift through during deliberations.

"Based upon your examination of the building and noting the directions of fire travel, were you able to form an opinion as to the area of origin for this fire?"

"Yes. In my opinion there were two areas of origin. The initial area of origin occurred on the first floor in the back left-hand corner where I found the lowest and heaviest fire damage."

Derrick watched him point out the first area of origin on an enlarged photograph and diagram. He was more interested in the second area. Sergeant Brady claimed there was only one.

"Were you able to form an opinion as to the specific cause of the fire that had its area of origin on the first floor?"

Derrick leaned forward. Did this expert find an accidental cause? Faulty wiring? Would he say it wasn't arson?

Antico looked into the jury box, making eye contact

with Derrick. "In my opinion this was an incendiary fire. Incendiary means that the fire was the result of the deliberate act of a person."

The witness instantly gained credibility in Derrick's point of view. He was a paid expert, but he wasn't going to take the stand and say anything the defense wanted him to.

"Do you have a theory as to how that fire started?"

Antico gave Sarah a slight smile. "An open flame was likely applied to combustible materials. However, I reviewed Sergeant Brady's report and, in my opinion, it's quite a stretch to draw the conclusion that someone hung gasoline-filled balloons from the ceiling. Potato chips are highly flammable. In that scenario, the latex would've melted in midair."

Derrick also found it hard to believe that a balloon fragment was recovered in the fire debris. Was Sergeant Brady exaggerating? Was he trying too hard to connect the dots and build a bulletproof case against Amina?

Sarah walked back to the podium. "Where did you find the second area of origin?"

Derrick looked at Sarah. Why hadn't she asked Antico his opinion on the red latex fragment that was recovered in the debris? What was his explanation? Did Sarah deliberately dangle the question to get everyone thinking and possibly questioning Sergeant Brady's investigation?

Antico walked over to the diagram of the upstairs apartment. "In my opinion the second area of origin occurred in the upstairs back bedroom next to this window." He pointed to the upper right-hand corner of the diagram. "Right here."

"What factors led you to your opinion?"

"I measured the depth of the char adjacent to that window and determined that it was an area where the fire burned lowest and longest on the second floor. I ruled out a connection to the fire that had its origin in the first floor."

"Why did you rule out a connection to the fire on the first floor?" Sarah raised her voice.

"Fire burns up and out. The burn patterns indicated to me that the fire with its area of origin on the first floor vented up and out through the kitchen windows on the second floor. The long hallway here served as a fire wall." He traced his finger over the hallway that divided the upstairs apartment. "You see, this long wall temporarily prevented the fire from spreading to the right side of the second-floor apartment."

"In your opinion, did fire travel up through the bathroom pipes?"

Derrick inched to the edge of his seat. *The bathroom pipes.* Sergeant Brady had theorized that the fire traveled up through the pipes to the back bedroom.

"Fire did travel up through the pipes connecting the first-floor bathroom to the second-floor bathroom. However, in my opinion, the fire spread up through the pipes later on. A second fire started near the window in the back bedroom before the fire traveled through the pipes from down below."

Sarah cupped her hands together. "What caused that second fire adjacent to the window on the second floor?"

"I discerned a clear pour pattern in the shape of a wide arc on the floor and a chair. Based upon my review of the lab results, I formed the opinion that someone used an open flame to ignite acetone on the carpet next to the window and on that chair."

"Did you eliminate other possible causes for the fire next to the window on the second floor?"

"I found no evidence of faulty electrical wiring,

appliances, or other heat sources that could've ignited that fire."

"Did you examine the roof of the building?"

"Yes. I noted there's a ladder bolted to the side of the building next to the back bedroom window that leads up to the roof. The building has a flat rubber roof."

"You mean the ladder leads from the same window where someone started that secondary fire?"

"Objection." Marinelli rose. "Leading."

"Sustained."

Derrick watched Sarah introduce several photographs of the ladder into evidence. Did someone really light that second fire with acetone and escape out the window, up the ladder, and across the roof? If so, they were lucky the ladder was there. Derrick glanced at the defendant. Perhaps Amina was the lucky one. The existence of a ladder to the roof gave her lawyers an opportunity to create reasonable doubt.

"Did you make any other observations about the roof?"

"I noted that the buildings are connected. There are areas where someone could get down from the roof."

"Please describe the locations of these areas."

"Number 103 has a small balcony off the back. One could hang down from the roof and the drop to the balcony would be about six feet. Number 101 has a small roof deck with a stairway down to the kitchen."

"Do you know who owns that building?"

"According to the Registry of Deeds, the building is—"

"Objection! Sidebar."

Derrick watched the lawyers march to the judge's bench for a conference. Could someone else have started that fire, shot the fireman, escaped across the roof and dropped down to a deck? Did the homeless man actually see someone running across the roof and think it was an angel? Derrick looked around the jury box and wondered what the others thought. Jeanette was shaking her head in the second row, appearing frustrated with the sidebar. He and Christine exchanged a quizzical look.

"No further questions."

Derrick was left wondering who owned the building.

Nick rose for cross-examination. Sarah had done an excellent job preparing her expert and keeping his testimony simple. He admired Paul Antico's style. He didn't preach or come across as a know-it-all. Instead, he educated the jury like a favorite classroom teacher who knew his subject matter inside and out.

"Good afternoon."

Antico smiled. "The same to you, Mr. Marinelli."

Nick had his work cut out for him. The jurors were likely to choose one expert over the other. Antico had more experience than Sergeant Brady and a gentle way about him. Nick would do his best to elicit testimony that would paint Sergeant Brady in a favorable light.

"Mr. Antico, you wrote the book *A Fire Investigator's Guide*?" Nick grabbed the hardcover book from his table and lifted it in the air.

"Yes."

"In chapter two you wrote: 'The fire investigator should respond to a fire scene right after fire apparatus is dispatched.'" Nick looked at the witness after he finished reading.

"That's correct."

He flipped a page and read another section. "'The fire investigator should speak with the officer in charge and first-in firefighters as soon as possible.'"

"Yes."

"And it says here, 'He or she should survey the exterior of the building during the fire.' Correct?"

"Yes."

"In this book you stress the importance of immediately interviewing witnesses at the scene, such as line-of-sight neighbors, passersby, and reporting witnesses?" Nick extended the book toward the witness.

"That's right."

Nick paused and rubbed his chin. "But in this case, you didn't even make it to the scene of the fire on July twentieth of last year?"

"I did not."

"You didn't interview any witnesses at the scene?"

"No."

"You weren't retained until five days after the fire?"

"That's correct."

Nick circled toward the jury. "You reviewed Sergeant Brady's investigative report?"

"Yes."

"Did you speak with Sergeant Brady about his investigation?"

"I did."

"Sergeant Brady arrived at the fire scene approximately twenty-five minutes after the first alarm was called in?"

"That's what he said."

"He examined the exterior of the building as it burned and took photographs?"

"Yes."

"Sergeant Brady interviewed the officer in charge and first-in firefighters?"

"Yes."

"Sergeant Brady conducted his initial fire investigation in accordance with the model set up in your book?"

"Yes, but it's his—"

"Please answer yes or no." Nick couldn't give him any wiggle room.

"Yes."

"In fact, *you* relied in part on Sergeant Brady's initial fire scene investigation?"

"I did."

"You were not present when Detective Callahan and Sergeant Brady first interviewed the defendant in the command center at the scene?"

"No."

"Therefore, you were not able to assess Ms. Diallo's demeanor within hours of the fire."

"Correct."

"You're aware that Sergeant Brady conducted a thorough interior investigation of the building within the first twenty-four hours of the fire?"

"Yes."

"He spent hours shoveling fire debris and reconstructing the scene?"

"Yes."

"Once again, you were not present for any of this tedious work."

"No, I was not."

Nick looked at the jurors. He hoped they would side with Sergeant Brady based on the time and energy he invested in the case.

"Mr. Antico, you agree with Sergeant Brady that the fire on the first floor in the market was intentionally set, an incendiary fire?"

"Yes."

"It's possible that a bottle of nail polish remover could've toppled from the windowsill or the small adjacent stand during the fire and spilled?"

"In that scenario, the burn pattern would've been

smaller and more concentrated in one area, as opposed
to a wide arc."

"Did you or anyone else recover a plastic bottle of
nail polish remover in the back bedroom upstairs?"

"No, but acetone was present on the floor near the
window."

"But you can't tell us when that nail polish remover
was spilled on that floor, can you?"

"I cannot provide an exact time frame."

"The nail polish remover could've been spilled on
numerous occasions over the years when the defendant
painted her nails in her bedroom?"

"It's possible."

"Thank you, Mr. Antico." Nick smiled. "No further
questions."

43

"**I have a** great deal of respect for Antico, but I still
think he's wrong," Frank said. "There was only one
point of origin. That first-floor fire traveled up through
the pipes. Your client is guilty."

"Let's agree to disagree." Sarah had grown weary of
debating with Frank, who sat next to Uncle Buddy at
the conference table. They'd been arguing over the
evidence for fifteen minutes. "Will you be in court
tomorrow?" she asked. Judge Killam had allowed
all sequestered witnesses to attend the closing arguments.

"Can't wait." Frank grinned. "So, I take it your client
will not be testifying?"

"Anybody want a pistachio?" Uncle Buddy hovered over a ripped plastic bag of pistachio nuts.

"You're making a mess." Sarah pointed at the shells on the conference room rug. She felt her level of impatience rising. "And, you, stop begging." She pointed at Rehnquist, who sat next to Uncle Buddy with a paw on the table, whimpering for treats.

"He's not bothering anyone." Frank reached across the table and grabbed a handful of nuts. "Clancy, only you would bring a big bag of pistachios and a dog with a bow tie to a legal meeting. You're a peculiar one."

"With peculiar instincts," Sarah said. She and her uncle had opposing views on Grease Gordon. She wanted to keep her distance, while Uncle Buddy had a hunch that Gordon could be useful. He mentioned Gordon's interest in the Quincy fire to Frank and convinced him to attend a meeting with Gordon in Cambridge.

"Gordon better show soon." Frank fiddled with his cell phone.

"You're going to break that." Sarah pointed at the phone.

"The state'll pay for a new one."

"Not in this budget crisis." Uncle Buddy wagged his finger. "The governor's slashing jobs left and right. Have you seen the lines at the Registry of Motor Vehicles these days? All I needed was a sticker for my plate and I waited over three hours. You watch, he'll raise the tolls again and up the gas tax too. Most expensive gas in the country."

"You're probably right." Frank cracked a shell between his teeth. "My job's next if I lose this case, so what am I doing here helping you two?"

"No, no, no, you've got it all wrong." Uncle Buddy waved his hand and finished crunching a mouthful of nuts. "You see, we're helping *you* solve that old case. When the verdict comes back not guilty tomorrow, you'll have the Quincy case to fall back on, save face."

"Clancy—" Frank paused when the door to the conference room opened and Grease Gordon stepped in. Sarah wondered how all this would go down. She knew Frank had his own agenda for attending.

"Let's cut to the chase," Frank said, as soon as Gordon shook hands with everyone and sat down. "You asked to see the file on the old Quincy fire. I can't exactly do that, but I'd like to know why you're interested?"

"Because Ms. Lynch here wants to know who shot her." Gordon sounded defensive.

"I think we'd all like to know that." Frank regarded Sarah for a moment; his eyes lingered on her left arm where the bullet entered.

Sarah rubbed her arm. She had to discover who fired the shots during Amina's arraignment. Donna had sent her down that path. She had to forge ahead despite her hesitation over Grease Gordon.

"So far, I've yet to find any connection to our old Quincy case." Frank popped another pistachio from its shell.

"And this may be our only chance to find one." Sarah had to work on Frank. She knew he desperately wanted to solve that old case with the homeless victims. "If the LaSpadas had anything to do with that barn fire—"

Frank sighed. "They were ruled out."

"I know, but, keeping an open mind, *if* they hired someone to commit arson in the past?"

"And with success." Uncle Buddy tossed Rehnquist a nut.

"Chances are they'd hire the same guy." Sarah waited for Frank to reply, but he worked on cracking nuts instead.

"Can I have a handful?" Gordon pointed to Uncle Buddy's bag.

"Of course. I apologize for not offering you any. Here." He emptied the bag and slid a pile across the table to Gordon.

"Thanks." Gordon cracked several shells. "There's something I've always wondered about."

"What's that?" Frank looked up.

"I remember reading in the *Patriot Ledger* that a witness saw the homeless people smoking shortly before that barn fire?"

"Okay . . ." Frank shifted in his chair.

"I knew most of the folks who lived in the neighborhood. After I read the article, I asked, 'Who saw the homeless people smoking?' Nobody knew. I came up empty-handed. That's when I began to suspect something. I also think someone found out I'd been out there making inquiries. A week later I got nailed for bribery and had my own set of problems."

"You sure did." Frank leaned sideways, stroked Rehnquist, and pulled a manila folder out of a bigger worn brown cardboard file.

"So I'd like to know who saw the homeless people smoking around the time of the fire?" Gordon said.

Uncle Buddy tapped Sarah on the arm. "One of the neighbors Sarah and I just interviewed commented on the same thing. Remember?"

Sarah nodded as she recalled their meeting with Mrs. Donahue.

"As I recollect, the witness you're referring to was interviewed at the fire scene." Frank thumbed through several papers. "Here it is. A subcontractor working in the area." He shrugged. "That's why no one from the neighborhood knew him." Frank flipped a page. "Looks like his alibi checked out too."

Sarah knew they usually investigated witnesses who came forward. Some arsonists were known to return to the scene of the fire.

"Who was it?" Gordon asked.

Frank looked around the table until his gaze rested on Sarah. He appeared to be thinking, weighing his options. He rearranged the papers without saying a word, and replaced the manila folder back in the file on the floor.

Sarah knew Frank hated sharing information with anyone. She had discovered that the hard way. What would he do? Sarah exchanged a glance with Uncle Buddy. He gave her a nod. That meant: push Frank. *Now.*

"Frank?" Sarah spoke softly. "We've all hit a wall. Our case, your case, it doesn't make a difference. At this point, what do we have to lose?"

Frank locked eyes with her. "The man's name is Cole Sollier."

44

Nick watched Sarah stand before the jury for the last time and smooth her cream-colored suit. She wore her hair long and gathered just below the neck in a mother-of-pearl clip. Sarah looked stunning. Nick could tell the jurors admired her, but would they side with her? He still believed the scales of justice tipped in his favor. When Sarah and Clancy rested their case, he knew the jurors were disappointed that Amina had not testified in her own defense. She had the right to remain silent, and Nick couldn't comment on why she had chosen to exercise that right in his closing argument. He scanned the two rows of jurors. *A penny for your thoughts.*

"Good morning Your Honor, counsel, and members of the jury. This is an emotional case for everyone." Sarah spread her arms. "A firefighter died." She paused and made eye contact with each juror. "In fact, taking this case on was a life-altering decision for me. I attended Jack Fogerty's funeral procession and was overwhelmed when his casket went by on top of Rescue One. *Don't take the case.* That's what my emotions said. *Just don't do it.*"

Nick heard the subtle choke in her voice as if water had gone down the wrong way. He knew Sarah meant every word she said. He studied the jurors . . . they knew it too.

"So why am I standing before you when it would've been much easier to walk away from this disturbing, unpopular case?" Sarah grabbed Amina's red flowered bowl from the clerk's table. "I just couldn't do it." She rotated the bowl in her hands. "I couldn't live with that decision. My conscience told me I had to take Amina's case. There were too many unanswered questions, inconsistencies, and other possibilities."

Nick listened to the conviction in Sarah's voice. He'd have to argue harder when it was his turn. He eyed the stoic faces in the jury box. Sarah raised the bar. He'd have to do his personal best to outperform her.

Nick watched Sarah place the bowl back and walk behind her client's chair as she had done in her opening statement. This time she gripped Amina's shoulders.

"My uncle and I believe in Amina. We did when we first took the case, and we continue to believe in her." Sarah paused without removing her hands from her client. "I've learned something over the course of this trial: justice is worth fighting for."

Nick wrote that down. He could use the same line in his closing. *Justice for the victim.*

Sarah walked back to her spot before the jury. "Amina's fate is in your hands. Judge Killam will instruct you that your decision is not to be made on the basis of emotion or sympathy. You are the sole and exclusive judges of the facts. It is your job to weigh the credibility of each witness and analyze the evidence. And *that* is a grave responsibility. Another person's life hangs in the balance."

Nick recognized Sarah's strategy to empower the jury and make them feel important about being the ultimate decision makers.

"Like me, you chose to take this case on. You didn't come up with an off-the-wall excuse to get out of jury duty. You took an oath to uphold the American justice system. What is the foundation of our system? We are all presumed innocent until proven guilty. The commonwealth has the burden of proving each element of these offenses beyond a reasonable doubt before Amina can be convicted of any crimes."

Nick noticed how Sarah raised her voice and carefully articulated each word in the last sentence. The burden-of-proof argument was a defense attorney's meat and potatoes. Judge Killam would discuss that burden at length when he instructed the jury.

"Beyond a reasonable doubt." Sarah stretched her arm up high and leveled her fingers. "That's a very high hurdle. Based on the evidence presented in this case, the Commonwealth did not meet its burden of proof. The police lacked probable cause to even arrest Amina. They acted on *pressure* to make the arrest." Sarah slowly swung her arm around toward the gallery.

Nick looked back and recognized that very pressure:

the union officials, the governor, and all the firemen. *Pressure to arrest. Pressure to convict.*

"Let's take a hard look at both charges and you'll see how the police rushed their investigation and jumped to conclusions." Sarah's lips formed a tiny smile. "The investigators should've read my favorite quote by Charlotte Brontë: 'Think twice before you leap.' "

Good one. Nick had to refrain from smiling himself. He remembered Sarah's propensity for quotes when she worked at the DA's office.

"We'll start with the fire." Sarah's voice sounded businesslike. "Sergeant Brady came up with opinions and theories about how the fire started. He found a tiny piece of red latex saturated in pickle juice and leaped to the conclusion that gas-filled balloons were suspended from hooks above the potato chips. Paul Antico, an acclaimed fire investigator, found that theory hard to believe.

"Sergeant Brady also leaped to the conclusion that fire traveled up through bathroom pipes into that back bedroom, ignoring the acetone poured in an arc pattern next to the window with access to the roof." Sarah tilted her head to the side. "Why did Sergeant Brady ignore the evidence of a secondary fire upstairs? Because he had a suspect in mind and didn't want to accept the possibility that he had the wrong person."

Nick recognized another favorite defense strategy: go after the police. Make their investigation appear shoddy and incomplete. Jurors often fell for it.

"The police considered Amina the prime suspect way too early, before they even entered the burned building. She voluntarily left her son's bedside at the hospital at 3:30 a.m. to answer questions. Now, who wouldn't be nervous with two gun-slinging investigators firing questions and bringing a dog in? Still, Amina cooperated."

Nick watched several jurors nodding along with Sarah as she offered alternative explanations for the presence of gasoline on the slippers, floor mat, and driving gloves. Sarah was chiseling away at his case, breaking off little chunks, creating fissures. It was up to Nick to rebuild.

"Sergeant Brady testified that he made the arson arrest based on witness statements." Sarah flipped her palms up. "*What witnesses?* No one witnessed Amina starting a fire. Actually, the first witness corroborated Amina's version of what happened. The BU student saw a frightened-looking woman running from the fire and then disappearing without a flashlight. Amina explained to investigators that she heard noises below in the store, went down, saw the fire, and ran back up to find her son. Is that criminal behavior?" Sarah walked the length of the jury box. "No. It's a mother's instinct to save her son. Further, why would she shut off an electrical main and not carry a flashlight?"

Nick bit the inside of his cheek. Sarah was jackhammering now. He had to appear unfazed.

"Does anyone really believe the Russian, Alex Kryuchkov, who watched the trial on TV and then came up with a story about seeing a woman wearing a headscarf filling balloons with gasoline? Now there's a guy who ended up with a great deal for himself. No jail time for armed robbery and a good citizenship award to boot."

Nick spotted Quahog chuckling. The Russian robber was a bit comical, but so was Sarah's homeless man with his angels and elephants.

"When the firefighters first arrived upstairs, the camera screen showed somebody running in the opposite direction, straight down the hallway. Who was that? Nobody can say without *guessing*." Sarah stretched out *guessing*.

"Why would Amina make a full meal for a homeless man if she planned to light her store on fire a short while later? It would make more sense to cancel the dinner that night to eliminate a potential witness. We know Amina and her son were very close. Why set fire to the store with her son sleeping upstairs? They both almost died."

Sarah looked back at her uncle. "My uncle has chosen his outer-space tie today. He calls it *the great beyond.*"

Nick glanced sideways at Clancy in his large black outer-space bow tie with yellow stars, moons, and what appeared to be comets. He sat next to Amina with hands folded and chin slightly raised. Clancy looked proud of his niece.

"Uncle Buddy always wears the *great beyond tie* for closing arguments as a reminder of the commonwealth's great burden: proof beyond a reasonable doubt. Did the police even come close to that? I suggest not. Remember the quote, 'Think twice before you leap.' Sergeant Brady and Detective Callahan leaped without thinking, ignoring other possibilities, and leaving too many unanswered questions."

Nick watched Sarah standing quietly before the jury. He couldn't see her eyes this time, but he knew she was making the crucial eye contact. Sarah and her uncle were quite a team. Clancy had likely insisted she explain the significance of the tie. The jurors would remember that—the all important visual. A bow tie for the concept of beyond a reasonable doubt. Leave it to Buddy Clancy.

"Let's look at the murder charge." Sarah raised her voice. "Detective Callahan also leaped without thinking twice. He arrested Amina based on inconclusive ballistics evidence and an unstable witness. There is no evidence whatsoever that Amina's gun fired the shot that killed Jack Fogerty. There was no gunshot residue on Amina's clothes, hands, or slippers." Sarah sounded angry.

"The commonwealth relies on the testimony of Andy Larson, who claims he saw Amina pointing a gun in Jack Fogerty's direction. Andy is a sympathetic witness, who's dealing with tremendous guilt and pressure. But, is he a reliable witness? Andy never mentioned the gun in his report and can't recall whether he told anyone about the gun at the scene. He also fell, struck his head, and may have passed out around the time he claims to have seen the gun. Andy admitted that part was a little blurry. *A little blurry.*" Sarah pursed her lips.

"If Andy really saw someone pointing a gun at his partner, wouldn't he dash to his aid? I suggest that the pressure of the trial got to him. He analyzed the events of that night so many times in his mind that he mistakenly believes he saw Amina pointing a gun." Sarah walked several paces, appearing pensive. "That's understandable. But can you convict someone of murder based on *that* testimony? The answer has to be no."

Nick knew Sarah had to be careful. Andy's credibility rested with the jurors. They could convict if they wanted to. She couldn't tell them what to do.

"What really happened on that tragic July night? Again, the burden of proof lies with the commonwealth. We don't have to prove a thing. However, the evidence supports an entirely different scenario. Someone else set that fire downstairs in the store. The easy escape route out the storage area in the back was blocked due to a recent delivery. The BU student was out front. This unidentified person had no choice but to run upstairs and start a second fire with acetone in the back bedroom and escape out the window and up to the roof. Even Captain Russo, the commonwealth's ballistics expert, admitted it was possible someone else could've shot Jack Fogerty with a common .380 handgun and escaped across that roof."

Nick caught the foreperson rubbing his chin and nodding. *Not a good sign.* Nick studied the others. Were they buying into the defense theory of what happened?

"Remember Danny Sullivan, the homeless man?" Sarah clapped her palms together. "His testimony corroborates our theory. He may have a different perspective, like believing in angels, but I suggest he saw someone on that roof. The timing is perfect. Mr. Sullivan saw that figure moving down the row of buildings to his left not long after the first two firemen went in."

Nick watched Quahog cross his arms. He didn't buy the bit about the angel. *No way.*

"Someone else committed these crimes. Was it a random act of violence? I suggest not. The background of this case speaks volumes. Amina simply wanted to operate the business that she started and built for fifteen years. She's an immigrant who pursued the American dream. Mark LaSpada persuaded her to buy the building at subprime mortgage rates, where he'd receive the larger fee, even though she qualified for a less risky prime rate. The lender was affiliated with his father's conglomerate, the LaSpada Development Company. In fact, four lending companies that Mark LaSpada used in East Boston were affiliated with the LaSpada Development Company. Was Amina the target of a subprime mortgage scheme? A scheme in which the lenders foreclose and LaSpada gobbles up the properties? Divide and conquer becomes foreclose and conquer." Sarah inhaled deeply as if trying to catch her breath. "It's legalized stealing."

The foreperson and several other jurors glanced at Nick looking for a reaction. He made a conscious decision not to object unless Sarah blatantly misstated the evidence. Nick knew from experience that jurors didn't like interruptions during summations. He would have his turn.

"Amina confronted Mark LaSpada at his office and told him what she had learned from the investigative reporter. Amina threatened to expose him and the LaSpada Development Company. Two days later, the fire occurred. Remember the antique barn which mysteriously burned in Quincy? A LaSpada project. Think about it. Was Amina about to blow the cover on LaSpada? Who *really* had the motive to burn her store? No one wanted Amina to get in the way. Perhaps that's what happened to Jack Fogerty. He got in the way too." Sarah spoke slowly and with emphasis.

"Ladies and gentlemen, this was and still is an emotional case. Divorce yourself from that emotion. Consider the Charlotte Brontë quote, 'Think twice before you leap.' We're asking that you think twice about the commonwealth's lack of proof. Think twice about who had the real motive to commit these crimes. Think twice about the true meaning of justice. Please find Amina not guilty of these charges." Sarah clutched her hands together. "Thank you."

45

Sarah breathed a sigh of relief as she sat back down between her client and Uncle Buddy. She finished the hard part. It was Nick's final turn to sweat it out before the jury. His last chance to score.

"May it please the court, counsel, members of the jury. This case is about Jack Fogerty, a firefighter murdered in the line of duty." Nick sounded strong. Sarah watched him make eye contact with each juror. They peered back at him with respect in their eyes.

"Jack was a living, breathing human being. Like each one of you, he had feelings, he had desires, he had quirks. Jack told long jokes, taking forever to get to the punch line. He was a bad cook. Jack had a family: a wife who loved him and four beautiful children." Nick motioned toward the family seated in the front row. "I also attended Jack's funeral. I'll forever remember the lone bagpipe and the image of the children tossing red roses on their daddy's casket."

Sarah recognized his strategy to employ vivid imagery, humanizing the victim and injecting emotion back into the case.

"Death is an irrevocable act that cannot be undone. Maureen Fogerty will never have her husband back in this lifetime. Those four children no longer have a father. Jack's baby girl will never know him." Nick's voice boomed across the courtroom. Sarah saw the jurors peering at the family with pity.

"In my opening statement I promised to prove beyond a reasonable doubt that the defendant, Amina Diallo, committed arson by setting fire to her store and dwelling place upstairs. In addition, Amina Diallo deliberately shot and killed Jack Fogerty without justification on July twentieth of last year. The shooting was a premeditated act committed with malice aforethought. Judge Killam will instruct you that is the definition for murder in the first degree." Nick's gaze remained fixed on the jurors. "The evidence piled on and around the clerk's table together with the witness testimony has enabled me to keep my promise to you."

Sarah noticed how Nick specified the elements of each crime that Amina had been charged with. The judge would soon repeat Nick's exact words. Sarah knew that Nick wanted the jury to believe he understood the law as well as the judge. Thus, Nick had the law on his side, and they must convict.

"Let's review what happened on that tragic July night." Nick placed a hand in his pocket. "You heard from Tim Murray, the BU student, who first observed flames in the back left-hand corner of the store. He saw the defendant running away from the fire. She looked right at him but did not ask for help."

Sarah couldn't help but admire Nick's choice to retell the story from the beginning, keeping it simple and straightforward. The jurors would likely review the case in order and Nick knew that. His job was to make it easy for them and paint a mental image of that night.

"Andy Larson and Jack Fogerty broke through the door and rushed into that burning building without hesitation. They made it upstairs and split up to save the occupants." Sarah watched Nick move to the diagram of the upstairs apartment. *Good move.* Jurors liked props during closing arguments.

"What happened next is *crucial*. Andy checked the front bedroom right here." Nick tapped the diagram twice. "He heard a loud bang that sounded like a gun firing and ran back toward the living room. That's when Andy witnessed Amina Diallo squatting and pointing a gun in Jack's direction. He saw the defendant clearly on the thermal imaging screen. In fact, Andy told you, 'I know it was her. She's the one I saw.' " Nick pointed at the defendant, imitating Andy.

Sarah studied the jurors' faces, looking for any signs of doubt. Whether they believed Andy or not was pivotal.

"After that, Andy ran toward Jack, tripped, and may have blacked out. Remember, he's in an emergency situation where every second counts. His years of experience on rescue tell him to save the occupants. Why didn't he rush over to see if Jack was okay? He saw Jack moving and doing his job. It was up to Andy to continue on and check the other rooms. And, that's exactly what he did."

Sarah knew that Nick couldn't ignore the weaknesses in his case; he had to talk his way through them as she had. No doubt the jurors would wonder why Andy didn't rush over to Jack after he saw the defendant pointing a gun. The answer was obvious to Sarah: Andy Larson didn't see a gun.

"Andy checked the other rooms without finding anyone else. He returned to the living room to see his partner crawling along the opposite wall with the defendant's son in his arms." Nick made a cradling motion. "Jack was dying and in excruciating pain, yet still fulfilled his duties as a Boston firefighter." Nick looked back into the gallery of firefighters and nodded at Jack's widow.

Sarah saw her crying and the jurors would see it too. *The sympathy factor.*

"Now the defense wants you to believe that a mystery man lit the fire in the market, ran upstairs, started a second fire in the back bedroom, and escaped across the roof." Nick grimaced. "First, there is no evidence of forced entry. How did the mystery man get in? The firemen who tried to get in through the back storage area didn't see anyone climb out the upstairs window and escape across the roof. Those firemen are trained to spot activity at windows and rooftops. The BU student didn't see anyone running across the roof either, and he was right outside watching the activity. The defense relied on the testimony of an alcoholic homeless man who claims he witnessed an angel flying across the row of buildings. Remember, that's the same guy who saw a fire truck fall from the sky and elephants dancing on the big blue bridge."

Sarah returned several raised eyebrows from the jury without flinching. She expected Nick would ridicule Danny's testimony. Had she made a mistake putting him on the stand?

"I suggest the defendant's son, Malick, is not a reliable witness, either. He was doing what he could to help his mother when he claimed someone ran near him during the fire. He lied about watching the trial on TV. At one point he told you that *he* shot Jack and then denied it."

Nick released a tiny smile. "I have a favorite quote by Lord Halifax: 'If the laws could speak for themselves, they would complain of the lawyers in the first place.'" The jurors laughed. "So don't be distracted by clever smokescreens and talking bow ties. Defense lawyers often make the best magicians." The jurors laughed again and looked at Uncle Buddy.

Sarah wished she had the last word. Nick launched a decent counterattack against their theories. On top of that, he came up with a good quote. Who would be left standing when the dust cleared? That was for the jurors to decide.

"Let's highlight the hard evidence that proves Amina Diallo is guilty of these crimes. Sergeant Brady told you that the fire started in the back left-hand corner of the store." Nick raised an enlarged photograph showing the fire damage in the area of origin. "This was an incendiary or set fire in which an open flame was used to ignite the highly flammable potato chip display. Gas-filled latex balloons were suspended from hooks above the potato chips. The heat from the burning chips popped the balloons and dispersed gasoline throughout the area, accelerating the fire."

Nick displayed another photograph showing the damage up through the kitchen area. "The fire then traveled upstairs into the defendant's dwelling. It spread up and out through the kitchen and up through the connecting bathroom pipes.

"You heard each expert explain how the fire debris collected in these cans exposed the crime of arson." Nick grabbed a metal can from the clerk's table and held it high beside the photograph.

Sarah listened as Nick highlighted testimony from the chemist and canine handler. She watched him parade the pink slippers, driving gloves, automobile floor mat, and red balloon fragment before the jurors. She wondered what the jurors would say about that lone piece of red balloon allegedly lodged in the crack of the floor. Would they think Sergeant Brady exaggerated? Would they hold it against him?

"Alex Kryuchkov witnessed the defendant filling up red balloons with gasoline less than twenty-four hours before the fire." As Nick highlighted his testimony, Sarah watched for signs of doubt from the jury box. They couldn't possibly believe the Russian who ratted out his friend and pounced on the reward money. The only one who appeared skeptical was Quahog.

"Let's take a good look at the ballistics evidence." Nick retrieved the gun and bullet from the clerk's table, and gripped one in each hand. "Captain Russo recovered this gun from the desk drawer in the living room." Nick extended the gun toward the jury. "This gun is registered to the defendant, Amina Diallo. This is the bullet that killed Jack Fogerty." Nick pinched the bullet between two fingers and held it up. "Captain Russo testified that the markings on this bullet share the same class characteristics as the .380 recovered from the desk drawer: the defendant's gun." Nick waved the gun. "This gun right here."

Sarah noticed the jurors appeared to be riveted by the gun. They couldn't take their eyes away from that small black weapon that Nick continued to exhibit over his head.

"Captain Russo told you that this gun is capable of holding seven cartridges when fully loaded. Five were recovered from the chamber. We know one was accidentally discharged through the desk drawer due to heat from the fire. That leaves an extra bullet. I suggest to you that this is that extra bullet. *The one that killed Jack Fogerty.*"

Sarah heard the fervor in Nick's voice. It was evident he wholeheartedly believed in his case despite the grenades she and Uncle Buddy had tossed at it over the past two weeks. Confidence meant everything. The jurors would pick up on the slightest trace of uncertainty.

"It all adds up to murder, and here's why." Nick replaced the gun and bullet on the clerk's table. "Remember Jack Fogerty had a flashlight clipped to his waist? Amina Diallo saw him coming. She was located in the far right hand corner of the living room, next to that charred desk. I suggest that's where she was when the firemen saw movement on the thermal imaging screen when they first arrived upstairs. It's also the exact same location where Andy Larson saw the defendant pointing a gun at Jack after he heard a shot." Nick clasped his hands behind his back and paced for a moment.

"Now, this is important." Nick gestured with both hands. "We have a significant inconsistent statement from the defendant pertaining to the desk and the gun. At first Amina told investigators that she kept the gun in her bedside bureau. The gun wasn't there." Nick stressed each word and raised his eyebrows. "Captain Russo recovered the gun from that desk drawer in the living room. After he informed the defendant where they found the gun, she changed her story. Ask yourselves, was the defendant trying to cover her tracks? Cover up a murder?" Nick scanned the jury box.

"The evidence suggests that Amina Diallo fired the shot that killed Jack Fogerty and then placed the gun in this desk drawer because she was standing right next to it." Nick walked over to the charred desk and forced open the warped top drawer.

"Why would the defendant do this?" Nick lowered his voice to a whisper. Sarah could barely hear him. "Judge Killam will instruct you that I don't have to prove *why* she did it. However, evidence of motive rings loud and clear. According to Mark LaSpada, the defendant said she'd destroy the store herself before she'd let the lender foreclose. Amina couldn't pay her mortgage; she was backed into a corner with no way out. The insurance policy was her saving grace: *one million dollars*.

"Burn the store down, collect the insurance money, and move on with her life. That was the plan." Nick clasped his hands together. "What happened?" He raised his voice. "Boston Firefighter Jack Fogerty got in *Amina Diallo's* way."

Nick glanced at Sarah and back at the jurors. "I do agree with the defense on one theme: justice is worth fighting for. *Justice for the victim. Justice for Jack Fogerty.*"

Justice for Jack. Those words echoed in Sarah's ears. She blinked away the vision of his casket atop the fire truck.

"Please return to this courtroom with guilty verdicts on both counts. Dispense justice for a fallen hero: Jack Fogerty, a Boston firefighter, shot down in the line of duty.

"Thank you."

46

Derrick sat in the center of the conference table with five jurors seated on each side and one at each end. They had been provided with fresh notebooks and pens.

"Flip the switch if there's anything you need or if you have questions for the judge. That just about does it." The court officer placed the remaining evidence on a long table against the wall. "I'll check up on you in an hour." He shut the door.

Several jurors were having side conversations. Derrick stood. "Okay, let's get—"

"I say we take a vote." Quahog raised his voice above the others. He sat on the opposite side with his sleeves rolled up and elbows on the table. Derrick spotted a tattoo on his forearm. It was . . . a big purple . . . *clam.*

"Judge Killam advised against a vote, remember?"

Derrick was annoyed. He wouldn't let Quahog take over. After jury instructions, he had crossed his fingers that Quahog would be selected as an alternate. *No such luck.*

"Derrick's right," Christine said.

"But if we vote and all agree on a verdict, what's the point of having a long discussion?" Quahog spread his arms and looked from one end of the table to the other. "Let's make it easy."

"Yeah."

"Can't hurt."

"We probably shouldn't."

Derrick heard various opinions mumbled around the table. Should they take a vote on whether to vote? No, he had to put his foot down. "We'll discuss the case first and then vote."

"That's ridiculous." Quahog exhaled. "If we all agree—"

"We'll get out of here sooner." The woman with the New York accent finished Quahog's sentence. Derrick watched her flick the government-issue black pen aside and extract a silver engraved Montblanc from its leather case. She considered jury duty secondary to her real job.

Jeanette raised a finger. "I haven't made up my mind." She sat at the end of the table closest to the evidence.

"And I'm sure you're not the only one." Derrick smiled at her. Everyone liked Jeanette. One morning last week she smelled like chocolate chip cookies. Probably baked fresh for the grandkids. "Let's start with the first witness."

Quahog grunted.

"Andy Larson?" The FedEx guy waved his hand. "Now, he had a tough job up there."

"No, it was the BU student."

Derrick sat down and checked his notes. "Yes, the student, Tim Murray. Did everyone find his testimony credible?" He looked around the table. Most nodded.

"Communications," Quahog snorted. "He caught the Arab in the act of setting her store on fire. Yup, I believe him."

"The *who*?" Linda stretched her arm toward Quahog and shook her silver bangles.

"The Arab."

"First of all, Amina Diallo is African, not an Arab. Second, we should refrain from using such derogatory language."

"What'd I say?"

"You referred to the defendant as an Arab."

"So what? An Arab from Africa. Didn't you see the veils she was sporting every day?" Quahog traced the outline of a long veil hanging down from his head.

Derrick figured those two would butt heads. They couldn't stand sitting next to each other throughout the trial.

"We should call Amina by her name." Antiliano addressed Quahog. "If I were on trial, I wouldn't want to be referred to as the good-looking Latino who cuts hair for the Red Sox."

Several people laughed. Thank God for Antiliano, Derrick thought. He often added comic relief with his stories about the Dominican ballplayers. Quahog liked him because he wanted to score free tickets.

"Come on." Quahog nudged Antiliano, who was seated next to him. "How would anyone remember a name like Antiliano Estrella? If you were on trial, they'd have to let you off." Quahog laughed at his own joke. "Besides, what would happen over at Fenway? They'd all have bad hair."

"Good point," Antiliano said.

"Have you thought of a career in acting with a name like that?" The young waitress leaned over the table and smiled at Antiliano. Her long blond hair fell forward, ensnaring a pen.

Derrick heard several voices discussing Antiliano's name. "Let's get back on track."

"Yeah, speed it up." The woman with the New York accent snapped her fingers three times. "It bothers me that Amina didn't ask for help when she saw the BU student standing at the front door."

"Bothers me too," the FedEx guy said.

"It would only take a second to open the door and have the kid call 9-1-1." Antiliano mimicked punching in numbers on a phone.

Derrick agreed. Why didn't she open the door and ask for help? He wished Amina had taken the stand and explained her actions during the fire. Judge Killam stressed that they were not supposed to consider why the defendant didn't testify. Amina had the right to remain silent.

"Let's face it." Quahog jammed a finger against the table. "Communications caught her in the act."

"Well, he didn't see her light the match." Derrick had to set Quahog straight.

"He didn't have to." Quahog grinned. "The Arab—Diallo—had guilt written all over her face. That's basically what the witness said. And we all know what guilt looks like."

Derrick leaned across the table toward Quahog. "I suppose you thought Amina looked guilty before the trial started."

"So what?" Quahog leaned forward too. "Gotta problem with body language?"

"How many of you are mothers?" Jeanette came to the rescue. She raised her hand and looked around the table.

Derrick counted four hands, including Jeanette's.

"I have three grown children." Jeanette lowered her hand. "You have to consider a mother's natural instinct to save her child. If my house was on fire, I may have reacted the same way. Amina's eyes were wide and she may have been looking right at the BU student, but did she actually see him?"

"Good point." Linda's bangles jingled. "We really can't make any decisions based on the student's testimony. Maybe Amina was afraid of a stranger peering in her window. I agree with Derrick. Saying somebody looks guilty is prejudicial."

Quahog rolled his eyes. "Judge Killam told us to use our common sense, which includes noticing body language, so I can voice my opinion on whether she looks guilty or not."

Derrick listened as several jurors discussed what a guilty look looked like. The waitress referred to the TV show *Survivor*. Derrick wondered why she was chosen for such a big case. *Too young.*

"Let's move on." The woman with the New York accent pointed to the clock. Derrick couldn't believe it was three thirty already. Judge Killam had given long instructions on the law. He wondered how many jurors had zoned out.

"Yeah, let's talk about Andy Larson."

Derrick noted animation on nearly everyone's face.

"Who thinks Andy saw Amina pointing a gun?"

47

This time Sarah couldn't concentrate and played a terrible game. Her team was shut out, 4–0, and they should've won handily. She lumbered away from the bench as the next team scheduled to play skated onto the ice. Her legs felt heavy and achy.

"Are you joining us for pizza, Red?" Farls placed an arm around her.

"Maybe." They had the early five o'clock game, and everyone was meeting for pizza at the Warren Tavern. Sarah didn't feel up to it.

"Your trial's done. What's your excuse now?"

"Farls, you have no idea how stressful it is waiting around for the jury to reach a verdict. My uncle and I are on standby notice in case the jurors have a question. Every time the phone rings I think it's the clerk. When he calls, we drop everything and rush over to the courthouse."

"Have they had any questions yet?" Farls asked.

Sarah nodded. "They asked if Judge Killam would let them experiment with the same type of thermal imaging camera used by Andy Larson during the fire. Typically, jurors love to conduct their own experiments."

"They allowed to do that?"

"Judge said no."

"Hmmm. I bet they're hung up on whether that guy really saw your Arab pointing a gun."

"She's African."

"Arab, African, whatever." He shrugged. "Doesn't matter. I believed him. Anyway, you're coming with us this time, Red. You need to relax, take a load off, get drunk."

"Let me shower and change first." She forced a smile, and upped her pace to the locker room. Perhaps she could change quickly and slip out ahead of Farls. Sarah knew they'd all be discussing the trial over beers and pizza like a bunch of Monday morning quarterbacks.

As she undressed, she became preoccupied with the case again. Amina's fate was in the jurors' hands, and Sarah had a bad feeling. What else could she possibly do? Grease Gordon didn't appear to know anyone by the name Cole Sollier. Another dead end. Time wasted.

Something's bound to turn up, Uncle Buddy had said that afternoon. *Remember when I lost my keys?* Sarah had made an excuse to get away from the office. She couldn't listen to that ridiculous key story again.

Sarah jammed her hockey jersey into the duffle, and noticed a text message had come through on her cell. It was from Gordon, urging her to meet him in the parking lot after the game. She squeezed into her jeans, threw on a sweatshirt, and bolted out the door.

"What's going on?" Sarah called out when she spotted Gordon across the lot leaning against his pickup truck. Uncle Buddy's lost key story popped into her head. Maybe something turned up.

He didn't answer.

"Why did you text me?" Sarah rested her hand on his truck and dropped her hockey bag on the pavement.

"I know Cole Sollier." He folded his arms.

"But I thought . . . ?" Sarah couldn't believe her ears. "You actually know the witness who saw the homeless people smoking in Frank's old Quincy case?"

Gordon nodded. "I've known Cole for years. He was real tight with Salvatore LaSpada, the patriarch. In fact, I think they went to grade school together. I also believe he was the guy at the Mobile Mart."

"No way." Sarah felt her heart pounding. "But I thought you didn't recognize anyone in the video?"

"The cap gave it away." Gordon tapped his head. "A few years back Cole was part of the crew who landed a record tiger shark in the Vineyard's Monster Shark Tournament. I remember seeing him on TV."

"You got that from reading *Cast It* on his cap?"

He grinned. "*The Cast It* was the name of the boat that brought the shark in. I double-checked it online."

"Did you tell Frank?"

"No, not yet." Gordon shifted his weight. "It wouldn't be the best move. I've been thinking about it. Cole's had run-ins with cops in the past, and I know he wouldn't like Frank. I should feel him out first."

"No. I think we should bring Frank in right away." Sarah didn't want to waste any more time. They needed to act on this. If they turned up any evidence that exonerated Amina, she could possibly present it to the judge before the jury reached a verdict. "Know how to find him?"

He nodded. "I've been to Cole's place, fished on his boat many times. It's been a while, but at least I know him."

"Where does he live?" Sarah considered telling Frank herself.

"I'd rather not say."

"Come on. Let Frank make the arrest and get this Cole character to flip on the LaSpadas. Frank is one of the best at persuading people to confess. Believe me, I used to work with him. He has a gift."

"Too risky. If it backfires, you're sunk. If the LaSpadas find out, they'll kill Cole."

"It could backfire on you too." Sarah didn't like the idea of letting Gordon act alone. Too much at stake. She recalled the last time she ventured out to meet a dangerous witness. It ended in tragedy. She couldn't let it happen again. "Do you really think you're going to get anywhere with Cole? I doubt he'll come out and confess everything to you."

"I hear he's sick."

"Sick?" Sarah recalled Danny's devil being sick. "What do you mean? How sick?"

"He's dying of stomach cancer. That's why I may be able to get through to him."

"Why not let Frank do it?"

"I'm telling you, Cole doesn't trust cops." Gordon raised his voice.

Sarah could tell from Gordon's tone she couldn't change his mind. "Can I come?"

"With me? You crazy?"

"Desperate."

Gordon rubbed his temples. "I'll see him as soon as possible. You're going to have to trust me on this one. Okay?"

"There you are!" Farls shouted from the door of the hockey arena. "Thought you ducked out on me, Red."

"Shit. Hold on a minute, let me get rid of him. I'll be right back," Sarah said to Gordon. The distraction bought her time to think. Gordon's words *as soon as possible* must mean *now*. He was planning to meet with Cole next.

Sarah jogged over to Farls. "Order me a cheeseburger," she said out loud. "I need a huge favor," she whispered. "Don't look over there, but follow that guy I'm talking to."

"What?" Farls looked right at Gordon.

"Don't look over there. Please. Just drive up the street and watch for his truck when he pulls out of the parking lot. I need this more than anything. I have to know where he's going."

48

"**I agree with** Derrick, let's begin this morning with the evidence." Jeanette walked over to the table against the wall and grabbed plastic bags containing Jack Fogerty's coat and tee shirt. She removed the items and passed them to Linda, who sat on her left. The fireman's coat still smelled like smoke. Her fellow jurors appeared sullen as they examined the bullet hole.

"Shall we look at the autopsy photos now too?" Jeanette wanted to get that part over with.

Derrick rose. "Do you mind grabbing the photos while you're up, Jeanette?"

"Certainly." Jeanette gathered the labeled pictures that had been admitted during the medical examiner's testimony. She shivered looking at multiple angles of the pasty-white, naked corpse. *So dehumanizing.* Jeanette scanned the table and found several shots of Jack Fogerty with his family and one of him marching in the St. Patrick's Day Parade. She shuffled the photos like a mini deck of cards and placed them neatly on the conference table.

"Thank you." Derrick smiled at her.

"You're welcome." Jeanette liked Derrick. As foreperson, he was doing his best to keep them on track.

"Who could shoot a fireman?" Antiliano raised the coat.

"I don't know." Derrick grimaced as he flipped through the pictures. "Here's a guy posing with his family, and the next thing you know he's being dissected at the morgue."

"Do you think it could've been accidental?" Kara addressed Jeanette. She was surprised to hear from the petite Asian woman, who seemed so quiet and shy throughout the trial.

"We *know* it wasn't accidental." The woman with the thick New York accent took a cursory look at the coat and shoved it toward the next person.

"No we don't." Kara gave her a dirty look and passed the blood-stained tee shirt to the FedEx guy.

"If you were listening, the ballistics expert said the bullet that traveled through the drawer did not hit the fireman," the New Yorker spoke rapidly.

Jeanette wished that woman had been picked to be an alternate. She acted like an authority on everything.

"The real shooting could've been accidental." Kara raised her voice. "I'm not talking about when the gun went off in the drawer. Maybe a different gun fired accidentally from the heat."

"Hmmm."

"Interesting."

Jeanette noticed several jurors wrinkling their brows, considering the possibility.

"There's no evidence of that." The New Yorker waved her hand in dismissal.

Kara rose from her seat. "If it was hot enough for one gun to fire accidentally, why couldn't it be hot enough for another one to go off?"

Quahog cocked his head. "We're talking random guns lying around the house, fully loaded? Going off like fireworks in there? I don't buy it."

Derrick flipped through his notes. "When Jack Fogerty got shot, I don't think the room was hot enough for a gun to fire accidentally due to the heat."

"I agree with you." Quahog pointed at Derrick. "When the gun went off in the drawer, fire was coming up through that heat duct beneath the desk. Got real hot."

Jeanette was surprised to see Quahog agreeing with Derrick on anything.

"Okay, but what about self-defense?" Kara remained standing. "We know Amina bought the gun for protection. On the night of the fire, Amina hears noises, runs downstairs, sees the fire, and goes back up."

"Don't forget the BU student." The waitress waved.

The New Yorker rolled her eyes. "We've already discussed him."

"Amina may have been frightened when she saw a stranger with his face against the window." Jeanette felt like siding with Kara and the waitress on this one. "How would Amina know that he didn't start the fire?" Jeanette wished Amina had testified. She wanted to hear a more personal story, along with Amina's version of what really happened during the fire. "Consider Amina's state of mind."

"I would've been scared seeing a man outside in the middle of the night." Kara placed her hands across her chest. "So Amina runs back up to look for her son and panics because she can't find him. Then she sees a big figure coming toward her. She thinks it's somebody coming after her and Malick. Amina's scared. She panics. The guy keeps coming. Amina shoots him in self-defense."

Jeanette noticed how quiet the room had become.

Sarah sat in a booth at the Banshee in Dorchester and pretended to study the pub's lunch menu. Every time the door opened, she looked up, hoping it would be Gordon. The wait was killing her.

Once again, Sarah dwelled on the events from the night before. Farls had successfully followed Gordon's truck from the hockey rink down to the south shore town of Scituate. Gordon had parked in front of a run-down beach cottage along Turner Road and walked inside. Farls provided her with the address. She considered taking the trip herself or going to Frank with the information, but decided against both options on the chance that Gordon's instincts were right. Perhaps he could convince Cole to flip on the LaSpadas. But Gordon should've called her last night. Sarah had tried to get in touch with him for hours to find out what was happening, but all she got in return was a text message to meet him for lunch at the Banshee. Why the long wait? It must not be good. Had she made a huge mistake? Could she trust Gordon?

Sarah forced herself to read through the traditional Irish pub menu. Halfway down, somewhere after the beef stew, she lost her focus. Farls mentioned that Gordon stopped along the way to meet with a woman in a Stop & Shop parking lot. The woman's description fit Donna. Had he been working with the reporter all along? Why had he lied?

"Sarah." Gordon rushed in and sat opposite her. "Sorry I'm late." He sounded out of breath. "The food's good here. Hungry?"

She had no desire to exchange pleasantries. "You're not being straight with me. What's going on?"

"I met with Cole last night." Gordon paused as a waitress came to the table and ran through a list of specials. "Let's get shepherd's pies. They make the best in town."

"Sure." Sarah didn't care what she ate. "What happened?" she asked, when the waitress left.

"Cole is very sick, probably has a month to live. He also takes care of his mother, who's in her nineties and can't get around."

"Did you get him to talk?"

"When I first got down there, he thought I was back in with the LaSpadas. You know, that's how we met."

Sarah hoped it wasn't true. Could Gordon be working for the LaSpadas now? "What did he say?"

"Asked if Mark LaSpada sent me down, and if I had something for him. Why else would I be there, you know? So, he kept asking when I'd seen Mark last. Sounded desperate, like he's looking for cash. I bet they owe him."

"And?"

"So I told him I was there for another reason. That I'd heard some things through the grapevine about the LaSpadas' plans to hang him and his mother out to dry because he's going to die anyway. I said I was there to warn him because I'd been screwed by them in the past. He knew all about that."

"Did he admit anything to you?"

"Not really." Gordon drank from his water glass. "I got him thinking."

Sarah sighed. "How do you know he won't turn around and call Mark LaSpada? Get you killed?"

The waitress served the steaming shepherd's pies. Sarah watched Gordon making lines in his mashed potatoes with a fork. He was holding something back.

Sarah decided to be abrupt. "What is your agenda in all of this?"

Gordon dug into the meat and potato pie, blew on his fork, and filled his mouth. He didn't answer her question.

"Why did you meet with Donna on your way down last night?"

He stopped chewing. "You followed me?"

"I know exactly where you went, and now I know you've been lying about Donna. Everyone seems to lie about her. First Frank, and now you. What's going on?"

"I can't say."

"Fine." Sarah stood, crumpled her napkin into a ball, and threw it at him. "I'll get it all from Frank. Right now."

"You can't do that. Sit down."

"No. I'm not wasting any more time with your bullshit. I knew I shouldn't have trusted you from the get-go."

"Sarah, listen to me." He leaned over the table, glanced around the pub, and lowered his voice. "I'm working with . . . She's not who you think she is."

Sarah sat back down. "Not a reporter?"

"I can't say much. I'm not supposed to discuss anything at all, but I'm part of a federal investigation that's been ongoing. I've been placed in my job for a reason. It was part of a plea bargain."

"That's why you didn't get jail time for bribery." Gordon's role was making sense. "So, the feds must be after the LaSpadas too?"

"They're after someone even bigger."

"Who?"

"I can't say."

This time Sarah played with her food. No wonder Donna took off; she didn't want her investigation compromised.

"Now do you see why I have to take it easy with Cole? There's too much at stake," Gordon whispered.

"Amina's life is at stake. She's on trial for murder. Amina comes first for me."

"Why not wait to see if the jury comes back not guilty?" Gordon said. "Besides, you can have the verdict overturned if we discover she's innocent in the long run."

"I can't take that risk. What if Cole dies or gets killed in the meantime? Where does that leave Amina?"

"What do you suggest? I can't push this guy too much." Gordon dropped his fork.

"Take me with you to Scituate. I need to speak with Cole myself."

"No way. Absolutely not."

"You have no choice."

49

Quahog studied the two large pizzas, searching for the biggest slice. It wasn't going to be enough. If this crew had a hard time agreeing on the type and number of pizzas, how would they ever agree on a verdict?

"Excuse me." Quahog moved in for the kill. He slapped the largest piece of pepperoni on his floppy paper plate.

"Watch it. You just splattered sauce on my blouse." Liberal Linda pinched the material and jiggled it up and down. The rest of her jiggled too.

"Ahh, it's tie-dyed, Linda. The pizza sauce adds character."

"Rude." She huffed and dabbed the two tiny spots with a wet napkin.

"Let's sit down and work through lunch. Come on, everybody. Let's go. Let's go."

Quahog hummed, "Start spreadin' the news . . ."

Christine giggled. "Stop that, she's going to catch on."

"I don't care." Quahog crammed the pizza into his mouth. "That lady's always trying to rush us. What's a New Yorker doing on a Massachusetts jury anyway?"

Christine smiled. "I'm assuming she lives here."

"Another transient yuppie," Quahog said, with his mouth full.

"We'll take a look at this pile over here." Derrick gathered the pink ladies' slippers, car floor mat, and leather driving gloves.

Quahog nudged Antiliano. "Be sure and grab another slice before you sit down. They're going fast."

"We should've ordered more."

"Tell me about it. We got voted down, remember? Speaking of votes, I'd like to know where everybody stands. Feels like we're talking in circles."

"Ms. Yankee will move us right along." Antiliano grinned and Quahog groaned.

Quahog settled in his seat and removed the slippers from the plastic bag. "These here are the proof in the pudding." *And they'd voted down dessert too.* "The Arab spilled gas on her slippers when she was setting up the balloon scheme."

"Don't get pizza sauce all over the evidence." Liberal Linda's voice sounded so whiney that it squeaked. "And don't refer to her as *the Arab*."

Quahog grunted. He let that one slip on purpose.

"Who'd commit arson wearing slippers?" The FedEx guy looked around the table. "Wouldn't you wear running shoes?"

"Cuts both ways." Antiliano made a scissors motion with two fingers. "If Amina really woke up to noises in the store, don't you think she'd run down barefoot? Who'd have time to put slippers on?"

"Yeah." The blond waitress flipped her hair back. "She'd have to find her slippers in the dark."

"I wonder if they were on the right feet?" The FedEx guy held the slippers up with the toes pointing out. "I'd like to know."

Quahog had opened a can of worms with the slippers. "She was running from the spot where the fire started." Quahog bit into his second slice. "That's one crazy Arab caught in the act."

"Knock it off or I'll tell the judge." Liberal Linda clanged her bangles against the table.

"Go right ahead."

"I think it's significant that Amina didn't have a flashlight," Ms. New York said. "If you planned to shut down the electrical main and then run from a fire, you'd carry a flashlight."

The FedEx guy raised a finger. "Maybe she dropped it."

"Doubt it."

"The fire guy would've found it," Antiliano said.

"The batteries may've gone dead." The blond waitress shrugged. "Happens every time I lose power in a storm, and then I can't find any matches, so I have to sit in the dark."

Circles again. Quahog tipped back his Coke can and drained it.

"I don't think we can decide guilt or innocence based on the slippers." Kara stood and Quahog wondered whether it was custom for Asians to stand every time they wanted to make a point. "Both the canine handler and the chemist said it's possible to track through fire debris and pick up gasoline residue."

Quahog rapped the empty can on the table. "That's what Judge Killam called circumstantial evidence. It all adds up, another piece of the pie." He could go for a thick slice of Boston cream.

"Quahog's right." The FedEx guy raised his voice. "We've also got gas on her car floor mat and gloves. The Russian witness said he saw Amina get out of a white car, which fits the description of her car perfectly."

Jeanette raised her hand. "There are plenty of white cars out—"

"And the Russian said she placed the box of gas-filled balloons in the back." Ms. New York raised the mat. "I guarantee more than one balloon leaked gas through the box onto this mat."

"Well, I got a problem with the Russian armed robber." Quahog couldn't resist sharing his inside knowledge. "Do you all know why the judge made Clancy change his tie that day?"

Antiliano grinned.

"Don't tell. See if they picked up on it." Quahog looked at Antiliano and placed a finger on his lips.

"The tie had two big rats, insinuating that the Russian was a rat because he testified against his friend on the armed robbery," Derrick said. "Judge Killam told us not to consider actions of the lawyers. That's not evidence."

Know-it-all. Quahog gave Derrick a dirty look.

"We'd have a simple case here if it wasn't for the lawyers." Ms. New York twirled her silver pen. "Sarah Lynch and Buddy Clancy created as many smoke-screens as they could. That's what they're paid to do."

"I bet this one cost a lot." Antiliano whistled.

"Oil money," Quahog said.

"Just because you think she's Arab?" Liberal Linda wrinkled her nose.

"Absolutely." Quahog glanced around the table. Was he the only worldly one here? "Oil and fancy rugs. That's how they make their money, and they all got it tucked away somewhere."

"That's ridiculous even if Amina was from the Middle East." Linda huffed. "But we all know she's a Muslim from Africa!"

"Muslim, Arab, same thing. Oil and rugs." Quahog

wouldn't back down here because he knew he was right. How else would they fund all those terrorists? "Oil money is what she used to pay her lawyers."

"Come on. Let's move off that subject," Derrick said. "We don't need to speculate about how the lawyers were paid."

"Speaking of lawyers, Nick Marinelli knows she's guilty." The blond waitress twisted her hair around her index finger. "I can tell. I liked him."

"Yeah." The FedEx guy smiled at her.

He liked the blonde, Quahog could tell.

"The lawyers know a lot more than we do about the evidence," Antiliano said.

"The system here favors criminals more than any other state." Ms. New York looked at Liberal Linda.

"It's designed to protect the rights of the accused here in Massachusetts." Liberal Linda folded her arms. "Still hanging them in New York?"

Quahog would love to see those two paired against each other. Mud wrestling.

"I find it hard to believe that anyone who planned to commit arson would go to a gas station and fill balloons." Antiliano looked around the table. "What does everybody think?"

"I think the armed robber saw the trial on TV and jumped on an opportunity." The FedEx guy wagged his index finger. "Those Russians are wily. That guy grew up in a St. Petersburg orphanage, so I bet he's watching out for himself every chance he gets."

"How do you wrap a balloon around a nozzle, pump gas in, and not spill it all over the place?" Antiliano spread his arms. "Seriously?"

"I'd worry that someone would notice," the FedEx guy said.

"Yeah." Quahog crushed his Coke can. "Like a

Russian robber who just happens to be there casing out the joint at two thirty in the morning."

Everyone laughed. Quahog cursed himself for not pursuing a career in comedy.

Christine flipped through her notes. "They were blocking the clerk's view and pumping the balloons inside that box. I think they had a red gas can with them. It's possible."

"Maybe the Russian saw two Arabs filling up a gas can and embellished," the FedEx guy said.

"Maybe."

"What about that man who helped her fill balloons?" Christine looked at Quahog from across the table. "I wonder who he was and if they'll ever catch him."

"No offense." Quahog raised his palms and looked at Liberal Linda. "It was another *Aay-rab*."

"Of course *you'd* say that." Linda's bangles jingled as she pointed at Quahog. "I suppose you think they're all terrorists too."

"Most of 'em are." Quahog shook his head. "How many 9/11s is it gonna take before you and your fellow tree huggers get it? Close up the borders, that's my solution."

"Knock it off," Derrick said. "Amina's legal, she probably has a green card. We're getting way off track here."

"Gimme a break." Quahog looked around the table, knowing there had to be someone else who shared his views. People were just afraid of speaking out.

"Maybe the guy at the pumps was the son." The FedEx guy gestured with his pizza crust.

"Let's talk about that." Jeanette called out from the head of the table. "And then we should discuss the developer."

"Back to the balloons." Antiliano walked over to the

evidence table and picked up a metal can. "I was surprised this tiny piece of red balloon didn't melt in the fire."

"Do you think Sergeant Brady planted the balloon in the crack between the floorboards?" Liberal Linda's chin jiggled whenever she got excited. Quahog rolled his eyes again. She was definitely batting for the other side in more ways than one.

"You're forgetting about the pickle juice, Linda." Quahog smirked. "Preserved the evidence."

"I don't buy that."

"Don't buy them?" Quahog couldn't resist. "What's the matter with pickles, Linda? Are they contributing to global warming?"

Linda flung a crust at him.

50

Sarah gripped the can of mace in her jacket pocket and stepped out of her jeep. What was she doing down in Scituate without Frank or Uncle Buddy? *Was she insane?* Gordon waited for her on the porch of the weather-beaten shingled cottage. He had agreed to let her come only after a mountain of convincing, but only her. Sarah had decided not to tell Uncle Buddy. He'd never let her go alone. Besides, she reassured herself, he had to stay near the courthouse in case the jurors had another question or reached a verdict.

"Don't worry. His mother's in there too." Gordon gestured Sarah toward the door. He must've sensed her anxiety.

It was only three o'clock in the afternoon, yet Sarah noticed the drawn curtains. She climbed the partially rotted steps and followed Gordon across the porch and through the front door.

The living room looked gloomy with its wood-paneled walls and soiled, mismatched furniture. An old woman sat hunched over in a wheelchair beneath a mound of blankets in the far corner. She appeared to be sleeping with her mouth wide open.

The walls and tabletops were decorated with enlarged photographs of a thin-faced man in various poses on a fishing trawler. It smelled like hard-boiled eggs and mildew.

"He's in here." Gordon motioned toward a closed door. Sarah heard a television blaring in the background. She followed Gordon into a cluttered fisherman's study containing two windows with a view to the open ocean. A huge shark was mounted on the interior wall. A small menacing glass eye appeared to be staring right at Sarah. It gave her the chills.

"What's *she* doing here?" a scratchy voice called out.

Sarah jumped. She hadn't noticed the emaciated man sprawled out in a La-Z-Boy chair beneath the shark.

"Sarah Lynch, this is Cole Sollier." Gordon turned the television down.

"I can't believe you brought *her* here! What the hell is this?" The man coughed violently into a stained blanket. Sarah noticed a sickening fishy smell coming from his mouth. His black hair appeared wet and stringy.

"Remember what we talked about, Cole? The LaSpadas screwed us both."

Cole glared at Sarah. "I don't remember a thing."

"From yesterday?" Gordon's face contorted. "We talked about this for two hours straight."

"Must've been the meds they got me on." Cole shook an orange pill bottle, but kept his gaze fixed on Sarah.

"You're lying," Gordon said. "You called Mark after I left, didn't you?"

Cole shrugged his shoulders. "Don't remember."

Gordon paced between the windows. "What about your mother?"

"My mother?"

"When you're gone, the LaSpadas are gonna toss her out on the street like a bag of stinkin' garbage. Wheelchair and all."

"Get the hell out of here. Both of ya," Cole yelled and clutched his stomach.

"Listen to me." Gordon gripped both arms of Cole's ragged chair. "Sarah can help you . . . with everything . . . including your mother."

Sarah nodded. "I—"

"What's she got to do with my mother?" Cole pointed an elbow at Sarah. "I'm taking care of my mother."

"With what?" Gordon spread his arms, knocking over several pill bottles. "You can't even pay your own goddamn medical bills."

"Leave me alone."

Sarah listened to Cole's raspy breathing. She had to come up with a way to get through to him. If she asked the right questions at the wrong time, she'd get the wrong answers. Be patient, she reminded herself.

"Maybe the LaSpadas will put a bullet in your head. End it all for you." Gordon placed a finger to his temple and mimicked pulling a trigger. "If you're lucky, they'll buy you an extra large casket so you can be buried with that old shark of yours. Then you won't have to worry about your mother anymore."

Cole reached for a phone on his bedside table.

Gordon grabbed it away from him. "Why haven't they paid you? Huh? Have you figured it out yet, Cole? Was it because you screwed up and shot a fireman?"

"I didn't kill no fireman." Cole doubled over into another coughing spell.

Sarah had run out of patience. She decided to play hardball. "You set fire to the Senegalese Market."

"*Me?*"

"You filled those balloons with gas. I watched you on the surveillance video from the Mobil Mart."

"You're lying." Cole snickered. "I saw the trial. That camera wasn't working."

"The one behind the counter worked just fine." She pointed at him. "You were the one who paid inside."

"Out of your mind?"

"You were wearing that *Cast It* cap."

"The what?"

"*Cast It*. The boat from the shark tournament. You wore that hat."

"What the hell?" He raised his arms and addressed Gordon. "She's out of her goddamn mind."

"Tell Sarah the truth." Gordon crossed his arms. "Come on, you have everything to gain and nothing to lose."

Cole hacked blood into a stained cloth napkin. "She won't like the truth. It's not at all what she wants to hear." He jumped up and ran out of the study to an adjacent bathroom. Sarah heard him violently retching and throwing up.

"Okay, we'll take a vote now." Derrick had wanted to put the vote off as long as he could because he was still undecided. It was Thursday morning already, and they'd been deliberating since Tuesday. Would it look bad as foreperson to be uncertain of Amina's guilt or innocence? Did undecided mean he was leaning toward verdicts of not guilty? Not necessarily, he told himself.

"It's about time." Quahog refilled his coffee mug.

"Let's take it one charge at a time. Who thinks Amina Diallo is guilty of setting the fire?"

Quahog, the New Yorker, and the FedEx guy raised their hands at once. Derrick counted five additional hands, including Antiliano, the blond waitress, and his friend Christine, the nurse. Derrick was surprised; he thought Christine would go the other way.

"How many of you think she's not guilty?" Derrick looked up and down the table. Jeanette raised her hand. *The only one.*

"So the rest of us are undecided? Let's see a show of hands." Derrick put his hand up along with Linda and Kara.

"What about the murder charge? How many of you vote guilty for first degree murder?" The same crew raised their hands except for Antiliano.

"Antiliano, what gives?" Quahog elbowed him.

"I'm undecided on the murder." Antiliano shook his head. "The commonwealth didn't prove it to me."

"That's why I'm voting not guilty on both." Jeanette sounded determined. "I don't trust the developer. He hired someone to set that fire. I'm convinced."

"Anybody else for not guilty on the murder?" Derrick scanned the table. All hands remained down. "I assume the same people are undecided?"

Linda and Kara nodded.

Now what, Derrick thought.

· · ·

"I made a mistake bringing you here," Gordon said to Sarah as they watched Cole place an extra pillow next to his mother's head.

"That's right. Leave. Get the hell out." Cole gestured toward the front door.

"Yeah, come on, Sarah, let's go." Gordon headed toward the door. "This guy's all done. The LaSpadas know that too. They have no use for him now. Let's leave him here to rot in his own misery."

"I'm not going anywhere." Sarah's gaze remained fixed on Cole. "Let me speak with him alone."

"Won't do you any good." Gordon grabbed the doorknob. "Come on."

"He owes me this much and he knows it." Sarah spoke slowly and with conviction.

"I owe you?" Cole appeared incredulous. "I owe *you*?"

"You shot me in the arm." Sarah blurted it out. Both men stared at her. Maybe it was the wrong thing to say.

"Christ." Gordon shook his head.

Cole wheezed and headed back into his study at a brisk pace, holding his stomach. Sarah followed.

"You can go." Cole turned around and gestured Gordon out of the room. "I might get a kick out of this one."

"I need a cigarette." Gordon shook his head.

"Don't smoke near my mother."

"I'm going outside."

Sarah heard the front door close. Now she was quite alone, except for the mother, whatever good that would do.

Cole maneuvered into his chair and stared at Sarah for several minutes. He had small cold eyes like the shark mounted on the wall. She recalled Danny's words: *those eyes held demons. And they did.*

"Nice shark." Sarah pointed to the wall above Cole's head. She couldn't think of anything else to say.

"A female tiger." Cole regarded her for another long moment. "A beautiful thing. See the brown stripes on her back?"

Sarah regarded the stripes as well as the identical set of upper and lower triangular teeth. "Is this the shark that won the tournament?"

"No way. That was nearly two thousand pounds, and we didn't win. Missed the weigh-in by six minutes."

"Oh." Sarah wanted to keep him talking, build rapport as Uncle Buddy would do. "What's the story with this one?"

"That's my princess. She's a youngster. I hooked her fourteen years ago near Woods Hole. Seven feet two inches, 188 pounds." Cole grinned. "She loved to kill."

"Sharks *have* to kill." She met his cold stare and refused to look away.

Cole finally broke the silence with a hoarse, sinister laugh. "You're one hell of a lady. Fact, you remind me of my dear, beloved princess." He twisted around and peered up at the shark.

"Thanks." *A unique compliment.*

"Did I interfere with your hockey?"

"My hockey?"

"When I shot you in the arm."

Sarah stared at him. "I learned how to play righty."

"Righty." He choked. "Good answer."

51

"**D**id you people** watch the same trial?" Quahog eyed the undecided camp: Liberal Linda, the Asian librarian, and Derrick. "Come on." He wasn't worried about Antiliano being undecided on the murder. He'd come around. Quahog and the rest of the guilty camp spent all day Thursday trying to convince the undecided camp to join them. Quahog couldn't believe it was Friday morning and they were still deliberating.

"How can anyone say Marinelli didn't prove his case with all this evidence?" The FedEx guy swung his arm toward the evidence table.

"You're singing to the choir." Ms. New York rolled her silver pen between her palms. "This is getting ridiculous."

"We should decide soon." Christine looked sideways at Derrick. "I feel sorry for Jack Fogerty's wife and family. They deserve closure."

"They certainly do." Jeanette wrung her hands.

"I agree," Derrick said.

Quahog hoped Christine could get through to Derrick. He noticed they had become close friends. They needed the foreperson in their guilty camp. If Derrick folded, Jeanette would follow.

"If we can't decide, we'll be called a hung jury." The FedEx guy leaned toward Derrick. "The case will be tried all over. We can't put the family through this again."

"Torture," Antiliano said.

"We'd be letting the justice system down." Christine spoke softly.

"Like a buncha tree-hugging wimps." Quahog smirked at Liberal Linda.

"Don't look at me like that." She always gave it right back to him in that whiney voice of hers. "How would you feel about sending an innocent woman to jail?"

"That Arab's not innocent, Linda." Quahog was fed up with her. "You're just too wishy-washy to decide on anything."

"I take offense to that." She raised her nose in the air.

"Good." Quahog wondered why the lawyers picked Linda in the first place. Couldn't they tell by the outfits and jewelry that she'd be way out there?

"That's enough." Derrick removed his glasses and rubbed his eyes. "We're all getting anxious and tired. Let's try and work it out. I don't want a hung jury either, but we need to be sure before we send anyone to jail."

"Sergeant Brady did a thorough job on his arson investigation." Antiliano grabbed the last jelly donut. "Both the prosecution and defense agree that somebody deliberately started a fire downstairs in the store. I think Amina Diallo set that fire."

"Antiliano." Quahog faced the barber. "How can you be convinced that she committed arson, but not murder?"

"I think somebody helped her set the fire, and maybe that person escaped out the back bedroom window. I'm just not sure who it could've been."

"Remember the homeless guy who saw the angel?" Liberal Linda raised her hand and jingled the bangles like a gypsy dancer shaking a tambourine.

"Ahhh." Quahog could expose the loony now. "Yeah, the angel did it, Linda. Guess we can all vote not guilty and go home."

She glared at him. "I think he saw somebody escaping across the roof."

"And he also saw elephants dancing on the blue bridge, Santa Clauses running through the streets in their underwear, and believes in miracles." Quahog raised his voice. "Come on."

"Actually." The FedEx guy raised a finger. "I know for a fact when they were celebrating the opening of the Zakim Bridge, fourteen elephants stood in a line across it. I remember getting stuck in traffic that day."

"He's right," Jeanette said.

Ms. New York nodded. "They used elephants to test the Brooklyn Bridge back in the eighteen hundreds. My great-grandfather told me about it when I was a little girl. Elephants won't cross an unsafe structure."

The blond waitress giggled. "I wasn't going to say anything, but there's a pub crawl every year where the guys dress up as Santa Clauses and wear boxers."

"So maybe the homeless man wasn't so crazy after all?" Linda cocked her head toward Quahog and stuck her tongue out like a three-year-old.

Quahog rolled his eyes. Let her make a fool of herself.

Antiliano sighed. "The homeless guy was right about the Sox winning the series. Many thought it was a miracle."

Quahog had to agree with that, but he still couldn't trust anything that came out of the mouth of a drunk bum.

The Asian librarian rose. She was in the undecided camp. "Even if someone helped Amina set the fire and escaped across the roof, she'd be guilty of arson." She addressed Liberal Linda. "Amina had the motive to set the store on fire, and the evidence really does point to her."

Quahog sat back and let her review the arson evidence again. They were finally making headway.

"The murder count hinges on Andy Larson's testimony, whether we believe him." Antiliano looked around the table. "What does everyone think?"

Quahog wanted the first word. "I believed Larson when he pointed right at Amina Diallo with that black stick and said, 'She's the one I saw.'" He looked at Antiliano and then Derrick. "I've been around the block, grew up in the Old Colony project. Larson's an honest guy. I could tell by his eyes."

"Me too. I don't blame him for not putting everything in his report." The blond waitress smiled at Quahog. "Sarah was too tough on Andy, don't you think?"

"Yeah." Quahog hadn't liked the way Miss Hockey attacked him either. "After all, his partner was shot and killed."

"Sarah was doing her job," Derrick said.

"Still."

"But how could Andy omit the part about the gun early on in his report?" Derrick pointed to the gun on the evidence table.

"Sarah had a good point there." Jeanette raised a finger. "If Andy saw someone pointing a gun at Jack, wouldn't he rush over to see if his partner was okay?"

"We're getting stuck on that again." Quahog got up, grabbed the gun, and walked over to the charred desk. Someone had to set them straight. "This is Diallo's gun, which was recovered with five bullets in the chamber. It holds seven. Diallo shot Fogerty with the first bullet. She placed this gun back in this desk drawer. The second bullet fired accidentally. Then she lied about where she kept the gun. *Guilty.*"

Quahog could tell he had the undecideds thinking. If the guilty camp could get the undecideds on board, Jeanette would have to give up. He looked down the table at the prim and proper Italian grandmother in her yellow dress. Jeanette appeared upset that morning. Why would she side with the Arab and vote not guilty?

"You know." Quahog realized he wasn't supposed to voice an opinion on this one, but he couldn't help himself. "If I was innocent and on trial, I'd testify in my own defense. It says something about—"

"Stop." Derrick raised his palms. "We're not supposed to draw any inferences about the fact that Amina chose not to take the stand."

The room went quiet. Quahog knew they were all thinking about it. The Arab should've testified.

52

"**F**rank, where the hell have you been?" Sarah sprang from her office chair as he walked casually through the door. "Did you get my messages?"

"And good morning to you." Frank handed her a large coffee.

Sarah tore the plastic triangular tab off. "Why didn't you call me back?"

"I tried you earlier at home and left a message. It's just ten o'clock now. Relax." Frank sat in the leather client chair. "What are you so anxious to tell me about?"

"I met with Cole Sollier yesterday down in Scituate." Sarah drank the coffee and watched Frank's eyes widen as her words registered.

"Cole Sollier? He's the witness from my old Quincy case."

"Right, and I know he's the guy who shot me."

"What the—?" Frank moved too quickly as he

jumped to his feet, knocking a stack of loose papers from her desk. "Why didn't you tell me?"

"They didn't want police involved."

"They?"

"Yeah, Grease Gordon brought me down there." Sarah raised her hand before he interrupted again. "Listen, Cole's dying of cancer, but he's willing to talk. I think."

"We'll record him then. A video would be ideal."

"I doubt he'll go for that," Sarah said.

"I'll just tell him—"

"He won't talk to you." Sarah watched Frank's mouth drop open. "I'm going to handle this one alone."

"Alone? No way."

"Do you want your Quincy case solved or not?"

"This is ridiculous." He spread his arms and leaned across her desk. "Sarah, you don't know enough about it. Like what questions to ask. All that."

"Why do you think I called you?"

"There's something sinister going on here. *I feel it.*" Jeanette stood before the other jurors during lunch. She felt like it was her against the world. Maybe she could convince them otherwise. *Maybe.*

The rest of them stared at her. Did they perceive her as another wacky grandmother who'd lost her marbles?

"What do you mean, Jeanette?" Derrick broke the silence.

"There are too many forces at work against Amina Diallo. I grew up in the West End, which was taken by eminent domain. We didn't have a choice; all of us had to move out. Anyone who fought the powers that be, lost. Nothing's changed. Amina, a single mother, picked a fight with a big developer and she didn't even know it. Did she ever stand a chance?"

"Diallo was facing foreclosure, so burning the store was her last resort." Quahog finished the rest of his meatball grinder.

"Perhaps it was Mark LaSpada's last resort. They were worried she knew too much." Jeanette snapped her fingers. "This case is all about greed."

"Do you think somebody tried to kill Amina and her son by setting her store on fire?" Christine wiped the corners of her lips with a napkin.

"Somebody tried to take her out during the arraignment." The FedEx guy pointed with the corner of his turkey sandwich.

"We had that homemade bomb on the second day of the trial." Linda raised her salad fork. "Remember?"

"The homeless guy got attacked too." Derrick drained his Coke.

"Yes." Jeanette pictured the poor man. "God bless him." She slid her chair back toward the evidence table and reached for Amina's bowl with the pretty red flowers. It was a piece of evidence that hadn't been discussed. "Amina wouldn't set fire to her store after all she's been through. She had to raise her son all alone after her husband was jailed and deported. Amina wanted a better life for Malick, so she worked herself to the bone all those years to run her business and provide for him. Why destroy it all now? I believe deep down in my heart that Amina wouldn't do this."

"Jeanette." Antiliano spoke softly. "Amina had a tough go of it, no doubt. I know how hard it is to run a small business and raise a child. And to top it off, she was about to lose everything: her store and home." He paused. "I think the pressure finally got to Amina. *She cracked.*"

. . .

"This is what I'd concentrate on." Frank pointed half-way down the second page of a police report from his Quincy arson file.

Sarah and Uncle Buddy leaned over her desk. She had prepped with Frank for about an hour for her meeting with Cole.

"I still don't like the sound of this." Uncle Buddy placed a hand on Sarah's shoulder. "You're taking risks you shouldn't be taking. I have a bad feeling."

"Do you have any other suggestions?" Sarah heard the sarcasm in her own voice.

"Yes. Let Frank handle it."

"I agree." Frank looked up. "In fact, I could potentially lose my job over this. Or, worse, something could happen to you."

"I should never have told either one of you."

"You're probably right about that." Frank winked at her.

"Have you reached Donna?" Sarah changed the subject.

Frank rubbed the circles under his eyes. "I've tried all my contacts. No luck. They've got a tight grip on this one."

"I wonder who the feds are investigating?" Uncle Buddy tapped his lips with his fingertips. "I can't believe they're using Grease Gordon as some sort of informant within the state government."

"He knows just about everyone. Perfect for the job," Frank said.

Uncle Buddy nodded. "I have a feeling their case overlaps somehow with ours, and I've been racking my brain trying to figure it out. I keep getting stuck on those documents that were stolen from your kitchen, Sarah."

"Me too." Sarah chewed on her cuticles. "We're missing something. It bothers me that Cole said I wouldn't like the truth, that I'd be surprised. What could it be?"

Both Uncle Buddy and Frank appeared deep in thought.

Sarah decided to speak up. "That's why I have to get what I can out of Cole now. See? This is our big chance." Sarah couldn't let Frank or Uncle Buddy waffle.

Their legal assistant barged into the office, startling all three.

"What's going on?" Sarah asked.

"The jury's back. They've reached a verdict."

53

"**M**r. Foreperson, has the jury reached a verdict?"

"Yes we have." Derrick felt the weight of his words. He rose and all eyes zeroed in on him, the leader.

"Do you have the verdict form?" Judge Killam's voice sounded somber.

"Yes I do." Derrick relinquished the folded paper to Clerk Kelly, who walked it up to the bench. He scanned the crowded courtroom. Firemen packed the gallery in their dress blues. The widow and her eldest son sat in the front row with arms around each other, studying him.

Judge Killam unfolded the paper and read the verdict to himself. Did he agree? Derrick couldn't tell. The judge refolded the paper and poured himself a glass of water. He took a long drink and handed the verdict back to the clerk.

Clerk Kelly raised the paper with both hands. "Will

the defendant, Amina Diallo, please rise and face the jury."

Derrick watched Sarah and Clancy stand up. Amina rose between them. Sarah placed a hand on her client's shoulder. She still believed in Amina. Derrick could see the longing in her eyes. Clancy had the concerned look of a wise elder: *I hope you did the right thing.*

Marinelli appeared as anxious as Sarah. He believed in justice, which, for the young prosecutor, meant a guilty verdict.

"What say you, Mr. Foreperson, as to indictment number 121971, charging the defendant, Amina Diallo, with the burning of a dwelling place in violation of Massachusetts General Laws, Chapter 266, Section 1? What say you, Mr. Foreperson: is the defendant guilty or not guilty?"

Derrick swallowed first and then he gazed at Amina. "Guilty."

Cheers and clapping interrupted the silence. Jack Fogerty's widow cried and hugged her son.

Derrick's stomach contracted when he saw Amina's lips trembling. The evidence pointed to *her*. All twelve had agreed that Amina set the fire. *She did it.* The evidence spoke volumes. Derrick glanced back at Jeanette in the second row. Deep down, she didn't believe it. He knew that. They had worn her down. A doubt flashed across his mind. Derrick pushed it away.

Judge Killam banged his gavel and the courtroom settled.

"What say you, Mr. Foreperson, as to indictment number 121966, charging the defendant, Amina Diallo, with murder in violation of Massachusetts General Laws, Chapter 265, Section 1? What say you, Mr. Foreperson: is the defendant guilty or not guilty?"

"Not guilty."

This time the silence stretched longer before snapping into pandemonium. Shouts and jeers erupted from the gallery. Derrick felt sorry for the widow, who collapsed into the arms of another woman. Her body shook as she sobbed.

Jeanette had convinced them to vote not guilty on the murder and Derrick agreed. The evidence was too sketchy. The Commonwealth hadn't met its burden of proof.

"Order!" Judge Killam pounded the gavel three times. "Does the defense wish to poll the jury?"

"Yes."

Clerk Kelly stepped forward. "Juror number one, as to count one, is this your verdict?" His voice reverberated across the courtroom.

Derrick regarded Amina again. "Yes."

"Juror number one, as to count two, is this your verdict?"

"Yes."

Derrick listened as each juror rose and confirmed the arson verdict against Amina. What a diverse group: Quahog, Linda, Jeanette . . . Antiliano. They had divided into factions, sparred with each other, and united in the end. Despite all that, this jury would never work together again.

"Does the commonwealth move for sentencing at this time?"

"Yes, Your Honor."

"Members of the jury." Judge Killam leaned over the bench. "This was a very emotional case. You took your job seriously and paid careful attention to all the evidence. I know how difficult it must've been to decide upon a verdict. Thank you for your service. You may stay for sentencing if you wish."

Derrick chose to stay. The lady from New York was the only one who left.

"Do you wish to be heard?" Judge Killam peered down at the defense table. Derrick wondered if the judge had already made up his mind. His demeanor appeared unyielding.

Sarah centered herself before the judge. "Your Honor, Amina Diallo has no criminal record. She supports local charities both here and abroad. Amina has struggled to support herself by operating her own business in this country for nearly fifteen years. She is a caring and loving mother, responsible for the well-being of Malick, her fifteen-year-old son."

Derrick studied Malick as Sarah continued praising her client. The boy stared at the back of his mother's chair and twisted his fingers beneath his chin.

"I respectfully request Your Honor's leniency." Sarah rejoined Amina and her uncle.

"Commonwealth?" Judge Killam remained stone-faced.

"Your Honor." Marinelli rose and looked back at the widow. Derrick noticed she was still sobbing in the front row. "The jury adjudged Amina Diallo guilty of setting her store and dwelling place on fire. Boston Firefighter Jack Fogerty responded to that fire and lost his life in the line of duty. At this time I'm requesting the court's permission to call witnesses to present victim impact statements."

"What is the substance of their testimony?"

"To describe the impact that Jack Fogerty's death has had upon his family and the Boston Fire Department."

Judge Killam leaned back and gripped the arms of his chair. "The defendant was adjudged not guilty on the murder indictment. Your request is hereby denied."

Marinelli looked disappointed. "Your Honor, based on the seriousness of the offense and the facts presented in this case, I'm requesting a substantial period of incarceration. Thank you."

"Will the defendant please rise?" Clerk Kelly sounded grave.

Derrick watched Amina stand and face the judge with Sarah and Clancy at her side. He held his breath. How much prison time did this woman deserve?

"Amina Diallo, you are hereby adjudicated guilty on indictment number 121971 and sentenced to the maximum period of twenty years in the state penitentiary. You will begin serving your sentence immediately." Judge Killam rapped his gavel.

"Court is now adjourned," Clerk Kelly said. "All rise."

Derrick watched Amina bow her head. Sarah whispered something while the sheriff's deputy handcuffed her.

"Wait. Can I say goodbye to my mom?" Malick stood near the attorneys' section. Tears streaked his face.

Sarah ran over and attempted to console him as the deputy escorted his mother out.

The sun warmed Derrick's back as he walked from the courthouse toward his T stop at Quincy Market. He planned to get off at police headquarters in Roxbury. It was time to come forward on the shooting he had witnessed years ago. He hoped that eventually another jury would get that case and dispense justice. It was the right thing to do.

Derrick didn't need a jacket; summer was approaching. *Twenty summers inside a prison cell.* Would he think about Amina from time to time? Absolutely.

54

"**Y**ou have to be strong for your mother's sake." Sarah sat behind her desk late in the afternoon with Malick and Uncle Buddy. She was still in shock from the verdict. "She wants you to focus on school and go to a good college. It's your mother's wish."

"Why did she get twenty years? Why?" Malick sobbed and struck the side of his chair.

"Judge Killam's tough. I'll do my best to get the sentence reduced." Sarah knew that would be an uphill battle, but what else could she say? Someone knocked.

Sarah opened the office door.

Their legal assistant appeared worried. "There's a lawyer here to see you," she whispered and glanced at Malick.

"I'll be right back." Sarah walked into the reception area to see a male lawyer accompanied by a tall African man and a woman.

"Armand DePalma." The lawyer handed her a card. "I'm representing Lamine Diallo in the petition for sole custody of his son, Malick. I just filed an emergency motion in family court, requesting a hearing. Lamine would like Malick to return to Senegal. This is his cousin who will escort him."

Sarah stared at the African man.

"This is Wendy Hadley from the Department of Social Services." The lawyer motioned to the petite woman standing next to him. "She will bring Malick with her at this time."

Sarah had to think quickly. "He isn't available just yet."

"It's my understanding that he's here," the lawyer said.

"Malick has to come with me now." The social worker handed Sarah a business card and several papers pertaining to custody. "You have no choice in the matter."

"Hold on." Sarah left them standing in the reception area and returned to her office. She motioned Uncle Buddy to the door. "We've got a guy who claims he's a cousin, a woman from DSS, and a lawyer. They're here to take Malick away. What shall we do?"

"Delay," Uncle Buddy whispered. "Tell them I've taken Malick out to dinner somewhere, and you can't get in touch with me."

Sarah nodded. "I'm going down to Scituate right now. If I can get Cole to talk—"

"Not by yourself," Uncle Buddy said. "Get Frank to go with you. Please do that for me, Sarah."

55

"**C**ole?" **Sarah banged** repeatedly on the door. *Come on, please answer.* Frank was on standby notice down the street. This was it. She had to squeeze the truth out of Cole. She rested her forehead against the frame. *Twenty years.*

"You have to leave," Cole replied in his raspy voice. "I can't talk to you right now. I'm sick."

"It has to be now. This is an emergency."

"Go away."

"You owe me, Cole, remember?"

No reply.

"For shooting me in the arm?"

Nothing.

"Come on."

"Go away for your own good."

"I can't do that." Sarah pounded on the door, and wondered what or who had changed his mind. "I can have you arrested right now, Cole. You admitted shooting me. That's attempted murder."

"I'm dying." He retched. "I won't even make it to my arraignment."

"If you're dying, you can tell me the truth. I need to know who set fire to the store." She struck the door hard with the heel of her hand until it throbbed. "Who did this?"

"Didn't you hear the verdict?"

"You know she didn't do it, Cole." Sarah kept her voice firm. "Let me in."

No reply.

Sarah banged on the door again. "The LaSpadas will end up killing you."

"So?"

"But you care about your mother, Cole. I know you do. You need to make sure she'll be alright before you die." This was her best shot. "I'll help. We can get her into a good nursing home and set her up with a living trust. I know a lawyer who practices elder law." She drew a deep breath. "Come on. What really happened?"

"I already told you—" He unlatched a bolt from inside and opened the door a crack. "You don't want to hear the truth. The Arab has been lying to you."

Lying? What did he mean by that? Sarah smelled his sour breath. "If she has, I still deserve to know the truth."

"Why? It doesn't matter anymore. They're coming

to pay me." He rubbed his fingers together. "They got their verdict."

"If anyone comes now, it will be to kill you."

Cole met her gaze. He had a knowing, yet menacing, look in his black eyes. Still, he had opened the door. *Run with it. Think offense.* "I bet they'll kill your mother first and then you." Sarah pushed forward, widening the crack in the door. She pushed again, and this time he stumbled backward. She squeezed inside and quickly shut the door behind her. Something about Cole had changed; she felt it. A rancid smell struck her nostrils. He was holding a lobster pot half-filled with vomit. She gagged.

"What's the matter, can't handle being around a dying man?"

Sarah swallowed hard. "Let me record your statement, and I'll keep it just in case they kill you later today." She looked at his mother sleeping in her wheelchair, and decided to ease up for a moment. "I'm sorry for her. I'm sure she was a good mother to you, Cole."

Cole bowed his head for a long time. "Can you really help her?" he whispered. Sarah could barely hear him.

"Yes. I promise."

Cole nodded.

"Come on, let's set up in your den." Sarah seized the moment and walked into the room with the big shark. It looked hungry and ready for a kill. She felt a wave of dizziness. The odors were worse than ever. *Get it over with. Do it for Amina.* She forced herself to breathe through her mouth.

"You're right." Cole cleared the phlegm from his throat as he entered the den with his pot. "They'll kill me. What do they need me for now?"

"Nothing. You're a liability." Sarah waited until he

positioned himself in his armchair with the lobster pot between his legs.

Cole's eyes appeared drawn and his complexion had a yellow tint. "You'll take care of my mother?"

"You have my word."

He curled into a ball on his side. "Do what you have to do. Just hurry."

Sarah set up a portable video camera on an end table and aimed the lens in his direction. The shark's eye followed her around the room as if it were protecting its master. She despised the thing.

She started with a simple introduction: date, time, place. "Okay, tell me about your relationship with the LaSpadas?"

"Sal and I. School together."

"Salvatore LaSpada?"

He nodded.

"Did you eventually work for the LaSpada family?"

He nodded again and gripped his stomach with both hands.

"What did you do?"

"Took care of stuff." He belched. "Paid well."

If he weren't so ill, Sarah would've taken him back to the beginning of their relationship, but she needed to focus on the two relevant cases: the Quincy fire and Amina's case.

"Did you set that antique barn on fire in Quincy?"

"Yup."

"Did Salvatore LaSpada instruct you to burn the barn?"

"Yeah."

"What about Mark LaSpada?"

"No, not him."

"Did you know two homeless people were in the barn when you set the fire?"

Cole nodded. "They were sleeping off the booze—bourbon as I recall. With a carton of cigarettes."

A planned double murder. Sarah felt like vomiting in the pot. She hated Cole. "How much did they pay you?"

"Fifty grand." He threw up into the pot and wiped his mouth on his stained blanket. "That feels better." He peered out the window. "If anybody shows up, hide. They can't see you here. They'll kill us both."

Did he suspect they'd be coming soon? Sarah decided to jump right into Amina's case and get out. She had an uneasy feeling. "What was your role in the fire at the Senegalese Market?"

"I helped Mark LaSpada fill the balloons and paid in the gas station like you said." Cole forced a smile. "Mark looked good in that Arab getup. Next day, I went to the store, hid in the back in that storage place. Snuck the box of balloons in the back door."

"Did you stay in there until the store closed?"

He nodded.

"What did you do after that?"

"I came out and hung the balloons up." He shrugged. "Started a fire beneath the potato chips, just like they said."

Sarah felt her heart racing. She could get Amina out of jail with this. *Keep going.* "How did you escape?"

"The Arab came down, so I ran upstairs."

Sarah noticed Cole's heavy breathing. "Did you think about escaping out the front door?"

"Somebody was there."

The college student. Sarah was surprised he hadn't seen Cole run past. "How did you get out of the building?"

"Bedroom window. I ran across the roof and dropped down to a deck. The LaSpadas owned it." He grinned again. "Foreclosure sale."

"Did you start another fire upstairs with acetone?"

"I did!"

Uncle Buddy and she had been right all along. "You happened to have it with you?"

"Comes in handy."

As a young boy slept upstairs. Sarah hoped this man would spend his remaining days in prison. *A despicable human being. The devil. Danny had been right.*

"You were hoping Amina and her son wouldn't make it out? That was your plan?"

"The LaSpadas wanted your client dead." He paused. "What's that smell?"

The vomit bowl, perhaps? "That's why you tried to kill Amina at the arraignment?"

"That's what they wanted, but I missed and shot the lawyer, shot you. So I had to keep doing shit for them to make up for my mistake. If I'd been shot and killed that day in court, they wouldn't have paid my mother. I know that now. That's why I'm doing this. They screwed me."

"You also attacked Danny in his alley because he saw you run across the roof?"

Cole hacked blood onto his blanket. "I had to make sure you lost in court. That's why I broke into your apartment. They wanted your papers."

"Referring to the Corsett Trust." Sarah felt her fingers shaking; she was so close. *Push. Go in for the kill.* "Why?"

"Your friend Gordon knows. Why don't you ask him?"

"I'm asking you."

He pursed his lips, but she could see the tiny smile in the corners. "Connects Noterman."

"The governor?" Sarah lurched forward.

Cole nodded and commenced another long coughing

spell. Thank God they were almost done. He wasn't going to last much longer.

"How does it connect the governor?" Sarah spoke rapidly.

"Casino license. He'll grant it to the Corsett Group."

"How does that connect the LaSpadas?"

"It's one of their companies. Same guys, different names. They have the plans in place already."

"How can we find documents?"

"In a safe-deposit box. Black Rock Bank, Scituate."

"Do you have a key?"

"Me?" He raised his eyebrows. "No way. You know, you were awful close when you had Mark squirming in court. *So close* that I was actually rooting for you."

Sarah recalled all the various trusts and shell companies the LaSpadas had been operating, like a ball of tangled twine. They must've used one hell of a good real estate lawyer.

"So, let me get this straight. Governor Noterman will grant the casino license to the LaSpadas, and they'll build it in East Boston. That's why they've been grabbing up all the property they could through the foreclosures." Sarah pictured the casino with its luxury hotels and condominiums. *A goldmine.* "How will the governor benefit?"

Cole grinned. "I'm sure the LaSpadas will hire him on as a well-paid consultant after he steps out of office."

Sarah needed one more answer and then she could go. "What about the fireman?"

"I didn't kill him." Cole looked into her eyes. "I would never kill a fireman. My grandfather was a fireman."

Sarah froze. *He was telling the truth.* Did Amina kill him? Is this what Cole had been implying when he said she wouldn't like the truth?

"Tell me who did it."

"When I ran upstairs I heard somebody go past. I stopped to see where they went, looked around." Cole grabbed his stomach and grimaced. "I could barely see up there, but I know what I saw."

"What?"

"That's when they came."

"Who?"

"The firemen."

"What happened?" Sarah held her breath, fearing his next response. She squeezed her eyes shut. "Was it Amina?"

"Wait—" Cole jumped up, knocking the lobster pot over. "We got to get out of here. That's gas I'm smelling." He grabbed her arm and pulled her out of the room. "Go out the front. I'll grab my mother."

"Oh my God." Sarah ran into the living room; the odor of gas was overwhelming. "I'll help you."

"I got her." Cole scrambled behind the wheelchair and pushed it toward the door. "Go!"

Sarah made it down the front steps and onto the lawn.

The next thing she knew, she was lying on the ground under a heavy coat. Frank knelt on one side of her and Nick on the other. Flames consumed Cole's cottage. They were nearly a hundred feet away, yet she could feel the heat.

"Thank God you made it out." Nick squeezed her shoulder.

Sarah attempted to get up, but Frank placed a hand on her arm. "I've called an ambulance. You need to be checked out."

"What happened?" Sarah felt her body trembling.

"The place exploded." Frank shook his head. "You're lucky to be alive."

"Did Cole and his mother make it out?"

"He rescued his mother and went back in. Somebody saw him do it."

"How did you get here?"

"I heard the explosion and drove right over. A neighbor grabbed his mother's wheelchair, which was on the front lawn, while I picked you up off the ground."

Sarah felt chilled. Sirens wailed nearby. "What's Nick doing here?"

"He was with me in the car. I arranged to have him meet me down here because I figured you'd get a confession." Frank buried his face in his hands. "God, I didn't think it would end like this. It's all my fault. I never should've let you go in there."

"No, it was my choice. You and Uncle Buddy tried to talk me out of it."

"And you wouldn't listen," Nick said. "Even after the guilty verdict, you still believed in Amina."

"That's right. Because Amina didn't do it, Nick. Cole Sollier confessed to starting the fire. The LaSpadas hired him; the governor's involved. It's all about the casino." Sarah sat up. "Shit. The camera. I left it there. It's gone now. All we have is my word."

"Sarah, your word is all I need," Nick whispered. "You prevented a great injustice. Amina will be released today."

Sarah watched him staring at the burning cottage; the fire reflected in his eyes. He would learn from Amina's case, just as she had. The law was never black-and-white, only gray. You had to keep an open mind, as Uncle Buddy would say.

"Hey, are you okay?" a woman yelled in the distance.

Sarah turned toward the voice and saw Donna sprinting up the street. What was she doing here?

"Sarah'll be alright," Frank looked over his shoulder. "Here comes the ambulance now."

"Thank God." Donna knelt down and gave her a hug. "I'm so sorry. This is my fault. I shouldn't have let you handle him alone."

"What are you talking about?" Frank said. "You knew about this?"

"I had Sollier's home under surveillance. Wiretap warrant. We placed a video transmitter in the shark's eye."

"What?" Sarah knew there was something up with that shark. It really was watching her. "Did you get Cole's confession?"

"We have it all."

56

Amina gazed at her former market with an arm around Malick's shoulders. It was a warm spring day; tiny green shoots had sprouted along the edges of the sidewalk. Mr. Clancy and Sarah stood beside them. Rehnquist sat in the back of Sarah's jeep with his head sticking out the window.

"Can we go in for a moment?" Amina knew it was time.

"Inside?" Sarah exchanged a glance with Mr. Clancy. "Why?"

Sarah sounded incredulous, and why shouldn't she be? Who'd want to go inside the burned-out market and relive that nightmare? Amina had been released and was reunited with Malick. Justice had been served.

The LaSpadas were arrested, and a federal grand jury investigation was under way against the governor. The press called for his resignation. And there was a good chance she could get Lamine back in the country. Mr. Clancy had introduced her to an immigration lawyer who thought they had an excellent case.

"It's over now, Amina." Sarah gestured her toward their parked cars. "Time to move on."

"This is important. You will see." Amina walked toward the door. "Come with us. Please."

Malick kicked a piece of wood with his sneaker. Amina felt for her son. These events were something he'd have to live with for the rest of his life. She unlocked the front door and they all stepped inside. Their shoes crunched as they crossed over fire debris. The pungent odor of charred wood struck Amina's nostrils. She could taste it. It felt cold and damp and vacant. She shuddered at the thought of Jack Fogerty dying inside. *The man who saved them.* What had he been thinking when he drew his last breath? Amina imagined him praying.

"Watch your step," Mr. Clancy said. "It's dangerous. There's stuff all over the place."

"We shouldn't be in here," Sarah whispered.

Mr. Clancy placed a finger to his lips. "It's okay."

Malick fingered the charred cash register. "I didn't know."

Amina regarded her son. "Go on."

"I heard someone running down the stairs, and then I smelled smoke."

"That was me coming down here." Amina closed her eyes, remembering. "I'll regret it for the rest of my life. I should've checked on you first. I am so sorry, Malick."

"So I got up and didn't know what to do. I was looking for you when that guy ran by me. I got this bad feeling, you know? I thought he was burning down the store and trying to kill us." Malick picked up a black-ened sale sign from the debris and threw it across the store. Amina remained quiet. *Tell your story, Malick. It's time now.*

"Up there." He climbed the staircase to their old apartment and ran through the fire soot in the hallway. They followed.

Sarah appeared uneasy. "What's he doing?"

"It's closure," Mr. Clancy whispered.

Amina exchanged a knowing look with Mr. Clancy.

Malick stopped outside Amina's old bedroom. "The bed." He turned and addressed her with a look of hor-ror in his eyes. "You weren't there, mom. That's when I—" His face contorted.

"Keep going." Amina held his hands. "You must."

"I grabbed the gun from the drawer next to your bed. And then, I heard you calling me." Malick skirted around her and headed back down the hall. "It was so dark, and the smoke was everywhere. I remember coughing like hell."

"I know." Amina felt his anguish. "I prayed I'd find you in time." She remembered the black smoke closing in on them. *The sheer terror of it all.* She shuddered.

"I ran toward your voice." Malick walked backward through the living room. "I knew you were close. And then, and then . . . when I finally found you, I saw the light coming."

"I remember the light." Amina closed her eyes. *That light, that life.*

"He's going to kill us. That's what I thought. He's go-ing to kill us."

"I was scared too."

"There were no sirens, Mom. How could I have known?" Malick slouched down into the corner where they had huddled months before. Amina watched her son's internal struggle. He must've felt trapped. *No way out.* All he wanted to do was save us, *save me.*

"It just happened." Malick yanked his hair with both hands and cried.

It just happened. The truth enveloped Sarah. Yes, Andy Larson had seen someone pointing a gun on that thermal screen. But it wasn't Amina. *It* was *Malick.* She exchanged eye contact with Amina. Sarah pictured her wrestling the gun from Malick's fingers and sticking it in her desk drawer where the police ultimately recovered it. Malick had been ruled out as a suspect because everyone falsely believed he passed out early on. And Amina went along with it. *A mother's instinct to protect her child.*

"I didn't mean to kill him." Malick cried long and hard against his mother's bosom.

"You wanted to save me, Malick."

He nodded. "I think about the fireman and his family all the time. I'm so sorry."

"I know you are." Amina kissed him on the forehead. "You have to learn from it and move on, Malick. Live a good and noble life in honor of the man who saved *your life.*"

"I will. I promise."

Sarah felt tears forming in her eyes. She imagined Jack clinging to his life as he struggled to bring Amina and Malick to that lone window on the other side. Sarah made her way across the room to the very spot where she believed he died. She knelt in the soot.

Uncle Buddy joined her and placed a hand on her shoulder. "Do you know the Fireman's Prayer?"

She shook her head.

"The last stanza goes something like this: 'if according to your will I lose my life, please bless with your protecting hand my children and my wife.' "

Sarah hugged Amina when they were back outside.

"I'm inviting you and your uncle Buddy to the grand opening of my new store. But first, I'm going to make you a Senegalese meal," Amina said.

"In your tulip bowl I hope?" Sarah smiled.

"Of course, and we'll invite Danny."

"I'll hold you to it."

"And you'll get him a dog?" Uncle Buddy gestured toward Malick, who leaned inside the jeep with his face pressed against Rehnquist's floppy ear.

"Yes, a puppy." Amina laughed. "Right away."

"Good." Uncle Buddy gave her a hug and a kiss. "Take care of yourself, Amina."

"Thank you again for everything." She gathered Malick and headed toward their car.

Sarah waved and watched them drive away. She hoped Lamine could get back in the country, and they'd be reunited again.

Sarah dug into her purse for her keys. "I suppose we'll have to tell Frank what happened with Malick."

Uncle Buddy slid into the passenger seat. "I already discussed it with him. We both suspected it was Malick after watching the video surveillance of Cole's confession."

"Will they charge him?" Sarah climbed into the car and buckled her seat belt.

"No, they'll call it self-defense. Amina and Malick have been under fire long enough. Salvatore and Mark LaSpada are responsible for killing Jack Fogerty. They set the whole thing in motion. That's why they've been arrested for murder."

Rehnquist nudged Sarah and barked.

She ruffled his ears. "Okay, okay, I'm starting the car."

"You want something to eat, don't you, Rehnquist?" Uncle Buddy rubbed under the dog's chin. "Let's take him out to lunch. He was a big help on this one."

"Cheeseburgers?"

"With french fries and gravy. His favorite."

Sarah laughed. "And yours too."

Uncle Buddy rubbed his stomach. "Oh. I forgot to tell you. After lunch, we have to swing by the jail. There's somebody I'd like you to meet."

"Oh really." Sarah eyed her uncle. "With another story?"

"A real doozy." He grinned. "You in?"

Sarah raised her hand for the high five. "In."

Forge

Award-winning authors
Compelling stories

. . . .

Please join us at the website
below for more information
about this author and other great
Forge selections, and to sign up for
our monthly newsletter!